"I cannot stay. I

"But to where?"
"North. To Land o
"But what about t
him."
"Yes, it would be a hard trip for Little Soul. Too much dangerous. I cannot tell everything," Shanna said, her misty eyes meeting Kathryn's.
"Then you can't go. You shouldn't go. You should stay here, with us." Kathryn could feel tears running down her face but she couldn't hold them back; she wouldn't even try. What could she offer this young woman? She had offered her a home and she had rejected it. What more could she give her?
She stared at the water. The current moved peacefully. It didn't have any worries.
"No, I must go. But Little Soul cannot come. I must give him to good people. Please...I give him to you and Mama."
For a long moment Kathryn was numb. Confusion washed through her, instantly freezing her inside and out and making speech impossible.
"H-how long do you want us to keep your son?" Kathryn finally managed to ask.
"You will take Little Soul?"
"Of course, we will," Kathryn said, honestly sincere, elation mingling with sadness. Gazing into Shanna's sober eyes a mountain of pity for the girl rose inside her.
Oh, she's so very young–just a child herself, Kathryn observed. "Let the baby get old enough you can leave him, then Mama and I will take care of him while you go about your business. We'll take care of him until you return."
Distant tree limbs blew in the cool wind and shadowed Shanna's face, seemingly muffling her words–"Little Soul is your son now."

Bridged By Love

by

Patricia Lieb

An

Tsylett Press

Publication

www.TsylettPress.com

Tsylett Press

Edited by: Valerie J. Patterson
Senior Editor: Sandra J. Dugas
Acquisitions Editor: Fredrick Hunt
Cover Art by: Patricia Lieb

All rights reserved.

BRIDGED BY LOVE
Copyright © 2009 by Patricia Lieb
ISBN 1-934337-41-2

This is a work of fiction based on a true history of the author's personal family. Some of the names, characters and incidents depicted in this novel are the inventions of the author. Resemblance to persons (living or dead), organizations, locales, or events is mentioned in a biographical nature, without intended harm or malice.

No part of this book may be reproduced or copied, electronically, mechanically, or manually, to include photocopying, scanning, recording, or transcribing; nor may it be transmitted by any electronic or mechanical means; nor may it be stored in any manner on any electronic or mechanical device without the express written permission of the publisher.

If you received this book from any source other than the publisher, or a publisher-approved vendor, please be aware that it is a pirated copy, and neither the publisher nor the author received any payment for its sale.

Tsylett Press
www.TsylettPress.com

Published in the United States Of America
April 2009

Tsylett Press
3616 Devils Three Jump Road
Little Plymouth, VA 23091

Other Titles by Patricia Lieb...

BLUE EYES
MURDER IN THE SWAMPLAND

Coming Soon...

WAYS TO SAY I LOVE YOU
DANGER IN THE CLIFFS
MURDERS ON THE SUNCOAST

Acknowledgment

Wayne Adcock, friend from my teen-age years and now a Texarkana historian, thanks for allowing use of information you adapted from microfilm.

Dedication

Remembering Kathryn Madelyn Williams

※

Shanna's Gift

One

*D*OWN IN THE Caddo Parish marshlands, a young Indian stood in a tiny back room adjoining the butcher shop at Jake Minor's Fish Camp. She clutched a tarnished knife handle in her fist and rested the sharp blade against the feed-sack dress draped from her shoulders and over her protruding belly. The knife, hidden in her bedding the day before, had been a tool used in butchering a hog for one of the camp's regular customers. He had come late in the evening to pick up his pork. He had then left a steer—a steer that might hang in the smokehouse forever. Within the hour, neither she nor Jake Minor would be on hand to butcher it. She'd be gone and he'd be dead.

Her thoughts briefly touched upon the familiar face of the handsome young Mexican, Rowe...the only man she had ever trusted. Or loved. If only he could have taken her away. Now she had no choice but to continue this path.

On the other side of the rustic log wall, Jake's skeleton key scraped inside the door lock. Shanna braced herself, each screech freezing the sweat beads bubbling from her forehead. Then came the familiar click as the brass lock slid from the doorjamb. In less than a moment, Jake pushed and the door sprang open.

Shanna was too terrified to move.

The flames in Jake's icy-blue eyes flared at her through strands of straw-colored hair. Hair that circled his head like a fallen halo. Her body jerked in fear. What had she planned to do? But the knife seemed to have a mind of its own. Quick as a snap, her hand raised and the blade plunged into flesh covering Jake's heart.

Vacantly, she watched blood spew from his hairy chest like muddy water from a broken dam. For an instant, a scene of the Red River flashed through her mind. Her father, mother and brother had camped along its shore. That day, she was nabbed and brought to Jake's place by a terrorizing group of masked horsemen.

"You...c-crazy...sq-squaw," Jake stammered, barely able to speak. He stumbled, his white hairy arms reaching for her.

Her body seemed still, yet she felt herself backing into a crate box used for a nightstand in the dim room. Her focus stayed glued on the one who had owned her half her sixteen years. Now, she watched the scene unfold: the fat man gasped, his white stare rolling over something on the dingy plank ceiling above her. And then—WHUMP!—his belly smacked hard onto the dank floor, humping twice before it sank to a final climax.

"Jake Minor is dead now," she whispered, her unsure words bouncing from the four walls encasing her. Her psyche spun in and out of the scene. She stared at the bloody knife in her trembling hand. At the body lying on the floor alongside the narrow unmade bed where she had lain awake most of the night comprehending freedom. Now this panorama was surely a nightmare, even though she had accomplished this mission many times in her dreams. Jake Minor was an evil man, and death became him. Getting a grip on herself, her mind settled somewhat and she inched closer to Jake's motionless body. There had been so many nights over the last eight years she had wanted to destroy this bad man. And now that she had, she was mystified. She must run away from this Caddo Lake marsh, from this parish, from all Louisiana without hesitation. She must find the main stream of the Red River and follow it north through the Arkansas backlands, and then northwest to the Land of Indians.

She watched as blood slowly formed a pool around Jake's lifeless body. His obese lard-white trunk was now splattered with maroon, the muscles in his big arms useless to fight, and the thick pee-stained underwear covering his buttocks and legs now darkened with blood and muck. She had seen Jake passed out many times, but always from his consumption of too much corn-mash rather than death. During some of his blackouts, she had run away but had never made it out of the marshlands. Times when Jake had slept through her absence, his outlaw and whisky-making friends had hunted her down and brought her back like a trapped animal. After a painful flee attempt last winter, she had become too frightened to try again. Rather than for herself, she now considered the destiny of the seed ready to sprout from her womanhood.

Shanna put her hand to her stomach. "Soon you will be safe Little Soul."

Unexpectedly—was it stomping on the plank porch outside the store? And then the cowbell on the screened door dinged as somebody entered. Heavy boots jarred the soft pine floor so the joists cracked. Shanna slapped her knife-filled fist over her mouth.

Run, she told herself. She peered wide-eyed around the cluttered room. There was no exit. The only door led to the storefront. And Jake had nailed wooden bars over the window opening after her last escape attempt.

Her body stiff, she analyzed the knife in her hand, the body on the floor, and the four walls penning her in like a bound swine in a slaughterhouse. She saw two, now four, now numerous broken images of her life, of this room, of Jake zapping here and there. These fragments seemed to keep time with the thump of boot heels stamping through the storefront.

She had killed one man today. She really didn't want another notch on her knife, but should the intruder be one of Jake's Raider Outlaws there surely would be trouble.

Bert, from way down in the parish, was due in next week. Perhaps he had come for his meat early. But Bert's steer was hanging in the smokehouse and yet to be butchered. He would know that.

"Minor, you here? Might as well show your face."

Oh no! The demanding voice jarred Shanna like a lightening bolt.

Oh my Ayimat Caddi, she cried silently, and more to herself than to the Great Spirit. Why had this bad man returned? Yesterday, he and Jake had done business, trading guns, animal skins and whisky. It wasn't like one to return so soon.

"Minor," he called again. "You held out on me. You still owe me."

Shanna trembled at his words, then the silence, and then the ruffle of products being shuffled about over store shelves.

"You here Minor? Better come on out. I'm taking what you owe me with or without your presence. Come on out if you're not too drunk. Else I might take the wrong stuff."

His boot heels clunked louder on the plank flooring. Then Shanna heard his stepping onto the gray slate surrounding the black cast-iron stove. She heard the soup ladle sloshing in the crock-pot. The thick aroma of day-old gumbo steam and the shocking taste of human blood blended in her nostrils. Gagging, she refused to vomit, and swallowed the sour matter bubbling in her throat.

The intruder sipped and slurped loudly.

This time she heaved, and everything inside her flew from her mouth and scattered with the bank of blood. She held her hand to her chest and hoped the man in the next room had not heard the commotion.

As seconds passed, blood flowed less and less from underneath Jake Minor. Suddenly, Shanna's gaze fell to the sticky dark liquid now oozing like a nightmare underneath the door.

Maybe he won't see, she told herself

Holding the weapon in front of her, Shanna crept toward the doorway. And then a sound like that of shuffling echoed through her head. He was searching for something.

She clutched the knife handle so tightly that sweat dripped from her hand. *Be brave,* she told herself. She stepped to the side and pulled open the door just enough to peep at the goings on in the storefront.

Guns. He's taking Jake's gun, she observed, then she quickly pushed the door shut.

She must have made some sort of noise during this quick maneuver. She caught her breath as the familiar man paused suddenly then tromped across the storefront. "Why you hiding in there, Squaw Girl?" he questioned roughly. "What you hiding from me?"

Unable to dismiss the hard knot tightening in her gut, she quickly positioned her body to serve as a door prop. Perhaps he would think Jake was bedding her and would leave.

"Where's Minor?" he questioned, his voice louder as he neared.

"Jake's in my bed," she answered, her speech wavering with the lie.

Sudden laughter penetrated the log walling and filled the tiny room like a whoop of bad breath.

"Jake's in my bed," she said, more nervously than before.

"Let me in Squaw Girl." He paused, and laughed. "Minor's not apt to bed you. Not 'til you drop that papoose. It's beneath him," he said, his sarcastic voice generating chills to crawl like cold wiggling worms down her spine. She knew this man who did trading with Jake. She knew him too well and he frightened her.

"Come on, Squaw Girl, open up," he coached. "I don't aim to hurt you."

She said under her breath, *You hurt me many times.* She recalled episodes of torture at Jake's selling her to his evil customers, including this man. He had pinned her down and covered her mouth with his strong hand during his horrifying demands. Her cries had been silent through these excruciatingly painful ordeals.

"Come on, Squaw Girl."

Motionless, Shanna waited for whatever was to come. "Holy damn!" the man said, his voice shockingly louder. "What you doing in there? Where's all this blood coming from?"

Shanna looked downward. In wonder, she focused on the immobile body and the blood leaching from underneath it.

How much blood runs through one man's heart? Doesn't a human stop bleeding when he dies? Animals do.

"Where's Minor?" The voice was more demanding now. "Squaw Girl, I'm talking at you. Where's Jake Minor?"

Her eyes moved from Jake's big frame to her own dainty fist still holding the deadly weapon. The scene clearly detailed the horrid reality. She had killed the brawny man. She had killed Jake Minor. He was white. She was squaw. She would hang for this. Her life didn't matter much, but what about the innocent soul more than eight new moons in her belly?

"Open this door or I'm knocking it in on you," he commanded. Then paused. "You do something to Minor? You surprise me Squaw Girl." There was a brief silence, then a laugh. "Minor shoulda known you'd do him in sooner or later." He paused again, and laughed again.

"Please, just leave me be."

"Not on your life, Squaw Girl. Might as well open the door. I know what's happened in there. You probably killed Minor in his sleep." Shanna cringed at the heavy breathing coming right through the door. "I'm not going anywhere Squaw Girl."

Shanna's own breaths came in short gasps, but the air around her swarmed like attacking bees.

"There's a bunch of mean men on their way here right now. Minor's outlaws are coming. They aim to ride today." He spoke precisely and slowly. "What they apt to do to you Squaw Girl? When they see this blood? Whoo-oo, they'll be pissed. Whoo-oo. Minor's outlaws won't be a liking this a'tall. Not a'tall." Again, he laughed.

"They 'bout twenty minutes behind me," he went on, dragging his words like a sick puppy, as if he were waiting for his statement to catch up. "Now open the door and let's make us a deal." He waited. "You need me Squaw Girl. I can help you, you know."

Shanna gazed at Jake, and then at the knife. She had fought men all her life and had always lost, except this time. Finally, yet much too late, she had gotten the best of Jake Minor. Now the time had come to scrap again. Could she fight this man and win? At the moment, there was only one thing to do. She moved from the door just as her intruder pushed it open. Obviously stunned at the scene, the tall thin man paralyzed. His appearance was more like a tall oak carving than human. He began to rub the couple day's growth of black whiskers protruding his thin jaws and chin. He took in the scene for moments that seemed like hours, and then he pushed his hands into the pockets of his gray linen jacket.

His jet-black pupils peered from the bloody mess on the floor to Shanna's dark eyes. "Looks like you're in a pickle barrel, Squaw Girl" His thick brows lifted. "Guess its up to me what happens to you now."

※ ※ ※

A short while later, Shanna stepped outside the storefront. She stood a moment on the creaky wood porch to breathe in the fresh, crisp air. Light from the full moon lit the moss-green bayou. She licked her lips and let her mind wander. She didn't know how long she stood there. This scene could be yesterday, but it wasn't. This was a new time. The tinge of a sudden dawn hovered over the tin roof covering the plank boathouse so it resembled a painting stored in her mind's eye. She stood looking for a moment, and then she hurried from the storefront and across the sloping terrain. Reaching the small structure, Shanna lifted the metal latch and pushed open the thick wide door. Two days ago, while anticipating this moment of escape, she had stored the canoe she favored, along with fishing nets and lines, on a bottom boat rack. The idea had been to do what she must and then run far, far away. She struggled to move about as her cowhide moccasin bogged in muck on the water's bed. Her arms around the end of the canoe, she pulled it from the shed and lugged it into the marsh. Her feed-sack dress sucked up water so that the garment weighted heavily on her tight belly. As it slipped from her shoulders, she grasped the earth-tone shawl, the one she had so carefully finger-knitted from golden straws and black sheep wool. She tossed the garment into the canoe. *Must keep it clean for the Little Soul*, she told herself.

In haste, she pulled the canoe through the tall grasses to the deeper water. Finally, she crawled over the hull and began to row. She pushed the oar through the swampy water on one side of the canoe and then the other. Her best chance at survival was to get many miles into the swamp before Jake's outlaws came to take her, as they had done so many times before.

The morning sun had moved from Shanna's face and settled on her back. She realized the day was hurrying by. Traveling northeastwardly, she maneuvered the canoe as fast as she could row through the midst of Cyprus stumps and trees.

"Be brave," she whispered.

Seeing a movement in grasses along the bank, she feared an intrusion of snakes. She rowed toward the center of the bayou and out of the stagnant green moss. And then a hard, tight pain like she had never experienced cut deep inside her abdomen.

"Oo-oo-oo-ooooooooo," she howled. A contraction? But nearly as quickly as the pain had come, it vanished. *Little Soul must wait*, she coached herself. *Little Soul must not come now.*

Jake's outlaws and their dogs had surely arrived at the store by now. They had surely found Jake dead. Surely they had started tracking her scent. Should they catch up, they would hang her.

She must use haste in putting distance between herself, the camp, and the dead man.

"Oo-oo-oo-ooooooooo!" She held her belly as another contraction cut her inside, like a sharp knife splitting the gut of a swine. How could she stop herself from birthing out here in the middle of the Caddo Lake swamplands?

Two

THREE, MAYBE FOUR, hour pony ride northeast of Caddo Lake, the freight train's elongated whistle blew and its iron wheels clacked and banged, breaking the forest tranquility. Kathryn stood before the woodpile and raised the chopping ax so the handle touched her shoulder, then slammed it into the last log she would chop this day. She lifted the ax again, this time aiming the sharp edge so it pierced an old stump. Being September, cool winds could overtake summer's remnants any day now. She gazed at the pile of logs she must cut soon. But at the moment, there were other chores to do. Already the sun was finding its way from the Arkansas border to the Texas foothills west of the homestead.

"Ka-Ka-Ka—."

Kathryn rested her hands in the pockets of her overalls and waited for the stuttering voice to pronounce her name. Without turning, she knew it was the old tramp.

"Moldie," she said, her chin jutting as she turned just enough to catch his glimpse. She raked her fingers through her hair and pushed curls off her neck and into the loose twist at the back of her neck. She figured Moldie had just jumped from the passing freighter. "Wednesday already?" she asked, knowingly. He had a habit of stopping by the homestead on Wednesdays for handouts. On different days, Moldie called on other folks in the backwoods.

"Believe ss-ss-so," he said, lazily resting his head to one side.

"Moldie, I work for my supper. You gotta work for yours."

Moldie's work was unworthy of a recommendation, but heck, he wasn't feeble. Wasn't working for needs God's intention for folks put on this Earth? This loafing old goat was slow in the head but he was strong. Ought to do him good to chop. Physical exertion always got her blood to circulating.

"Whatcha want me to do, mm-ma'am?" he stammered, his hazel, red-veined eyes squinting to block the sun.

For a moment, Kathryn detected the smell of alcohol. But where would Moldie get money for moonshine? She hadn't known him to booze it up since her former husband left town. Back some eight or so years ago, Alex traded Moldie liquor for favors.

She eyed him for a moment. "Go over there and start stacking logs upside the house." She pointed to a short stack a few feet from the stump.

"Get the ones I've already split."

Moldie's gaze wandered from the woodpile to the pasture, which was practically burned up by the summer drought. Then he looked west, as if he were expecting something to emerge from the nearby pine forest. Soon, he glanced toward the fine log house Kathryn and her Mama shared. But, Kathryn was quite sure he hadn't heard much she had said.

"Put them right over there on top of the others," she continued, watching as Moldie held his black felt hat in front of him. His pink fingertips grasped the brim and turned it slowly. Kathryn had given him that hat. She had given it to him long along with a feed sack of other clothing that Alex had left at the homestead when he deserted her. "And Moldie, don't call me ma'am," she said, the drawl in her voice deepening.

She didn't know if he understood her orders, but it really didn't matter anyhow. She glared at the old tramp for a moment. Then she grinned, turned, and hastened the ten-or-so paces to the back porch. She glanced at Moldie once more, grabbed a water bucket, and hurried on across the back yard to the well.

She let the rope slither through her hands so the well bucket dropped through the deep dark chamber. Her gaze lingering on the rough twine, she allowed her thoughts to turn again to the man she had married at seventeen. After a short marriage, he had broken her heart mercilessly.

Being pregnant had been the best part of the marriage. The excitement she had known at the moment she realized that her monthly curse had ceased, now sloshed hurting memories through her brain.

At that time, some eight years ago, Kathryn was in Milton's Woods cutting pine timbers. The idea of being pregnant was too good to keep from her husband. She hurried to the field stable to fetch Sugar, her palomino. Quickly, she swung the saddle onto the blond mare and tightened its belly belt. Soon, she was riding over the sandy trail the ten-or-so miles to the homestead.

"Alex," she called, allowing the screen door to bang shut behind her. She practically ran to the bedroom. Alex had his dress suit spread out on the bed and was placing other garments into a small brown-and-tan checked carpetbag he used for traveling. "Why you packing?" she asked in confusion.

"Tell you what Little Gal. I'm heading out west. To Arizona and Colorado." Kathryn disliked the nickname Alex had dubbed her, but confronting him about it would lead to sour feelings. He had scolded her in the past for trying to correct his choice of words. Best just to let the nickname go in one ear and out the other. She didn't want to argue with Alex. Especially now that she was expecting.

"Arizona? Colorado? You've never mentioned going west."

"You know what they're saying, 'Go west young man, get rich?' That's what I aim to do." Alex had a habit of sing-songing his words when he thought he was on to some kind of self-serving deal. "Buffalo hides are bringing big bucks. The west is full of buffalo right now but they won't be around long. I should have stayed there the first time I went, even if I did have to fight red skins." He paused, and stood silently for a moment while he shook creases from a white store-bought shirt. Then he carefully folded the garment and placed it in the footlocker. "Got to get my hands on as many hides as I can. And while I'm in the west, I might even do a little gold prospecting."

"It's so far. Why so far?" Kathryn asked, her eyes on the tall, thin man's large hands as they carefully placed an extra pair of undergarments, straight razor, and shaving mug into the suitcase. His expressionless, clean-shaven face was slightly browned from sun exposure, and his black eyes stayed focused on his packing.

"Lots a man can do in the west. Yes, I should have stayed when I was there, but like a fool, I came here where's there nothing but rotten cotton. I'll go west and get rich and then I'm coming back to fetch you Little Gal." He winked, his dark eyes holding a hint of a flirt.

Oh Alex, she thought. *You're leaving and I got a little life growing inside me.*

How could she tell him? He wouldn't change his plans anyhow. She wouldn't even ask him to. She knew he loved rambling more than he loved her.

And Kathryn knew when Alex made his mind up to do something there was no stopping him. He was like her in that respect. She was stubborn as a mule, a red Irish mule, so folks often said.

Kathryn kept the news of her baby to herself that evening. Before dawn, Alex had tied the carpetbag to his horse's saddle and was off. He claimed he would pawn the horse in town for enough money to catch a train to Dallas, then journey on by some unforeseen means from there.

Calendar page after calendar page, Kathryn's belly ballooned more and more. Still, she continued working in Milton's Woods with her partner, Leonard—a good man who lived down the road a short piece from the homestead. In the evenings, she did home chores with Mama. All the while, she wanted desperately to hear word that Alex would soon return to her.

She heard nothing for nearly five months, and then totally out of the blue, Alex was waiting at her back door one cool afternoon when she arrived home from Milton's Woods.

"Here's what I've decided," he said, without giving her time to grasp the surprise. "I've found a way to make us rich. Tomorrow, we'll go to the courthouse in Texarkana." He paused, his black pupils seemingly piercing her brain. "Little Gal, you'll be so happy with my plans."

"What'cha saying Alex?" Kathryn asked, her head tilting in uncertainty. She could feel her face stiffen in worry.

"With this homestead in my name, I can get some loans," he said, the tone in his voice holding authority. "With the money, I can start me up a business in Dallas. I already talked it over with a banker in town. I can go into dealing furs with rich people from here to England. Dallas is growing, 'bout as fast as Texarkana. It'll be the new frontier. Be getting all kinds of businesses now that railroads are running through." His dark eyes looked into hers with a familiar greedy gleam.

"With money, I can dress you up," he bragged, then slapped her across the butt. "I can make you a city gal." Grinning, he pushed his black felt hat from his forehead and winked. "There'll be no end to things I can do."

"Alex, haven't you noticed anything?" she asked, pleadingly.

"Something different?" His voice was low, and wrinkles formed around his eyes.

"Look at me," she said, rubbing her hands over her belly.

"You look good, Little Gal. Healthy," he commented, his thick brow lifting as he eyed her up and down.

"We're having a baby," she whispered. Her lips puckered to curve her excitement.

"Well now, doesn't that just beat the drum? You'll be a mama."

"And you a papa," she said softly, with an unavoidable smile taking her face.

"Now what about that? You'll be a busy gal," he said, his voice low and singing. "We better get all this legal stuff done before we start making family plans. We can get the papers signed tomorrow. I've already checked."

"Checked?" she asked, the dismay in her question apparent. She felt her face become straight, and her brows lift in bafflement.

"Yes. I went to the courthouse this morning."

"I'm not sure what you aim on doing?" Already, the abundance of joy over the baby had drained from her being.

"Just go with me. All you have to do is sign papers changing the name on the homestead deed from Williams to Andrews."

"Mama won't agree to that," she noted, trying to rationalize this sudden notion that seemed so important to Alex.

"She doesn't have to. You're the breadwinner here. I've checked everything." He hesitated. Grinning, he patted her hand.

"Where you off to?" she asked, as Alex straightened his hat.

"Now don't you go worrying your pretty red head about it," he said, his dark gaze suddenly piercing hard into her eyes. "I got to ride with the boys. I'll be back sooner or later."

Kathryn stayed up late that night considering her husband's expectations. Alex expected her to obey his every command. But regardless, she would not give ownership of the homestead to him. Finally, and long after Mama had slipped off to bed, Kathryn fell asleep in a front room rocking chair. She didn't know what time Alex got home. But the next morning, she didn't bother to wake him when she dressed for work.

Throughout the morning and on into the afternoon, Kathryn worried about defying her husband. But what about Mama? Mama would never understand if the property she and Papa had worked hard for was taken away. Going behind Mama's back would be un-family.

"You're sure quiet today, Kitten," Leonard said during their lunch of biscuits and honey Kathryn had brought from home. Leonard, who was probably a good ten years older than Kathryn, had started calling her Kitten when she was a kid about six. Back then, he often drove a horse and wagon to the homestead so his mother could do quilting with Mama. Leonard readily did nice things for folks. Once he hung a rope from the limb of an oak tree and made a swing for her. He would push her and play tag and other games with her as long as she wanted him to. She smiled, now, and thought about how she used to cry when he had to leave her. He would say, "I'll come back to see ye next week, Kitten." Kathryn never knew why Leonard called her Kitten, but the warmth in his voice when he pronounced the name brought her pleasure.

She smiled lightly at her friend. "I'm sorry. Just got stuff on my mind."

Later that day, Kathryn felt her stomach turning sour. Moments later, the biscuits and honey came up.

"Kitten! What's the matter with ye?" Leonard called anxiously. He dropped his ax and hurried toward her, his long legs leaping over sappy trunks of fallen pines. And then, he grasped her head between his strong hands and held it while she heaved.

Slashing pains ripped through her abdomen and blood started to flow. Holding her stomach, she fell to the ground in agony, her head burying into a pile of sawdust.

"My baby. Leonard, help me," she cried. "I'm losing my baby."

The pain was unbearable. In the midst of this anguish, Kathryn lost consciousness and remained out until the next day. When awareness returned, Alex was at her bedside. He patted her hand, the expression brotherly, distant, perfunctory.

"Don't feel so bad," he said. "You hurt now but you're strong. You can have another baby when the timing's right."

Kathryn's body pained more than ever before, but not as badly as her heart. Alex had just presented her a whammy.

Why are you so cold, Alex? You're not at all the man I thought I loved.

Alex had been a different person when they wed only two months after their meeting. Or perhaps she just hadn't known him.

"Please leave me," she said, turning to face the window. "Leave me alone."

Alex left all right. He didn't even look at his dead son wrapped in towels and laid for viewing in the company room. He left the homestead that very evening without even saying goodbye.

The day after the baby's funeral, Doctor Adams came calling from the West side of Texarkana.

"To conceive again would be risky," he informed her, his voice stern. "You went through a lot. I was afraid we might even lose you."

"You mean—I can't—I shouldn't—." Tears filled her eyes and she tried to close her ears to the doctor's words. "Having a baby means more to me than anything," she pleaded.

Her baby, the baby she had so dearly loved and wanted had died inside her. Was this horrible misfortune her punishment for cutting pulpwood sun up to sunset? Would this terrible thing have happened if she had honored her husband, as she had promised in her marriage vows, had she signed the homestead deed over to him? She agonized inside, and then the thought of Alex's last words, "You can have another baby," sickened her to anger.

Three years later, Kathryn went to Texarkana to talk with her lawyer friend, Cavin O'Tool.

"I need your help," she explained. "I haven't seen Alex since I lost our baby. I want free of him."

Cavin obtained the divorce for Kathryn without any difficulty. And as far as she knew, nobody around town had seen hide or hair of her former husband in a coon's age. That was just fine with her. Any sight of Alex would only mean trouble.

The only reason he had married her in the first place was for the homestead. Of that, Kathryn was sure. But she would never let him or anyone take the property from Mama and her. *Alex is a thing of the long-gone past*, Kathryn assured herself. She smiled and looked across the rolling pastures that were, in the springtime, filled with grasses, blue bonnets and white-and-yellow buttercups. She glanced to the various shades of green foliage lining the forest and the peach, fig and plum trees in the back yard. One-hundred-and-sixty acres belonged to Mama and her. They weren't much, but her papa had claimed them nearly thirty years ago. Seven years later, he died for the Confederacy. The following year, when the homestead laws went into effect, Mama filed a claim.

Perhaps growing up without a father had strengthened Kathryn both physically and emotionally. Perhaps that was how she obtained her vigor and wisdom.

Still, there was a real woman with real desires and needs underneath the overalls she wore. There was a woman who longed for the man she loved. But John Allen, the handsome city man who had ridden a train in from the east three years ago, had never talked romance to her. And already she was twenty-six.

"Pooh," she moaned, placing the water bucket on the porch shelf. One of these days, her life would change. Kathryn hurried through the kitchen, the screen door slamming shut behind her.

"Mama," she called, walking across the rustic oak floor and on to the front room. Tables made of varnished persimmon and cedar sat spaciously among the sofa and chairs Mama had built and adorned with seat pads and cloths stitched from tan, brown and ivory store-bought fabrics. Mama was wonderfully talented and had handed her skills on to Kathryn. The beautiful whitewashed log walls were attractively decorated with drawings and photographs of late family members. Some were penned by Kathryn's ancestors and brought over on a boat from Ireland.

"Yes Kathryn," Mama said, acknowledging her feisty daughter from the rocking chair setting between the front window and the stone fireplace. A tin pan filled with green beans sat on her apron-covered lap. Continuing to snap, she looked up at Kathryn.

"Was that old Moldie I saw going around back a while ago?" Mama's voice was strong and her hazel eyes glistened knowingly.

"Yep, Mama. It's Wednesday already. He's out there now, stacking logs."

Kathryn uneasily turned toward the fireplace, her gaze moving upward to a gun rack her papa had made from a set of longhorns and mounted above the mantle. She reached for a shotgun and blew dust from the barrel. Then drawing it to her cheek, she peered down the sight, aiming at nothing.

"Now just what's that all about?" Mama questioned, lifting her chin and glaring lightly at Kathryn.

"I'm getting ready for those confounded wolves."

"I see. You say you're going to shoot them, but you won't. I've never seen you shoot anything yet."

"I'll shoot the wolves. Just you wait and see." She placed the shotgun back on the longhorns and turned, grinning teasingly at Mama.

"Did you tell Moldie he had to work for his supper?" Mama asked, her gaze still on Kathryn. "You know he's a cripple."

"Mama! Would I do any such?" Kathryn's brows arched. She waited a moment, but Mama said nothing.

"Anyway Mama. The old tramp's only missing one finger. That doesn't exactly qualify him as a cripple," She paused. "You know, I really should make him help me cut pulpwood for all the handouts he gets around here."

"Now you know good-and-well you don't have to go out working in them woods everyday. We can make it fine by just keeping this place up," she hesitated for a moment. "Rather than growing only vegetables, I'm thinking we can plant a few acres in cotton come spring. The price is sky high. I heard talk in town the other day."

"Cotton is always sky high," Kathryn agreed, softness playing in her voice. She placed her hand on Mama's shoulder and rubbed gently. "We can do cotton if that's what you want. But I like working for Milton. You know, if I didn't get my boots on and go off cutting everyday with Leonard, well, I'd just be lost," she said, her grin bringing fine lines to her face.

"And we got our truck farming to keep up with."

"I wish you'd marry Leonard," Mama said, suddenly blurting out the words. "He loves you. It's written all over his face."

"Mama!"

"I'm telling it true."

Kathryn pushed her hands into her overall pockets. Mama was just in one of those feeling-sorry-for-her-daughter moods. She would get over it. Mama knew she needed a man to share her life. But what Mama didn't know was that her dreams were of John Allen, and if she didn't haul logs to town every day or so, she would never see the man who owned her heart.

"I'll feed Moldie," Mama said. "The stove's starting to cool off but the stew's still hot."

"Want me to throw in another log?" Kathryn asked, starting toward the kitchen.

"Nah. Save it."

While Kathryn set the table, Mama stirred the chicken-and-potato stew so the scent of garlic and sage rose with the sudden spew of steam from the cast iron pot, then she ladled a goodly amount into the yellow clay bowl they kept especially for Moldie.

"Dang, Mama, the stew smells good," Kathryn attributed, turning toward the stove for a deeper sniff. She backed up just enough to allow Mama's gloved fist to pull an iron skillet of golden cornbread from the oven. She cut a crusty wedge, placed it on top of Moldie's dish, and carried it to the porch.

After supper, Kathryn went outside for a bit of relaxation. It was dark now. She could hear the song of crickets meshing through the pines and the loud croaks of frogs calling from a distant pond. Night sounds made her cheerful.

"Did you have enough to eat, Moldie?" she asked, leaning against a porch post.

"Ye-ye-yes. It sho 'nough was good ta-ta-too." he said. "I'll be going na-na-now."

Kathryn's gaze followed Moldie as he sauntered down the path alongside the house and on to the trail in front. He was starting to look like an old man during the past few seasons. His strawberry-blond hair was streaked with gray and thinning above his drooping brows. His pink, wrinkled skin was splotched with patches of brown. Kathryn had known Moldie and his twin brother, Bill Junior, might near all her life. Both boys had been a bit slow, in her opinion.

She grinned, recalling a really weird happening that occurred when she was about five. The twins, the best she could figure, were twelve or close to. Mama had paid the boys to chop a stack of wood while she went about other chores in preparation for winter. Bill Junior was chopping and Moldie was dancing around, aggravating Bill Junior the best he could, it seemed. Several times Moldie put his hand down on the chopping stump and dared his brother to whack it.

"Put it back. Just put it back again and I'll cut it off," Bill Junior warned.

"Cu-cu-cut it off, cu-cu-cut it off," Moldie teased. "Cu-cu-cut it off and I'll tell mo-mo-mommy," Moldie stuttered. He stuck his right index finger on the stump again. That was a mistake. Bill Junior slammed down the ax and Moldie's finger went flying into the pile of wood chips Mama used for kindling.

When the twins became teens, Bill Junior wandered off to Louisiana somewhere. Folks talked about what may have been his fate, but nobody knew for sure. Some folks said they believed Bill Junior had fallen off the planet. Moldie swore he didn't know the whereabouts of his twin. He stayed in Arkansas and developed his panhandling routine.

Focusing on the tattered overalls covering Moldie's pudgy body, Kathryn's mind drifted into the future. What would she be doing in the next year, or next spring? Or even tomorrow? Her life may change but she would never be like Moldie, out begging for handouts. Not as long as she was halfway healthy and could work at all. The good Lord had given her two strong hands and a strong back. She could do a job as well as any man and better than most. And she was right smart, too. She had more common sense than lots of townspeople and could go a long way in figuring stuff.

Kathryn smiled to herself. Besides being smart, she looked about as good as anybody else in these parts, even though her hair was almost orange in the sunlight and her face wore a mask of fading freckles. And she was healthy—hardly ever sick—and a good pulpwood cutter and farmer. If only she could conceive. *John*, she thought. *I want you. I'd die having your baby if you asked me to.*

Three

"Ayimat Caddi," Shanna cried to her god as another pain cut through her abdomen. She braced herself, but her head dropped over the canoe hull and her long hair rode the mossy water like a lily pad. The hard, tight throbbing was long and intense. The pain suddenly passed. She lifted her head slowly. She stretched, pulling her body back to the center of the canoe. And then, "Ayimat Caddi," she screamed as another contraction ripped inside her. "Oh God of the heavens and earth, how long will I hurt?"

Was there anyway she could delay birthing? Delay the unbearable taut ripping of flesh? She wailed, louder this time, as another knife-like cut came. "Ayimat. Ayimat." She held her hands tight on her belly. "The baby is coming. Ayimat Caddi. The baby is coming." She clenched her teeth. "Help me my God. Ayimat Caddi. Help me."

Dogs yelped more rapidly now, but on this huge lake forked with bayous and marshes it was difficult to know just how far off they were. And could they trail human scent through all the water and murk?

"Oh my Ayimat Caddi. Baby is coming."

Water spilled from her body. In agony, she maneuvered the canoe the few more yards to where a sea-green current encompassed a bubbling spring.

The water here is clean, she told herself. *But will buzzards smell blood and be circling by sunup?* She recalled a time in her early childhood when a woman in her tribe lay paralyzed for two days after giving birth before all the blood drained from her body and left her fingers frozen like icicles hanging from a bayou bridge. The infant had lived and was taken by a tribal family. What would happen should she join that mother in the life after? There was no one other than the outlaws in this Caddo Lake marsh, not even in the parish, to take this new member and raise him to be free.

"Oh-oo-oo-ooooo," she cried out. Moments later, the contraction stopped and her body fell limp.

Again, dogs barked and yapped. For a while, it seemed, they had been silent. Or had her cries of suffering toned her ears to silence all else? Dogs, it now seemed, circled her. She must contain her cries. She must not let the dogs and outlaws find her.

She willed herself to silence, to accept the ghastly throbs coming more often and lingering for longer intervals inside. She reached for a tree branch and broke off a hard twig. She clutched the wood in her fist tightly. As the next contraction came, she jammed the small timber into her mouth.

She grasped the stick with her teeth and bit as hard as she could. The hurt was long. And then the pain subsided.

She allowed memories of early childhood to come to her mind. She recalled her people's love of fresh water. Fresh water from springs and creeks was cleansing to the body and spirit. Powerful chiefs, councilmen and braves often bathed in the flow prior to hunting. Would such a wash in this lake do her good now? Would the lake help in birthing this new soul? Would the moving waters keep the newborn safe in this wilderness? Would the waters prevent the smell and taste of birth from the nostrils of beasts, dogs and outlaws?

Without realizing her moves, Shanna fell over the canoe into the cool spring, the wood still planted between her teeth. The calm surge was soothing; still, the horrid pain lingered. Her hands on her belly, she waited for the long recurring ache to ease and then she waded to a slightly emerged rock.

She held on for a moment, her silent screams lodging in the wood. Seconds passed, then another contraction ripped through her abdomen. Then, another.

She crawled onto the big gray rock. Using the boulder for a birthing stool, her hands grasped the clean edges, as if the stone had been chiseled over time for this very moment.

The pain. *Oh Ayimat Caddi*, the torturing pain. *But this hurt, like all else, will pass.*

Forcing her body to relax, to let all her muscles fall limp, she panted short rapid breaths past the twig clenched tightly with her teeth. A hurt, like she had never dreamed could be, ripped her apart.

At the very same moment, a miracle unparalleled occurred.

She lifted her knees and reached between her thighs. Her hands clutched the protruding life and held it. The infant's tiny head rested between her fingers, then tiny shoulders emerged. At this vast expulsion, her delicate body parts ripped inside and out. She could not breathe, could not move nor cry. Her spirit had fled her being and took its space above her lifeless body, shading her suddenly pale face from the full moon.

And then, her hands were full of life.

"Oh. Oh my God, my Ayimat Caddi," she cried, this time in pleasure more than pain. Suddenly, it seemed a muse released her from this difficult task. Without realizing, she forced her finger into the tiny mouth and cleared out mucus. Holding the infant to her chest, she moved to the canoe and grabbed hold. She inhaled long through her nostrils so the air sank to the pit deep in her gut. In another moment, she reached into the canoe and before she knew what was happening, her fingers swiftly tied the newborn's belly cord with fishing string, and then with her sharp fingernails, had snipped the attached length. Shanna carefully placed the baby on the wool-and-grass shawl on the canoe bed. Already the infant stretched his tiny arms and his fingers spread. "My boy. So smart," she whispered, her eyes taking in the magic. Smiling, Shanna tightened the shawl around the infant. Again pain struck her abdomen. Again she sank to the birthing rock and fought to control her breathing for the next million moons, it seemed, until the placenta was clean from her womanhood. She struggled to the canoe and climbed inside. The full moon's glow lit the lake so it twinkled like a heaven of stars. She reached into the current and scooped a handful of water and brought it to her mouth. It tasted so good. No one would know a baby was just born here. All traces of birth were far into the marsh by now; this would surely confuse the hounds. Lying in the canoe hull, Shanna's body nearly filled the length. She cuddled the newborn to her bosom.

Just a little time for rest, she told herself. *We'll be gone before the dogs come.*

※ ※ ※

Tromping through wetlands, their long black coats sucking up swamp water, their guns in their white-gloved hands, and with barking dogs running wildly—the outlaws, only a handful of miles behind Shanna, kept their sights fixed for anything that moved.

"That's sure a pitiful sight back there," one said of what they had just seen at Jake Minor's store.

"You ain't telling me nothin'. If'n I didn't know better, I'd say it was some wild animal done got hold of Minor," another said through his lip of snuff.

"Somebody sure had it in fer him."

"Yep. Pitiful."

"Think it was the squaw?"

"She probably revengeful enough."

"Whoever done it can't be too far." He spat so brown liquid splattered the yellow matter topping the moonlighted marsh. "The dogs'll catch 'em."

"Yep. There's lot of swamp out here though. Might take days ta find the no-account."

※ ※ ※

Shanna opened her eyes and stared upward through Cyprus branches to the full moon. Where was she? Then she remembered. She was in the swamp. What was happening? The infant. She had given birth. She smiled downward at the newborn lying in her arm. "Oh Little Soul, I have delivered you into a world so full of misfortune." And then came voices. Jake's outlaws were upon her. She covered the infant's face with the wrap. "Oh for love of life, don't make a sound," she whispered, as if the child could understand.

Their calls meshed louder through the wall of marsh grasses. Shanna shivered. "Over here, Morton. My dog's got a scent."

There was rumbling in the marsh beyond the wall of shrubs separating the canoe from the outlaws. Shanna dared not breathe.

"They's smelling something going this way."

It sounded as if the horses were walking slowly in circles around the barking dogs. Had they discovered her? Had they found the smell of birth?

"Look 'ere, Morton."

There was more rambling in the marsh.

"What'cha find?"

"Don't know. Looks like blood."

Oh God, Ayimat Caddi. They've discovered afterbirth. Please God. Please keep this Little Soul safe.

"There! There! In the bushes." A pack of dogs yelped continuously. "Shoot. Shoot." And then bang. Bang again. And then a third shot fired. "You get 'em? Morton, you get 'em?"

"Think so."

The rumbling became louder.

"You idiot!"

"What? What?"

"You didn't get 'em. You just blew hell out of a coon."

"How's I s'posed ta know?"

"Now you done warned the squaw, or whoever got her."

Still not breathing, Shanna closed her eyes. *Thank you God. Thank you my Ayimat Caddi.* She listened to more chatter among the riders as their horses sauntered away from the bank, gaiting southwardly, further into the parish. "We'll be safe Lttle Soul. We'll be going north. She closed her eyes again. She would rest a little longer, and then they would be on their way.

A yellowish glow of morning light found its way to Shanna's eyelids. She pulled back the finger-knitted wrap and glanced at the infant lying still against her breast. She took a more intense look to make sure he was breathing, and seeing that he was, a smile came to her lips. "We go now, Little Soul," she whispered. The infant opened his eyes and rammed his fist into his mouth. "You hungry. But I can't help you now." She tightened the wrap around the tiny body and laid it in front of her on the canoe bottom. Listening to his soft cries, she began to row and sing: "Shush Little Soul now don't you cry; Shanna's gon'ta keep you safe and dry. Shush Little Soul now please don't cry; gon'ta make you happy by and by."

At about mid-morning, Shanna maneuvered the canoe under a bridge used mostly for cotton wagons to cross the bayou. As long as she didn't happen upon any of Jake Minor's outlaws, she and her child should be safe here. She paddled to the bank. Already, she was tired from rowing and her legs and back ached, but she couldn't stop now. She must continue on. She crawled over the canoe siding and scooped her baby into her arms. Holding the child securely, she waded through the marsh to the adjoining dry land. *I must stop. Just for a moment*, she thought.

Feeling slight, Shanna grabbed hold of a willow branch and held tightly. *Don't faint*, she told herself. *Don't faint*. Still holding onto the branch, and keeping her consciousness, she bent forward and laid the infant on the ground near her feet. Moments later, a big ball of gook plopped from her womanhood and dropped to the yellow grass below. She felt her eyes widen in wonder—a gob of mushy blood; and now more clunks were dropping. She took quick breaths, and parted her legs to allow clogs to expel. She sank to the ground and lay motionless for a brief while; and then feeling she had gained energy, she stumbled back to the canoe and pulled out the fishing line. She then returned to the willow where the infant lay. She looked about, her eyes lingering on bolls of cotton near the trail that had fallen from passing wagons. She hurriedly gathered a handful. Using fishing line, she strung bolls into a thick pad to fit between her thighs. She wrapped the string, which hung from the pad, around her hips and tied it at her groin. This contraption would ensnare blood blobs before they dribbled down her legs. Feeling more confident about her condition, she collected the newborn and walked north along the trail toward the city. Still, she stayed close to shrubs that hugged the road edge. In case of danger, she could duck into the bushes. As morning lurked, Shanna ignored cries from the infant. She knew he was hungry. And she would feed him in time. But as yet, her milk had not come. "Oh Little Soul. I'm so sorry," she whispered.

In the early afternoon, with the infant restless in her arms, Shanna came upon a spring jutting from fall leaves inches above a shallow brook. She hurried to the water and laid the child on a clean bed of leaves. She stooped and lowered her head and allowed the cool liquid to fall over her lips. She hesitated, and took a deep breath. She then let cool drops of water seep from her fingers into the infant's eager mouth. When it seemed his thirst was satisfied, she gathered him into her arms and lay near the creek. Sometime later, Shanna was jarred by a noise on the trail. It was just round the corner and coming from the south. Realizing she had been sleeping, she quickly got up, the baby in her arms. Hidden from the approaching wagon, she stole closer to the trail. The cart, loaded with cotton, neared. She waited until the driver's face was clear. It was an older man. But he didn't look dangerous like the men she had known from Jake Minor's store. She waited until the wagon was only a few feet away, then she stepped onto the trail. The driver halted the team of two mares. Pushing his hat from his face, he gazed at Shanna. Shanna swallowed. "You're going my way." She waited a few seconds for the man to speak, but he said nothing. "I have Little Soul here. Born in the moonlight."

The man squinted and, tilting his head to the side, stared at Shanna. Still, he was silent.

"Maybe you give me a ride. North."
"Going to Texarkana?" he asked.
"Not so far. Just a ways up the road."
"Show me the young'un if you got one."

Shanna walked closer to the man. She pushed away the wrap to expose the infant head.

"Well I'll be a crawdad sucker. You sure 'nough do have a young'un."
"You give me ride?"
"Get on up here."

❋ ❋ ❋

The winter's worth of firewood finally chopped, Kathryn stood silently on the porch and allowed the cool night air to chill her skin. This was her hour, with her work and home chores behind her. She wasn't too good a Christian, like most folks here in the backwoods, but she was kind and, in her own way, quite tolerant of aggravation that sometimes found its way into her life. The Lord was good to her. She was blessed with a dear mama and her good friend Leonard. She had a fine place to live, and plenty of food to eat. She was rather comfortable.

With eyes closed, she inhaled long and hard so her nostrils flared and the humid taste of dusk dropped through her throat and into her belly. And then, out of the blue, a ruffling in the bushes startled her. A wolf behind the fig trees, she supposed. She hurried across the porch toward the screen door. Reaching just inside the kitchen, she grabbed a shotgun. Lifting the weapon to her face, she rested her jaw to the gun-cheek so her eyes aimed down the sight.

More ruffling commenced.

"Somebody there? Show yourself before I shoot."

And then, out of the bushes, a human figure emerged.

Four

SOMEWHERE IN TEXAS, Rowe—a young Mexican—slept restlessly. His mind webbed thoughts with frustration and confusion. In his reoccurring dream, an Indian girl's arms clamped tightly to his waist. He slapped the Pinto onward, attempting to escape Jake Minor and his small band of riders. The Pinto's hoofs stirred sand into a whirlwind that cut his flesh like a tight noose. He had heard of these outlaws. They were deadly men. Killers. But Rowe would do whatever necessary to save the girl from the life of torment she suffered at the hands of Jake Minor—a horrific life for any young woman.

Fast running dogs surrounded the pony, nipping at its hoofs. The Pinto neighed just as a rider yanked Shanna from its back. She clutched at Rowe's shirttail, ripping it from his body. In Shanna's hand, the white cloth waved like a surrendering flag in a cloud of gray dust at the outlaw's stallion's side.

Rowe reined the Pinto toward the bad-man, but, as if trapped in the air, the Pinto reared higher, neighing louder. A sharp stinging pain pierced Rowe's shoulder. He fell forward, his head dipping into the pony's mane.

"Ye-aah! Ye-aah!" Rowe yelled, slapping at the pony's neck. "Ye-aah!" As the pony's hoofs touched the ground, a rifle butt slammed into Rowe's head.

He fell facedown to the ground, and the gritty earth and blood rolled on his tongue. All went black. The dream changed. What had happened? He willed that the nightmare return. But no, it rolled on. To another place and time. He wasn't on Caddo ground anymore. He wasn't even in the parish. That time—how long had it been? an eternity ago—more than a year? Now, he was captive in a calaboose somewhere in Texas.

※ ※ ※

A short piece from the Williams' homestead in a lumber-framed house, Leonard sat with family at the kitchen table. Using a freshly baked biscuit, he sopped up the last bites of creamed potatoes and milk gravy from his supper plate.

"Mighty good eating," he said to Cameron, his brother's wife. He lifted a hand-towel from his lap and wiped his mouth, then excused himself from the table. He left the large kitchen and went into the front room.

Bridged By Love

From a wall near the long fireplace, Leonard picked up his fiddle and slid the bow up the scale. The evening ritual at the Whites' home most evenings consisted of Leonard playing the fiddle, his brother, Jordan, picking the guitar and Cameron and her daughter, eight-year-old Becky, usually adding their voices.

Leonard had been in the front room for about ten minutes when Jordan and Becky joined him. Becky quickly put words to a new tune Leonard had fiddled up.

"I love you like wind. I love you like rain. I love you like a stormy night," she sang. Before more words came, she glanced at her uncle and smiled.

Leonard grinned. "Now what kind of love is like the wind on stormy nights? Think that's the best lyrics for this tune, kiddo?"

"I like stormy nights. I like wind and rain."

"Okay. Who's the 'you' in your song?"

"My dog, Uncle Leonard. I love Bacon like the wind on a stormy night."

"Then I guess it's all right to sing about it," Leonard said, his head bobbing slightly to his musical words.

To Leonard, family and music brought a bundle of pleasure. Still, he was happiest when, on glorious evenings, he rode with Kathryn from his workplace in Milton's Woods to her home. He'd stop at the Williams' homestead for any reason he could strum up. Helping Kathryn and Mama with men's work, and then having a bite to eat with the women, always seemed to lift him right up to the heavens.

Leonard loved Kathryn. He had loved her since she was a kid. The first time he laid eyes on the curly-haired toddler was during a memorial service held for countrymen whose bodies were believed buried in a mass grave at Shiloh. After that, he'd seen her often when he drove his mother to the Williams' homestead to do quilting with Mama Williams. After his mother passed away, Leonard still checked on the Williams' and kept them supplied with fresh pork, beef and wild game.

Leonard was a good ten years older than Kathryn, but he so wanted her for his wife—to love her, to provide for her, and to keep her safe.

Nearly a decade ago, he had almost popped the question, but out of nowhere, she up and married Alex Andrews—practically a stranger in town. The news had come to Leonard like a knife to the heart. Soon after the marriage, word of Andrews' ungodly doings became the talk of Texarkana. Word spread rapidly of his involvements with women, cheats and outlaws. Andrews had been bad for Kathryn.

Excusing himself from the family music-making session, Leonard put his fiddle on its stand and went out onto the long front porch. The moon was big tonight, a full glowing ball of light up there in the heavens with the awesome stars.

Kitten, you are always on my mind and in my heart, Leonard thought.

He looked up and pronounced her name aloud, as if she were waltzing amongst the planets. "Kathryn, if I asked you to marry me, would you make this man the happiest alive by saying yes?"

※ ※ ※

The moon and stars, like bright torches, lit up the land around the Williams' back porch, bringing focus to the human figure moving from the fig thicket toward Kathryn.

"State your business," Kathryn demanded, the shotgun staying on the subject.

"I come visiting."

Surprised at the quick girlish voice, Kathryn lowed the gun. "You lost out here?"

"Been traveling from Caddo with Little Soul."

As the girl neared, Kathryn eyed the young woman with dark hair hanging to her waist. She wore a feed-sack wrap draped from her shoulders and carried a blanket-covered bundle near her chest.

"Come on over here," Kathryn said. She watched the woman climb the four steps and stop at the porch edge.

"Where's your family?" Kathryn asked, studying the woman's youthful face. "What'cha doing running around the backwoods, it being night and all? Don't you know there're bandits out there? Bad ones."

Kathryn moved to the back door and held the screen open. "Come inside." She followed the stranger through the doorway. "Sit there." Her eyes glanced to a chair near the eating table.

"Mama," Kathryn called, poking her head into the front room. "We got company." She turned back to Shanna. Then, her breath stopping in her chest, she found herself staring at the bundle—at the head of an infant protruding into view.

My God. This young woman has a baby!

Kathryn froze, unable to move even her lips. She wanted to speak. She wanted to get closer. She wanted to reach out and touch the infant. She felt tears coming.

Where did you come from? she said under her breath.

Mama hurried into the kitchen and gasped, "Oh my! Who are you?"

"Called Shanna."

"You lost?"

"No. I'm finding my way to the Territory. Going to my people. Have this Little Soul now." She hesitated, and looked pitifully from Mama to Kathryn. "I'm tired."

"We have room. You'll sleep here," Mama said.

"Yes, yes," Kathryn interjected, her eyes searching beyond the wrap in Shanna's arms. "You hungry?"

"I eat on trail. Peaches. Pears."

"Come," Kathryn said, motioning Shanna to follow her down a hallway to a room near the back of the house.

"This is the company room." Kathryn pushed open the heart-pine door leading to a room warmly furnished with persimmon and cedar fixtures. She had helped Mama match the décor in this room with the rest of the house's interior.

"You and the infant can sleep here. It's a feather bed. Should keep you comfortable." Kathryn peered at Shanna, her brows lifting. "I'll bring water. If you need more, you can get it from the porch bucket." Her fingers brushed a big blue bowl with red flowers painted on the side. "You can use the pitcher and washbowl here on the basin."

Kathryn breathed hard, trying to loosen the knot tightening more and more in her throat.

"What all do you need for the baby?" she asked, finally.

"Cloth for wrap," Shanna replied, tapping the newborn's bottom through the woven blanket.

Kathryn swallowed painfully. She had baby clothes, lots of them. She and mama had sewed and knitted booties, sweaters, dresses and blankets for the child she had conceived. Through the years, she had kept the tiny garments, perhaps inwardly expecting a day like this would come. "I'll fetch some clothes. And I'll fix you a bite of supper before you bed down. You look weary."

※ ※ ※

Weary, according to Shanna's condition, was too casual a description. She had canoed across the massive Caddo Lake and sprouting bayous, given birth amidst the alligators, snakes, outlaws and dogs. She had tromped through swamplands and backwoods before finding her way to Kathryn's place. But these days had not been the worst she had known. The most horrendous had been her life with Jake Minor.

At age eight, outlaws had stolen her from her family while their tribe traveled north along the Red River somewhere in Arkansas. To this day, the happenings surrounding that frightful event were vivid in her mind.

Shanna closed her eyes, easily drifting back in time...

Shanna left her parents side at the sight of plump berries along the river bank. Horsemen by the dozen approached through a clearing beside the river, riding stallions twice the size of the tribe's ponies. Fear pricked at her stomach and she hunkered down, hiding inside the thick sticker vines, trying to remain out of sight. A rider dropped back, allowing the others to pass him. Then he turned around, rode back to her, and scooped her up without ever once slowing or stopping. At first, too frightened to scream, fear gave way to panic and she found her voice. She kicked furiously and pulled at the long black coat covering her face.

"Ayimat Caddi! Ayimat Caddi!" she screamed to the Great Spirit. "Ayimat Caddi! Ayimat Caddi!"

Her wet face sobbing into the horse's rump was the last she remembered before the ghoulish man clutching her rode amidst the others. Then, all riders stopped in sort-of a circle.

"Ayimat Caddi," Shanna cried, more breathlessly now.

The man dropped her to the ground and the others laughed and leered and roared out coarse words she didn't understand. Too frightened to move, her knees went limp and she plunged to the black bottomland earth. She sobbed and pleaded, "I want my daddy; I want my daddy."

The demon who had nabbed her talked really fast and pointed his white-gloved fingers at first one horseman and then another. She couldn't understand his words, but she knew it was bad stuff from bad spirits. Then he took money from a rider on a horse that neighed uneasily near her feet.

"Sold!" the man said.

They laughed louder. Before she knew what was happening, the fat man who had paid the money scooped her up. Her own spirit must have left her then, for when awareness returned, she was laying on a cot soaked with her own maiden blood in the room she later came to know as her own little prison...

Shanna had soon learned the riders in long black coats and white gloves and hats were a band of outlaws that stole, raided, and robbed without reason. They had slaughtered many Negro people in the northern parishes and in the eastern lands of Texas and western Arkansas. Those same riders had visited Jake Minor's store often since the horrible day they had taken her captive.

Shanna squinted to block off a sudden dribble of tears. She pulled the fresh-smelling colorful quilt around her shoulders and cuddled the infant to her breast. Tonight, she felt safe. But she knew this bliss would not last. She must savor the moment. Soon she would be forever on the run.

❋ ❋ ❋

The wick in the oil lamp burned, its light flickering so the brown, tan, red and yellow colorings in Kathryn's festively decorated bedroom glowed. Her mind was on the young woman sleeping in the company room. The idea of the woman traveling alone with a newborn seemed peculiar. Where was her man? She was very young, but surely she had a man someplace; she had a baby. Didn't Indians usually keep their families together? Perhaps she had gotten lost from her people somehow. Kathryn sighed and scolded herself for her intrusive thoughts. This girl's doings were none of her business.

Kathryn rolled over and stretched so the moonlight shining in the window seeped through the thin nighgown covering her body. She rubbed her hand gently over her breast. It would be nice to have a man to love. She needed a man. And the man she needed, wanted and loved was John. "John," she whispered, touching her nipples soothingly. "I want you." But, she wondered, would he ever want her?

❋ ❋ ❋

Lying on the bed in his room at the S. Wagner Boarding House in Texarkana, John Allen hurt for a woman. A good woman. One who would respect him and provide for his most manly desires.

He ran his hand over his male organ. His erecting manhood wanted more than he could provide himself. If only he were attracted to the widow, Sharleen Wagner, sleeping in the room adjacent to his. But she was homely, too old, and a bit bossy.

Then there was Kathryn Williams. She wasn't bad to look at, in fact she was quite fetching, and she was right nice to talk to, but she had her bloody faults, too. She just didn't seem to be the kind of woman a man could live comfortably with. She wasn't a woman a man could dominate, as men were supposed to do. She was the type of woman who would ask questions. She was too curious to belong to a man. Maybe she would be good in many ways, but he was afraid she'd want to wear the pants. And that was certainly not what he wanted in a woman.

Forget Kathryn before you even think about her, he told himself.

As on other nights like this, when the moon was full and its light shining in his window, he thought of beautiful Lilly and wondered what had ever happened to her. But their meeting had been three years back, when he was coming to this land of the new frontier. He'd never find Lilly now, of that he was most certain, but just thinking of her made his manhood bubble over; and that certainly eased the hurt and provided some sexual relief. *Beautiful Lilly.* He held her memory as if she were with him now as she had been so briefly so long ago. "Lilly," he whispered. "Lilly."

On the train traveling west from Boston three or so years ago, John Allen relaxed against the hardened leather that covered his seat. His goal was to travel to Texas and settle in Texarkana, the new frontier. In the city, he would develop a lucrative career as a carpenter and carver. Also, he wanted to find a good woman. A woman who would always be there for him without his asking. One who would never leave him no matter what. A woman with eyes focused only on him. A classy one on the train caught his eye and captured his soul. John was almost sure he'd lock onto this bold and beautiful lady's hand through life. Strange, how things happened, though.

"I want to know all about you Mister Allen," pretty Lilly had whispered, snuggling closer to him and slipping her hands into his jacket pocket.

Lilly obviously enjoyed something about the way he talked, for she asked him the same questions over and over and over between Boston and St. Louis. Throughout the ride, the two stayed at each other's side constantly, not leaving for even a minute except to perform personal hygiene duties. Smiling at the pretty woman with lips the color and size of a spring plum and eyes as black as her raven hair, he knew for sure that this was love.

"Tell me how you came to America," she pleaded again. Her dark lashes flickered and her lips puckered within an inch of his own.

"I came by way of Ireland," he said, reaching to touch a lock of hair dropping from under the brim of her wide green hat. "You might say I'm Scot-Irish. Really English. My ancestors left England because of poverty and religious problems. In Ireland, I was among the sprouting limbs of the Allen tree. But nothing was any better for us in the new land than it had been for our fathers in England." He paused, looked down at her, and grinned. "Sorry, I do have the tendency to ramble on."

Lilly's eyes were like mirrors. He could see his reflection in them.

"When I saw an opportunity to catch a boat bound for America, I climbed aboard. I didn't have any money, but the captain was kind and allowed me to work my way to Plymouth. Then I toiled around here and there and put a few dollars together. I got on this train southbound out of Boston, and that's when I found you, my pretty one."

He caressed her rosy cheek with his hand. This was love, instant love.

He was sure when her hand, concealed in his jacket pocket, found his most private body parts. His stare caught her eyes and sucked her into him, deep into him. Sucked her all the way to the most demanding organ, sucked her until the fountain of love opened, shooting to the surface a liquid substance and allowing it to spew over, leaving him weak and unaware of the world passing by the clacking of train wheels.

He remained in awe as the helm came to a screeching halt, while people paraded with baggage through the aisle, while the conductor punched holes in tickets of passengers who had just boarded.

"Lilly," he whispered, his eyes closing and rolling about under his eyelids. "Lilly."

Love was grand. In his thoughts and dreams, he relived the wonderful sexual experience again and again. He awoke, his gaze dropping to his hand-covered crotch. He was wet and warm. He looked to his side, at the seat where lovely Lilly had sat. It was empty. He stared through the train car for a moment, and then felt inside his jacket pocket.

Lovely Lilly had vanished.

So had his wallet and all the money he had earned in Plymouth.

"Porter, tell me. The lady with me earlier; did you see where she went?"

"Yes sir, I's sho 'nough did. The lady done gots off the train with a gentleman that was a riding in the next car down. Gots off just west of St. Louis. Sho 'nough did." The porter paused, and straightened his snow-white cap. "I'z didn't think yas knows whats is a'happenin'. I sho 'nough didn't." The porter gazed for a moment at John. "Tells yas whats though. The man won't go far. He rides this train plenty times. Sometimes goes all the way to Dallas. I's better not talk more. Don't wants to get caught up in the midst of a group of outlaws."

Outlaws? The porter hadn't elaborated further and John hadn't asked him to. This whole ordeal with Lilly was too hurting. A hurt he would live with for a long time, of that he was sure.

He should have known a woman as beautiful as Lilly would be difficult to keep. Now, after all this time, he should give up on ever seeing the awesome woman again. But he never would.

Nowadays, when John got hard up for a woman, he could always go a few paces down the street to the House of Chances and get him one. Or even to one of the gambling saloons. However, he would never marry a whore.

Finding somebody to marry here was a task. Kathryn Williams was the closest to wife material as he had found. She was a right pretty Irish woman: hair the color of a chili pepper, pale freckles and slim frame. Oh she wasn't nearly as pretty as Lilly, but she was attractive and smart looking.

If only she were not so head strong and so set in her ways. And after being in love with the smartly dressed and beautiful Lilly, even briefly, how could he settle for a woman who dressed like a cowpoke and worked on a log wagon? Why didn't she just stay home and sew?

John smiled and closed his eyes. He knew Kathryn would marry him at the snap of his finger. Her longing for him was so obvious. The woman was bloody funny for him. That was a fact, but she could never satisfy him. Never.

Certainly not after his experiencing Lilly.

Five

At the Williams' homestead everybody had always gotten up with the first crow of the rooster. Today was no different. Kathryn yawned to ward off sleep and slowly pushed the red-and-yellow patch quilt off her shoulders. She yawned again, stretching her arms so the straps of her white nightgown fell from her shoulders.

As the first glows of dawn seeped between the drawn-back yellow-ruffled curtains, Kathryn smiled and welcomed a new day. She briskly got out of bed, straightening the quilted spread behind her.

The well-structured furniture in Kathryn's bedroom matched the groomed persimmon and cedar furnishing scattered through the dwelling. As long as she could remember, she or Mama had chopped branches from choice trees to build their own furniture, as did many people living in the backwoods.

She sat on the red-dyed wool-cushioned stool at her vanity and, looking at her reflection in the mirror, brushed her reddish hair from her lightly freckled face and rolled it into a twist at the back of her neck. From her cedar wardrobe, she selected a blue-plaid felt shirt and denim overall. Pulling a pair of thick cotton socks from an accompanying drawer and picking up her brown leather boots, she scurried to the kitchen.

Mama was also an early riser. Already, she had a fire going in the black iron stove, making the room warm and cozy.

Kathryn smiled. "Morning Mama."

"Morning," Mama replied. Her focus moved from the table-size chopping block, though she continued kneading a short mound of biscuit dough. Mama wore an ankle-length dress made of store-bought cotton fabric the color of a brown eggshell. It had long sleeves and a gathered skirt that fell over the tops of her black boots. Kathryn remembered watching Mama sew the dress so many years ago.

Smiling, Kathryn noted how gracefully Mama had aged over the years, never gaining or losing weight, and her gray-streaked hair accenting the loveliness of her gentle face. A good woman, she was always ready to give of her possessions or time to help one in need.

Kathryn dropped her boots, the pressure of the fall making a quick thump on the plank floor. She pulled a straight-backed chair from the table and, hearing footsteps behind her, turned just as Shanna strolled into the kitchen. "How you doing this morning?" Kathryn asked, her eyes moving upward just a little. She sank onto the woven-seat and pulled on her socks.

"Rested," Shanna said, but her voice held a weak quiver.

"I didn't hear the baby last night."

"He sleeps good." Shanna's eyes met Kathryn's and her thick lips puckered into a smile. "Handsome boy child."

"Yes, handsome," Kathryn agreed softly. She smiled, but couldn't prevent a sharp pain of sadness sweeping through her and swelling in her heart. She must hide her own sorrow and let happiness for this woman and infant show.

"Well, I'll just bet you'll feel even better after you down some coffee," Mama interjected, her smile deepening the thin wrinkles near her hazel eyes.

Suddenly, it seemed, the aroma from the steaming coffee filled the air.

"Sounds good." Shanna smiled lightly and pulled out a chair. She sat cautiously, as if in pain. Kathryn watched the young woman as she pulled her long hair to her cheek and tied it with a string.

"Where did you come from, Shanna?" Kathryn asked as she slipped into her boots.

"Two nights that way." Shanna pointed southwardly.

Mama turned from the stove. "Walking? Riding?"

"Canoe one night. Wagon one night." She hesitated. "I borrowed a ride in the wagon. I leave when the wagon man sleeps."

"Did he want money from you?"

"Don't know. Didn't ask. Didn't want him see me go. Didn't want him to follow."

"I see. It's getting to where a body can't even trust her own shadow," Kathryn said, getting up to leave the room. "Be right back."

Outside before daybreak, Kathryn hurried to the chicken coop. She stepped into the small plank-framed henhouse. Here, box nests of about one-foot-by-one-foot containing a slight layer of fresh straw lined the east wall and spread the taste of fall flavor to the tiny hut. On the west wall, four long, wooden rails placed like stair steps served as roosts, however, the chickens were already outside and scratching in cool places for bugs and worms. Next spring, substance collecting on the dirt floor would be used to enrich the garden soil, she noted, turning back to the nests. In one nest, Kathryn found a Rhode Island Red setting, even though winter was near and the survival of biddies might be difficult. From the remaining nests, she collected six eggs.

"Hens did good," Mama said, her eyes watching as Kathryn put the eggs on the kitchen counter.

"Quite a handful." Kathryn smiled. "You know, that old hen Rodey's setting."

"More chickens...can't complain," Mama said.

Kathryn exchanged a look with Mama, then glanced over at Shanna.

"I know you said you're heading out west, but travel ain't exactly safe for a woman alone, you know. You're welcome to stay on with us, if you like."

Shanna regarded her solemnly. "Maybe that would be good. To rest. For a few days."

Kathryn nodded. "It's settled, then."

After breakfast, Kathryn put butter and honey inside eight leftover biscuits and wrapped them in a clean, white rag. This would be lunch for Leonard and her. Then she left the homestead and began the three-mile hike through the forest to where she and Leonard had stopped cutting pulpwood the day before. Usually, she would have saddled Sugar and ridden her, but of late the palomino had been favoring her left foot. She would have to check the mare over and maybe apply a remedy when she returned home this afternoon.

The walk was extra beautiful and rewarding this morning. It was as if she were seeing nature for the first time in many years. She stood motionless for a moment and listened to the singing of winds moving through the yellow and rust leaves. A thumping noise sifted through the dried shrubs and fallen twigs and drew Kathryn's attention. She breathed deeply and smiled at the sight of a half-dozen or more squirrels scampering over the brush, their jaws carrying acorns. At a rustle coming from the right, she glanced over her shoulder. A brown rabbit, so unafraid, stopped and gazed at her.

"I love these woods," she told herself, smiling broadly.

In an oak tree just ahead, a handful of honeybees hovered over a hive. It seemed odd she had never noticed it. Perhaps, come Saturday, she could get a couple pints of the honey and a piece of the cone.

Another rabbit, this one scampering alongside a stand of wild plumb trees took the spotlight, then another, and another. Cottontails were plentiful. The first killer frost would destroy the sick rabbits; the ones left would be safe for eating. Leonard would supply Mama and her with all the meat they'd need. And then, *Oh my goodness, such a beautiful doe!*

She smiled. *I could stand in this lovely place and dream forever.*

But she knew she must hurry to work. As the golden glow of morning light seeped through the yellow maple leaves and cast a hue on the beaten path through the Williams' property, Kathryn broke into a run. She must get to the wagon yard soon or Leonard would surely head on to Milton's Woods without her.

Leonard was a hard worker, worth the pay of two men. And he could lift so much weight. Of course, he was stronger than she. He was at least six-foot-three and muscular. Many times she had seen him pick up a pine tree trunk all by himself. But next to Leonard, she was indeed the most valuable pulpwood cutter in the county. And she was the only woman with guts enough to spend time at the sawmill yard in Texarkana with all those men. But she had never been intimidated or worried. Men treated her with respect and kept their distance.

Kathryn slowed her pace as she started down the hill that led to the wagon yard. From here, she saw Leonard loading their wagon with cutting gear. She watched him lap his long legs over the railing and slide onto the seat. He grabbed up the reins and slapped at the two mules.

"Lord-a-mercy, I'm late," she said aloud, and again broke into a run.

Catching up with the wagon, she grabbed hold of the back end, held on and ran with it until she picked up enough speed to jump and swing her body upward. Then she quickly drew her legs over the plank railing. She dropped into a clear section of the wagon bed and sank down to sit silently for a moment, her breath coming and going too rapidly to speak. A moment later, she crawled to the front and sat on the bench next to Leonard. Laughing mildly, she reached into her overall bib and pulled out the cloth containing the biscuits. They were smashed. "Ah-hh," she squealed.

A grin spread over Leonard's leathery face. The pleasing look from this older man presented her a special feeling of worth.

"Where in tarnation did you come from?" he drawled, his smile deepening the crowfeet around his hazel eyes.

"Bet you thought I wasn't coming in today." She laughed, and glanced over her shoulder at the man she knew adored her. Her eyes stayed on him for a moment while she brushed sweat curls from her cheeks and tucked them into the roll at the back of her neck.

Leonard nodded. "I should-of knowed you'd be here."

"You didn't aim on waiting for me though, did you Mister White?" At her teasing, she laughed and shook her head. Leonard was an exceptional man, very sweet and compassionate. He was one-of-a-kind. A true treasure. They'd been the best of friends since she could remember.

Kathryn closed her eyes and let the music of rolling wagon wheels carry her over the fields. *Now count your blessings*, she told herself. *One, a good life. Two, good health. Three, Mama and Leonard. Four, my mare, Sugar, and my homestead. Five...Five*, she swallowed hard. *Five, the girl and her baby.*

By the time Kathryn had mutely thanked God for his daily gifts, as she usually did during the ride to the jobsite, the wagon arrived at the spot where Leonard and she had quit working the day before. In hardly any time they had chopping tools unloaded and each of them were at an end of the two-man-saw. Their bodies rocked back and forth while sawdust flew wildly from the first pine.

"There she goes!" Leonard shouted as the tree wobbled. Then came the slow whisking fall.

Kathryn jumped back. "Hey, hey," she called. Her laughter was loud above the cracking of timber as the crisp pine needles and branches swished into the shrubs of a plum thicket. Seeing the tree had fallen before the saw had cut all the way through its trunk, Kathryn took her ax and hacked away the interlocking twigs. Then she stood straight and smiled at Leonard.

"This is about a fine looking piece of pulp," she acknowledged.

"Yep," Leonard agreed. "We're off to a good start all right."

Kathryn tilted her head and winked.

The sun straight up and the wagon filled, Kathryn wanted a break. She rambled about gathering brushwood while Leonard arranged dried leaves and twigs for fire starter.

"We'll have us some coffee here in a bit," he said, his head bobbing while he talked. "I think we better be driving on to the sawmill after we eat. We've about got all the timber these mules can pull."

"You're right," Kathryn agreed, her brows lifting with her satisfied grin. "It's a fine haul."

After their meal, Kathryn took the driver's seat and held the reins while Leonard tromped on the fire to smother the flames. He removed his denim cap and rubbed his thinning brown hair from his broad forehead, then climbed onto the sitting bench beside her.

For a while, there was silence as they rode through the clearing toward Texarkana. Soon, Leonard broke it.

"You know, Kathryn, I'm a lonely man."

"Now how can you be lonely with that nice family you have living at your place?"

"A man can be lonely. Don't make no difference if the house is full or empty. A man needs a woman."

"Oh, guess what Leonard," Kathryn said, deliberately changing the subject and shifting the direction of conversation. "We have guests at our place." Without looking, she could see the dismay in Leonard's eyes as he squinted to conceal emotions.

Maybe she should talk romance with Leonard. Maybe she should give him the chance to propose marriage. But to do so would be unfair while her dreams were of John.

She held her breath for a moment, hoping he would not speak the words she knew his mind held.

Six

ALEX ANDREWS STOOD in a stand of young oak trees and watched his former wife and Leonard White until the wagon loaded with logs was out of sight. *The Little Gal has no shame*, he mused as the clacking of the medal wheels rolled over the wagon trail toward the sawmill in Texarkana.

Wonder if that hick has asked her to marry him yet, Alex thought. *Everybody knows he loves her regardless of her hen-pecking ways. No need to worry about that, though. She doesn't love him. She'll never marry Leonard White or any other man. Not as long as I'm in the picture. And I'm here for the duration.*

Even if Kathryn should accept a proposal from Leonard, he would see to it that the two were never hitched. Whether Kathryn knew, she and he would retie the knot she had so boldly unleashed. Hell, he wasn't in love with the feisty little redhead. Not at all. Didn't have to be. But seven years ago when they'd gotten hitched, it was for better for worse. And although he saw fit to leave the tri-states, those vows still rang clear in his head.

Alex chewed the past over to himself:

So maybe he wasn't the best husband a woman could want, but he wasn't really bad either. He drank a little more whiskey than necessary, played a mean hand of poker, got just about everything he wanted by wheeling-and-dealing, and he liked the young painted ladies. Didn't matter if they were pretty. But his profile was much the same as every other man alive, except perhaps that of Leonard White.

And he had never hit the Little Gal. Hell, if he had, she'd have likely beaten the tar out of him.

Indeed, she had divorced him. He knew all about the actions she had taken after he left the homestead. After she lost the kid.

That week, Alex had ridden down to Caddo Lake to do a little business with Jake Minor. From there, he had gone to Texarkana and left his stallion with an old boy to ride, feed and board for him. He had then caught the Union Pacific to Dallas, then on north to the Colorado and Arizona territories.

Riding the rails had been unkind to Alex. Several times he had drunk a little too much whiskey and barely escaped death while playing poker. But he had come through with a bundle of money before slipping off the train, without being seen, someplace in Colorado—wherever he was, there was a big whoop-dee-do about statehood going on.

There, he prospected for gold. He would have stayed longer than he did and found enough nuggets to get rich had it not been for the excruciating, back-breaking, slave-hard labor.

But now things had changed, and much for the better, he mused. He could get just as rich here in these backlands and it wouldn't take nearly as much sweat.

First, he must make Kathryn his wife. He had a scheme that would work. He had bait to lure her in like an anxious fish jumping for the worm. There would be no stopping him now.

"Damn you're smart Alex Andrews," he praised himself. Grinning, he listened to the clacking of the log wagon's wheels fade away.

Only a matter of time 'til Kathryn will be eating out of your hands and you'll get exactly what you want, he marveled.

A sudden whip of wind loosed a spray of brown leaves from the oak limbs above him. He stood there for another moment thinking of his victorious plan before turning to his stallion.

He said aloud: "Now Alex, it's time to play your ace in the hold and ramrod your next move."

Alex's plan at the moment was to find old Moldie's brother, Bill Junior, and do some conniving. And then he needed to grab that squaw... "You're not going to like it Squaw Girl, but you and I are hopping a train headed west, and you're gonna help me get what I want," Alex said aloud. He raised his brows in glee, and then laughed boisterously.

※ ※ ※

In the Texas jail, an acute pain shot across Rowe's back, as if someone had used a sharp knife to cut a deep gash into his flesh. He flexed his shoulders and hunched them forward toward his chin. Another cutting pain came, this worse than the previous. Rowe gritted his teeth. His skin split and a warm substance gushed down his spine. He hurt good and finally was able to breathe. He reached behind his back and felt the liquid. Puss, he realized, looking at his hand. He reached back again and pressed the inflamed muscle. A hard lump, about the size of a pecan, popped from the lesion onto his fingers. This sore had lingered on Rowe's back since the time of his capture. It would never heal without cleaning. Also, whisky should be applied, he understood. He slumped forward on the dingy mattress covering the narrow cot and put his hands behind his head so his elbows spread outward like wings.

"Ye gettin' up at all today boy?" the jailer asked, glaring from the small table serving as a desk on the other side of the jail bars. "Ye been having fits all mornin' boy. Just like a mad dog."

Rowe stretched his legs and allowed pain to shoot through the whole of him. If only he could get out of this cell. First thing, he'd grab up that bastard jailer and set him out for the buzzards.

"Ye heared me? Think ye done got mad dog fever."

"How about some whisky and a rag. This damn infection's getting worse. You better keep me alive or the outlaws will hang you instead of me," Rowe said, taking pleasure noting the probable outcome of his own frightening fate.

"Ye already used up ever thang we had. Ye jest have to suffer now."

"What kind of dump is this?" Rowe rose from the cot, one hand holding his ribs to keep in a protruding bulge. "You got no grub. No tolerable water. No shit house. No alcohol. Nothing to make a bandage." He glared aimlessly from corner to corner of the untidy facility, then down at the cot. "Hell, you don't even have any bedding in here."

Rowe paused briefly, unnoticeably eyeing the jailer. "You ain't cleaned up this jail cell. You don't even got sense enough to give me soap and water to clean it myself." He paused again, and again glimpsed at the jailer. "You aren't doing a thing except keeping me locked up. You don't even have backbone enough to come inside here and duke it out with me. You're scared of me as crippled up as I am. You're nothing but a yellow coward."

"Ye jest wishing me to unlock ye. Ye jest wanting to break away and run off. Mind ye, that ain't happening. So just settle yer-self down."

The day will soon come, Rowe said under his breath. *Things will be as they once were.*

At age twenty, before wandering into Caddo Parish and meeting Shanna, Rowe had traveled through Texas in search of water and minerals. Born a Texan, his mother was Mexican-Mayan and his father a white politically involved rancher. Rowe had completed high school with Caucasian students in Laredo, just a stone's throw across the Rio Grande to Nuevo Laredo. Through school, he had received high marks and upon graduation was quickly accepted by the Waco-Laredo Water and Mineral Search Company. Headquartered in Laredo, the business associated with water-and-mineral companies as far east as St. Louis. No, Rowe had not always been locked in this musky jail cell, his hair and beard getting longer by the minute, waiting for outlaws to come hang him. He had been a man of class, culture and character. And he would be that again.

That day will come. But first, I'll be one hell-raising son-of-a-bitch!

Seven

"You're nice to let me stay last night," Shanna said as she entered the kitchen where Mama stood by a washbasin with a kettle of boiling water in her hand. She poured the water so it fell over Mason jars, scalding them in preparation for canning.

"I must return a favor."

"You owe us nothing, dear. We've been helped before ourselves. We like doing for others."

Shanna caught a whiff of the pinto beans and saltpork steam coming from a large crock.

"You canning beans?"

"Yes. We'll have a goodly amount of vegetables in the cellar. Enough to last through the cold spell."

"I can help. Need garden picked?"

"I've 'bout got it cleaned out." Mama laughed lightly. "Just about everything's canned already."

"I'm very good hunter. I learned many years ago. Haven't got to hunt in a long time."

Mama smiled and looked from the hot kettle to Shanna. "Why not?"

"Was not allowed. Man who owned the camp wouldn't let me hunt unless I was being watched. He feared I'd shoot him, I think."

"Oh my. What would give him such an idea?" Mama's voice held concern. "You wouldn't have shot him—would you?"

Without answering, Shanna squinted and gazed at Mama. If Mama only knew the truth about her. That she had pushed a butcher knife into Jake Minor's heart. However, if she could have gotten her hands on one of his loaded guns, she would just as soon to have shot him as to look at him. It would have been so easy for her. Regardless of how it had happened, though, she had put the bad man to rest. He was out of her life for good.

"I can use your gun. I'll get a opossum or a coon."

"Sure you can," Mama smiled at Shanna. "Take the rifle from the rack in the front room. We like to keep this gun here by the back door in case we need it real quick.

"You come with me to hunt?"

"No. I'm sure you don't need me." Again Mama eyed Shanna as if studying her motive. "I'll tend your baby."

"Yes," Shanna agreed. "I go alone."

38

Bridged By Love

"Just be back to feed him when you think he's hungry."

"I don't have milk. I give Little Soul white gravy you make this morning."

"Oh my," Mama said, worry in her voice. "I'll–I'll get some liquid into the little fellow."

Shanna didn't turn to see if Mama was watching her. She walked straight to the front room and took the rifle from the gun rack, then hurried out the front door.

Shanna held the gun with both hands as she slipped about in the forest surrounding the Williams' homestead. If a raccoon or an opossum should happen along she would shoot it, but the real reason she wanted to get out with a weapon was to see if the outlaws and dogs had caught up with her. If so, one would probably be hiding out and waiting for her to show face.

After about an hour and seeing nobody, she discovered an old tree stump near a stream and set down on it. She smiled and held her head back so the gentle breeze meshing through the trees cooled her face. She breathed deeply through her nose. The air refreshed her lungs and produced energy.

Then a scampering noise caught her attention. A critter was near. Quietly, she waited until the raccoon reached the water.

Shanna held the rifle to her cheek, aimed at the game, and pulled the trigger. BOOM! She had taken the small creature out with one slug. Getting up from the stump, she moved toward the animal. The shot was clean. The strike had gone through the scull so the raccoon had not suffered.

"Little friend forgive me. The meat you give will nourish bodies of good people," she whispered.

She picked up the game and walked a little way down stream where the water ran more rapidly. Here, she took a knife from the pocket of her feed-sack smock, sliced open the animal's stomach, and then using her hand, pulled out its innards.

As Shanna washed her hands in the stream, she watched the current take away blood and guts. She sat quietly on a log of petrified wood and let the cold water wash over the meat. Then, carrying the raccoon by the hind legs so its head dangled at her side, she started through the forest to the Williams' home.

Just then she heard more scampering. The noise, sounding like that of a horse, was getting closer. Her hand still clutching the raccoon, she leaped into a thicket of plum bushes and hovered close to the cool damp earth. The clomping of hoofs came closer. And then she saw the bad man who did dealings with Jake Minor—the bad man who had caught her standing over Jake's bloody body back at the fish camp—riding on his big white stallion.

Shanna cried silently: *He wasn't supposed to come. He said he'd leave me alone. He wasn't supposed come. Why did he follow me to Kathryn?*

The deal had been that he would take Jake's guns and sell them in Dallas. She would not tell anybody of him stealing the guns and he would say nothing of her. Shanna stayed hidden until the sound of hoofs had disappeared in the opposite direction of the Williams place. Then, watching her steps carefully so not to get surprised by him or any other rider, she hurried toward the homestead. She must be aware of everything around her and make plans to leave the area, to go off where she would not be found. It wasn't safe for her to stay longer. Not for herself and not for the good women.

At the homestead, Shanna raked kindling into a pile under the black iron wash-pot in the back yard. With her back to the wind, she bent forward and blew lightly on sparks until flames came. The afternoon was cooling, she noticed, and hurried to the well for water. She drew up two buckets full and poured them into the pot.

"Looks like you got a coon," Mama called, stepping from the kitchen onto the back porch. She walked across the rustic planks and stood at the edge.

"Yes. Got a coon. A nice one." Shanna pointed at her take lying on the grass near her feet. "You got lye and salt?"

"Sure do."

In only moments, Mama was at the wash-pot with a bar of lye and two long blades. Shanna picked up the raccoon and dipped it several times into the boiling water, and then she laid it on a carving table near the wash-pot. Immediately, she and Mama scraped off bristles.

"Like the hunt?" Mama asked, her eyes again studying Shanna's expression.

"Hunt was good. Forest was cool. Nice," she paused. "Little Soul wake up?"

"Yes. I fed him. Gravy's gone now. Gave him water."

"Little Soul needs milk."

"Our cow is dry. Have to get milk from somewhere though," Mama said.

"I can cook squash. Mash it soft."

After about a half-hour, the women had the raccoon scrapped clean and rubbed all over with salt.

"We'll hang the meat in the cellar," Mama said, and the two walked to the door leading downward into a space built into a mound of earth on the cool side of the house. "We'll cook it in a day or so."

Shanna followed Mama down the steps into the cool cellar. Just then she heard a loud ruckus coming from the front of the house. "Dogs coming," she said to Mama.

"Yes. Don't get dogs often around here. Sometimes hounds lose their way when they take off after a deer that doesn't drop right away."

"Dogs coming for me," Shanna said, her voice a sudden tremble.

"Why would dogs be after you?"

"'Cause I'm running from dogs. Outlaws, wearing black, want me."

Shanna paused. "Little Soul," she whispered. "I don't want Little Soul harmed."

"Why would outlaws be after you?" Mama asked, now more concerned than before. "Men in black—do you mean the Raider Outlaws are looking for you?"

"Yes. Jake Minor's outlaws. They wear black coats, white gloves."

"Oh my goodness, Shanna. What have you done?"

Yelps grew louder, seeming to barge right through the cellar door. A line of daylight emerged through a crack and into the cool room. The beam allowed Mama to focus on Shanna's face. "How would the Raiders know you're here?"

"Outlaws chased me through lakes and bayous. Forests, fields. They want to hang me. They heard me shoot the coon. They followed me."

"We got to figure out what to do," Mama said, putting her eye to the crack to see outside. "We're in this hole and the baby's in the house." She paused. "And the rifle's propped up out there by the work table."

Eight

*W*ITH JOHN ALLEN a regular customer at the sawmill, Kathryn could look forward to seeing him on her trips to town. And for her, seeing John was the highpoint of any day.

She sat straight and smoothed her hair so the reddish strands that had fallen from her twist lay neatly behind her ears. Looking around, she guided the mules down busy Front Street, keeping the team far to the right and out of fast-moving trolley traffic. Three men in front of a gambling hall were swinging fists at each other. This action was not uncommon in this growing metropolis. A short piece farther, she reined the mules over a wide row of streetcar tracks and made a quick turn north on Third Street. Smiling, she waved at people passing in rugged work wagons as well as those riding fancy carriages.

Texarkana had grown profusely since becoming incorporated some ten or so years ago—to the tune of about 8,000 people, give or take. Most of the growth was due to the building of the Texas and Pacific Railroad, which ran parallel with Front Street on the south end of town. Then came an abundance of other train lines, thus generating much business to the twin cities. The town's growth was also, in a vast way, due to numerous cotton growers and buyers.

At the intersection of Third and Broad streets, Kathryn waited for a row of cotton wagons to pass. So much of the crop still on the streets showed growers had prospered this year. Her focus moved over the fat bales on what must be at least a hundred horse-drawn carts. Growing cotton, as Mama had suggested, might be a good idea, Kathryn mused briefly. But for her, anything other than her truck farming and pulpwood cutting just didn't seem right. She steered the team north a short ways to the sawmill yard. Bracing herself in anticipation of John's presence, she guided the mules over the board-covered gully and into the sawmill yard.

Without turning, Kathryn absorbed the surroundings in her peripheral vision. There, John stood beside Milton outside the one-room sawmill office. His hands rested in the pockets of his charcoal-colored suit jacket so his matching vest and starched white shirt provided him an appearance of class. John always dressed and carried himself in a sophisticated air. It was hard to pull her stare from this man who made her feel so womanly inside.

Kathryn shook the reins, her head dipping slightly as the wagon passed the two men. She smiled inwardly and remembered three years ago, the first time she had seen John. He had just gotten off a train arriving from the east.

"Excuse me Miss," John had said, pronouncing his words in an accent unrecognizable to Kathryn. On that day, after she and Leonard had delivered their haul to the sawmill, Leonard had personal errands to attend and she had gone to the depot just to watch trains arrive—a pastime she thoroughly enjoyed whenever she had time to spare. "I do hope you can help me," the handsome stranger had said, tipping his dark gray hat with the thin satin multi-colored band. "I'm looking for a rooming house."

"The Cosmopolitan Hotel is over on the corner of Texas and Broad," Kathryn said. She turned slightly and pointed west. "You can't miss it. It's three stories high and takes up might-near the whole city block."

"Oh, but I prefer a rooming house since I plan to make my home here."

Kathryn tilted her head. This had to be the best looking man she had ever come to face. Most of his smile favored the right side of his mouth and his blue eyes twinkled. "You're not from around these parts, are you?"

"No, I'm not. Come here from Boston. Before Boston, Ireland."

"Goodness gracious, you've come a long ways." She hesitated, smitten with his charisma and the way his eyes kept moving over her approvingly. "Well, let me see now," she paused for a moment, then added, "S. Wagner's Boarding House is right over on Hazel Street. You better catch yourself a horse trolley; it's a pretty good ways." She paused again. "Just got off the train, didn't you?"

"Yes. Riding was such a wonderful experience. The train traveled over a huge river bridge at a place called Fulton. This is my first time in Texas," he said, pointing at his own chest and laughing mildly. "I hope I don't run into any cowboys with six-shooters. But I hear a man is quite safe unless he deals in cattle."

Kathryn smiled through tightly closed lips. She didn't want to offend this friendly gentleman, but still she wondered where he had gotten his information. Somehow, questioning him about it didn't seem right, though. "Well now, you just got off the train and walked to here. To this very spot," she said, glancing at the suitcase near his feet.

"Yes, only moments ago."

Suddenly a hint of shyness came to her. She smiled, feeling her eyes betraying her by flirting with this foreigner.

"Well, I don't know how to break the news to you." Her southern draw teased a bit more than usual. "But this isn't Texas. When you ride in here on a train from the west, you get off in Texas, but when you ride in here on a train from the east, you get off in Arkansas. It's kind-of crazy, I guess. But that's just how it is."

"So I've not stepped foot in Texas?"

"No. Come on." She motioned the man to follow, and then she stepped about three feet to the west. "Now, you're in Texas."

"Can this be?" he said, more a statement than a question. "So you can just walk from state to state."

"Yes, when you're at the divide. The street leading north in front of the depot is the divide." She positioned her feet about a half-foot apart and did a sort-of two-step dance. "This side in Texas and this side is Arkansas," she said, positioning her hands from side to side to demonstrate her explanation. "Anyway, why'd you come here?"

"Greener pastures," he had answered, one corner of his mouth raised in the tantalizing smile.

Kathryn sighed at her recollection. As if it had been yesterday, her first meeting with John lived vividly in her mind. She had surreptitiously loved this man every moment since that very impressive day.

Her focus stayed on John now, and her tongue dallied lightly over her bottom lip.

"Kathryn," John said, waving frivolously.

Goodness gracious. She caught her breath. He was walking toward her.

She dropped the reins and climbed over the buckboard. John's sky-blue eyes seemed to dance when he reached for her hand. He took a step backwards, then removed his hat and using his fingers as a comb, swept his light brown hair from his fair face. He looked first at her, then at Leonard.

"Looks like you have quite a load of pulp here. Did you cut it all this morning?"

"Sure did," Kathryn bragged.

"Isn't that work much too heavy for a lady?"

"Nope."

"As I've told you time and time again, a lady as lovely as you shouldn't be cutting pulpwood." He brought her hand to his lips and kissed gently. "A lady like you should stay inside the home. You should wear fancy clothes. Appealing dresses and bonnets. Teach piano." He paused. "You do play piano, don't you?"

"I got a bit of an ear for it." Butterflies fluttered in Kathryn's stomach. Did John know how very much she cared for him, how his presence sent chills through her blood, and how his voice made an ache for him play in her stomach? But fancy clothes and piano lessons? Who did he think she was?

"There are no other pretty ladies working for Milton." Even his teasing made a tingle bubble inside her.

"Someday," she paused, searching for words. Someday she would like to have a family: a husband, a child. But she knew that was not possible. Hearing Leonard slip to the middle of the wagon seat and take the reins, Kathryn turned from John.

"Where you going, Leonard?" she called, her voice raised so to be heard over mill clamor.

"Over yonder where they'll be stripping logs tomorrow."

Bridged By Love

"I suppose you're going to help unload the wagon," John jested, dimples deepening his cheeks. He smiled, replaced his hat, and straightened the brim.

Kathryn didn't answer right away. She just stood there like a knot on a log and marveled at John's charisma. And how could one man have such an exceptionally handsome face? He was about a head taller than she, and slim yet strongly built. Without touching, she knew his skin was smooth, his handsome nose slightly oversized, brawny chin and high cheekbones. She would so like to rub her fingers over his face and wrap her arms around him and crush him to her breast. And she figured, from the way he looked at her at that very moment, he would like that, too.

Seeing John's eyes move over her like he knew her private thoughts, she blushed again. What must he think of her? She tried to remember what they had been discussing a moment ago? Work? They had spoken of her job. He had asked if she was going to help unload the wagon. *Say something*, she told herself. *Say something, you fool!* It was hard to concentrate when John was so near.

"John," she said, nervously trying to cover the emotions flipping around inside her. "Somebody's got to unload that wagon; I'm about the most likely person to do it since I'm the one Milton is paying."

"It just isn't work for a lady, Kathryn," he said, his words so soft and his eyes warm. His gaze set blaze to the kindling already sizzling in her stomach. Suddenly, a wistful breeze blew over her, freezing a sweat that had risen between her breasts, and her heart beat rapidly. Desires shredded her insides like lumber shavings. *Oh goodness gracious*, she thought. Would she go to hell for the lustful fantasies overpowering her body and her mind?

Her limbs, trembling with frustration, wouldn't allow her to stand there any longer. She had to walk off. Her want for John was out of control. She took a deep breath to regain her composure, and then walked painfully toward the wagon.

A young boy she had not seen around the lumberyard was helping Leonard unload. For a moment she wondered why the Thatcher boy, from the homestead near her place, wasn't there as he usually was. She started to ask but was interrupted by Leonard's voice.

"We can get it, Kathryn," he called, lifting one end of a piece of pulp.

"All the same, I'll help. Make way."

"Never mind, Kathryn," Milton butted in, his voice exerting authority.

She turned to face him, her eyes moving from his khaki pants and shirt to the glare of gold teeth that matched his bronzed skin and burnt-orange hair. "I'll do my share," she said, her voice stern.

Milton pointed toward the open gate, his arm hair as thick as an ape's and shining like copper in the sunlight. "You've done your share. Now go on. Go shop and spend some of that money I'm paying you."

Kathryn left Milton and tromped across the dusty sawmill yard. She sensed the sound of somebody approaching her from behind and knew it was John. Soon he caught her, almost prissy, gait. Glancing up, her eyes fixed on his handsome face.

"Did you have something to do with that?" A flirtatious smile came to her lips. At this moment, she felt quite womanly.

"You'll never know," he teased.

Determined not to let her desire for him get the best of her as it had a few moments earlier, she slipped her hand through his curved arm and together they walked from the sawmill yard onto busy Broad Street. This, like other streets in town, seemed to grow bigger everyday with businesses booming from all corners. Tall brick and stucco buildings blocked the western horizon. People, horses, cotton carts, milk wagons and horse trolleys paraded like cowherds. A few blocks farther, she observed that members of the Salvation Army had begun a crusade against the corset, a device of the devil, they believed. Of course, Kathryn would never wear a corset anyway.

She and John turned north onto State Line Avenue, coming face to face with many women in long dark dresses and ruffled bonnets with satin bows. Many greeted John by name and she couldn't help but feel jealous.

Hurrying along, they passed several upstairs buildings on both sides of the border.

Reaching the State Line Cafe, they stopped. "You must be thirsty, Kathryn, after such a busy morning."

"I am. Yes."

John put his hand on her back so it rubbed lightly over her overall straps and guided her across the floor to a cast iron table near a front paned window. This created a distance between themselves and a group of noisy cattlemen. The group had clustered around a long marble-top bar. She looked for a moment at the cowmen, at their long gray dusters, and then to the reflection of their boots in the shiny marble floor. They would likely disappear into the back room for a few hands of poker before much longer. Already they appeared three sheets in the wind.

"Would you care for tea?" John asked. He pulled out a chair and offered it to her.

Kathryn laughed lightly and shook her head. She had, since meeting John, found listening to his speech amusing. For instance, the way he used some terms, such as saying tea when he actually was speaking of grub.

"I ate dinner in the woods a couple hours ago. Ought to keep me going 'til suppertime. I'll have a mug of cold cider, though." She pulled a nickel from her pocket and flipped it onto the smooth black-marble tabletop.

"Keep your money." John winked, and walked to the bar.

Waiting for him to return with the cider, Kathryn gazed out the window. Cavin O'Tool, the lawyer who had represented her divorce proceedings, emerged from a building across State Line Avenue, heading for the cafe. He spied her in the window and she waved. His face seemed to light up before he continued on to the door. In moments, he was beside their table, reaching down to shake her hand.

"Where you been lately?" she asked.

"I've been up in the Indian Territory for a spell," he said.

"Well, sit on down and tell me all about it." She waved him toward the empty chairs just as John neared with the two mugs of cider. "John, do you know Cavin O'Tool? He's been out of town for a right smart while. He helped me get my divorce, you know."

John put the drinks down and extended his hand to Cavin. "John Allen," he said.

"Good to meet you," Cavin returned.

"Please, take a seat." John waved to one of the vacant chairs.

Kathryn sat between the two men, glancing at one and then the other. At the moment, and with the two best-looking men in town as her company, she felt as if she were the belle of the ball—even though wearing overalls.

"Cavin," she said to the tall blond man at her right. "You've been off to the Indian country lots now. What's all the hippy-do that's happening in the Territory? How'd you get there anyway?" Kathryn raised her voice to be heard over the loud cowmen.

"Buggy. I went by buggy. I've been checking on land in the Territory. Let me tell you something, one of these days, and it won't be too far in the future, there's going to be the biggest run for land that you ever did see." Cavin placed his hand inside his tan suit coat and pulled out a cigar. He chewed at the end. Glancing casually into Kathryn's eyes, he smiled, then removed his brown dress hat and put it on the table.

"You've been gone for better than a month, haven't you?" Kathryn felt her eyes dancing in the excitement Cavin must have experienced.

"I left here in July. The fifth." He raised his thick brows so they rubbed blond curls on his forehead.

"My goodness. When did you get back?"

Cavin bent forward and raked a match down the grit between two slabs of black floor marble, then placed the flame to his cigar. "Yesterday," he said, nodding, then slowly exhaled short puffs of smoke.

"You mean to say you've been up there loafing around all this time. Well, whoever's been taking care of all that law stuff you do?"

"Now hold on a minute, Kathryn. I haven't been loafing around. I've been up there on business. I've been working with Indian agents. My young assistant, Gerald Thompson, has been handling my practice here."

Kathryn nodded, and smiled casually. Guess he wasn't too worried about losing business to any of the new lawyers who had opened practices in town. Even the new female lawyer from Chicago was getting enough cases to keep her stylish. The two cities were growing like nobody's business. But, she had to admire Cavin to just up and take off whenever the notion struck his fancy. Her former husband used to do that, but whatever his real business was he never revealed. She had come to realize that Alex Andrews lived two lives, one she saw and one he kept secret. Thank goodness he was out of her life for good. She glanced again at Cavin and smiled.

47

"Lots of Indian folks in the Territory, like we hear?" she asked.

John smiled, and Cavin laughed lightly through a cloud of smoke.

Kathryn thought about Shanna and the infant. Perhaps she had started off for the Territory. But going all that way? And with an infant?

"Kathryn," John said, and nudged her arm. "Didn't you hear Mr. O'Tool?"

She shook her head. "I'm sorry. What was that?"

Cavin took another drag from his cigar. "I asked, 'Why are you so curious about the territory?'"

"I've just heard talk."

"You want to ride up to the territory with me, Kathryn?" he teased, the cigar protruding from one side of his mouth. "Bring Mama Williams, too. She might get festoon ideas. I know she likes woodworking." His eyes stayed on Kathryn for a moment, and then he took the slightly smoked cigar from his mouth and smothered the fire out in a sand-filled ashtray on a stand near the table. "You can see what's going on up there for yourself. I'm going back in about a week."

The tip of her tongue slid over her bottom lip and she felt her eyes widen. The very idea of seeing it all for herself...! Of course, he was only joshing her. Heat warmed her cheeks. "I have no reason to visit the Territory." She smiled, her head dipping slightly.

Actually, it wasn't Cavin she wanted escorting her to the territory. Though if she should go rambling off with John, even with Mama riding along, talk here in this cattle town would color her as red at the Scarlet Letter. Folks already thought of her as loose, her being a divorced woman. Her working in Milton's Woods with Leonard and being the only woman ever showing face at the sawmill had smudged her reputation in a big way. She glanced at the amused expression on John's face. Could he guess what she was wishing?

Cavin got up and brushed wrinkles from his suit pants. "I'll be running along now. It was a pleasure meeting you, Mister Allen." He rubbed his hand gently over Kathryn's shoulder. "And if you decide to satisfy your curiosity and ride north with me, just let me know." He gave her a wink.

At the cafe table with only John, the idea of traveling to the Territory vanished from Kathryn's thoughts, leaving only the strong feelings of love exploding inside her for this man. She could barely pull her stare from his face. The longing she had for John ate at her insides and made casual conversation impossible. If only he had for her just a touch of the feelings she had for him. Would he ever care for her? She would like to stay with him forever, going wherever he wanted her to go, doing whatever he wanted her to do. But he had never talked romance to her. Sometimes his eyes told her he wanted to kiss her, perhaps even go farther. She wished he would kiss her. Long and hard. She breathed deeply to lighten her thoughts.

Hating to face facts, Kathryn realized she had been gone from the sawmill for more than an hour and she knew Leonard would be waiting.

"Got to go now, John. No telling what's been happening at the sawmill. Bet Leonard's ready to go by now." Her eyes met John's. "Want to walk back now?"

"No, no." His voice was distant as he spoke and his eyes seem to search for something beyond her. He leaned back on his chair. Then all of a sudden he said, "I have some things to take care of back at my room."

Kathryn glanced out the window to see what might have John's attention. A woman in a long blue dress, fancy bonnet, and carrying a matching umbrella was looking about, as if she were lost, then she hastily disappeared into a storefront across State Line Avenue.

Sudden jealously swelled inside Kathryn and chewed at her stomach. She swallowed and turned quickly away. She must not let anybody see how she hurt. She must never reveal her foolish feelings for this man.

※ ※ ※

"I'll make a run for the rifle," Shanna said, hovering close to Mama in order to peek through the cellar door crack to the outside.

"I don't see anybody. You sure somebody's after you?"

"Yes. I know."

"Why? Why would men with dogs be looking for you? Did you get yourself in some kind of trouble?"

"Yes. Much trouble."

"Want to talk about it?"

"Better if you don't know. Better if I run far."

"Be kindly hard for you to go running off with a newborn."

"It would," Shanna agreed.

In silence, the two women gazed at each other. The dogs had stopped yelping. Mama slowly opened the door and stepped from the cellar.

Shanna moved up the plank steps behind Mama. As soon as she was out the door, she ran to the butchering table and grabbed the gun.

"Hey y'all," a familiar voice called from front of the house.

"I'm in back," Mama yelled. And then, "Don't shoot, Shanna. It's a neighbor done come calling."

Nine

Kathryn stepped from the cafe onto the flat-timber sidewalk. She pivoted, slightly moving into her shadow to glance through the cafe window at John, still sitting at the café table. She waved goodbye. Making a smile come to her face, she hurried south along State Line Avenue. But the ache lingered in her heart and mind for John before erupting and bubbling through her person like poison.

Did John know the fashionably dressed dark-haired woman who had gone into the modern insurance building? She walked a few paces, and then turned. John had come out of the café now. He was just standing there facing west, as if waiting for the woman. He must know her. Oh how this jealousy hurt. Turning east on Front Street, she swallowed and tried to hold back tears. She must get hold of herself before returning to the sawmill.

Within fifteen minutes Kathryn had reached the sawmill. Without surprise, she saw that Leonard and the boy had unloaded the wagon. Leonard held his denim cap in one hand and scratched through his thinning brown hair with the other.

"Ahh-hh, here she comes now," Leonard said. The crowfeet at the corners of his eyes emphasized his grin and his head bobbed to the musical words of his voice.

"Been waiting long?"

"Nah," Leonard said. The light in his eyes glowed.

Kathryn knew he wouldn't complain about her. Even if she had taken a trip to the moon, he was always anxious to see her return. It wasn't fair for a man to feel for a woman the way Leonard felt for her without getting some affection back. Perhaps someday a woman would love Leonard the way that she loved John.

Catching a glimpse of Milton coming toward them, Kathryn smiled and turned in his direction. His khaki pants and shirt were quite a bit dirtier than they had been an hour or so earlier; and his feet drug slightly as he walked, stirring up a small cloud of dirt and sawdust.

"Kathryn, I see you found your way back. We moved all those logs over there while you were off flitting around," Milton jeered, as usual seeing just how much teasing he could get by with.

"Hey, I'm still getting my pay? You're the one who told me to take off. Wasn't my idea, you know."

Bridged By Love

"Think you've earned a day's pay?" Milton teased. In sparks of light shining through branches of a persimmon tree, the big man's burnt-orange hair flickered like on fire.

"Confounded right I do," she said, her voice a bit teasing. "And if you don't think so, well, I'll stay in the woods an hour later this evening and do some extra chopping—maybe at some of those young pine seedlings you got growing."

"You've earned your pay, Kathryn." Milton laughed.

She glanced at Leonard and winked. They both knew how Milton liked to taunt about her work, but they also knew he would not want to lose her.

Leonard slapped the reins and guided the mules from the dusty sawmill yard, turning south for a few yards, then west on Front Street. They drove alongside the busy brick street, the iron wagon wheels rattling over a set of trolley tracks.

Kathryn shivered. The afternoon had cooled considerably and she wished she had brought a wrap. Of course, she dared not mention her chill to Leonard or he would worry about her. She glanced at his face, at the contentment it held, like he didn't have a worry in the world. She smiled, and gazed about at the last of city stores as they drove from town. Soon Leonard reined the mules onto the quiet, sandy road lined with cedar and pine trees that would lead them home.

The breeze meshing through the larches tinged Kathryn's arms. She lifted her face to see gray clouds drifting under the sun that had now become so distant. And for a moment, she dreamed of John. *John, you're always in my dreams and in my heart*, she mused.

The mules made a final turn on the rutted wagon trail toward the barn in the equipment yard in Milton's Woods. They neighed suddenly as a yellowish creature cut across the trail in front of them. "Hold it Leonard!" Kathryn quickly reached under the wagon seat and pulled out a rifle. "That's likely one of the wolves that's been killing my chickens!"

Leonard yanked at the reins and brought the mules to a neighing halt.

Clutching the shotgun, Kathryn jumped over the buckboard and pushed her way into the thicket. She paused at the edge of the brier patch. Something moved. She raised the gun to her shoulder and rested her cheek against the wooden stock so her eyes peered down the sight. Her finger tense on the trigger, she waited for the varmint.

The wolf moved again, then dashed from behind a bush. It leaped into the briers just a few feet ahead of her. The weapon still at her cheek, Kathryn's body swerved and the gun barrel followed the movement in the bushes, her finger ready to squeeze. Suddenly she heard soft whimpering. "Pups," she whispered, loosening her grip on the trigger and lowering the gun.

She knew good and well the right thing to do would be to shoot the whole litter right then and rid the woods of such dreadful beasts. She just couldn't, though. She swallowed, and turned from the briers.

"It get away?" Leonard asked, raising his brows as if he didn't expect an honest answer. He grinned slightly, his amused, hazel eyes glowing in the shadow of his cap bib.

"Wasn't sight of that confounded beast anyplace," Kathryn lied. She climbed over the buckboard, her gaze staying on the trail ahead. She hoped with all her heart she didn't have to face another wolf or any other beastly critter this day. To kill was not her thing, anyway. She'd rather have thoughts of John, or the baby and the girl, or the pleasant fiddle music Leonard could make—anything else, anything nice.

Once music came to mind, Kathryn noticed the ruffling of crisp oak leaves being strummed by the wind. This reverberation and slight clanging of the wagon's wheels as they rambled over ruts, presented a delightful composition. But too soon, Leonard pulled the reins, ending the rhythm, and brought the mules to a halt. The day would soon be over. For the most part, it had been good. She had earned her pay and had spent precious time with John. Now she was going home. Home to a house that had changed overnight.

Kathryn watched Leonard, his body hardly bending, as he flung his long legs over the side of the buckboard.

"Where's yer mare?" he asked, his eyes squinting as he looked around.

"Sugar has something wrong with her foot. I thought it best not to ride her for a few days."

"I'll put this here cutting gear away. Won't take but a jiff," he said musically. "Bequeath me a few minutes and I'll fetch ye home."

Kathryn loosened the bridles and removed the bits from the mules' mouths, swung them over her shoulders, and carried them to the barn. She followed a few paces behind Leonard.

"It'll be just as well if I walk. I don't mind. Anyhow, it's a good two miles out of your direction."

"Never ye mind that," Leonard called, glancing back at Kathryn. "Been meaning to get over yer way anyhow. Sprint can use the exercise."

As the falling sun made shadows three times their size, Kathryn climbed on Sprint's back behind Leonard and the horse pranced peacefully down the narrow trail toward the homestead. Most likely, by the time she reached home, Mama would have fed the livestock, as she often did when Kathryn worked late.

On the trail to the homestead, Sprint went into a trot and Kathryn clamped her arms tightly around Leonard's waist. Without realizing, she rested her cheek against his strong back and let her mind wander into the words of a never-before-heard tune he was singing. Next thing she knew, she was waking from sleep. Sprint was halting near the front porch at the homestead.

"You awake?" Leonard asked softly.

Kathryn dismounted quickly to hide the fact she had dozed off.

"Leonard, do you want to come take a look at Sugar's foot?"

"Sure 'nough do."

At the pasture gate, Kathryn lifted the two-by-four latch and the mare came walking slowly toward her. "See how she's favoring her left foot?"

Meeting the mare, Kathryn rubbed its mane. "Hey Sugar," she said, and placed her hands on each side of the mare's face. "How's my girl?" Bending, she lifted the palomino's foot.

"Look at this mess," she said, turning to Leonard. "Guess I'd better clean it out." She reached in her pocket and brought out a knife, then carefully scraped at a hardened clay clog.

"It's tender," she said, and then let the mare's foot drop to the ground. "Mind keeping her here 'til I get a compress?"

Kathryn hurried to the house and crawled a few feet underneath the plank porch to where a goodly supply of red potatoes was stored for winter. She fetched a small one and, returning to the pasture gate, pulled her knife from her overall pocket and sliced off the top.

"This'll have to do," she said. She lifted Sugar's foot and rubbed it with the juicy end of the potato. "Sugar wouldn't keep this contraption on even if I should tie it."

"That ought to bring the poison out anyway," Leonard noted. "She'll be good as new; just got to give this old foot time to heal."

"Now that Sugar's taken care of, how about staying for supper? Mama hasn't seen you in a spell. I know she'd be powerfully delighted."

"Oh, I don't think I'd better impose. Yer mama's not expecting company."

From the corner of her eye, Kathryn watched Leonard as they walked to the porch. He removed his cap and scratched through his thinning brown hair. He always scratched his head when something was on his mind and he was trying to find words. Kathryn had an idea what those words were but she didn't want to hear them, not from him. Too bad she didn't adore him as he adored her. But she just couldn't imagine herself ever caring for anyone other than John.

Kathryn felt she must say something before Leonard talked marriage to her. Her lips parted. "I told you about Shanna, our company, didn't I?"

Leonard's crowfeet deepened. "Sure did."

"She's a young Indian. Don't know what tribe. Stopped by last night with an infant. Can't be more than a couple days old." Kathryn glanced around at the property. "And she isn't much more than a child herself."

Leonard sat on the doorstep and rested his back against a porch post. He stretched his long legs. Before turning to Kathryn, he shook his head slightly, and then held her gaze with his.

"There's something I want to tell ye," he said, softly. "I don't quite know how to go about it, though. Every time I attempt, for some reason or another, I can't seem to get it out. But I've commenced now and I aim on going ahead with it."

"Look, there's Mama and Shanna now," She said, quickly pointing at the two coming toward them from the Blackberry Lane path, so named for its groves of blackberry vines.

Shanna was carrying the tiny bundle in her arms. And Mama had a long string of fish. "Where in tarnation did y'all get all those fish?" Kathryn called.

"The creek down by the Red Bailey Bridge," Mama said, excitement in her voice. "Cameron White came calling this afternoon. We went fishing with her. She's got a string just as long." Mama hesitated, holding the catch of bullheads up in a bragging jester. "You should see how Shanna catches fish with her hands."

"It looks like you'll have to stay for supper now," Kathryn said, her laughing voice addressing Leonard. "I know how much you like a fresh mess of catfish." Glancing at Leonard and meeting his stare, she smiled and winked. "Think we can get 'em skinned?"

Mama placed two wedges of hickory in the stove then mixed some flour, freshly ground corn meal, yeast and water heated in the kettle into a big bowl. Normally, she would have used milk rather than water, but that wasn't possible since the family cow had gone dry. She stirred the mixer, then cracked four eggs and blended them into the contents. She set the pan on the butcher block to let the yeast start to rise, and took an iron skillet from a wall hanger near the stove and spooned a goodly amount of lard into it. As the grease heated, pork bits sizzled and smoke rose from the skillet and moved in a thick cloud through the kitchen. Mama poured the cornbread mixture into the skillet slowly, giving the blend a chance to rise even more as it fell into the hot fat. Using a stove iron, she pulled the oven door open, and then placed the heavy skillet inside. Already the mouth-watering aroma of pork and cornmeal wafted through the house.

Next she poured a canister of ground yellow hominy into a pot of boiling water on the back burner. Hearing the screen door screech, Mama turned from the stove. "Nice looking bunch of filets," she said with a smile. "Didn't take ya'll long at all."

"Thanks to Leonard. He skinned about three to my one. It's all in the way his big hand grips the pinchers."

"He's a good man," Mama said, eyeing Kathryn. She took the pan of filets and placed them on the butcher block. "You go on back out there with Leonard," she cajoled.

"Don't you try getting something started here, Mama. You know Leonard and I got friendship. That's all."

"Just get on out there. I'll call you when I finish frying."

Kathryn started for the door, then hesitated. Shanna had taken her baby to their room, but Kathryn sure wished she'd come out and join them, so she wouldn't have to be alone with Leonard. An idea came to her and she made a side trip to Mama's bedroom to fetch Papa's old guitar.

Leonard jumped to his feet when she stepped through the door, a huge grin spreading on his face.

She handed him the guitar and tried to sound carefree when she asked, "Got any new songs written?"

Leonard always had new songs. If he didn't have lyrics already lined up in his mind's eye, he would compose aloud as he picked. However, for the most part, the newly created words were usually heard only once.

"Well let me see," Leonard said, taking the guitar. He picked and turned the keys to tune the instrument. It hadn't been used since he'd stayed for supper with Mama and Kathryn a couple weeks back. He picked and played over the scale, then smiled at her.

"Here's a song I been working on," he said, nodding slightly. "Goes like this:

There's a lovely butterfly I see.
Her beauty suits me to a tee.
In my heart she's the only one to be.
Through life and eternity with me."

He strummed the melody again.

His eyes on Kathryn brought an itch to her body. Why had she asked him for a new song? Why hadn't she suggested something that would make her comfortable, like the hymns he usually sang?

"Very nice, Leonard. Pick something else now. Pick one of the church songs you like."

Leonard's eyes were pleading with hers, into her face, into her total being. She had to do something to make him stop, otherwise she would cry, or scream, or take off running. Her face stiffened so she could barely move her mouth to talk. "Pick..." she hesitated. "Pick *I'll Fly Away*."

Half-dozen or so hymns later, Mama opened the screen door and poked her head out. "Y'all come on in. I've cooked up some grits, tomato gravy, and cornbread to go with the bullhead."

After supper, Kathryn heard a soft cry coming from the bedroom. "The baby," she said.

Shanna glanced at Kathryn. "Yes. Little Soul is hungry."

Kathryn watched as Shanna helped herself to another spoon of grits, added a few drops of water, and left the kitchen with the plate in her hand.

"She isn't planning on feeding grits to the baby, is she?"

"Never you mind," Mama reprimanded. "She's the child's mother. She knows how to take care of him. That kind of thing comes natural." She turned to Leonard. "More coffee?"

"No, thank you, ma'am. I ought to be going." He rose from the table. "Thank you for the fine supper."

"Thank you for cleaning the fish."

"See you tomorrow, Kathryn," he nodded in her direction.

"See you then," she replied. She watched him let himself out the door, relieved on the one hand, sorry on the other. Sooner or later she was going to have to talk to Leonard and make her feelings clear. She just wasn't sure what to say so she wouldn't hurt his feelings. He was the dearest friend she had and she didn't want to lose his friendship.

She got up and started gathering dishes.

Kathryn and Mama were just finishing cleaning up the supper table when Shanna returned to the kitchen.

"Is he sleeping?" Kathryn asked anxiously.

"No, Little Soul is awake. Looks like he smiles." She hesitated, and for a moment stared at Kathryn. "If you want, you can tend Little Soul."

"Really? I'd love to hold him. When?"

"You can tend him now."

Kathryn stood frozen for a moment. Shanna made no effort to accompany her to the bedroom. "I'm ready," she said, unable to stop the grin that made her feel so silly.

"You don't need me. You can tend."

Unable to speak, she nodded and hurried to the company room.

Baby boy was so small lying on the blue-and-tan quilt on that big feather bed. Kathryn sat on the edge and leaned toward the infant. "Hi there baby," she said, and barely touched his creamy-brown cheek. Shanna was right. He did smile a lot. She slid her hands underneath the bundle tightly wrapped in the yellow baby blanket Mama had knitted for Kathryn's child. The child Kathryn never saw alive.

She held the bundle to her chest and allowed her lips to gently brush the infant's tiny crown of soft black hair. The oddest sensation came over her. It was as if this child belonged to her. Warmth filled the crevices in her heart created by the loss of her own child. "Sweet baby boy," she whispered. "Sweet, sweet, boy...if only you were mine."

Oh Lord, Kathryn stop it, she scolded herself. *He's not your child.*

No, but if only...

Ten

HER MIND FULL of awe, Kathryn got little sleep that night. The baby stayed on her mind. The baby wrapped in her baby's yellow blanket, wearing her baby's long white dress and the white booties she had crocheted herself with so much devotion. Shanna's baby sleeping in the room that would eventually have been decorated for her baby.

Oh how she adored this infant. For a moment, only a moment, Kathryn's heart was full of envy. Shanna had what she wanted more than anything in the world. Shanna had a baby. "Oh Lord forgive me for coveting," she whispered.

❈ ❈ ❈

In his room at S. Wagner's Rooming house, John stared at light shining from the large wall globe and flickering on the ceiling. The fleshy blonde lying on his arm snuggled alongside him. "Joanna, sweetheart," he whispered, his mouth nudging her ear. "Where do you go from here?"

"St. Louis. Business is better there."

"When do you leave?"

"Next train from Dallas is tomorrow."

Memories of his ride through St. Louis three years ago came to mind. He had been with the beautiful Lilly. No woman could ever fill her shoes, he had told himself a million times. Now he was here with Joanna, his favorite House of Chances whore, whom he had known for the last year. Joanna was a bit bigger than he liked but she was soft and warm and treated him the way a woman was supposed to treat a man. Some women he had known undressed in the dark and waited for him to make all the moves. But Joanna was aggressive with her lovemaking. The light flickering on her large creamy breast seemed to make her so bold. She disrobed like a stripper and paraded to the bed edge where he waited anxiously, then she'd push her own ample breast to his mouth. He had never slept with Lilly, but she had put her hand in his trouser pocket and thrilled him more than one could imagine. The thought of Lilly now gave him overwhelming pleasure though Joanna was lying beside him. Joanna moaned and rubbed her hand over his stomach, then from there to his manhood.

"Come with me to St. Louis, John," she whispered, almost purring like a cat.

"Sweetheart," he hesitated for a moment, and searched for an excuse. He couldn't tell her the truth, that she was just his whore, nothing more. He couldn't express these feelings while she was doing things that excited him so. "You know that I have an edifice company here," he said, finally. "I'm busy now on that big house going up on the west side of the Post Office." He chuckled. "The house with a name." He rubbed Joanna's shoulder to encourage the strokes she was performing with her fingers.

"Come with me, John. I'll take care of you."

"Sweetheart, I can't go now. Business is too good here," he paused, still thinking of the unusual house being built. When completed, the heavy stone accommodation would be four floors high. The unusual thing, this mansion was being built in the form of the Ace of Clubs symbol. The carriage house was a mansion on its own. The whole shebang was being constructed with funds the owner won in a poker game. Uncanny luck. "The gambler laid down an Ace-high Club Flush," John said, amused. "That's how the house got it's name: the Ace of Clubs House."

"Yes, Johnny boy," Joanna moaned. "There's lots of talk about the house and its owner." She rubbed over his pubic line and whispered, "You'd like it in St. Louis."

"Sweetheart, you can stay here," he whispered. He waited for her to speak, and when she didn't, he stirred his fingers into her curly blond hair. "You can do all right here. The Ark-la-tex is booming. Stay and I'll come to visit you more."

"I'm going back to the house I worked in St. Louis," she said, practically mumbling her words. "Tried Dallas, but I didn't care for it. Too much a cow town for me. And Texarkana's got some bad desperados. I like a chic city and fancy clothes. I'm not one for cow towns and dust."

"You think Dallas is too dusty and Texarkana is too rugged?"

"That's it. St. Louis is elegant, and big, and lighted." Her hand moved over his thighs, over his stomach, to his chest, and started down again. This treatment was making him crazy. Joanna might be worth pulling up his stakes and traveling with to St. Louis. But then, he couldn't be seen with the whore in public. And what if Lilly came looking for him? Better to stay put.

※ ※ ※

In Milton's Woods, Leonard marveled over Kathryn's unusual quietness. "You're not talking much today," he said, resting his ax in an upright position at his side. He removed his cap, pulling a bulky white handkerchief from the bib of his overalls to wipe sweat from his forehead.

"I know," Kathryn replied, and continued hacking a limb from the small pine that had just fallen. "I know."

"You're thinking about that baby back at yer place, ain't 'cha?"

"Yep, I am."

"Your Ma says he's a fine looking lad. And he's right healthy."

Kathryn swallowed. "Yes, he is," she said, lightly, trying to conceal her emotions. If only the baby she had carried had lived. She swallowed again. It didn't seem fair that she could never give birth.

"Leonard, I hope Shanna will stay on with Mama and me. Everything's good with that little baby at our house. It's like the child is the pot of gold at the end of the rainbow."

"You know, Kathryn, you ought to have a family of your own, the way you like little ones."

A hard lump filled her throat. Oh, how she wished she could. Leonard just didn't know she could never give birth.

That afternoon while she and Leonard unloaded the logs at the sawmill, she looked around for some sight of John. She wanted to tell him about Shanna's baby—how he moved his arms and spread his fingers. How his little fist would ball up. How he looked at her eye to eye. She tried to remember the conversation they had yesterday. Had she mentioned Shanna? No, she didn't think she had.

Where was John today? He was usually at the sawmill figuring materials, for some reason or another. Why was he not here now? The dark-haired woman in the blue dress. That was it. John had gotten with the fancy dressed city woman!

Why was John always drawn to a woman, any woman it seemed, except her? Why had he never courted her? She was the one in love with him.

"Is something wrong?" Leonard asked as they lifted the last log from the wagon.

She smiled up at Leonard. "Still thinking about the baby," she said, her voice soft and clear. "I'm ready to leave for the woods now if you are. I'd like to get home early this evening."

Leonard offered Kathryn a ride to the homestead that afternoon but she refused. She really just wanted to walk. Being alone in the woods with nature and critters was satisfying to her mind. It made her feel fresh, even young and beautiful. But then, everything seemed more beautiful since the arrival of the baby boy tucked away in the company room in her house.

Nearing the homestead, she turned and started running toward the well, toward Mama drawing up water.

"Why Kathryn, you're home early."

"Anxious to see the baby."

"He's fine as can be," Mama bragged, lifting the water bucket and starting toward the house. "Nothing wrong with that young'un." She smiled, bringing wrinkles to rest at the corners of her mouth.

Kathryn's face was cracking with so much glee that her skin hurt. She was unable to restrain the strings connecting her mental pleasure and those controlling her facial expression. This awesome feeling she got from the very thought of Shanna's child was overpowering.

"He's a dandy," Mama said as Kathryn took the bucket from her and started to the house.

Reaching the back door, Kathryn followed Mama into the kitchen. She put the bucket on the counter top and nodded hello to Shanna who was entering from the front room doorway.

"Shanna," Kathryn said, her breath short. "You're on your feet so much after giving birth. Shouldn't you stay in bed for a few days so your insides can move back into place?"

"I'm fine, Kathryn. Please don't worry. I must travel soon."

"But you really need rest, and you're certainly welcome to stay with us. For as long as you want." Kathryn paused. Shanna couldn't leave. She couldn't take her baby away. She had to stay with Mama and her. "Raise your baby here. Send him to school down the road," she said quickly. "There's a school just a short piece down the road. On College Hill. Nice school, so they say." Kathryn had never seen the school, but she had definitely heard talk of it.

"Can't stay. I must go north."

"A body does need to rest after having a baby, something you've sure not done," Mama cut in. She poked the black iron handle into the latch on the stove door and pulled it open, allowing the aroma of chicken pie to fill the air. Kathryn noticed the veins in Mama's face protrude as she pushed the coals back and threw in another log.

"You can't get too far by foot in these parts," Mama added. "And if you plan on getting on a horse, you're mighty apt to start hemorrhaging."

"I must leave after next sun."

"Tomorrow night?" Kathryn questioned.

The very thought that Shanna and her baby boy would leave practically after just arriving, was totally devastating to Kathryn.

This is horrible, she thought, then spoke out rapidly: "You're going to take your new born baby out already? And it'll be turning cold before too long. Don't you know that's a disgusting plan?" She hesitated, her eyes pleading. "You can't leave. You just can't leave, Shanna."

"Kathryn," Mama scolded. "It's not like you to tell a body what she can and can't do."

Shanna's dark eyes quickly darted into Kathryn's. "Next sun, we go fish."

Kathryn looked at Mama, then back to Shanna. "How can you think of fishing at a time like this?"

"We go?"

"What about feeding the baby?"

"Little Soul will be fine. You go with me?" Shanna asked again, her voice becoming wary.

"Yes, if it means so much to you. My mare is lame so we'll have to walk."

With dawn still east of Arkansas, Kathryn prepared for the four-mile walk to Red Bailey Bridge. Before coming into the kitchen she slipped into her coveralls. Mama was up already and sitting at the table sipping hot, boiled coffee when Kathryn walked barefoot into the kitchen. She pulled a chair from the table and sat down. Dropping her boots to the knotty pine floor, she started pulling her thick socks over her heels.

"Looks like you'll be going with Shanna," Mama said.

"Yes, I suppose I will. I don't think she's apt to change her mind. Must really like to fish," Kathryn said, her voice holding disgust. "Just don't think she ought to leave the baby and go off. Not just yet."

"The boy's gonna be fine." Mama peered over her coffee cup at Kathryn.

Kathryn heard a stirring sound coming from Shanna's room. She raised her brows and looked at Mama. "She must be feeding the baby now. We'll leave soon as she's done. Ought to be back here by nine o'clock. Will he be hungry before then?"

Mama watched Kathryn adjust the socks over her ankles but said nothing. Just then Shanna appeared in the doorway.

"We go now," she said, straightening the burlap draped from her shoulders as she hurried into the kitchen.

"I got biscuits ready," Mama said, removing the hot pan from the stove. "Want to eat a bite before you leave?"

"No," Kathryn said, stepping to the kitchen pantry. She took out two bamboo poles and a can of fishhooks she'd made last winter. "We can take biscuits along with us. I want to get on so we can be back soon." She turned to Shanna. "Guess we're ready."

"Why do you really want to fish?" Kathryn asked as they walked down the back porch steps.

Though it was too dark to see, Kathryn sensed Shanna's dark eyes staring somewhere into the distance.

After a long pause, Shanna said in a soft voice, "I give my son this gift."

Kathryn frowned. "What gift?"

"Later. I tell you, later."

Eleven

Dawn came as Kathryn and Shanna neared Red Bailey Bridge, Kathryn's boots leaving prints in the sandy road smaller than those made by Shanna's moccasins. The cloth sack Kathryn clutched had not been opened.

"Want a biscuit?"

Shanna nodded and reached into the bag. "Mama makes biscuits good. I like Mama."

"Yes," Kathryn agreed. "Mama is a good woman. She follows the Golden Rule. 'Do unto others as you would have them do unto you.' I can never remember her turning anybody away when they needed her."

At the bridge, Kathryn scampered down the creek bank. She stopped where the earth was damp and pulled a knife from her jacket pocket.

Shanna's shadow, straight and tall, devoured Kathryn as it swayed on the current.

Kathryn pulled out two worms and started to bait her hook.

"No," Shanna said. "We need no pole."

"What 'cha mean, Shanna?"

"We need no worm. We catch fish like this." Cupping her hands, Shanna lifted them toward Kathryn.

Kathryn laughed. "Maybe you can, but I've never caught a fish with my hands."

"I teach." Shanna slipped out of her moccasins and waded into the clear stream.

"Can't a body ever say I wasn't willing to learn," Kathryn said, dropping the poles. She pulled off her boots and socks and followed Shanna into the cold creek.

"Walk light," Shanna said. "Make no mud." They moved on until the water swerved around their knees. "Now we wait."

"In this cold water? We're liable to end up with pneumonia."

Shanna grinned at her.

Bubbles soon surfaced. Shanna cupped her hands as before. "When fish come, move hands like this," she said demonstrating a swift snap. "You must be fast."

"Watch," she whispered as a small rockbass swam near. Bending, she placed her hands in the water and when the fish came closer, she quickly snapped them together. Water streamed through her fingers as she lifted her hands and held the captured fish toward Kathryn. She smiled, and then pushed her catch into a pocket lining the breast of her wrap.

Kathryn shook her head. "You make it look so easy."

"You get the next fish."

"I'll do it!" Kathryn found herself actually having fun. Of course, she felt the fun wasn't deserved because they had left the baby at the homestead when he should be in the arms of his mother.

Kathryn slowly placed her hands in the water as Shanna had encouraged. She remained still, anticipating the quick movements of an oncoming rock-bass getting nearer, then with the twist of her wrist— "Hey, I got it! I really got it!"

And then Kathryn saw the satisfied look on Shanna's face, and she realized—the young woman hadn't come to the bridge to fish at all. She had come only to teach. Kathryn threw the fish back.

"Come on, let's get out of this water before we catch our death." She helped Shanna slowly wade from the water and step onto the slippery bank.

Shanna straightened her skirt. The fish she'd caught started flapping about her breast. She reached into the pocket, pulled it out, and flung it into the creek.

"We talk now," she said. She climbed a few feet farther up the bank and sat down on the trunk of a fallen Red Oak.

"Talk, eh? And why do I get the feeling that's what this was really all about?" Kathryn picked up the fishing poles and secured them under her arm, then collected her boots. With her free hand, she held onto a branch and pulled herself up the bank to sit on the grass alongside the log. Squinting in the morning sunlight, she leaned back on her elbows. "What's on your mind, Shanna?"

"You fine woman, Kathryn. You work hard, you and Mama. You take care of horse. You learn fast. Many cannot catch fish with hands."

Raising her brows in embarrassment, Kathryn said, "I appreciate your kind words. It's not everyday that folks speak so highly of me."

"I must find my family," Shanna said, her focus moving from Kathryn to the trail alongside the creek. "But trail is so hard. Too hard for Little Soul."

Oh my God, what is she saying! Kathryn prayed silently and swallowed the huge lump of disappointment trying to choke her.

She and Mama didn't own much, but what they had they would share. They would share their home and their love. Shanna and the baby could find happiness here in this backwoods country. She and Mama lived a good life and had never gone wanting. But if Shanna left, and she took Baby Boy...

"Shanna, don't go. Stay with us. You can live with Mama and me," she pleaded, placing her hand on Shanna's shoulder. "Oh, Shanna, we have so much space in our house. You've been comfortable here, haven't you? And it would be a dream-come-true to have a boy grow up right before our eyes. Please Shanna. Say you'll stay."

"I cannot stay. I must go."

"But to where?"

"North. To Land of Red People."

"But what about the baby? You say the trail would be too hard for him."

"Yes, it would be a hard trip for Little Soul. Too much dangerous. I cannot tell everything," Shanna said, her misty eyes meeting Kathryn's.

"Then you can't go. You shouldn't go. You should stay here, with us." Kathryn could feel tears running down her face but she couldn't hold them back; she wouldn't even try. What could she offer this young woman? She had offered her a home and she had rejected it. What more could she give her?

She stared at the water. The current moved peacefully. It didn't have any worries.

"No, I must go. But Little Soul cannot come. I must give him to good people. Please...I give him to you and Mama."

For a long moment Kathryn was numb. Confusion washed through her, instantly freezing her inside and out and making speech impossible.

"H-how long do you want us to keep your son?" Kathryn finally managed to ask.

"You will take Little Soul?"

"Of course, we will," Kathryn said, honestly sincere, elation mingling with sadness. Gazing into Shanna's sober eyes a mountain of pity for the girl rose inside her.

Oh, she's so very young–just a child herself, Kathryn observed. "Let the baby get old enough you can leave him, then Mama and I will take care of him while you go about your business. We'll take care of him until you return."

Distant tree limbs blew in the cool wind and shadowed Shanna's face, seemingly muffling her words–"Little Soul is your son now."

"No, Shanna. Don't you even think like that."

"I must go. I cannot return."

"Oh Shanna, why must you go? Why can't you return? Why can't you take your baby? The baby needs his mother." She bowed her head. "Oh what is going on with you?"

"Better if you do not know. I am in much trouble. If Little Soul is with me, he be in trouble, too." Shanna put her arm around Kathryn's shoulder. "Will you take him? Give him home? Be family?"

Kathryn wanted the baby. More than breath she wanted him. She jumped up and gave Shanna a hug. "Yes! Yes! And we'll give him a good home."

Yes, she would take the baby. Oh, Lord yes, she would take him. She would never forsake him. Never! Not as long as she had life. She would love him and care for him. She would teach him to fish.

Suddenly the sun was warm and the wind blew and Kathryn heard the creek ripples hurrying downstream, like the words that ripped through her mind: *"I give my son this gift."*

※ ※ ※

Shanna had known she would take the baby. She had taught her to fish with her hands knowing that someday she would teach this method to her son...Aaron. A smile bloomed on Kathryn's face. Aaron would be his name. Aaron, a name from the Holy Bible. Aaron, Hebrew, meaning Enlightener. Aaron Zebadiah, a gift from God.

Their clothes had dried by the time they reached the homestead. Mama sat on the front porch in the swing. "Did the baby wake up?" Kathryn asked as she started up the steps.

"No," Mama answered. "He's been sleeping the whole while."

Kathryn wondered if she should mention what had occurred between Shanna and her? Perhaps it would be best to wait until Shanna went to feed the baby. She had no more time than that to debate the matter. Shanna broke the news when she said, "When Little Soul wakes, you tend him. It is good his mother feeds him."

Not knowing what to say, Kathryn looked at Mama. *She knows*, she thought, seeing Mama's confirming expression. Mama was aware of Shanna's gift.

Suddenly the enormity of Shanna's sacrifice, and this new responsibility, overwhelmed her. Shanna had been the one to feed him. She'd never fed a babe a day in her life. What if she did something wrong? What if...? What if...? She turned back to Shanna. "Please don't leave tonight."

The Indian girl smiled. "All will be well."

Kathryn swallowed. She wanted Aaron now as much as she had wanted the child she had lost. But to take him and then do something wrong. What in the world was going to happen?

"Oh," she cried, tears choking her. "The good Lord only knows how much I want this child. But how will I feed him? What about milk?" She looked from Shanna to Mama. "Mama, I don't know how to feed a baby."

"Well I reckon I can remember enough to get by," Mama replied with a twinkle in her eye. "Though it would be better if he had milk. I just don't know anybody you could find to nurse him. Ain't nobody around here had a baby for quite a spell. Of course, babies have been raised on cow's milk."

Kathryn paced across the porch, rubbing her hands up and down the sides of her hips. Sure, cow's milk would be fine from a healthy cow.

She whirled back to Shanna. "Shanna, what if I say I can't keep Aaron? What will you do?"

"Aaron?"

"The baby's name. The name I've picked for him."

Shanna stared into the distance as she walked to the porch edge.

"Oh, Shanna, I don't know the right thing to do."

"If you cannot keep Aaron, then I must take him to orphanage in city."

Oh my Lord! Kathryn screamed silently.

"I cannot take baby Aaron to land of Red People," Shanna said, her words stressed, her eyes tearing. "If I could, I would. But is too much danger. Please understand."

Kathryn swallowed. Then she held her head back and breathed deeply. What was happening to this poor girl? Wasn't there some way she could help her? What was she running from?

But more than that, what agony was ripping her apart, for giving up her son?

"I'm sorry, I didn't mean to distress you. Of course, I'll keep Aaron and he'll be my own son," Kathryn said, her voice low and final.

Kathryn moved absently to the front door, and then turned back to Shanna. The two women's misty gazes met. She offered a wordless, reassuring smile and then entered the house.

An awesome chill slapped at Kathryn as she crept into Shanna's room and looked down at Aaron sleeping so peacefully. He didn't know what was happening. Someday he would ask, but with all the love and care he'd get from Mama and her, he would accept everything. She reached for the yellow baby blanket and pulled it over his tiny body. He was the most beautiful child she had ever seen and already she loved him more than breath. She touched his head and tears filled her eyes. "My son," she whispered, her words choking. "My own precious son."

Backing from the company room, she left the door open slightly so heat from the fireplace could circulate through, and then she hurried to the kitchen. She would get a pail and go down the road to the Thatcher's place. Their cow had birthed a calf several weeks before. They would have milk to share.

Kathryn stepped from the living room to the front porch. Shanna had not moved from her position. Kathryn could only imagine the hurt she surely felt at this moment. If only she could help her. If only Shanna would stay. But she had pleaded with her already to no avail. The thing left to do now was to love and care for Aaron.

Kathryn started down the steps. She turned abruptly to Shanna. "If I don't get back home before Aaron wakes up, will you feed him from your breast once more?"

"I cannot feed from breast," Shanna said, keeping her eyes fixed on the trail. "Aaron eats table food. Mashed and chewed. I don't make milk."

"Dear Lord," Kathryn whispered. She would have to do something quickly or Aaron would starve. She'd lose him so soon.

❈ ❈ ❈

Half-a-dozen horses with men on their backs followed a pack of yelping hounds through Northern Caddo Parish swamps and bayous. The team, in pursuit of the squaw they believed had pushed a blade into Jake Minor's chest, scurried like a meandering tornado. The men reined their horses to the right as the dogs made a quick turn into the thick timbers of Arkansas. Then the dogs stopped abruptly.

Pulling his horse to a halt, one barely opened his mouth and let words whistle through a space where three teeth used to be. "Figured them-there dogs would lose the squaw's scent in the water, but they jest keeped on running."

"They got a whoop of something back there in the marsh," another interjected.

And then another remarked, "Looks like they finding something rights ch'ere." His horse paced slowly a few feet toward the sniffing dogs.

"Looks like blood. Somethang been bleeding here."

"Must be the squaw. Maybe she done found her somebody else to chop," one said, scratching his balding head. "Don't see no signs of camps here anywheres."

The men gathered around the sniffing hounds at the bloody site. Within minutes, the dogs started yelping, and with their noses to the ground they took off running again.

"Dogs going north. Let's ride."

Twelve

Somewhere in Texas? Perhaps.

Yes. He was in a Texas jail. His captives had brought him here. And they had taken the Indian girl, Shanna.

Rowe lay on a cot in the small cell awaking from another seizure. Seemed he'd been having spasms often these days and nights. How long had he been here? Months? A year? How long had he laid unconscious before awaking in the first place? His hair and beard had grown long and straggly and cuts and bruises covered his thin body.

He had been here too long. Of that, he was convinced. Somehow he would escape, though. When he did, he'd go after Shanna.

He rose from the cot and slipped into his denim breeches, then pulled on his knee-high alligator boots.

"Why ye getting dressed-up? Where ye think ye going?"

"When you aim on letting me out of here?"

"Now Rowe, I done telled ye time after time that they's paying me to keep ye here."

"For how long?"

"'Til they come fer ye."

"Did they have a girl with 'em when they dumped me off?"

"Now boy, ye done asked me that ten-dozen times and I always telled ye—no Injun squaw.'"

"Be best for you if you let me get away. You can't trust those brigands. Anyway, you let me out and I can do more good for you than they can."

"Well theys done sayed I'z to keep ye here. Theys sayed ye stealed a horse and a squaw and some eats. Now boy, ye ought to know ye can't go stealing a feller's stuff," the jailer said, grinning like a dumb-ass. "Yer mighty lucky they didn't go shooting at 'cha. I don't know what theys aim on doing with ye but theys sayed theys be coming fer ye when theys ready. Boy I don't know what theys figuring on doing with ye." He was still grinning, as if he enjoyed being the barer of bad news.

"Come on, open the gate. Let me go."

"Can't do it, boy. Theys the ones that tells me what to do."

"I won't hurt you if you let me out."

"That ain't what 'cha sayed before."

"I promise. Let me out and I'll leave here without even turning around," he waited a minute, but got no response from the jailer. "I'll send rewards."

"Can't let ya out, boy. Can't do it."

Rowe eyed the jailer. Maybe not today, maybe not tomorrow, maybe not even next week, but sooner or later he'd get out of this poor-excuse for jailhouse. Sooner or later he'd get even with the beasts that put him here—regardless of their ropes, guns, and regardless of the revenge their long black coats and white gloves represented.

The jailer neared the cell with a pan of pintos and rice.

"It don't bother you at all, mister jailer, to eat your grub over there at that table with all the stink from this shit pot blowing right over to you, does it?"

"Nope," the jailer answered, pushing the tin bowl underneath the bared door.

Quick as a sudden streak of lightening, Rowe stepped on the jailer's fingers, overturning the rice and beans.

The jailer screamed, "Ye low-crawling rat!" His fingers meshed into the beans and rice like a slice of wormy pork. "Yer paying for this," he cried, trying to pull from the hold Rowe's boot had on his fingers.

"Gimmie the key," Rowe said.

"Ain't got it."

Rowe put all his weight on his foot and moved his pointed toed boot from side to side as if squashing a cockroach.

The jailer fell to the plank floor. He pushed his feet against the jail cell and pulled with massive strength, freeing his hand from Rowe's hold. "Yer gonna pay fer this, boy" he cried, holding his broken hand and fingers with his good hand. "Ye be sorry ye ever knowed me. Yer gonna pay."

The corner of Rowe's mouth turned up in a slight smirk. "Maybe so," he said with humor in his voice.

✳ ✳ ✳

Kathryn could hear the Thatcher's cow bellowing long before she arrived at their place. Her run slowing for the first time since she had left the homestead, she practically fell into the yard gate. She stood for a jiffy to slow the pounding of her heart, then raised the latch and entered.

The cow sauntered toward her. Its bellows echoing painfully through the stillness and its bag hanging low with milk to waste.

"George," she called, hurrying on to the weathered plank house. "Anybody here? Molly?"

Kathryn ran up the flight of six steps to the long narrow porch. "Molly. George."

She banged on the door. No answer.

Must have gone someplace, she thought. But it wasn't like George and Molly to leave without informing Mama or her. And where was the Thatcher boy, Billy Don? She recalled he'd not been at the sawmill Thursday nor Friday.

Kathryn turned and walked slowly down the steps.

In dire need of attention, the cow waddled to her and rubbed its head against her arm. "What's the matter, Nellie? You're wanting rid of some of that milk, aren't you girl? She reached underneath the cow, placing her fingers on a teat and pulling to relieve it. This cow had not been milked in days. Had George and Molly gone away without having someone look after their livestock? The chickens could go unattended for a good spell, but to go off and leave the cow. And where was the calf? By the looks of Nellie, milk had been building up for days.

"Come on Nellie," she said, placing her hand on the cow's neck. "I'll take you on over to my place."

Kathryn grabbed a rope from a fence post and lapped it over Nellie's neck, then led her to the porch. She'd leave a note for George and Molly.

Kathryn recalled that the Thatchers always kept an extra house key underneath the water bucket on the porch shelf. Lifting the bucket, she frowned and curled her nose at a settlement of bugs floating lifelessly on the water.

"This is disgusting," she whispered, and tossed the water out. She took the key and, for a moment, stared at the door. A sudden weird kind-of fright pounded within her. She felt she was being watched. *Oh, Kathryn, don't be silly,* she told herself. *There ain't no one around. Who'd be watching you?*

She shook her head to dismiss the sudden apprehension, but then putting the key into the lock, her mind conjured thoughts of horrible things that could have happened. Perhaps George and Molly had been robbed. Somebody could have stolen the calf and killed the family. She took a step backwards. Maybe it would be better to take the cow and head on back to the homestead. But should she do that, and then if somebody else found the Thatchers dead, folks might think she had killed them just to steal the cow. She again scolded herself. *Stop it, Kathryn! Don't be so simple!*

I've got to get hold of myself, she thought. She had always been brave.

The lock clicked, and then she opened the door, guardedly, and crept inside.

The front room, spaciously furnished with plain oak furniture, seemed to be in order. She opened the door to the bedroom. The empty bed was neatly made. She turned back to the front room and hurried to the desk. Taking a pen from the inkwell, she composed a note; then she went out to the porch and replaced the key underneath the bucket. She smiled with relief and hurried down the steps. She didn't know where the Thatchers were now, but the fact they weren't dead inside was a pleasing thought.

"Let's go, Nellie," she coaxed, reaching for the rope that dangled from the cow's neck alongside the cowbell.

As Kathryn led Nellie to the trail, she noticed a man coming toward her a short distance ahead. "Moldie," she said with a sigh. Was this his day to come calling on the Thatcher's for a handout? Perhaps he would know the whereabouts of the family.

His pace hastened somewhat. "Ka-Ka-Kathryn, that you?"

"Yes of course it's me," she snapped.

He came closer. "What ye da-da-doing with da-da-cow?"

"I'm borrowing her. Anyhow, she needs some attention. She hasn't been milked in a coon's age." Kathryn tilted her head, a frown creasing her forehead. "Moldie, do you know where the Thatchers are?"

Stopping in front of her, Moldie removed that black felt hat he so treasured and Kathryn could almost hear his small brain wiggle about as he scratched. "They we-we-went over to El-El-El Dorado," he sputtered.

"El Dorado! Why would they go way over in Arkansas? And without telling anybody?"

Moldie kept scratching. "'Bout a-a-a week ago. I-I-I been wa-wa-watching after the place he-he-here."

"You have?"

"I-I-I sawed them on the way off. Th-th-they sayed tell somebody to watch the place. Th-th-they jest been so good to me, I-I-I decided to jest take care of it mm-mm-myself."

"Why'd they go to El Dorado?"

"Molly Th-Th-Thatcher's daddy died. She sayed it was all of a sudden. Je-je-jest up and took a coughing spell."

"So you're looking after the place, huh, Moldie? Well, maybe you can tell me what happened to Nellie's calf. Her milk bag looks like it's about to pop."

"I-I-I guess the wolves got it. I ain't seen it in a da-da-day or two."

"You mean you're watching after the place and you've let something happen to the calf?"

He lowered his head and nodded it nervously in admittance.

Kathryn bit lightly at her bottom lip then rubbed her tongue over it a couple of times. She stared at Moldie, her eyes squinting. Moldie was such a liar. She didn't know if she should believe him now or not, but she couldn't keep standing there thinking about it. She had to get home to Aaron.

"You ought to go out hunting for that calf, Moldie. When you find it, bring it on over to my place. I'll be keeping this cow for a spell." She paused. "You take it on yourself to do somebody a favor, then that's what you do," she added, in a voice of authority.

It was late afternoon by the time Kathryn reached the homestead. She tied Nellie to a front porch post and hurried into the house and peeked anxiously in Aaron's room. He was lying on his stomach, sleeping soundly with his little arms tucked underneath his body. She stood there for a moment and allowed a happy smile to linger on her face.

Shuffling in the kitchen caught her attention. She pushed her hair from her face and hurried through the house. Mama stood by the stove. Using a long ladle, she was scraping in the iron soup pot.

"Whoo," Kathryn remarked at the dominant scent of garlic and onion rising from the chicken stew.

"Supper's about ready. You ought to be hungry by now."

"Did Aaron wake while I was gone?"

"Yes. I fed him carrot juice."

"He took it okay?"

"Like a hungry boy."

"Where's Shanna?"

"I don't know. Outside somewhere, I guess. Or she could have left already. I tried to get her to stay on here. Told her she wouldn't be charity. Told her she could help us out in the garden. She just won't hear to it." Mama's voice seemed anxious and held a tone of confusion, or perhaps just plain disappointment. "Get milk?"

"I brought the cow home with me."

"I kindly figured they'd let'cha have it when they heard about the baby."

"They weren't home. I saw old Moldie on the road. He said Molly's daddy died. They've gone over in Arkansas for a bit."

"Oh my," Mama said, slowly stirring the stew.

"Moldie said he took a coughing spell."

"I'm sure sorry to hear that. Guess you have to expect such when you get old. Molly Thatcher's a right smart older than I am. Her daddy was getting up in years. The good Lord only put us here for a while."

Kathryn washed out the pail she used for milk, and then went to the front yard. She sat down on the porch steps near Nellie and rubbed her neck to steady her for milking. Little Aaron would wake up soon. He would surely be hungry. How could he have lived for two days without milk?

"Let Nellie's milk agree with my baby," she prayed, and ran her hand along the cow's side. She held her head back and let the sunshine sink into her face. The warm tinge rejuvenated her skin and stirred movement into her blood. September had always been her favorite month. September days had cooled from summer's heat. Brisk winds blew from the north. The sky was clear and blue. Night heavens were filled with twinkling lights. She loved September, especially this September, for this September she had Aaron.

A noise on the trail broke her reverie. She looked across the front yard. Something in the distance moved.

"Shanna!" she called, but the silent figure disappeared into the forest.

※ ※ ※

Shanna knew Kathryn saw her slip from the clearing adjacent to the homestead and into the thick growth of trees and bushes. She was again on the run. If she stayed at the homestead, as Kathryn and Mama had pleaded she do, sooner or later the riders in black would find her. And what would these horrible men do to Aaron? With her out of the picture,

Aaron would be safe at the homestead. Nobody would try to take him from Kathryn and Mama. The white women would love the son she had birthed. They would be kind to him and teach him respect and goodness. Aaron would live in a decent household. He would never have to run from outlaws.

Even if he could survive the life she must now live, having an infant would slow her down and likely get her caught and hung. They would take Aaron and make him their slave.

In haste, she must move far from the swamplands of Caddo Parish and the timbers of Arkansas. Suddenly, a weird feeling came over her. It was as if she were being followed. She ducked behind a wide oak tree and stood totally still. Was it a horse prancing toward her? *Oh please*, she thought, *don't be the white stallion.*

Go 'Til You Find the Indians

Thirteen

THE BIG MOON lit the forest like daylight. Shanna could easily make her way through the trees and shrubs. At the same time, the light put her on display for marauders.

And she knew somebody's eyes were on her now. She could feel the mystique flowing with the cool breeze around her. She was being followed. If only she could make it to the city where perhaps she could hide among the crowd and go unnoticed long enough to find direction to the Land of Red People. The Territory lay northward from the big city, she had heard.

Scampering westward, Shanna tried to keep tread with the moon. She stopped occasionally to listen for movements that might be of threat. Focusing through the moonlight and seeing no immediate danger, she picked up her pace again, swiftly moving on toward Texarkana.

After a while she came upon a tiny creek and followed its flow to a spring. There, she fell to her hands and knees and crawled to the clear water. The cold liquid numbed her lips as she drank.

"Ahh," she said, moving her face from the dribble long enough to catch her breath. Then she drank more.

She crawled away from the bank into the surrounding brush, careful not to crush the natural cover. She pulled the grass-and-wool wrap from her shoulders and spread it on the cold brown leaves, then rolled over onto her back and closed her eyes. A moment of rest before going on would do her well. She lay on the wrap that had, just days ago, covered Little Soul after she had birthed him in the swamp. She didn't want to think of Aaron right now. She was too tired; she was too drained. But thoughts were hard to stop.

She turned her face upward to the moon and rubbed her hands over her belly—over the area she had only last week felt movements of the Little Soul who was about ready to see the light of day.

She missed Aaron. Kathryn had picked the proper name for her son. Aaron was a gift from God and he would be an enlightener for all around him—Shanna knew this already.

"You'll be okay, Aaron," she whispered.

But then, a noise, what was it? Footsteps on the fall leaves? Her eyes flung open and she stared upward.

"I've been waiting for you, Squaw Girl."

No, she thought. *No.* Her vision blurred in the moonlight as she gazed, unable to see anybody, but she recognized the haunting voice that emerged from this man she so disliked, this man who had caught her red-handed at the scene after she had fed the knife to Jake Minor's heart.

Don't panic, Shanna. Don't panic, she demanded of herself.

"That you, Alex?" she asked finally, trying to remain calm. She held her breath.

"That you?" she asked again, presenting a welcoming tone she hoped would disguise her fear.

※ ※ ※

In the South Arkansas backwoods, the band of tracking dogs walked in circles sniffing the earth. Alongside them, outlaws in black gazed mystified at each other.

"I think they've lost the trail," one said, his breathe short.

"Knew we shouldn't have stopped to rest," another interjected.

Another rubbed his straggly beard and grinned. "Let's go for the Mexican."

Laughing loudly, the group whipped their horses around and galloped off in the direction they had come.

※ ※ ※

Alex was standing over her. It had been he trailing her through the backlands. Shanna had hoped he'd lose her trail, for he was might-near as bad as the dogs and outlaws.

"You weren't trying to hide from me, were you Squaw Girl?"

"Want to find Land of Red People. You said go to Kathryn. You said I would be safe there. You said you would take Jake's guns and sell them in Dallas. Now why have you come to me?" she hesitated to get a grip on words. She knew she must sound brave.

"I know the way to the Territory. I'll take you there. You just do what I tell you."

"But you said you would go to Dallas." Shanna blinked and her eyes began to focus on Alex.

"I see the papoose is out of your belly. What did you do with it?"

Shanna swallowed. She was unable to speak.

"You give it to my wife?"

She nodded. All was silent then. But in a moment she spoke bravely. "You said you'd not bother me if I be quiet about Jake's guns."

"I'm here to help you Squaw Girl. I helped you get away from the fish camp. I told you the way out of the swamp. I told you who to leave the papoose with. Now I'm helping you get to the Territory. You'll find I'm not so bad.

Alex's piercing eyes seemed to rape her face, then her body.

"Get up if you want to. I'm not bedding you here."

"What now? What you want from me?"

"Squaw Girl, I don't think you trust me. Told you—do as I say and I'll help you."

"Help me how? You keep me from dogs and outlaws?"

"I will. And I'll take you to the Territory. I know right where your people are."

"Why you do this?" Shanna asked, her tone defensive.

"Because you want to get there. And I want to take you."

"You were never nice before."

"Let's get going," he said, lifting his brows in a mystic fashion.

"Are riders after me still?"

"You bet. Pink-face riders in long black dusters and white gloves." He paused, and then spoke in a low frightening voice, "With hungry dogs. Lots of dogs. They're after you all right. Let me tell you, they're getting closer every minute. They're not liking what you did to Jake Minor. He was one of their own." Alex hesitated. "They find you they'll skin you alive. Then they'll go after the papoose."

"How would the outlaws know where I left little Aaron? You promised not to tell."

"So, was the papoose a boy?" Alex said, sounding somewhat amused. Light from his eyes beamed through the night to Shanna. In a moment he said, "The outlaws won't know unless they find you. They'd know how to make you talk."

The tone in Alex's voice was that of excitement. As if he were getting a high from his image of torture she might face.

Shanna kept her eyes on Alex while she got up from the spring and lifted her wrap from the dank leaves. She didn't trust this man. Not at all. But at the moment, what could she do other than go along with him until she could find a way to escape. She was better off with Alex than she'd be if caught by the outlaws.

But Shanna knew that, for a price, Alex wouldn't hesitate turning her over to those horrible men and dogs. Alex and his dealings with Jake Minor were evil. Now, if Alex were doing something for her, he would be rewarded somehow. He wasn't the type of man who would help a body just to be nice. But what could he possibly want from her?

Shanna trailed along at the white stallion's side over the soggy forest bedding for many long miles. So far, Alex was traveling as promised—northward, according to the moss and ferns growing on the north side of oaks. But out of the blue—what was that echoing somewhere in the distance? Dogs!

Dogs!

Breathlessly, she stopped in her tracks. Alex reined his stallion to a stop also. He glanced at her, his face a grin, but said nothing.

Barking dogs pounced closer. She swallowed, fear overwhelming her. Her eyes blurred and her body went limp. Barely moving one foot in front of the other, she staggered toward a tree, her arms reaching out, her hands falling against the trunk. The mossy ripples of dark bark focused in her eye's view, then everything blackened.

❋ ❋ ❋

Squaw Girl was out cold. That was good. Alex slapped at the girl's face but she didn't move. Then he yelled, "Okay, Bill Junior. Come on. She won't see you."

In only moments, Bill Junior rode up on the Pinto that Alex had given him last year in return for devious favors. He grinned at Alex, his blond skin shining in the moonlight.

Alex laughed. "Where'd you get the dogs?" he asked, nodding at a half-dozen or so skinny hounds.

"Did like ye said. Put out traps."

"Good God, what's that smell?"

"Chickens. Gots a couple dead chickens in my saddlebag. That's how I keeped the dogs with me." He eyed Alex. "Ye said fer me to have dogs with me. Ye wanted dogs to be barkin'."

"You did good, Bill Junior. Now you can let them go. Don't need them anymore. Just needed to scare the squaw."

"Want me to take her back to Minor's place?" Bill Junior asked.

"No. I got plans for her." Alex stood by his stallion. "Tell you what. Take my horse. Keep him for me 'til I get back. I'm gonna take the squaw to the Territory. She'll be a good tool to use if I need safe passage."

Bill Junior grinned. "Ye be needing all the tools ye can get to fight off them Injuns. They don't like the looks of ye much, Alex."

"They don't exactly care for you either Bill Junior. You've done more to them than cut off their fingers like you did to your own brother." A smirk came to Alex's face. "But I'm not faulting you none. I'm sure old Moldie had it coming even if he was a little dummy."

Bill Junior laughed. "Yep, I ain't seen the likes of Moldie in a long spell. Ye still got him doing favors fer ye, though, ain't 'cha Alex?"

Alex laughed, and then said, "Course I do. Right now I got him calf rustling."

❋ ❋ ❋

"Hunters after you al-right, Squaw Girl." Alex's voice aroused Shanna from the world of sleep she was hiding in. "I protected you this time. You just stay with me, now. Don't you try slipping off and I'll get you to the Territory."

What had happened? She must have passed out. How long had it been? It was still dark but the moon had moved far to the west. Morning would come soon, wouldn't it?

There were no riders. No dogs. Where had they gone? If they were friends of Jake Minor's, they would have taken her, wouldn't they? Perhaps the dogs and riders were a part of her dream. Perhaps they were of a different pack, possibly pursuing game. Could have been dogs other than the ones that had tracked her through the swamps and bayous. After all, she was many miles from Caddo Lake now.

"Where's your stallion?" she asked, rubbing her head in confusion. The last she remembered was the barking of dogs and a horse coming to a halt.

"Outlaws took Fire. I gave them my horse to save your hide," he paused, his brows rising and his eyes peering at her demandingly. "Now you really owe me, Squaw Girl."

"Why would you save me?" She lowered her head wondering what Alex expected of her now. Already, he had her over the barrel.

"You just don't trust me Squaw Girl. I'm really a nice fellow." He grinned. "I like you, Squaw Girl. I've known you a long time. You're like my little sister." His grin became broader, and then he laughed. "I wouldn't let the outlaws have you. See, I care more about you than I do my own horse." He paused, again lifting his brows. "Now there aren't many men who would trade a horse for a squaw."

In the distance a train whistle blew, reminding her of the trains she had heard on meat deliveries she and Jake had made in the city. She had never been close to a train, but she had often dreamed of being on one and going far from the swampland.

"Our train's calling," Alex said, quickly grabbing her arm and moving toward two long iron railings lying only a few feet ahead.

"Our train?"

"Yeah. You're about to have the ride of your life," Alex said, pulling her even closer to the tracks. "The train will be coming along here. When I say jump, you jump into the boxcar opening. Hear me, Squaw Girl?"

Shanna nodded, but she wasn't sure she could jump. Her strength was drained and blood was still spilling from her womanhood. Right now, putting one foot before the other was a task. But as the train got closer, a spirit zapped her like a magic wand. Without hearing Alex's yell, an aura of energy lifted her in the air and she was flying through the large opening into the moving boxcar.

At the same time, Alex leaped, grabbed hold of bars, and clung to the side of the moving freighter.

Shanna's chest slammed painfully on the wooden flooring; and her legs and feet dangled in the air through the wide opening. All her strength rushed to her hands, and she pushed so hard she thought her fingers might bore holes through the planks and dig all the way to the gravel lying between the tracks. Cold winds whipped briskly at her legs and her feet hung so close to the whizzing earth below, they stung. It was the strength in her hands that saved her from slipping out the opening. Pushing harder into the flooring, she raised herself upward and swung her lower torso into the boxcar.

She turned just as Alex, still hanging onto a bar outside the boxcar, reached through the wide opening, grabbed hold of something, and pulled himself through.

"What y'all running off from?" a male voice drawled from a dark corner.

Shanna peered at the stranger.

"Who's talking?" Alex asked, his voice casual.

"Hobo just ridin' the rails," the man said of himself. "Be changing boxcars in the train yard in Texarkana. Got lots to choose from," he added.

"Been there a few times myself," Alex declared. "First time in a boxcar, though. I usually ride in the coach. Not sure I want to ride in a coach car with Squaw Girl, here."

Shanna glared at Alex and wondered what part she actually played in his plan.

"Where y'all come from?" the hobo asked, his voice trembling, as if he were frightened or chilled.

"From all around. Went to Colorado a few years back to do a little gold mining. Went on west to gather buffalo hides. Stayed there 'til I heard how good things were in Wyoming. Went up there for a spell. Left about a year ago." Alex paused. "You hear about the massacre up in Rock Spring last year?"

"I heared somethin' 'bout that. Happened when a bunch of miners had a fit, 'cause they figured they was owed more pay. They killed a bunch of Injuns or something like that."

Goosebumps popped up on Shanna's arms at the conversation. Alex had been fighting Indians over buffalo. The miners killed a bunch of *Injuns*.

"No. You got it all wrong," Alex said, nonchalantly. "The miners killed a pack of Chinks."

"Any 'ticular reason?"

"'Cause they could," Alex said, his voice somewhat raised. "'Cause the damn foreigners were hogging all the labor. They work cheap. Cheap labor gets the jobs. I swear I don't know why they're in this country."

"I heared it was a big mess up there. All the killin' and burnin'. Whoo-wee. A mess."

Alex gazed at Shanna as a sudden beam of morning light glowed through the boxcar opening.

"I didn't have a thing to do with stuff that happened up there. Just figured it was time for me to move on. Got better things to do around here." He paused for a moment, and then returned his attention to the hobo. "First I'm going to deliver Squaw Girl, here, to her people. They're in the Territory."

"What's yer dealings here?" the hobo asked.

"You're getting kind-of personal."

"Jest camaraderie. Tryin' to be friendly like."

"Well, I'll tell you what. You be around here this time next year you'll be hearing a lot about Alex Andrews. Just keep your ears open."

Shanna shivered. What did Alex have in mind now?

Bright noon sunlight flooded the open door when the boxcar banged and jerked Shana awake, some hours later. Alex was hunched, facing the wide opening as the train rambled and clacked alongside a sight Shanna had never seen—many more boxcars standing still that looked like the one in which she was riding.

"Squaw Girl, we're getting out here," Alex said as the train slowed.

Shanna followed Alex's lead. She had never traveled like this. Was this the path to her people?

The boxcar clanged so loudly the sound could have been mistaken for thunder. Then it came to a slow jerking stop.

"Let's go." Alex jumped from the train. Following his advice, Shanna climbed down behind him.

She followed Alex a few yards west where they approached a boxcar on a different track. Through the two-inch openings between the planks, steam rose into the cool air from just released cow manure. Shanna slumped forward and gagged.

"No time to get sick, Squaw Girl," Alex said, sliding the big gate open just a little. "Climb in."

Putting her hands on the flooring, Shanna lifted herself into the freight loaded with mooing jerseys.

"Tell you what, Squaw Girl. You hide in the back there somewhere in the hay. You're going for a ride. I'll come for you when its time to get off."

"We going to the Land of Red People now?"

"Sure are," Alex said, his eyes peering through black curly hair that had fallen to his forehead. "Now Squaw Girl, I'm leaving you for a while. I'll be traveling in another car. No matter what, you stay here. I'll come for you when it's time to change directions."

"How long before we find my people?"

"Few days. I got some stops to make along the way. You just do as I say."

As the train started to move, Shanna pushed her way to a corner and pressed her forehead to the wood railing so sun shined through the cracks onto her face. She closed her eyes and for a moment, it seemed, lost sense of all happenings around her. Awaking with a start, she realized just how thirsty and hungry she was. Her last meal had been a couple days ago. She had eaten a piece of biscuit while with Kathryn at the fishing bridge and her last drink had been yesterday evening at the spring where Alex had found her.

Today, at the homestead, Mama would cook the raccoon the two of them had dressed. By now Mama would have a fire going in the cast iron stove. She would put the meat and water into a pot and place it in the oven. When half done, Mama would stuff the critter with fried corn bread and sizzling fat drippings. Then she would add peeled sweet potatoes to the pot. Kathryn would bring Leonard to her house to eat. Kathryn and

Mama would say a prayer. Kathryn would mash spuds and gravy and feed Aaron from her finger.

Jolting her mind back to the present, Shanna felt a cow's belly rubbing against her face. Barely able to move in the tight space, she reached over and grabbed a teat. She squeezed and pulled it gently generating a fountain of warm milk to fill her mouth.

"Mm-mm. So good," she whispered. She satisfied her hunger, and then she hovered near the railing and covered her head with her wrap. She put one hand on her tummy and, leaning her head on the railing, closed her eyes.

"I miss you Little Soul," she whispered. "I'll not allow anybody to harm you, ever. I promise. Everything I do is for you, Aaron."

Fourteen

*L*EONARD HAD TOLD her often to take her time getting to work and this morning Kathryn did just that. For her, this was no ordinary day. Last evening, she had thought about the future until late in the night. Then at dawn, she had discussed her plan over breakfast with Mama. Presently, she would tell Leonard what had happened between Shanna and her at the Red Bailey Bridge—how she now found herself with a child.

Kathryn smiled and reined Sugar over the horse trail where the sand was clear of small rocks that might upset the mare's weak hoof.

"Who in the world?" she whispered in amazement. It was a bit out of the ordinary to see an unfamiliar rider on the trail. Looked like a rider on a Pinto leading a white stallion. She pulled the reins to slow Sugar to a strut. She didn't recognize the rider or Pinto. But the stallion?

No. It couldn't be!

If she didn't know better she might think the stallion was Alex's horse Fire. *No, it can't be.* Just then the rider turned off the trail, breaking the team into a run through the grove. Quite baffled, Kathryn rode on beyond the wagon yard and into the timbers where she heard Leonard chopping. At her approach, he put down his ax and reached for Sugar's reins.

"Hey there," he said as she dismounted. "I was a bit fretful fer ye, Kitten. Thought I'd ride over to yer place to see 'bouts ye before going in to town. Looks like yer okay though. Everything all right at yer place?"

"Everything's more than all right." She rubbed her hands down her overalls and let her head dip to the side as she often did when thinking. She wondered where to start her say. Finally, examining Leonard's anxious expression, she began her story.

Leonard said he understood and assured Kathryn that to take a work leave was the proper thing to do. "Lot of things more important than making a buck," he said. "If ye need anything, I'm always here."

"Guess this means I won't be seeing too much of you," Kathryn said, resting her hands on her hips and looking into his hazel eyes.

"You have enough funds to tide ye over?"

"Don't need much. Got plenty enough oil for the lamps, ample staples in the pantry. Got beans, potatoes, flour. Got plenty vegetables canned. Got smoked meat in the cellar."

"Never-the-less, I'll be stopping by after my hunting expeditions," Leonard said, his head bobbing with the music in his voice. "Got to make sure ye got fresh meat for the table." He paused, grinning. "Somebody'll have to be coming around so that little feller won't think there's just women in the world. Somebody'll have to teach him to hunt."

※ ※ ※

At Union Station in Texarkana, dressed in a brand-new three-piece charcoal-colored suit and white shirt, Alex stood in the long spacious depot fingering through a deck of cards he had just purchased in the tobacco shop. Squaw Girl was settled in a Texas & Pacific cattle car headed farther west. She wouldn't likely be spotted before time for her to de-board. However, if she were to get caught and arrested for stabbing Jake Minor, she couldn't point the finger at him for taking the man's guns. He'd be riding coach on the Missouri Pacific and trying his hand at a little five-card stud. He hadn't gambled in a while and this new deck felt hot.

Though leaving an hour or so after Shanna, the passenger train would reach Dallas in plenty time for him to catch up with Squaw Girl. Alex put the cards in his vest pocket and walked casually to the teller window.

"One-way to Dallas," he said, and flashed a roll of bills he'd gotten from a Texas gun trader.

Dallas, on a high-speed train like the Missouri Pacific, was just a hop-skip-and-jump across the Texas border. Thanks to modern technology, once the train stopped and did its business in Boston, Texas, there was no holding it back. Alex had ridden this route several times to attend to business in the west and to visit his good friend Lilly.

Though Lilly had settled down somewhat over the last couple years, she was still beautiful and full of life. She just wasn't much for stealing anymore. At one time, the two of them did quite well by taking wallets from passengers riding west from St. Louis.

In the modern coach car, Alex found a comfortable padded seat where he'd catch some rest. Before a serious poker game, he needed total relaxation and confidence, both of which would require only about an hour in time and perhaps forty miles of train track. Once he became involved in winning, which he was sure to do, time and miles would fade with the east as it was eaten up by darkness.

Alex leaned back and closed his eyes, and as his mind lingered in a dazed state, he went over his plans. While in Dallas, he would visit a furrier who he traded with regularly, call on Lilly, and then catch a stage northeast to the Choctaw Land. Sure, it would have been closer to take Shanna to her people by going northwest on horses; the Territory border being some forty miles—give or take—from Texarkana, but he couldn't let Squaw Girl know how easy the trip really was. By taking the long way through Dallas, Squaw Girl would be totally lost. She'd never find her way back to Kathryn's homestead if she tried. Alex smiled and nodded off.

※ ※ ※

"Not so long ago people thought this neck of the woods was Arkansas," Alex said later that evening, as he shuffled the cards. He put the stack in front of the man on his right to cut. Clayton tapped the top.

"Then Texas got statehood. Sure made a mess of things. Now people with property around here don't know if they live in the United States or Mexico. They're going round and round like clock hands," he paused, his eyes focusing on first one player then another. "Five card stud. Deuces wild. Ante ten," Alex said, and passed a card to the first player on his left.

"King of spades bet." And then, "an ace of spades; that messes something up. Ace bet," he said, lifting his brows. Alex plopped more cards before the gamblers. "And now a deuce of clubs. That screws somebody up. King of diamonds here, and I'll have—ah, another deuce. My bet, throw in ten on the three queens."

❋ ❋ ❋

Shanna hovered in a back corner of the cattle car. She shivered. The night air coming through the openings between rails chilled her skin. She pulled the straw-and-woolen wrap tighter around her head and gazed through a space near the bottom railing. The clanging blended with the sparks of fire continuously flying as the train wheels scraped over the tracks. *Think nice thoughts*, she coached herself; perhaps then time would pass faster. Shanna's thoughts wandered from Aaron and Kathryn and Mama to the swamps of Caddo Lake to the Mexican boy she had loved. *Rowe*, she whispered. *Are you alive somewhere?*

After Shanna had ridden for a full day and evening in the cattle car, the train stopped with a loud bang, generating the iron wheels to scrap up more sparks than before. She gazed through the cracks. And then a sudden, hard confusion swam in her brain. Where was she? This didn't look like a village for Indian people. She remembered Alex's orders: "Stay 'til I come for you." But she wouldn't do as Alex said. She would break away from that low-life carpetbagger and find her own way. She would find her chance to get out of the cattle car and mix with cowpokes.

But then, there—Alex. He didn't look the same. He was dressed in rich clothes so unlike the worn suit he had on the last time she saw him. She watched him step over several tracks before he reached the boxcar. He slid the big door so it opened slightly.

"Still here, Squaw Girl?"

It was too late to ditch him now. She'd wait until the time was right.

"Back here," she said, pushing her way through the herd.

He frowned as she neared. "Squaw Girl, you smell awful. You need a bath if I'm gonna help you out of this town."

She glared at Alex, and then climbed from the boxcar.

"I know a place you can wash up without anybody asking questions. You smell like a milk cow," he said, still frowning. "Now you stay behind me. Don't walk too close. Don't want anybody thinking you're with me."

Shanna followed Alex across the tracks and along a rocked path between a stand of tall structures, then up a narrow plank stairway. He waved, directing her to stand back, and then he knocked. A woman with hair the color of charred oak greeted him at the door.

"Lilly girl," he said, hugging the woman.

The pretty woman flung her arms around his waist. She stood on her toes and kissed him on the mouth. Then she glanced over his shoulder.

She must have flexed, because Alex drew back.

"Lilly girl, I need a favor. I got some business with the squaw, but I can't complete it with her smelling like a cow pen." Looking back at Shanna, his brows raised. "She needs a bath."

"You want her to bathe here?" Lilly asked, curling her nose.

"I'll make it worth your while. I got some money now, but I'll have a lot more next time I come through."

"And you pay the water boy now?"

"Sure will," Alex assured, and pulled his roll from his jacket pocket.

The warm bath felt good, even if Alex were the one arranging this luxury. Shanna sank into the long tin tub of soap bubbles, head and all, and stayed under the surface until the last bit of breath left her lungs, then when she saw the water boy returning with more warm water, she held her head back so he could pour the relaxing liquid onto her long hair. She sat in the water for a long time and tried not to hear the act of sex being shared behind the thin curtain separating the bathing tub from the sleeping quarter.

Too soon, Alex and Lilly rose from bed, then Shanna heard the rustling of clothing. She got out of the tub, wrapped herself in the towel Lilly had put out for her, and went to an open window where she had laid the burlap dress and her grass-and-woolen wrap on the adjacent roof to air out. The garments felt damp.

"You can't wear that, girl," Lilly said, appearing from behind the curtain. She pitched a red-and-gold garment to Shanna. "Put this on."

Shanna stepped to the side and partly hid herself behind the curtain divider to dress. Jake's friends, including Alex, had seen her nude and had taken her sexually, but she had always hated it. She put on the long thick dress. It felt good on her skin. Made her feel like a new woman. "You can keep this dress," Lilly said, smoothing the linen fabric so it hung straight over Shanna's hips. "And here's a shawl for you. Not as unique as the shawl you came here with, but it's nice and clean."

"Thank you," Shanna said, glancing at the fine yellow threads. She hurt at the idea of parting with the wrap she had made as the Little Soul had developed inside her. But Aaron would never need it again. His new family covered him with clean-smelling clothes and blankets.

She raked her fingers through her long hair like a comb and pulled it over her shoulder. Separating the hair into three strands, she began to plait, working her fingers like knitting needles until her hair hung in one long braid to her waist. Finishing, she noticed Lilly watching her. Lilly smiled. Lilly was nice. Why was a good woman like this with Alex?

"Time to go Squaw Girl. You do look better. Might even let you ride inside the stage."

"Stage?"

"Yep, we'll be riding north on a stagecoach," Alex said, his voice dragging somewhat. "Or, maybe I should say that I will. Don't know if they'll let you ride with white people or not. Just have to wait and see."

"She's a beautiful girl, Alex. Why wouldn't they let her ride inside?" Lilly's unexpected words embarrassed Shanna.

Alex's brows rising, he said, "She's Indian. A knife-stabbing Indian. Can't trust her."

"If you can't trust her, why you have her with you?"

"I got my reasons. Might tell you next time I'm in Dallas."

Shanna eyed him hard. *He's the one who can't be trusted.* She knew she would have to keep up her guard against him.

❋ ❋ ❋

Squaw Girl behind him, Alex hurried along downtown Water Street to a mud-brown adobe with a cluster of glass windows.

"Stay back," he said, turning briefly to the squaw. The girl didn't know where she was now but, all the same, he didn't trust her. She would take off or even put a knife in his back first chance she got. "Wait right here. I'll be watching you from inside the store."

"Watching me? Why?"

Alex laughed. "Why, I don't want any body bothering you. I'm here to protect you, Squaw Girl." Alex was sure Shanna didn't believe him for an instant, but if she thought he was watching she would stay put. Inside the store, Alex quickly spied Newberry Jackson in the back of the large room with a stack of furs on a table in front of him. "Jackson, I got some dealing to pass your way."

"Let's hear it," Jackson said, continuing to sort articles.

"I'm heading to the Territory. Got a tip on a load of furs." Alex paused, looking straight into Jackson's eyes. "Interested?"

"If the price is right, I'm interested."

"We can deal. Want the whole load?"

"They cured?"

"They are."

Jackson nodded. "Good. When can you get them here?"

"Soon. In plenty time for shipping," Alex said, mentally noting that Jackson would want a good assortment of American pelts to send to Europe. The market was booming right now.

"Bring 'em on in. I'll take all I can get over the next couple months."

❋ ❋ ❋

Bridged By Love

At a busy stage stop, with a horde of horses and wagons coming and going, Shanna stood back and kept an eye on Alex. He chatted with a man hooking a team of two horses to a fancy wagon with a top on it. This, she supposed, was the stagecoach Alex planned to ride.

"The squaw's civilized." Alex was speaking of her.

The horse-keeper scratched his head and ogled her, then turned back to Alex. "I don't know 'bout her. Thought all the Injuns was sent up to the Territory."

"She was raised by a white man in Louisiana. Had her since she was a kid."

"Sure she ain't mean? I don't trust no Injuns."

"She does what I tell her," Alex said, eyeing her.

Shanna listened to what Alex had to say and was sarcastically amused. He didn't know her as well as he thought. He couldn't trust her any more than she could trust him, which was none at all.

"She won't be giving us any trouble, I'll assure you that much."

The horse tender scratched his head again. "I want ye to know, this ain't no regular stage line. It's just a trip I contracted. I say ye ride, ye can ride. I say ye can't, ye can't." He scratched his head some more, now in a different spot, as if maybe he had bugs crawling in his ratty hair. "If she offends anybody," he continued, pointing at her, "she goes on top."

Alex nodded and handed money to the man.

"Now ye know that means if a woman at any stop wants to ride, the squaw goes up." He looked again at Shanna. "I don't like this much. If there's any trouble over the squaw, she be off completely. And she rides on top 'til we out of town, that's fer sure. We be leaving soon as I load my shipment."

"What kind of shipment?"

"Don't know. Don't care. We be heading out in 'bout a hour."

Alex motioned Shanna to come. She obeyed, quickly following his long gaits to a large oak tree. "Now tell you what, Squaw Girl. Anybody ask any questions, I do the talking."

Shanna watched Alex and, keeping a straight face, passed him a quick nod. She was sure she wouldn't have any reason to talk with people on the stagecoach anyway. All she wanted right now was to lose Alex and find her people.

"How long before we reach the Land of Red People?"

"Now, Squaw Girl, why you care as long as I keep you safe from outlaws and law people."

"I need to know. I need to plan."

"You plan?" He laughed. "What you aiming to do. Your last plan was pretty damn deadly. You aim on sticking a knife through my heart like you did to old Minor?"

Was Alex fooling around with her or did he suspect she might actually knife him? She said nothing and then his glare lingered for a moment in her eye. But she couldn't answer his question because she didn't know what was to come.

Atop the coach, Shanna hovered between two large footlockers and covered her head with the fancy yellow shawl Lilly had given her. The stage was on its way out of Dallas. She visualized the horses trotting and the big wheels rolling along brick and stone streets thickly lined with large magnolia and elm trees. Suddenly, she realized how tired she was. She closed her eyes and tried to forget that Alex had control of her now.

※ ※ ※

Alex pulled two cigars from his vest pocket and offered one to the well-dressed man sitting across from him.

"Don't mind if I do," the man said, quickly accepting the smoke. He put the Cuban-wrapped tobacco in his mouth and Alex passed him a light. "Doc Wilber's the name." He reached to shake Alex's hand.

"Andrews here. Alex Andrews."

"Where you headed Andrews?"

"Choctaw Land. Taking Squaw Girl up there. I'm trading her off." Alex caught Doc's gaze through clouds of gray smoke coming from each side of the older man's mouth.

Doc stared suspiciously at Alex. Then, "How you aim on trading her. You can't own an Indian. She'll just naturally go on the reservation."

"All the same, Squaw Girl will get me where I need to be. Right spot at the right time. Nobody knows what Nation she belongs to anyway."

"There's no need for her to be riding atop," Doc said matter-of-factly. "Shouldn't you bring her on inside?"

"Nah. Squaw Girl is fine where she is. Don't really want to fall asleep with her too close. Don't trust her. The squaw's full of fire."

"Seems quiet to me," Doc said, and puffed his cigar.

"She's quiet all right. That don't mean you can trust her. I've seen what she's capable of," Alex paused, lifting his brows to pass a knowing eye at Doc. "Squaw Girl can carve up a man just like she can carve a steer."

Alex lowered the leather roll-down curtain so it deferred the evening sun. Actually, he didn't think Shanna would pull anything right now, not as long as she needed him to find her people. Besides, she wasn't fool enough to start a hullabaloo on the stagecoach after being put through the wringer by the driver.

※ ※ ※

In a Texas jail, Rowe wrapped the striped Mexican blanket around his bare shoulders and walked the six feet across his cell to the tiny barred window. Nothing there to see but grass dried from lack of water. But he couldn't tell if it was spring, summer, fall or winter. The only thing he knew for sure was that this place was a hellhole.

"I got to get out of here," he said aloud.

Before he had made chopped meat out of the jailer's fingers, the skittish man had talked with him some. Now he just gave him go-to-hell looks and made threats to emphasize his power.

Rowe rubbed his hand through hair that grew to his shoulders, then to the straggly beard around his mouth and chin. He gazed out over the rocky terrain. What was it, riders in the distance heading toward the jail? Holding the blanket tight to his chest, he stepped closer to the bars and rested his forehead against the cool iron as two horses galloped nearer.

The clamor of hoofs on the gravely terrain woke the jailer. He jumped from his comfort chair and grabbed a rifle.

"They comin' fer ye Rowe. They comin' fer ye," he said, holding the weapon close to his body and doing some sort of a hip-hop dance.

"Might as well open up," Rowe said, walking to the cell door.

"Can't do it boy."

"Let me out. I'll help you. I won't let them get to you. We can shoot it out."

"Can't do it boy. Can't do it."

The jailer stuck the rifle, aimed at Rowe, under his right arm to carry it and scuffled to the cell. He pulled his jingling keys from his belt loop. The gun still pointed at Rowe, he put the key in the lock.

"Git back, Rowe. Git way back there by the winder," the jailer whined joyfully, keeping a stupid-looking grin on his grime-smeared leathered face.

Slowly Rowe backed toward the wall.

The rifle still pointed at Rowe, the jailer turned the key then quickly switched the rifle to his left hand, his shooting finger on the trigger. The jailer kicked so the door screeched open.

"Don't 'cha try nothing funny, ye hear me? Git on out of this 'ere cell and do it real slow like."

The racing horses' hoofs, sounding more like a thousand than two, thundered louder as they neared the jail. And then the noise came to a stifling halt.

Got to get out of here, Rowe thought. *Got things to do. This can't be the end. Not here. Not now.*

The jailer's gun waved, ushering Rowe from the cell to the center of the room.

"Come on, man. What's in this for you? Let me go and I'll make it worth your while." As Rowe spoke, he picked up his dingy shirt and put it on.

Before the jailer could reply, the door swung open and two mean-looking grubby cowpokes wearing long black dusters and white gloves entered. Rowe twisted the ends of his long beard around his finger but his focus was on the huge Colts arming the men.

"I keeped him fer ye. Jest like ye said fer me to." The jailer lowered the rifle and held out his left hand. "I keeped him fer ye."

"What you want you ignorant fool?" Brown liquid sprayed from between the man's spaced yellow teeth as he spoke.

His hand still extended, "Little bit more money. I keeped him longer than ye paid me fer. I had to feed him, mind ye."

"You hear that, Morton?" The man spit a wad of chewing tobacco toward the wall and laughed out loud. "He wants money."

"Oh, yeah? Gold or silver?" Morton laughed. "You'll get what's coming at 'cha," Morton assured the jailer. He then nudged his Colt into Rowe's side. "Move boy."

Moving carefully, the gun still poked in his side, Rowe started toward the door as directed.

The quick clicks of a gun chamber rolled and Rowe stopped instantly. Were they going to shoot him right here? But it wasn't Morton's gun. It was a six-shooter that the jailer had out-of-the-blue pulled from his desk.

"Stop. Stop right here, right now, or I aim to shoot ye."

Morton laughed, and suddenly, like a bolt of lighting, fell to his knees, aiming his Colt revolver quicker than the eye could witness and firing so the bullet sped into the jailer's chest.

The outlaw laughed again, and again Rowe felt the gun barrel pushing into his side.

"Where you taking me?" he asked, the Colt nudging him toward the door. He glanced back to see the jailer falling to the floor.

"Move," the words came as the Colt pushed hard into his back.

Fifteen

THE HORSES MOVED at a steady pace. Eight miles every hour, according to the driver, and the darkness didn't seem to slow the team any. Shanna lay curled in a fetal position between the two footlockers; the fancy yellow shawl Lilly had given her wrapped around her body like a blanket. She watched the stars and moon dancing in the heavens. The moon was like a glowing ball bouncing from one side of the sky to the other as the stagecoach rocked about over the terrain like a fishing boat on fast-flowing bayou waters.

Far from the bayous now, far from Caddo Lake, far from Caddo Parish and the whole state of Louisiana, she would soon reach the Land of Red People. She would find her Nation. She would find life with her people. She didn't have Aaron but he was with Kathryn. Aaron was safe. He would never fall into the hands of Jake Minor to be sold or traded or enslaved like she had been.

It must have been hours later that she opened her eyes again and found the moon had ceased to bounce. And then, "Wooo," the driver called to the team. She raised herself as the horses sauntered to a stop at a long tying post in front of a log storefront. Hickory smoke from the chimney filled the air.

Shanna could almost taste the chicken pie Mama had cooked a few nights ago. If she had jewels or furs now she would trade them for food.

The driver hitched the horses to a long railing while the passengers got out.

"Gonna let the horses rest and catch some shut eye myself," the driver said. "I'z been driving this rig since Houston. He removed his cap and raked his fingers through his matted hair. "Y'all can cook up something if ye want to. There's some rice and saltpork in a tin back there," he babbled, pointing to the boot at the back of the coach.

"Don't get too comfortable here, though," he continued. "I ain't stopping fer y'all, I'm stopping cause I need a bit of shuteye. Be ready to load up whenever I call at 'cha."

Shanna climbed from the top and in a moment stood face to face with Alex. "Earn your travel, Squaw Girl. Cook up some grub."

Shanna despised taking any kind of an order from Alex, but right now, she was hungry and had no problem in obliging. This would be food for her stomach, too.

Looking through the moonlight, she saw a stream to one side of the storefront. She grabbed a pail from the stage boot and caught water from the crystal waters, which she then added to the rice and saltpork. She secured the crock on stones circling a fire Doc had started. Already, the aroma rose with the steam and the thick sticky rice and pork lingered on her taste buds.

After grub, Shanna lay awake for hours listening to the three men snoring when, sometime before dawn, the stage driver began to rustle about on his bedroll. Finally, making several loud unwanted bodily noises, he arouse. "Y'all load up," he called out.

Getting to her feet, Shanna shook grass from the red and gold dress and fine wrap Lilly had given her. She put her foot on the boot to climb atop the stagecoach.

Doc, about to board the coach, stopped and glanced at her. "Come ride with me," he said.

Stunned, Shanna's wide eyes stared at the older man. He, too, had boarded in Dallas, but she had already been situated on top and had not spoken to him, or he to her until this moment.

"Yes, I'm talking to you," Doc said, his voice holding a friendly tone.

"I must ride on top," she said, and smiling lightly, nodded.

"Says who?"

"Driver says so. Alex says so."

"I'm a paying passenger and I got say, too."

Doc must be out of his mind, Shanna thought. She couldn't do something as bold as ride in the coach after overhearing words that had transpired between Alex and the driver back in Dallas. Her eyes moved to Alex, now standing behind Doc and waiting his turn to get into the coach.

"Come on, Squaw Girl," Alex said. "Don't want to dispute Doc here. Wouldn't want to upset him and then find out he's really the notorious Doc Holliday."

"I just soon ride atop," Shanna said, quickly climbing up.

"Best keep her up there," Alex said, a mischievous grin on his face. "Never can tell what Squaw Girl is up to." He shook his head, and directing his statement to Doc, said, "Can't trust that squaw."

As the morning passed and the stagecoach moved over unfamiliar grounds, Shanna enjoyed scenery much different than the swampland areas around Caddo Lake and the bayous in Louisiana. During this peaceful tranquility, her mind moved through a valley of thoughts: Aaron, Kathryn, the Territory, and her people. All were good thoughts. She smiled and relaxed.

Then the conversation that penetrated the open windows and invaded the cool comfort of solitude disturbed her terribly.

Alex was referring to Indian people as savages. But they weren't savages, were they? Since being taken from her family, she had known only whites, those who came to Jake Minor's store, and the Raider Outlaws—they were savages; and a few Mexicans who had wandered up from the south, mostly working their way north through sugar cane fields. She sighed. Soon she would find her people. And she would find a way to get Alex out of her life.

Blending with the music of wildlife somewhere north of Boston in the East Texas wilderness, Doc's voice emerged through the pleasant songs of nature. "That girl don't seem savage to me. Seems quiet," he said.

"Don't let her innocent appearance fool you, Doc. I've seen what that squaw can do."

Shanna's body stiffened. *Alex dislikes Indian people. Alex is white.*

"Sometimes I think Indian people are pushed too far," Doc continued, his voice in and out of her ears with the rocking of the stage moving over road roughness. "Take those Indians in the Panhandle about a decade back, for instance. All they wanted was to hunt the buffalo to eat; then get their hides. Hunters of our kind, I mean white as you and me, went in and destroyed the buffalo and got the Indians all riled up."

Doc paused, or his voice faded, Shanna couldn't tell which. Then she picked up his words again.

"Let me tell you something right here and now. The good life for the Indians ended with the Red River War."

"Well Doc, don't you think the white people had a right to live without being massacred by the savages? All they wanted to do was set them a livelihood."

"Oh bull! White people moved in, lots of 'em being buffalo hunters. Then they cried to the government that they needed protection. So the government set up forts."

All was quite for a moment. Then Doc said, "If the north and south had kept fighting, the Indians would have been all right."

"How you figure?" Alex questioned, a sarcastic tone in his voice.

"Well hell," Doc commenced again. "When the north and south were fighting, the military withdrew from the west to fight for the north, or the south, which ever they were told to. Then white people who had moved west started crying to the government again."

All government people are white men, Shanna mentally recorded.

"Well, them Indians got plenty more than they should've. One way or another, they always get something for nothing," Alex said.

"Nope, nope, nope. The Indians didn't make out on anything. The ones that didn't end up dead were sent to the Territory. The Comanche and Kiowa went to one reservation and the Southern Cheyenne and Arapaho went to another. The government's supposed to provide them their needs. Even guns and ammunition for hunting. Goods are supposed to be allotted to the tribes every year for the next three decades."

"Guns and ammunition," Alex said with excitement. "How you know so much?"

"They don't call me *Doc* for nothing."

"So you're an educated man?"

"Reckon I am."

"Then tell me, why does the government give the Indians guns when we won the war against them?"

"'Cause the tribes I just mentioned, they're supposed to get to hunt anywhere south of the Arkansas River as long as the buffalo roam."

"It'll never work. They're too savage."

"Ten chiefs signed the treaty and a whole slew of Indians agreed to stop raids on settlers. Lots of them moved to the Territory. 'Course, nothing good has come of it yet."

Just who's this Doc, person, who knows so much? Shanna wondered.

"'Cause of the Indians, I'm sure." It was Alex's deplorable voice now polluting the country air.

"Nope, because of commercial buffalo hunters."

There was a long pause. Shanna strained to hear.

Doc spoke again, "Hunters slaughtered buffalo by the thousands and sent the hides east."

Alex's voice got louder. "We got a right to buffalo hides. It's our country."

"I figure you know a bit more about that war in the Panhandle than you let on."

Alex laughed. "All that stuff about the Indians claiming the buffalo and wanting to keep the west for themselves is a bunch of hog-wash if you're asking me."

"Nobody asking you, Alex."

"Just so you know, Doc. The Indians started that war. It was that one that said he was some kind of god or something, called himself Isa-tai, or something like that, who instigated the whole ordeal." Alex paused briefly, but before Doc said anything, commenced talking again. "You're forgetting about the fort at Adobe Wells, aren't you Doc? You're forgetting that a band of Comanche's attacked the post and got this whole tornado-war thing going. At least that incident showed the white people they can't trust the Indians. Best place for redskins are on the reservations—someplace to hold them so they can't bother anybody any more. Best thing Texas ever did was send them off."

I get frightened by Alex; he's an evil man. I must get my freedom soon, Shanna thought.

"Sounds like you had a hand in the trouble with the Indians, Alex."

"Wouldn't be ashamed to admit it if I did. Like General Philip Sheridan said about the Removal Campaign of Seventy-four, it was 'successful.' And that's what's important. The Indians lost that Red River War."

There was more mumbling below but Shanna couldn't make out who said what until Alex's loud voice shot up like a whip. "I'm not ashamed to say I've done my part to get rid of Indians during the wars. By fighting off Indians I've protected white folks."

Sure, Shanna thought knowing any protection he gave to anybody was for his own gain.

Bridged By Love

"Maybe so," Doc said. "But tell you what, Alex. Might be interesting to hear you discuss the episode at a Comanche council gathering."

Alex laughed loudly. When his laughter calmed he said, "Doc, I don't know if you're fooling or talking serious."

"I'm serious, Alex."

Alex laughed, even louder than before.

"I'll set it up so you can speak to any of the tribes. You can tell them all about your days of fighting Indians."

"What you talking about Doc? Sounds like you're working with them."

"I do work with different tribes." Doc paused. "Don't think they'd take to you too much, Mister Andrews."

Again there was silence except for the wheels rolling over the rocky trail. Soon Alex said, "So I was buying a load of hide from a buffalo hunter when a band of Quahadi Comanche came barreling toward Fort Sill. I could tell by looking at them their fight was gone. They were too weak to do anything other than surrender," he said, and then paused.

"I can tell you don't agree with me Doc, but I'm saying my peace. There's nothing wrong with buying and selling hides. Now you know that." Alex's defensive tone penetrated the coach clearly.

"Did you have contact with the Quahadi?" Doc's voice carried a hint of anger.

"Not a bit. No reason to," Alex said. "But the Quahadi went down then, and now Geronimo's gone down." Still laughing, he added, "Never thought I'd see the day. One thing about Geronimo, he was a hell-raiser."

"So, you know Geronimo personally. Did you fight him?"

"Just heard of him. I'm glad to say there's not any more chiefs out there like him. We wouldn't be safe traveling up here right now if there was."

There was a long silence and then Alex's voice came filtering up again. "I been gathering and selling hides off-and-on since I was a boy. Had a few other ideas working in my favor, too. I've made a good bit of money with my wheeling-and-dealing. And I plan on making a lot more in the next few months. You can bet on it." There was a paused. "I got a fortune waiting for me across the Red River."

"Speaking of the Red River, looks like we're about to cross it," Doc said.

Shanna looked to the river running alongside the trail, rolling in clay-red ripples. She trembled. *Will there be outlaw riders in the Land of Red People—in the Indian Territory?*

Shanna kept her eyes on the rolling river on the north side of the trail. Still, Doc and Alex's conversation sifted along with the sounds of moving waters to the stage top, but now their words were barely audible. What were Doc and Alex talking about, really? They had been speaking of a war between Indians and white settlers that had occurred more than ten years ago. They had discussed things that happened when she was a little child, even before she was kidnapped from her family and taken to Jake Minor's place. At that time, Alex had been one of the outlaw riders who called often on Jake.

Shanna signed. Most white men frightened her. Doc was white, yet he seemed nice. She wasn't afraid of him. Leonard had treated her very kindly. She wasn't at all afraid of Leonard. Some white men were good—like the white women she had come to love: Miss Shearon and Kathryn and Mama and now Lilly.

Rowe was good. But Rowe was Mexican.

"Oh Rowe," she whispered loud enough the wind could carry her voice to him. "Where are you Rowe?"

※ ※ ※

Two against one isn't that big a deal, Rowe told himself as he rode a gray stud between his two captors. Morton had proven he'd kill in a heartbeat. This other desperado looked equally calloused. Sooner or later, though, he'd make an escape. Already, they had been riding for hours. Would they stop to sleep? Morton had slowed his horse to a steady walk, making it necessary for the other rider to do the same.

"Slow up here, Cowboy," Morton said to Rowe. "I want 'cha to know right here and now, if'n ye go trying anythang, I mean anythang a'tall, I aim on shootin' ye."

Rowe looked to his right. Evening shadowing Morton's face showed an even darker side to the outlaw. "I'm riding unarmed between two armed men. Now what you think I'll try?"

"Jest so ye know I ain't 'fraid to shoot. And don't 'cha think for a minute ye can outrun bullets." Morton paused, brought his hand to his face and scratched through a thick growth of black whiskers.

Surely, Rowe thought, *they won't shoot me for talking.* "I'm curious as to where we're headed. And where are we now?"

The rider on the left laughed. "Mean ye ain't figured out where ye at. Figured by now ye'd have learned where ye lived fer might-near a year."

"Been that long? Time passes fast when you're happy."

"Happy, huh," Morton butted in, his voice sarcastic.

"Felt like home." Rowe waited but neither of the other men spoke. "So you don't plan on telling me where we are now, huh?"

"I know what'cha thanking. Yer thanking if ye know where ye at, ye have a better chance if'in ye break loose," Morton said, turning to face Rowe.

"I'm thinking no such thing."

Morton slowed his horse to a very leisurely pace. His partner did the same, which forced Rowe to follow suit.

"Yer slowing up too much, Morton."

"Ready to make camp?" Morton questioned.

"Might as well. We too tired to go on. Ain't getting no wheres no how."

"Looks like this is as good a place to stop as any," Morton said.

Bridged By Love

The riders pulled the reins, halting their horses. Rowe could see both men were tired. Likely, more tired than he was. He watched Morton play with the Colt revolver, which was nearly constantly aimed at him, while the other man held a rifle at his side.

Where the hell am I?

"Get on down here," Morton said, waving the Colt.

I don't think so! "Yooo-ooo," Rowe yelled out, kicking the stud in its ribs so it reared and bucked, spinning sand and fine rocks so the scene became a whirlwind.

"Shoot him! Shoot him!" both men screamed to each other. Bullets fired furiously at Rowe's back.

Rowe slumped suddenly. Something, maybe a rock, flew from the horse's hoof. The blow was powerful. A stinging commenced between his neck and shoulder. *Heaven forbid! I'm hit!*

"Yoo-oooo!" he yelled, slapping the reins quickly from one side of the horse's neck to the other. Galloping hoofs folded in behind him as he charged on eastward. Soon they were like ghouls speeding through the big-moon night.

※ ※ ※

Though Shanna had seen the Red River where it ran through Arkansas during her childhood and in Louisiana during attempted escapes from Jake Minor, the body of water now had new meaning for her.

Land south of the Red River was part of Texas, but the north was the commencing of the Territory.

Once crossed, they would actually be in the Land of Red People, she marveled. As yet, however, the driver had shown no signs of crossing the flow. But, she wondered, when the time came, how would the stage get over?

The stage rolled along the trail as it meandered along the twisting vegetation-covered banks. Shanna pulled her wrap tighter around her shoulders to ward off bugs that accumulated in the trees and shrubs adjacent the water.

In what seemed the longest time, the stage pulled close to a log building. This was a store, a trading post, much resembling Minor's place.

"Whooaa," the driver called, slowing the team. And then, "Everybody out. And you," he said, turning to Shanna. "Off."

Shanna climbed down just as Alex and Doc exited the coach.

"What's up?" Alex asked the driver.

"I want ye to help me unload the stage. We gonna have to take the mules and coach through the water. Don't want it bogging down."

Shanna, along with the three men, began to unload the heavy shipment of what-ever-it-was the driver was taking someplace unbeknown to her.

"Squaw Girl, get up there and push those boxes to the boot," Alex ordered.

Shanna climbed atop the coach and following Alex's demand, pushed the crates toward the boot. *Guns in here*, she told herself. She could tell a container of guns a mile away, having been exposed to such time after time by-way-of dealings at Minor's store.

She watched as Alex climbed on the stage footer and pulled the crate toward him. A familiar sly look covered his face. This meant he was considering a shady move. *He's knows there are guns here*, Shanna thought. She raised her brows and pushed another crate to the back. She knew the stage driver had better watch his back or Alex would take off with the shipment before anybody could as much as blink an eye.

The crates unloaded, the driver gave Shanna two ropes, each with one end tied to a mule's bridle.

"Take 'em cross," the driver said. "The water's down. Hadn't been any rain in a coon's age. Right here's yer low point," he said, pointing.

Shanna looked hard at the driver. "Sure mules can make it across?"

"Jest never ye mind. Don't need to be nosey."

After the long ride from Dallas, which Shanna suspected had taken Alex and her miles and miles out of their way, she was too fed up with him and the driver to hold her tongue.

"I am Indian. You be in land of my people across the river." By speaking her mind, had she foolishly overstepped her bounds? But she must not look intimidated. She glared even harder at the driver.

"Jest let me put it this way, if ye don't lead 'em across yer apt to die right here."

Shanna narrowed her eyes. It wasn't that she had a problem leading the mules across the water; it was just that she was sick and tired of being ordered around by callous men. Kathryn and Mama and Leonard and Lilly had treated her human. Good people were unlike this filthy stagecoach driver and Alex.

"The girl's got a reasonable point. Why can't the mules go on the ferry?" Until now, Shanna hadn't noticed Doc paying attention to the situation.

The driver turned to Doc. He leaned his head to the side and hesitated, as if fishing for words. "The raft's rotten. Coming apart. Got ta withstand the cargo."

For the first time since this conversation started, Alex spoke. "Sounds reasonable to me, Doc."

"Nobody asked you, Alex," Doc shot back.

"You're getting kind-of huffy, aren't you Doc?" Alex said, almost jokingly, and with his black eyes aimed on the older man.

"So I am," Doc said, his voice holding a bitter tone.

Shanna didn't want to see Doc and Alex get into a ruckus here. Alex might hurt Doc. And right now, he was the only person here she could consider even close to being human.

"It's okay Doc," Shanna said. "I'm satisfied the mules and carriage can't cross on the raft. Should the raft go falling apart the mules would spook."

"Well, what intelligence you have, Squaw Girl," Alex said, raising a brow as if in amusement. "Didn't know you could say more than a three-word sentence."

Giving Alex a tired look, Shanna took the ropes from the driver and started toward the sloping bank. Surprisingly, the mules followed without hesitation into the river. She waded to the point where the clay-colored river crept to her shoulders, and then she treaded water for a couple minutes before breaking into a sidestroke.

I can do this, she told herself, drawing one knee up and then kicking. Still holding the rope, she swallowed a gulp of thick muck. Gagging, she felt herself sinking into the thick waters. Her eyes wide open, she saw an array of churned-up brown and reddish particles flowing through the sun-lit water like schools of minnows. Her life seemed a million miles away. She was someplace in the sunset, someplace where she may spend eternity.

Weak and immobilized, Shanna watched particles spiraling in the light beam through the syrupy mass. Then, from nowhere, a power came over her like a lightening bolt and whipped through her long throat chamber until she coughed furiously. She upchucked until her windpipes were as clean as the God-given flow in Caddo Lake where she had given birth to Aaron. She could do anything now. She was strong. She was phenomenal. She commanded massive power.

I will myself on, she said in her head. *I will myself on.* She was only a half-a-river crossing to the Land of Red People—to the Indian Territory and freedom.

Her eyes aimed straight ahead, she led the team onward.

Shanna didn't know how long she lay on the slippery riverbank before she heard commotion on the water. She turned. The driver and Alex were maneuvering the raft across the river. Doc and a man she had not seen before were crossing in a canoe.

Moving her attention from the men back to the earth on the north side of the river, she lowered her head so her mouth touched the soil, kissing in rapture the slippery red loam. She had made it. This was her land. She was home.

Shanna got to her feet and lifted her face to the sky. She closed her eyes and breathed in the Red People's air. She breathed in the air of her land and the freedom it held. She lowered her face and gazed at the man stepping from the raft to a rocky incline built at the water's edge. Now that she was home, she must figure out the best way to get rid of this beast of a human, this white demon disciple of Jake Minor's ghost. Alex Andrews was her only hindrance to freedom.

Sixteen

ONLY THE CLACKING of iron wheels disturbed the natural music of the forest. Shanna listened from atop the stage as it rolled through the hilly terrain where unspoiled crests were alive with animals and greenery. She smiled at a doe and two fawns standing perfectly still, their big brown eyes aimed straight at her as the stagecoach passed. And then in a stream, a half-a-dozen raccoons washed and ate roots. A rustling to her left drew her attention. Behold, a bear cub. Not at all frightened. Not budging. Just reared up on its hind feet, its front paws in the air, as if waving hello to the passing team and sniffing to see who'd come calling.

She was glad she had chosen to ride on the stage top rather than accept Doc's kind offer to ride with him in the coach. The top was peaceful. And at the moment, there were no voices emerging from inside to disturb her solitude.

As the stage moved on to the northeast, Shanna marveled at the abundance and variety of trees: pecans, hickory, walnut, hazel nut and chinquapins. There was no wonder the forest was alive with rabbits, squirrels, raccoons and opossum. Every now and then a flock of bobwhite quail, wild turkey and prairie chicken scampered from alongside the trail into the high grasses. And from time to time, a flight of pigeons darkened the sky like storm clouds moving in. Already Shanna loved this land.

Three or so hours after crossing the Red River, the horses halted, bringing the stage wheels to a dirt-crunching stop. Shanna looked over the railing. Three young braves stood beside the trail. Two climbed on top while one stood near the team and spoke with the driver. Then the brave pulled something from the pocket of his buckskin pants and handed it to the driver. Shanna didn't try to see what was passed, as it was none of her business and she didn't care anyway. Once the team pulled off, Shanna found two of the young braves spoke English as well as she did. The third never said anything loud enough for her to hear.

"What tribe you belong to?" One asked, only minutes after climbing aboard. His beady black eyes sank into hers.

"So long ago I don't recall. I was very young. My family was moving in a number count on two-hands. We traveled along the Red River. Somewhere in Arkansas, I remember."

"My name, Snakeskin," the brave said, his trigger finger pressing his chest. "You?"

"Named Shanna."

"Shanna," he repeated, and grinning he shook his head. "Not Indian name."

Shanna said nothing. She had given herself that name after being called every name from Squaw Girl to Pussy Lips. She shuttered at the recollection. But good thoughts came at remembering the white woman who was for so long at Jake Minor's place during her early years. Images seemed to blur together now, but she remembered the good woman's name was Miss Shearon. She spent much time at the store back then. When Miss Shearon didn't have a man hanging on her, she visited with her—the squaw kid—and taught her to read and write and do arithmetic. Miss Shearon was kind and, when she said it was time she must leave Caddo Lake, she pleaded with Jake Minor to allow Shanna her freedom, too. But the possessive man said no.

Oh how she had wanted to flee with the kind woman, she thought, remembering the hurt that had filled her soul. After that, Shanna pretended to herself she was the woman's daughter, and that Miss Shearon would return someday and the two of them would fly away together. A smile came to her face recollecting, but then Snakeskin's voice broke her reverie.

"You know your people?"

"Have a brother." Shanna drew her hand to her chest and said, "I was younger."

"Know his name?"

"Moon Hunter."

Snakeskin's brows lifted. "Moon Hunter lives with the tribe a short piece from the river."

No. This couldn't be true. Shanna's breath hung in her throat, choking her consciousness to reason. Finally, she asked, elated, "You know my brother Moon Hunter?"

"We get off tonight when we come to village. I take you to Moon Hunter."

Shocked, Shanna was at loss of words. Could she trust this brave? And what were Alex's plans for the night? If the braves could take her to her family, she must try to get away from Alex. What would he do then? Look for her? He had told Doc he had a fortune waiting for him once he crossed the Red River. So where was this wealth? Right now, she must think of the best thing to do.

"We get off at Pell Junction," Snakeskin said, breaking her thoughts.

Snakeskin knows my brother. The thought played in Shanna's mind. Should she talk, ask questions about her family? Shanna let her head drop so that her eyes focused on her folded arms. For a long while she was silent with her reveries and meditations. Then when courage came, she wanted to talk and ask questions about things that could have frightening answers.

It had been such a long time since that haunting day she had left her family and had stopped to pick blackberries in a brier patch away from the riverbank. She wondered now if she would know her brother or her parents when she found them. And, equally important, would they know her?

"You know my Moon Hunter. You know my tribe?" she renewed the topic.

"Think Moon Hunter runs with renegades."

"You mean he deserted his people?"

"Not that. He just do his own thing. Takes orders from nobody. Not from chiefs, not from soldiers."

"So he has no tribe?"

"Lives in land of Choctaw and Chickasaw." Snakeskin looked deep into her face and said, "I think Moon Hunter come with mixed blood."

"What is mixed blood? Mixed Choctaw and Chickasaw?" Shanna asked, Snakeskin's words having brought confusion. "My parents and Moon Hunter's are same. I am Choctaw and Chickasaw? What do I say when I search for my people?"

"Moon Hunter lives in land of Choctaw and Chickasaw. He not sure which tribe he belong to. So he choose both. Moon Hunter is good renegade. Trader with the white man. He help his tribes," Snakeskin assured her.

"How can he be renegade and trader, if he helps Indian people? If he helps two tribes?" Shanna felt her face draw wrinkles of dismay, her mind becoming more confused than before.

"I think Moon Hunter has white daddy."

She slammed her hand over her mouth. *NO!*

The shocking idea Snakeskin beset upon her sent her mind spinning in a wayward trance. Her Moon Hunter didn't have a white daddy. She barely remembered her daddy, but she knew he was caring and kind and every bone in his body was good. He wasn't like white men she had known—mean, evil and taking.

Unable to say more or even hear the conversation Snakeskin kept going, she lay back on the coach roofing and let her mind carry her to a time when she had been with her family. Where had they been then? Somewhere along the Red River in Arkansas going to—

Where were they going? To the Territory? No. They had been in the Territory already, hadn't they? Where were they going? Where? Her daddy? Her daddy was there with her. And her mother. She saw her mother's long black braids in her mind's eye, her eyes as dark as cinders, her skin brown as an autumn leave, and her face as beautiful as a cactus rose. Her daddy? She conjured the man taller than the other Indians with a bearded face, unlike the other Indians, and skin as tan as a newborn fawn. The man she saw in her mind was an Indian, wasn't he? He wasn't white, wasn't pink like Jake Minor, or with freckled spots on his face like Leonard. He wasn't as maroon as the cage of grape brandy behind the butcher block as Jake Minor's store, like Rowe. So if her daddy was not an Indian, then what was he? And where had her family been heading? Shanna closed her eyes. Her family had been hiding. But from what? White men, white men wearing black.

She remembered something: "Moon Hunter," her daddy had said. "Go back. Go home." The boy, Moon Hunter, was much taller than she was. "Go Moon Hunter. Be safe," her father re-enforced. And that was the last time she saw her brother. The next day, she believed, was the last she saw of her mamma and father. She had left their camp on the riverbank to follow a thicket of blackberry vines. And that was when the outlaws found her and took her with them.

Sitting atop the stage, her eyes wandered over the three braves now chatting among themselves in a language she didn't understand. She played with the long black braid falling onto her lap. She didn't know to which tribe she belonged, but she did know she was an Indian. Her mother was an Indian. Moon Hunter was an Indian. And her father was an Indian, too.

That evening, when the stage stopped at a little store building at Pell Junction, Shanna watched the braves get off.

"We here. Come," Snakeskin said while lowering himself via the wooden side rails.

Shanna hesitated. Her eyes followed Alex from the stage to the storefront, followed him through the doorway, followed him until the log door shut and he disappeared inside. She wanted to go with the braves. But what would Alex do if she ran again? Find her? Tell the outlaws her whereabouts? Report her to authorities? Go with evil intentions to Kathryn—oh God—to Aaron?

"Come," Snakeskin repeated.

In a flash, and a sudden burst of courage, Shanna scrambled to the edge of the stage roof. "Must hide quickly," she said. "Man in store will hunt for me."

Snakeskin extended his hand to Shanna. Unaccustomed to such kindness, she hesitated for a moment before accepting his helping her to the musty ground.

※ ※ ※

For nearly two weeks now, Kathryn had lived in total awe. She had lost every feeling she had ever known of loneliness, of being childless, of yearning for a baby. She had forgotten how to want, to need, to seek. Aaron coming into her life was pure bliss.

On this mild fall day, the front porch swing swayed gently. Kathryn cuddled Aaron to her breasts. She smiled down on the sweet innocence. This child was the love she had for so long desired, a love that she could never have imagined. Holding him closer, she pushed the thin blanket from his infant head and gently kissed his dark scalp. She whispered devoutly, "I love you baby boy."

Seventeen

TWO BRAVES WHO had been riding atop the stage rode off on ponies that had been tied at the storefront, but Snakeskin and Shanna darted into the forest. Running was something she had come to know too well, it seemed. Why, now that she had crossed the Red River, must she run and hide? Of course, she knew the answer to that.

Here now, alongside Snakeskin, she was surely running as fast as a deer being chased by wolves, whizzing through the forest by clusters of trees, twigs, and bushes. Without even seeing it, Shanna found herself leaping over a shallow creek and then dashing on through the thicket. They were miles from nowhere, it seemed, when they stopped.

"You know this place?" Shanna asked.

"Here, we pick up ponies," Snakeskin said, pointing to a house that looked as if it were made of grass.

"How far to Moon Hunter?"

"Don't know. Maybe half-sun. Maybe he be gone."

"Gone. No!"

"Not to worry. If he gone, we go another trail," Snakeskin said.

"But we will find him?" Shanna questioned, worry in her voice.

The brave nodded. "Moon Hunter back and forth, tribe to tribe. We find him. Don't worry." Snakeskin smiled and patted her hand. "Let's get ponies now."

※ ※ ※

Alex shook his head in wonderment. He should have expected Squaw Girl to take off first chance she got now that she had reached the Territory. She was a runner. But he'd find her. No doubt about that. He would get what he wanted with or without the squaw. However, with her at his side, the Indians would find him more sincere and be more easily convinced of his offers.

"You see which way my squaw went?" Alex asked Doc as he re-positioned himself on the stage seat.

"Didn't see a thing."

"You were here all the time. Sure you didn't see or is it you just aren't talking."

Doc grinned. "Maybe she knows you don't like her kind. That perhaps you treated the natives mean in the past."

"She'll know just how bad I can treat her when I find her again," he paused and twisted the ends of his mustache to present a more groomed look. "Don't know if I told you this Doc; Squaw Girl is running from the law. She stabbed her foster daddy in the heart with a butcher knife."

Doc jerked quickly and stared at Alex, and then in a moment said, "That young girl? I wouldn't have thought it."

As the stage rolled on over the hilly territorial terrain, Alex mentally calculated the moves he would make now that he didn't have Squaw Girl to use to bait the Indians—to use as a trading tool. He needed Moon Hunter's furs and hides. He had promised them to the dealer in Dallas.

※ ※ ※

After being with Snakeskin atop the stage and now alone in this isolated section of Territory, Shanna found herself coming to respect this friendly brave. Not only for helping her, but also for the way he moved rapidly with both words and actions.

"You not to worry," Snakeskin said, his low voice breaking her thoughts. "I trade for ponies."

Later that evening, Snakeskin pulled the reins so the gray pony he had traded for stopped. Shanna stopped her gray also.

"Tomorrow we travel to camp where Moon Hunter comes. Now we rest."

Shanna couldn't prevent a joy blooming inside her. "Tomorrow?"

Snakeskin nodded.

"Why not travel on tonight?" Shanna asked, suddenly confused.

Snakeskin reached for her pony's reins. "I got other plans," he said, his face straight and unsmiling.

Shanna held her breath. What was brewing in Snakeskin's mind? Had she made a bad move in giving him her trust? She looked him straight in the eye but said nothing.

"I build fire here so you stay warm."

"You stay here with me? We leave before sunup."

"Okay."

Shanna watched Snakeskin's every move as they gathered wood and then as he rubbed sticks to get the fire started. Her eyes heavy, she realized how incredibly tired she was. She laid her head on a cool pile of dried leaves. This day was over, she reckoned, calculating actions that had transpired.

Early in the morning Shanna, awake and ready to tackle the universe, arose to find the warm coals turning to cinders. Glancing around, she wondered where Snakeskin had gone. Had he stayed the night at the campfire? Had he traveled on without her?

Unexpectedly, she heard movements in the dark forest and turning quickly, she saw Snakeskin scampering toward her, a skinned rabbit in one hand and a pole in the other. "Got grub," he said loudly. "We eat and then travel."

Shanna nodded, and instantly began tossing sticks onto the dying fire. Until this very moment, she hadn't realized how hungry she was.

"Rabbit dressed?" she asked.

"Yes dressed. Ready to cook." Snakeskin said. Coming to a stop at the fire, he poked the pole through the rabbit cavity. "Ready to roast."

Shanna gathered more sticks and tossed them onto the fire, all the while her face holding a grin.

While they ate, Shanna watched Snakeskin suck charred rabbit dripping from his fingers. "Meat tastes good," he said. Afterwards, as dawn hinted that the hills would soon be lighted, Snakeskin said, "I take you to Moon Hunter now."

Could this be? Shanna wondered at the sight. She and Snakeskin had just stopped at a forest edge bordered by an open field. Anticipating this place, Shanna had envisioned her people gathering to discuss peace treaties or talking of a big hunt. But what she found were braves barely dressed in hides covering their fronts and wearing long tails in back. She frowned. Her people looked a lot like a herd of cows. Yet these were the Indian Territorial Lands of which she had for so long searched. Were their actions for real? Besides their funny appearance, weren't these silly-looking braves chilled? After all, they were nearly nude.

Bewilderment must have shown on her face. She just stood there saying nothing.

"This is good game," Snakeskin finally said, nodding toward the actions occurring in the field ahead. "This my favorite sport. Moon Hunter's favorite, indeed. He out there."

Still, Shanna didn't speak. She watched as an Indian in a long headdress went to the center of a ring.

"That medicine man," Snakeskin said, indicating the man on show.

The medicine man tossed a small ball into the air. And then braves tried to hit the ball with long sticks that appeared to have deer hide handles.

Shanna scrutinized some couple dozen braves. They moved so fast that she couldn't really see their faces. One of these players was Moon Hunter? Which one? How could he perform in this childish game? She needed to talk with him now. To talk about important things, like what had happened during the past eight years. The turmoil she had suffered. Where had he gone when their father sent him away? The awful life she had lived from the day of her kidnapping until this very moment. And most of all, her being compelled to give away her newborn son.

Shanna's attention turned to the women—who appeared just as unconcerned as the men—standing outside the field cheering the funny sport on. Every once in a while one would hurry to the game ring and pat a brave on the back as if he had committed so daring an act.

Keeping her eyes on the happenings in the circle, Shanna observed the ball was never touched by anybody's hand, but always by hitting or catching with the sticks.

"Why they do this?" she asked Snakeskin, who was quietly watching the action.

"This fun. It game. I like this. Moon Hunter like this, too." Snakeskin paused, and Shanna felt his stare cutting deep into the skin on her face. "Tribal people have hard time in the past. Time to relax. Enjoy." He pointed at the players. "They all full-grown."

"This is the way of my people?"

"This is the way."

"We go now and talk to Moon Hunter?"

"Not you. I go first. He maybe can't talk to you." Snakeskin turned briefly to Shanna, and then patted her hand—a comforting she found most delightful.

She watched Snakeskin saunter from her and stop at the circle edge. He waited until the game paused, then he motioned to one in the field. A good-looking brave ran forward and upon their meeting, the two embraced. Shanna held her breath. This was surely Moon Hunter, her brother. She waited patiently until Snakeskin turned and started back to her. Moon Hunter was at his side.

※ ※ ※

Alex frowned. Yesterday evening and this morning had been annoying, with Doc poking fun at his losing Squaw Girl. "Don't be surprised if someday somebody don't go knocking that opossum sneer off your face," he said, glaring from underneath his hat brim at the stage passenger sitting across from him.

"You speaking at me?" Doc asked, turning briefly to address Alex.

"You know I am."

"Why is that girl so important to you?" Doc asked, removing his gray hat and placing it on his pin-stripped suit pants. "She's just an Indian kid. Don't see how she can help you out anyway."

"Told you before. I plan on trading her off."

"Can't be done," Doc said. "Tribes up here may not be as street-smart when it comes to spotting crooks as they ought to be, but I think if you go trying to trade them one of their own kind, you might not like their decision." Doc leaned his head on the backboard and closed his eyes.

Perhaps Doc was right. Perhaps if he had shown up with Shanna and offered her to them for their furs and hides, they would have done him harm. He'd get the stuff one way or another, though. Just a matter of time. Still, he would have to punish Shanna for betraying him.

And he knew just where to find her and the loot he wanted.

Alex watched Doc snooze. How could this man of medicine sleep in an upright position? He couldn't sleep right now even if he were in comfort; Squaw Girl's cleverness in leaving him was burning a hole in his mind. But he would get even.

Doc was still sleeping when the stage driver reined the team close to a fence railing at another trading post. "We're stopping here," he said, halting the horses. He crawled from his bench. "Better stretch a leg while ye can."

This was Alex's chance to get the load of guns. He got off the stage and followed the driver to a pit where he commenced building a fire.

"You aim on taking them guns to some Indian renegades. Right?" Alex asked conversationally.

"So what if I am? They paid fer 'em."

"I know where you're taking them. These guns are for Moon Hunter and Snakeskin. Right?"

"How ye know 'bout that?"

"I'm not dumb. I heard you talking to Snakeskin back at the Pell Junction."

"Like I said—'so what?'"

"Thing is, Indians are all up in arms right now. They'd just as soon kill the sight of you as to look at you."

"Why ye saying this stuff? Ain't nothing I can do to change it."

"No, but you can get somebody else to deliver the guns."

"Who'd do that if what yer saying is so?"

"I'll do it."

"Why would you do it if there's problems with the Injuns?"

"'Cause they know me. We've done trading before. They trust me."

"Yep, but can I trust ye?"

"'Course you can. You saw me coming from Jackson's Furrier back in Dallas. You know what a respectable businessman he is. Now would he be doing business with me if I weren't trustworthy? He sent me up here with all this money," Alex paused and pulled the wad of bills from his vest pocket. "All this is Jackson's money and I'm buying furs and hides with it."

The stage driver scratched his head. "He must trust ye pretty good."

"Yeah he does." Alex put the wad back into his vest pocket. "Now tell you what. I'll take the guns off your hands and when I go for the furs, I'll deliver them for you."

"That might not be a bad idee."

"Tell you what. Come daylight, I'll pick up a horse and wagon, load the guns on it, then you can be on your way to wherever it is your headed."

"Back to Dallas. I'll be heading back to Dallas."

He will be going back to Dallas and I'll be tromping on Shanna's heels, Alex thought. And he realized that his grin, not Doc's, was surely the first cousin to that of an opossum's.

❋ ❋ ❋

Shanna listened as Moon Hunter told her stories about the life they

Bridged By Love

had led with their parents. Their paternal grandfather, with a strong count of Scottish blood flowing through his veins, had been a traveling Baptist preacher and had met their Chickasaw grandmother in Choctaw-Chickasaw lands in the Territory. Their son had taken a Choctaw maiden for his bride. So Shanna and Moon Hunter's father was mostly Chickasaw and their mother was Choctaw.

"Where's our parents now," Shanna asked.

"Never saw them after the day they told me to go home. They send me back to the Territory. I've looked. Never found." He turned so his eyes met Shanna's. "I looked for my sister, too. Never found."

"You think our mother and father are dead?"

"Don't know what to think. Just look and hope to find. Come," he said. "Tonight, you sleep in my hut. Tomorrow we build your house."

"My house?"

"Yes. We build you a hut of logs, mud, grass, much like you sleep in tonight. You be comfortable."

At dawn the following morning, Moon Hunter, Snakeskin and Shanna went to the forest where they cut logs and dragged them the short distance to the settlement. To Shanna's surprise, within the hour, a congregation of young people had joined them, bringing axes and hunting knives, and working as if they were building the hut for themselves.

"This how we do it," Moon Hunter assured her. "They help us. We help them. Everybody profits."

In no time, it seemed, the structure's rectangular-shaped log wall, joined at the corners and with mud pushed into the cracks, stood near the wood edge. Then, before Shanna realized, the hut was nearly built; a slanted roof made of roughly cleaved flat slabs of wood was pegged over the walls, a door opening toward the settlement was hinged with wooden pegs, and the back window was covered with shutters.

"For now, earth floor is good," Moon Hunter said to Shanna on their third day of labor. "We build floor a later day."

Shanna smiled. This hut was a facility of wonderment. She had been in the Territory only four days and already she had a brother, home and friends. And though her heart ached for Aaron, she knew he was in good hands with Kathryn.

But where was Rowe? It had been many new moons since they were together. He would have returned to her if he could. Now, if he should look for her at Minor's Fish Camp, she would be gone. She could only hope they would be together in their next life. *I'm sorry, Rowe*, she said inwardly.

※ ※ ※

I think I've lost them, Rowe told himself as he reined the horse to a stop in a valley of trees. Finally catching his breath, he felt stinging pains gnawing at the muscle topping his right collarbone. He felt to check the damage. The wound hurt like hell but he realized the bullet had not seared the bone. There was no bullet in the flesh, either. In time, the tear would heal without much attention.

But where was he? He needed to move on. He couldn't just hang around and wait for the outlaws to show him the way out.

East. How does a cowboy know which way is east? He rubbed his chin and gazed at the starry night sky. Grinning, he held up his hand. He pointed at the moon, and then with his finger, trailed its path.

"That way," he said with a laugh. "Yooo-ooo."

※ ※ ※

"You should have known I'd find you," Alex said, appearing out of nowhere like a rat that came calling while she slept.

Shanna stiffened. She couldn't move. Her body had frozen to her cot, like in a nightmare. Like when men came to her in the storeroom at Minor's place. This was a nightmare, wasn't it?

"Aren't you going to greet me, Squaw Girl?"

This was worse than a nightmare. That was actually Alex standing over her cot. She sat up hastily. "What you want?" she asked in fear and anger.

"Why'd you run off from me, Squaw Girl?"

"You got no hold on me now. This is Land of Red People. This is Indian Territory."

"That doesn't mean the law will turn its back on a murdering squaw. That river back there might separate the states from the Territory, but the government still has say as to what goes on here."

"I don't think government will come looking," Shanna said, assumingly.

"The government may not give a damn about you, Squaw Girl, but let me tell you right here and now, the outlaws in black are anxious to get their hands on you. They're ready to string you up real fast like."

"Then so be it," Shanna said, not thinking how Alex might take the thought. Her real concern all along had been for Aaron. Now that he was safe, she wasn't too worried about getting strung up; it surely would be better than ever returning to the life she had known in the bayou bottoms. She gazed at Alex's face as he moved about in the beam of moonlight that shined through the window.

"You don't mind getting hanged?" he asked sarcastically.

"I didn't say that."

"You said, 'so be it.' That's the same as saying you don't care."

"Please leave. I never hurt you."

"I'm not going away yet, Squaw Girl. I'm staying right here with you. You keep me hidden in this fine hut of yours. When the time's right, I'll be on my way."

"Why you come here?"

"You'll see soon enough," he hesitated, and she could see him twisting the ends of his mustache. "I'm going to camp right over there in that corner. If anybody comes in, we'll say you're my squaw."

Shanna said nothing but her eyes followed Alex to a darkened corner in the hut. Didn't he realize what she was capable of? Hadn't she set an example with what she had done to Jake Minor? Didn't Alex realize she could just as easily put a knife through his heart? Didn't he know she could hack him up just as quickly as she could slaughter a pig?

"Don't even think about it, Squaw Girl," Alex said as if reading her mind.

※ ※ ※

Alex knew that Shanna would ram a knife into his heart just as quickly as she had rammed the knife into Jake Minor's, and she'd be glad when it was over. But would she try to kill him right now? He didn't think so. Not in haste. She was a squaw who crafted her moves to cover every tiny crack in the big picture. No doubt she had planned the fate of Jake Minor, probably for months, before jabbing him like a piece of raw meat on the butcher block.

Alex stayed awake the rest of the night. Before dawn, he got up from his chosen corner and quietly left the hut.

He needed to find the hides the Indians kept in this village. That was his whole purpose for being here. He didn't have time to waste. This group of mixed-bloods had more hides and furs than any buffalo hunter he had ever dealt with and he aimed to make them his. It wasn't like he planned to steal the merchandize. He had already paid for everything when he purchased the information—fair and square. Now, all he had to do was locate the cooler, "a hut cut in the hillside," his source in Dallas had explained. And camouflaged with trees, shrubs and vines.

Alex walked along darkened paths around the settlement for more than an hour making a mental note of shelters to check out later.

He returned to Shanna's hut before dawn and entered through the window, as he had on his initial call. He lingered for a moment over Shanna's cot. Her wide-open eyes stared at the ceiling, but she said nothing. He grinned, returned to the corner, and bedded down. Morning would come soon and he had much to do.

※ ※ ※

Just before daylight, Alex picked up his grooming pack and left the hut. He hurried to the nearby stream where he bathed and shaved his face. He even took special care in trimming his mustache. Feeling inside his suit coat pocket, he fingered the roll of bills. Then he started out to meet all the day might entail.

He hurried to a cave a few hundred yards from the stream where he'd hidden a team of horses and a wagon that he'd bought to carry the guns.

He wasn't too concerned if it was discovered, though things would be easier if it wasn't, but he figured Shanna could help him explain it away in any case. From the wagon bed he took a long barreled revolver and stuffed it under his suit jacket. Then he returned to Shanna's hut.

"What's cooking, Squaw Girl?"

"Not your slave here. This is Indian land," she said, rotating a hunk of buffalo.

Alex grinned. Squaw Girl had developed herself a smart-assed mouth. "When will the meat be ready?"

"Grub is for Moon Hunter. He comes here soon."

"Oh, is that a fact?"

"Moon Hunter knows you here."

"Oh. You told him?"

"He saw you sneaking out of here before sunrise."

"Tell him you're my squaw?"

"Did not."

"Who does he think I am?"

"White man who helped me get here."

Alex laughed again. "You told him right. You're clever, Squaw Girl. Why does he think I'm here now?"

"To buy hides."

"Did he say where the hides are kept?"

"Didn't ask."

That was just as well. Alex would gain Moon Hunter's trust. Moon Hunter would take him to the cellar, either voluntarily or at gunpoint. Didn't matter much to him.

Eighteen

*T*HAT EVENING WHEN Moon Hunter came to Shanna's hut, Alex pulled a wad of bills from his vest pocket. "I've got all this money to purchase hides," he said.

"Rather have guns than dollars," Moon Hunter quickly advised.

"Then you'll get guns."

He surely took the guns from the stage, Shanna thought, glancing fleetingly at Alex. That had been an easy call.

※ ※ ※

Rowe reined the horse to a stop and pulled the canteen from the saddle pouch. He drank short, then replaced the canteen. He rubbed his shoulder. Already it was starting to heal. How many days had he been riding now? Three? Four? He had lost count.

He gazed at a path beaten through remnants of summer vegetation. Greenery here had turned to weeds and brown grasses. It was only a short distance between him and the swamplands of Caddo Parish. He was now in the vicinity where he had lost Shanna to the outlaws—where he had been captured.

Rowe could find his way to Minor's Butcher Shop easily now. But what would he do when he got there? He certainly must stay out of sight. He would find Shanna and take her away once and for all. Even if that meant doing away with Jake Minor.

※ ※ ※

The following day Alex left Shanna's hut early and went to the wagon. He checked to make sure the guns were still there. He smiled and recalled how cleverly he had obtained them. How he had swindled the stage driver; that man was one dumb coot. Now the object was to do as well in his dealings with the Indians.

He tightened the horses' harnesses and climbed up onto the wagon seat. He shook out the reins and the horses obligingly stepped off, out of the cave and into the sunlight. He had everything under control. He laughed and shook the reins again.

Alex followed the directions Moon Hunter had given him. At the settlement, he guided his horses to the structure built into the side of a hill; it was a type of cellar. He looked at his gold pocket watch. He was on time. Moon Hunter and Snakeskin met him at the door.

"You bring guns?" Moon Hunter demanded.

"Got them right here," Alex said, turning and motioning at three crates.

Alex quickly moved from the driver's seat to the wagon bed and started pushing the crates to the back so Moon Hunter and Snakeskin could unload them without hesitation.

"Now for the furs," Alex said.

"Here. This way."

Alex followed the two braves into the cool shelter lit by oil-burning lamps that lined the long walls. Furs, fabulous furs, hung from log ceiling rafters.

"Your furs here as promised," Moon Hunter said, motioning to a mound of hides.

"What about these?" Alex questioned, looking upward at a unique white bear and red fox furs.

"Uh-uh. Already promised."

"I see," Alex said, nodding. "Then let's load these on."

Later that night, after Moon Hunter and Snakeskin had closed the furrier, Alex returned with the wagon. He looked around to see he wasn't being watched; then he got off the wagon and hurried to the cooler, raised the latch, and pushed the door open. He stood at the entry for a moment to allow his eyes to adjust to the darkness, and then entered. For just this white bear and the red fox furs, Jackson would pay oodles of dollars. And there they hung just as pretty as they had today. The only difference, now they were his.

Alex pondered over his take for a moment longer. He grinned as he hurried to the furs and gathered them into his arms like a beloved child.

Now he would have to get the hell out of the Territory as quickly as he could. He needed to be well into Texas before Moon Hunter and Snakeskin found their prize furs missing and before they realized they had traded a mound of hides and furs to him for guns they had already purchased from somebody else.

Stupid redskins.

The grin frozen on his face actually ached his skin. But there was no way to be anything but happy now that he had everything he had come to the Territory for. He had simply happened upon the guns, which made obtaining the furs much easier than he had anticipated.

Hee-hee! How could he do anything other than grin now?

※ ※ ※

Rowe's horse slowed to barely moving one foot before the other. "Whoa," He called softly, and patted the mount on its neck. "Whoa there."

That's Minor's Fish Camp. Got lot of business for this time of night.

Rowe glanced up at the moon. The wee morning hours had come. Why were so many people at Minor's place at this time of night? If he could get closer, perhaps he could see what was going on. Slowly, Rowe dismounted and crept to the storefront. This wasn't wise, he realized, and then ducked to the side of the building. He must go around back and find Shanna. Keeping out of the moonlight, he tiptoed close to the log structure to the back room where Minor kept Shanna and peeked through the tiny barred window. "Shanna," he whispered. He waited a couple seconds, and then in a louder voice called, "Shanna." Still nothing.

Why wasn't she answering? Why couldn't he see her? She wouldn't be butchering a kill at this time of morning, would she? The storefront. He must see inside the storefront. Quietly, he made his way back around the mossy edifice. He stepped onto the front porch and crept to the window, then looked around to be sure nobody was with him. Moving closer to the glass pane, he peered inside. Several men were sprawled out on blankets on the floor. Two were seated near the stove. It looked as though they had set up camp. Rowe stood there looking in, waiting for somebody to say something. Finally, one said, "They ought to be getting back here with that boy by now."

"Ye think so?"

"What ye 'spects keeping 'em?"

"Ain't got the faintest."

"Think he was still there?"

"Fur as I know. The jailer had him last I heared."

"I'd hate to miss the hanging but I got business in the city. Can't wait here much longer." "If ye need to go, then go."

"I'll give 'em 'til tomorrow."

They're talking about me, Rowe realized. *They're waiting for their friends to come back with me. They aim to hang me.* Rowe stood there, frozen like a block of ice. Where was Shanna? Where was Jake Minor? One of the men stood up. He had been blocking Rowe's view of another man near the stove. The fat man's face was turned from the window and a cap covered his head, making it impossible for Rowe to identify him. Rowe waited to see what would happen next. Then the fat man spoke. "Don't kill 'em yet. We need 'em to get the squaw back. Then we'll kill 'em both." He pointed to a cot at a back corner where a man lay propped on pillows. "We owe it to Jake."

Rowe couldn't see the bedded man's face. And where was Jake Minor?

Shanna has escaped. Shanna isn't here. She got away and that's why they sent for me. Shanna got away and they think I know where she is.

Rowe couldn't prevent his smile escalating to a silent laugh. She had outsmarted Jake Minor. She had outsmarted that old bastard, hopefully once and for all. *She outsmarted you, Jake Minor. Shanna outsmarted you, you bastard!*

But where was she now? Would he ever again see her? Did she need his help? Did anybody know which way she went? She had once talked about finding her family. She had believed her parents had gone to the Indian Territory. Could she find them? The Territory covered endless miles of varied terrain and numerous tribes. Where would one start to look? Rowe turned to leave. It was certain that Shanna wasn't at the fish camp. He didn't know where she was, but she wasn't here. Then—what was it nearing the storefront? Riders— the Raider Outlaws from whom he had escaped had caught up with him. The two riders came closer. Rowe ducked quickly into a stand of undergrowth alongside the porch.

"What was that?" somebody called from inside. "What's going on here?"

Then the riders' horses stopped at the porch edge. The men inside the storefront hastened across the room to the front door.

※ ※ ※

Alex kicked dirt clunks from his boots and then walked into Jackson's Furriers in Dallas. "I was hoping you'd be here tonight. Got you the load," he said of the hides and furs he had taken from the Indians.

"Took ye long enough. Been wondering if ye'd bring them or not," Jackson said, his eyes staying on a pad with a checklist.

"Have I ever let you down?"

Jackson glared at Alex for a moment. "You're pretty decent at delivering," he agreed. "But I was starting to get concerned. I got obligations, ye know. Folks overseas waiting for stuff. If they don't get it from me, they be looking elsewhere."

"A month's not that long when it comes to going to the Territory and then having to look over your shoulder all the way back."

"The stuff hot?"

"'Course not. I got them fair and square."

"Well, bring 'em on in."

Alex went outside and got back onto the horse-drawn wagon, then guided it around back where Jackson had opened the carriage house door.

"Cast your eyes on this," he said, getting down and uncovering his haul.

※ ※ ※

Rowe held his breath as the outlaws dismounted and stepped onto the porch. Three brigands rushed out to greet them. They all talked at once; still he heard the most important parts of the conversation.

"Where's the Mexican?"

"Y'all ain't gonna like this a bit," Morton commenced. "Had to shoot the boy. He tried to run off."

"What you mean, 'had to shoot the boy?'"

"He had a gun tucked in his britches. When we bedded down, he pulled it out and started shooting," Morton said, defensibly.

Bridged By Love

"The two of ye couldn't fetch one Mexican?"

"I told ye, he pulled a gun."

"Ye thank ye killed 'em? Where 'bouts?"

"Texas."

"Texas! That's telling me a whole lot. Where 'bouts in Texas?"

"'Bout a hundred miles south of Dallas."

"Hell, ye shooted 'em soon as ye picked 'em up."

"I told ye. He had a gun. The jailer musta give it to him. We had to kill the jailer."

What a bunch of bullshit, Rowe thought. The clatter of talk meshing through the bushes got louder, making it difficult to understand anything they said. Finally, the group went inside.

Again, Rowe crept onto the porch and looked through the windowpane. Two men, who had previously been lying on pallets, had gotten up and joined the conversation.

"I figure the Mexican's dead. Else he'd be hunting the squaw. Now, if'in ye was that boy, where's ye be hunting?"

"Don't know," one said.

"Seems he'd be coming right 'chere first thang."

"I figure yer right, Judd. He be coming here. I figure he'd be here by now if he was alive."

Let's figure your right, Rowe said to himself. Yes, he was looking for Shanna and he was here now. But Shanna wasn't here and this bunch of outlaws didn't have any idea where to look for her. But he did.

More than likely, Shanna had gone to find her people. Where would she start her journey? He had tried to help Shanna escape previously. They had gone into the swamp. Shanna knew the swamp, but Jake Minor had caught up with her during past escape attempts. How had she gotten away this time? How long had she been gone?

Rowe studied the faces through the pane. Did they all know what he looked like? Two of them did, those being the two who had come to Texas after him. But what about the others? They all knew he was Mexican.

A gun. He needed a gun. He'd wait until the men were sleeping, or gone, and go for one of Jake Minor's many guns.

"So what we s'posed to do now?" It was Morton's voice breaking the rhythm of chatter.

"Go to Shreveport. And Texarkana. Nail up them wanted posters. Ask questions. See if anybody seen the squaw."

Wanted posters! They have out wanted posters for Shanna? Rowe could hardly believe what he was hearing. These men certainly wanted Shanna back. Jake Minor would have never let her go. But to circulate wanted posters seemed a little much? Minor was the criminal, not Shanna!

Rowe had heard enough. He would stay in the bushes all night and day, if necessary; he would stay hidden until the men were either asleep or gone, then he would get a gun and set out to look for Shanna. The men were passing moonshine now. They should be out cold before much longer. Rowe returned to his hideout in the bushes. All he could do now was wait.

Nineteen

OCTOBER DAYS IN the backwoods were much colder than folks in the tri-state lands had predicted. Outside the house, the late afternoon sun gave a false reading to the cold day. Inside, things couldn't get much worse.

Kathryn fought to hold her tears. She had protected Aaron since his birth; still a hot fever had come to plague the child barely six weeks old.

She sat in the living room rocking chair with Aaron on her lap. She had wrapped the baby head-to-toe in a thick blanket in hopes of bringing sweat to his tiny body.

"I'll be back soon as I can," Mama said, passing through the living room and then making her way through the kitchen.

"Get the doctor soon," Kathryn said, crying.

Aaron was silent. His eyeballs moved, rolling upward in his head, as if trying to see the roots of his black hair.

"Oh God, let him live. Please don't let this baby die," she prayed aloud, her words muffled with a head of tears.

Placing her fingers inside the blanket, Kathryn touched Aaron's tiny chest. Still hot. So hot. The potato compress she had put on him earlier was still in place but much warmer and drier. Time for a new compress, she figured.

She got up from the rocking chair, Aaron still clutched in her arms and, making her way to the kitchen, stopped at a noise on the back porch steps. And then came a strong knock. She knew Leonard had come calling.

Leonard didn't wait to be invited; he just pushed his way in.

"I come as soon as I heard," he said, removing his cap and hurrying to Kathryn.

Kathryn wanted to talk, but words choked in her throat.

"I saw Mama heading for town. Told her I'd go for the doctor, but she said, 'Get to Kathryn. She needs you.' I was on my way here from work anyway." He turned to the counter where red potatoes lay on a clean towel. "Making a compress for the little fellow?"

Still sobbing, Kathryn nodded. A rush of tears spilled down her cheeks and flooded over her nose.

Leonard read her unsaid words and, picking up a carving knife, quickly sliced the potatoes into halves.

"I'm afraid if I cut them smaller they'll dry up before they can draw out the poisons."

Kathryn nodded, and watched while Leonard drenched the white cotton cloth in vinegar and then positioned the potato pieces on it.

"Want to get the old compress off the little fellow?" Leonard's voice was not much more than a whisper.

Kathryn held Aaron in a lying position on one arm and pulled the blanket from his chest, allowing Leonard to replace the used cloth of potato compress.

"Don't want to fan the covers," Leonard said. "Want the fever to break."

Kathryn carefully rewrapped Aaron with the warm blanket.

"All we can do now is wait and hope the little fellow breaks out in a sweat," Leonard said, lightly touching Aaron's head.

"He's got to be okay, Leonard. Aaron has to live."

"I know, Kitten," he said, his hand rubbing lightly across her shoulders.

※ ※ ※

For John Allen, days were endless blurs with what appeared as mannequins wandering about the streets of Texarkana in the place of people. True, he had not pursued a meaningful relationship with Kathryn. He had not considered her a marriage prospect. For the last three years, he had wanted to find the beautiful Lilly. He had wanted to find that she had not run out on him, that she had not been the person who had stolen his wallet during that poignant train ride. He had hoped that an earth shattering something had come up that had caused Lilly to get off the train in St. Louis. He had hoped she would show up in Texarkana looking for him. But he had not rediscovered Lilly and chances were that he never would.

Time to face facts, John Allen, he told himself. *You'll never have Lilly.*

Time to take a wife was beginning to run out for him, he decided. He had kept his eyes open since his arrival in Texarkana but had not found a woman to marry. The beauties, like Lilly, were married by the time they were thirteen. Even the ugly ones were married before sixteen. Except for the whores. Well, there were Kathryn and Sharleen. Kathryn was divorced, which many considered a disgrace, though that didn't bother him. He just couldn't see her as giving up wearing the pants in the family. Now, Sharleen would be willing to give up head of the household status, but was quite a bit older, a widow with two half-grown daughters. Neither of these two were virgins, though he didn't think it likely he'd find a virgin to marry—as Lilly had claimed to be.

Between the two available women in town, Kathryn was the one to corner, he decided.

Now was the time to make his move. But he was a little concerned. Kathryn had not been to town in more than a month. She had that

Indian kid out at her place, taking care of him as if he were her own, and obviously thinking of nothing or anybody else. She had been bloody funny over him since they had met...was she now losing interest? Was the child taking all her energies? *Can't have that*, he said to himself. Got to propose to her now.

John went to the carriage quarters attached to S. Wagner's Rooming House. He hurriedly hitched his horse, Blaze, to his buggy. Leaving the premises, he passed the construction site of the house shaped like a four-leaf clover. Imagine winning enough money in a poker game—an ace-high Straight-Club-Flush—to build a mansion, John marveled as he passed the edifice commotion.

Turning south at the next corner, he reined Blaze down State Line Avenue; thus, remaining on the Texas side of the city while traveling to congested Broad Street. At Broad, he waited near the tracks for a street-trolley to pass before making a left and entering Arkansas.

While he reined Blaze among the heavy traffic, he rehearsed how he would propose to Kathryn. *Kathryn*, he would say, *I want you to be my wife.* No. Such common words would be out of character for him. He needed to think of something original. *Beautiful Kathryn. I have loved you from the moment I laid eyes on you and I have longed to touch your face.* He would lift his fingers to amiably touch her. Then he would say, *I so long to kiss your lovely lips but I don't dare without first asking you this question: My dear beautiful lady, will you give me the honor of being my wife?*

A grin spread over his face. He could see her now. She would fall into his arms and smother him with kisses. She would cry out: yes, yes. Kathryn would forever be the woman he could depend on no matter what. She would love him as she had never loved before. They'd be married by this time tomorrow.

John's buggy rolled on past storefront after storefront in the busy town. Soon, he guided Blaze to the right and across a row of railroad tracks.

There—the mare in front of Doctor Adams's place—didn't it belong to Kathryn? He pulled the reins, bringing Blaze to a stop, his gaze on the lumber-framed house. People were standing at the front door. Then Doctor Adams turned and entered the house. The woman moved about impatiently. Who was she? She turned for just a brief moment so John caught an image of her face. Golly be, it was Mama Williams. What was she doing at Doctor Adams's place? Moments later, Doctor Adams returned to the porch, this time carrying his medical bag. Then the doctor turned and started to his carriage house and Mama Williams hurried toward Kathryn's mare.

"Mama Williams," he called as the older woman mounted Sugar. "Why'd you come for the doctor? Is something wrong?"

She turned, apparently seeing John for the first time since he had stopped near the doctor's gate.

"Oh yes," Mama cried. "The baby's bad off. Could be dying."

Stunned, John could only stare at the woman addressing him, her face flushed. "I must hurry back, Mister Allen," she said, fluffing her long skirt and then shaking the mare's reins. She called back, "I'm worried about Kathryn as well. She hasn't slept or eaten enough to keep a fly alive in days."

John watched Mama ride off. So, Kathryn had not eaten or slept in days. She must be a wreck. He would wait a spell before seeking her hand. This certainly would not be a good day for wooing.

※ ※ ※

Leonard sat on a straight chair—his head bowed as in prayer and resting on his hands—while Kathryn rocked and whispered lullabies, all the time her eyes not leaving Aaron's flushed face.

"Please God," she cried, the words flowing like tears. "Please let Aaron live."

Leonard raised his head slightly, but said nothing. Kathryn felt the infant jerk in her arms. She looked at him, her mind and body holding a fear like she had never known. Aaron jerked again, this time so hard the blanket started to drop from his hot body. His body jerked again, and then again. Clutching Aaron, she quickly stood; thus upsetting the blanket and compress so much that potato slices flapped onto the pine plank floor.

"Leonard!" She looked down on the tiny face but saw nothing but white eyes.

"Please God, let Aaron live. If I must give him up, let it be to Shanna. Please, not through death."

Suddenly Aaron's body stiffened and Kathryn's own sobs hung in her ears. Leonard grabbed the taut child from her arms.

※ ※ ※

Shanna rubbed her stomach, now as flat as that of a teenage girl who had never given birth. She hovered near the fire she kept going inside the hut. It had been more than a month since she had come here and she was becoming accustomed to the ways of her people. Sometimes it seemed as if she had never been separated from this life. But on some days, like today, she ached for the Little Soul who had seeded inside her so many moons ago. Today, more than days before, she felt Aaron needed her. Something was wrong with the infant she had birthed.

Baby is sick. Dying. The words jammed through her eardrum as clearly as if someone had said them. Fear overwhelmed her being. The medicine man came to mind. She could go to him? Could he help her? But how could he help Aaron, the child being many moons from the Territory? The medicine man couldn't touch him from here.

She recalled Moon Hunter's telling of her father. He had been the son of a traveling Baptist preacher. But, like Moon Hunter, her father had put much faith in tribal medicines.

Shanna tightened her yellow shawl around her shoulders and left the hut. Sunset rode the shoulders of the hills to the west. In quick long paces, she hurried toward a log house some five minutes away and built partly into the hillside. Here, she had noticed, was the medicine man's home.

Though she had been very young when taken from her family, she held an image of a true medicine man in her mind. She couldn't remember where or when the incident had occurred, but her vision held an ornamented man moving about before a fire and touching her, thus forcing away images of huge beetles and spiders crawling above her. The next thing she had seen was the face of her mother looking into hers.

With memories of so long ago coming to her, the walk up the grassy trail was brief. Without her calling, an old man walked from the log house to greet her.

"Baby in another land is dying," she uttered without hesitation. "I know you can help. How can we save this child's life?"

"Come, child." He turned to reenter his house. Shanna followed.

Not long after, Shanna re-emerged and climbed higher up the hillside, evening's chill fast approaching. She found a cousin to the May Apple tree growing out of season in the shade of many trees, just as the medicine man had predicted she would. With her bare hands, she dug down alongside the special tree until she felt roots; and then, without damaging the foliage, she gathered tiny sprouts. Once gathered, she washed the roots in a spring bubbling among the thick vegetation and, in haste, returned home. Back in her hut, Shanna placed the roots in a pan of water and boiled them, bringing the strengths that had been a part of the delegate shrub to settle in the liquid.

"Powers, move from the root to the water. Be so that I can drink. So that I can feel the life and strength move from my body to my child," she chanted, repeating the lines over and over.

Almost exhausted from anguish, Shanna removed the liquid from the fire and poured it into a tin cup. Then carrying it with her, she went out into the evening. Holding the tin cup of powers, she looked up and reached toward the heavens in an offering. Moments later, she drank quickly.

"Powers, move this enhanced strength from my body to that of the Little Soul I birthed," she whispered, her words becoming chokes through the mass of tears covering her face. An abundance of energy fled from her then, and she fell, her face to the cold earth.

"Aaron," she whispered, only once.

She closed her eyes and felt a cold sweat building a river around her.

❈ ❈ ❈

Kathryn heard noises on the front porch. Opening her eyes, she found herself lying on her bed. *How did I get here?* And then she realized that Aaron had stiffened in her arms.

My baby. My baby's dead, she cried silently. She had felt such pain before, when she had so long ago miscarried the child inside her. But this was the worst pain ever bestowed on anybody, she knew. *My baby is dead.* She turned her face to the window, unable to rise from the bed. The sun was fading now, like her heart, like her being.

"I don't want to live anymore," she whispered.

Where was Mama now? Why had she not returned with Doctor Adams? Why had he not come to save her baby?

And then she heard movement in the living room. People had come.

"It's all over," Leonard said, to somebody, his voice low. "Come take a look."

And then she heard a low crying. It was Mama. and a man's voice, "Let me see here."

Doctor Adams had come.

"Where's Kathryn?" he asked.

"She passed out about a half-an-hour ago. I put her to bed. I been keeping an eye on her. She'll be okay."

Leonard's words vaguely penetrated her eardrums. She swallowed as a fresh trail of tears flowed. And then the rumbling of more movement came, somebody walking across the floor. Kathryn got up, and though weak as a dying rose, she fled down the hallway to the living room. Leonard, Mama and Doctor Adams turned, their eyes gazing at her as if she were on display.

"It's all over now," Leonard said.

"I know," she whimpered. "My baby's dead."

"No," Leonard said, hurrying to her and putting his hand on her shoulder.

"He's dead," she cried, all the pain in her coming to the surface. "He died in my arms."

"No. He's there sleeping," Leonard said, his voice finding its musical flow, yet holding a tone of worry. He pointed at Aaron lying silently on the davenport. "Come see. He's wet as a water-rat but the poison came out."

"He's going to be all right," Doctor Adams chimed in. "After having that bad cold, then coming down with the fever, the little fellow just couldn't escape going into convulsions."

Kathryn swallowed and walked to her precious baby boy. Aaron was alive. That was all that mattered.

She remembered the words she had prayed to God. *If I must give Aaron up, let it not be through death.*

Twenty

Finally, all was quiet at Minor's Fish Camp. Rowe slipped from the shrubs and stepped cautiously onto the plank porch. Scrunching down, he crept on to the window. The men inside were out cold. He moved to the entrance and pushed open the heavy log door. Its screech seemed louder than normal. A bandit moaned unconsciously. Rowe stood still for a moment and let his eyes move over the room.

A gun. He must get a gun. He tiptoed across the room to the wall where Jake Minor kept his guns displayed. But where were they? He looked around the room. They were gone, and right now, he didn't have time to look for them. He just wanted to arm himself and get out. Pausing at the cash register, Rowe decided to take the chance that opening the loud contraption wouldn't awaken the gangsters. He pressed a lever and the drawer sprang open. Eying the green, he scooped up a generous handful of bills. Rowe looked at Morton, all sprawled across the floor, his magnum at his side. It was a good gun. Rowe had already seen it demonstrated when Morton gunned down the jailer.

He inched toward Morton, stooped, and picked up the weapon.

Hurrying to the door, he heard a moan, but without turning to see what was going on, Rowe ran from the storefront to the nearby woods where he had left his horse.

※ ※ ※

Through mid November, the backlands were unusually bright with colorful trees and sunshine. Kathryn, in the back yard splitting wood for the cooking stove, paused to stretch her shoulders forward to allow the sun to penetrate her shirt, to allow it to sink through her flesh all the way to her backbone. It felt so good. She dropped her ax and reached to remove the pin that held her hair at the back of her neck.

She'd just shaken her hair free when she spied Moldie coming toward her. She guessed he was making his usual tour for a handout.

"Well, look who's here," she said.

Moldie grinned cautiously and removed his hat.

"Where you been all fall? I thought you must have died or something?"

"Well, I-I-I been on down ta-ta-ta Louisiana. Went on down there and stayed with my brother for a wh-wh-while."

Bridged By Love

"You found your brother? Bill Junior?"

"Ye-ye-yes. Down in Ida woods."

A guilty, or was it a worried look that spread over his face. Moldie hadn't spoken of Bill Junior in years, as far as she knew. But it was for sure he had been staying someplace for the past couple of months.

Most likely, he had been in hiding because of the heat. George Thatcher had officially accused Moldie of stealing his calf while his family was in El Dorado. He was pretty angry about it—angry enough to take Moldie to court over the ordeal.

"You wanting some lunch? We got pintos."

"Ye-ye-yes, Ka-Ka-Kathryn. I-I-I could use a handout."

"Well then," she said, pushing the ax handle toward him. "You can split this wood for me while I get it for you."

Without looking at Moldie, she rubbed her hands down the sides of her coveralls and started for the house.

Rather than stopping at the stove and spooning out grub, Kathryn went straight to her room and lifted Aaron from his bassinet. She held his tiny body against her breast and brushed her lips across his forehead. "Aaron," she whispered. "I love you."

Since the day Shanna had disappeared into the forest, Kathryn had spent most of her time with Aaron. She had not left the homestead at all. Mama had gone with Molly Thatcher to town twice, and Leonard had come to visit often.

But John, her dear, beloved John. The last time she had spoken with him was that day at the State Line Café, which seemed an eternity ago.

She thought for a moment: There was still plenty canned food in the pantry and the chicken pen was full of young roosters; plus Leonard kept them well supplied with prime cuts from wild game he rounded up after work and on weekends. The flour and cornmeal buckets were nearly full. Actually, they didn't really need anything store-bought unless maybe some seeds for Mama's truck-farming.

Certainly, going to town today wasn't a must-do, but she did need to see John. Did he know about Aaron? Did he know Aaron was her very own baby now—her very own son. If he knew, surely he would have come calling, or surely he would have sent a message of congratulations. John loved children, didn't he? He was ridiculously silly over Sharleen Wagner's two straggly daughters, practically teenagers now. Aaron was a fine boy, healthy and strong.

And then Kathryn wondered if John might think badly of her for taking in an Indian child. He didn't appear to be a prejudiced man, but one never knew for sure about anybody nowadays.

Now that she had allowed thoughts of John to come, they flashed through her mind with every heartbeat. She must go to town this very afternoon. She must tell John of her son, of Aaron.

She could visualize herself walking in the sunlight, her red hair shining with streaks of gold. She would leave it hanging loose rather than rolled in the usual twist. She dipped her head and reached to touch a golden strand. She remembered a pink flowered dress Mama had made for her last summer. It had a black sash that fit tightly at the waist and a gathered skirt that swept her ankles. The neck opening was round and low, exposing cleavage. She could visualize John offering his hand to her and his desires overflowing with lust. She'd prove to him she was a real woman.

Kathryn was spooning milk into Aaron's tiny mouth when Mama came into the house from the front porch.

"Kathryn, I thought you were out back chopping wood."

"No, it's Moldie."

"Why's he chopping?"

"I told him to."

"Kathryn Williams, you know I don't want to make the old tramp work for his handouts. We can always spare food for the hungry."

"You don't make him work, Mama. I'm the one doing it. Good-Lord-a-mercy, Mama. It's not going to hurt him to do a little something. Maybe it'll clear his conscious some. He never brings anybody a mess of fish, nor a rabbit, not even a coon. Besides, he's a thief."

"Now you don't know that for a fact."

"It's surely evident. He sold Thatcher's calf to Saul Jones down about Kibler and swore to me the wolves got it. George and Molly won't be getting over that for quite a spell."

Kathryn stood up and, turning from Mama, walked quietly to her bedroom and put Aaron to bed. The sound of the ax splitting into the wood had stopped.

She returned to the kitchen and pulled Moldie's clay bowl from the cabinet and filled it with hot pinto beans and a goodly slab of saltpork. She put a hunk of cornbread on top and carried the steaming bowl to the back porch where Moldie had perched.

"Sm-sm-smells good Ka-Ka-Kathryn."

She handed the bowl to him and then gazed aimlessly across the pasture.

"You been in town lately?"

"I-I- yesterday."

She pulled her pants legs up a little and sat down on the porch edge so her feet dangled over the side. Moldie didn't look at her. He lifted the bowl to his face and sipped. Moldie should know if John was out and about these days.

"Did you go to the sawmill?" she asked, casually.

Removing the bowl from his lips, he nodded shyly.

"Who did you see there?"

"Wa-wa-well, I-I-I sawed Billy Don Thatcher."

"I see."

Now she understood Moldie's hesitation about spilling out information. Billy Don had more than likely chewed him out a good one. And he surely should have.

"Who else was there?"

Moldie didn't answer. He turned instead to watch Mama pull a chair through the back door to the porch. "Who you wondering about, Kathryn?" she asked.

"Nobody especially. Just wondering how things are down at the sawmill."

"You've missed going to town, haven't you Kathryn?"

"Ah, I've thought about it a bit." Her voice was distant. "But Mama, you know I'm the happiest woman alive now that I have Aaron."

"Think you might not be going back to work?"

"I will when and if the time is right. Don't know, though, if I could stand to leave Aaron. Maybe when he's older."

"Th-th-they're needing some workers at the sawmill," Moldie stammered.

Kathryn felt her face quiver. "How you know that, Moldie?"

"I-I-I heard Milton telling John."

John! Kathryn hesitated for a moment, wrapping herself in her own world of awe at the mention of the man she loved. In a little while she stood up and, lifting her arms, stretched lazily.

"Sitting around the house so much is making me a tired woman," she said, and glanced slyly at Mama.

"I haven't seen you doing much sitting," Mama said with humor in her voice. "Land sakes, it seems to me you're busy all the time."

Kathryn glanced toward the trail. "I'm going to town in a little bit."

"Taking Aaron?"

"Will you keep him here?" she asked, though she knew Mama's answer to that question. She'd love to take Aaron with her but first she wanted to tell John about him, gauge his reaction. There was plenty of time for them to meet later.

※ ※ ※

The chilled winds brought tightness to Kathryn's face and its force twisted her hair into damp curls about her neck. She straightened the pink and white flowered printed dress over her legs and sat straight in the saddle.

"It's about time I rode you." Her voice was pampering while her hand slid over Sugar's silvery mane. She clutched the leather reins in her hand and, giving them a quick shake, called to the horse. "Eee-ii."

About an hour later she rode along the busy street adjacent to the sawmill yard. She looked casually toward Milton's office. Not seeing John, she rode on to Smith's Dry Goods Store on East Broad Street and lapped Sugar's reins over a post at the street edge. She raked her hair from her face as she moved toward the store.

Laughter from behind brought a sudden stillness to her. She knew it was John and, glancing back, she saw he was with Sharleen and her daughters. The oldest girl, standing nearly as tall as her slender dark-haired mother, yanked on John's arm while the younger child danced around him. Kathryn listened but couldn't make out words the kid was singing.

Kathryn, unable to take her eyes off all the mounds of red rouge Sharleen wore on her lips and cheeks, managed to smile in spite of the painful jealousy flaring inside her. She swallowed the tight knot that had come to her throat and hurried on into the store.

Inside, Kathryn purchased a sack of flour in a soft blue bag. Mama would use the supple cotton fabric to stitch rompers for Aaron.

Noticing a headline on the **Daily Independent**, Kathryn picked up the newspaper, laid it on the counter, and stated to read:

As stated by our West side contemporary, yesterday was the 11th anniversary of this city, and when we see what has been done in the past eleven years, it gives us great hope for the future. Let our people remain united in the advocacy and support of public schools and all public enterprises, and Texarkana will ere long become one of the most prosperous young cities in the southwest.

She smiled, and put the newspaper back on the stack. It was good to know that the public school system was growing here. She lived in the country. Still, good schooling would be available for Aaron by the time he was school age. Kathryn heard Sharleen and her daughters enter the store, but John had remained outside. He was coughing now. She held her chin up and nodded a casual "hello" at Sharleen as she turned to leave.

"Kathryn," John said, removing his hat as they met in the doorway. "It's really you?" His eyes moved the length of her body several times, drawing up a want for him in her heart and then releasing it over her entire being so she ached completely.

She smiled and softly spoke, "How are you, John?"

"Right now, I'm engrossed with you." He reached for her bag and tied it to Sugar's saddle. "Are you in a hurry to get home?"

She tilted her head slightly, her eyes flirting. "No hurry."

"Good. Let's get some cider."

At the State Line Café, Kathryn and John stopped at the bar and picked up two glasses of hard cider. John pointed to a quiet corner.

"John, do you know about Aaron, my son?"

"Everybody in town knows. They're saying you took in a papoose. I was quite surprised, myself."

"Surprised? Why?" she asked, puzzled.

"Forgive me, Kathryn. I don't mean to be disrespectful. It's just that I find it hard to imagine you taking in an infant Indian as your own child."

"I've always loved children." Kathryn could not prevent the abundance of disappointment that suddenly came over her. This wasn't the reaction she'd hoped for.

"I'm sure you love children, but an Indian?" He quickly shook his head. "I shouldn't have said that. I just thought you'd be more concerned about talk." His eyes slowly traveling over her bosom brought a blush to her face.

Bridged By Love

Then he smiled and held his glass near his lips and peeked over the rim. "Tell me all about the tot."

"He's precious, John. Come out to the homestead and see him."

"Is that an invitation?"

"Of course, John. For-goodness-sake, don't you know you're always welcome at my home?"

"I'll come," he said, reaching across the table for her hand. "I will. I've been wanting to visit you."

"Today. Please, John," she said, instantly knowing she had appeared overly anxious.

"I'd like to ride out with you now. Certainly. Just let me do a couple chores. I'll meet you at the sawmill?" John's words lit a flame inside Kathryn that not even a gulp of hard cider could put out.

She and John parted outside the café, him going to the S. Wagner's Rooming House to fetch his horse and buggy and her going to have a quick chat with friends at the sawmill.

Billy Don stopped working when he saw Kathryn. He held his hand up in a greeting. "Hi Kath-ern," he slurred."

"Hey, Billy Don. How're your folks doing? Did you hear anymore about that missing calf? I hear y'all are filing charges on old Moldie for stealing it."

He shook his head so his blond hair fell back from his face. "We found out Moldie sold our calf to Saul Jones and that's a fact. I caught up with him on the trail this morning and I told him off good-and-proper. He gonna pay for it one way or another." He spit thick brown tobacco juice onto the sawdust-covered ground. "Kath-ern," he slurred, "you ain't gonna believe what I'm 'bout to tell you. Moldie said that Alex gave him a nickel to lead that calf off. Then Saul Jones bought it from Moldie."

"Alex! Not Alex Andrews!"

"That's what the old fool said."

Kathryn frowned. "Well, he's an old fool all-right. Everybody knows that," she said, assertively. "That's the stupidest, confounded thing I've ever heard. Alex has been gone from here for–," *seven, eight*–she counted under her breath. "He's been gone for seven or eight years now. He wouldn't have any reason in the world to come back all of a sudden. And he certainly wouldn't have any reason to give old Moldie a nickel to lead a calf off."

"You know, a body can't believe anything old Moldie says."

Jangling harness and creaking wheels from John's buggy caught Kathryn's attention.

"Gotta go, Billie Don. I'll be seeing you."

As the carriage passed S. Wagner's Rooming House, Kathryn smiled. She was quite happy she was the woman sitting next to John now.

Then she caught sight of a work wagon headed toward the sawmill. Buoyed with her euphoria of the moment, she waved boisterously at Leonard as he passed. He saw her all right, and his stunned expression evaporated all her joy. She'd always known Leonard loved her despite her attempts to discourage him. She couldn't prevent the sadness her heart pumped into her veins.

But how could she be sad? How could anything temper her happiness when she was sitting beside John, the man she loved so dearly? And yet, the depressive sensation continued...long after they'd left town and Leonard was out of sight.

She tried to focus on the drive home, on the lovely light breeze, on the birdsong in the trees. The afternoon sun penetrated through the oak branches and felt warm on Kathryn's skin as the carriage moved on a good five miles toward the homestead. "I've been here many times," John said, bringing the horse to a halt.

"You have? Why didn't you come on out to the homestead?"

"I've always decided that perhaps it wasn't the thing to do."

Kathryn's hand fell on John's knee. Realizing the accidental and certainly uncharacteristic move, she quickly jerked it away. Then John touched her fingers and clapped his hand on hers.

"Kathryn, I know how you feel about me. I've always known. And I can tell you quite honestly that I've missed seeing you in town during the last couple of months. When I come here it's to think about you."

Kathryn watched his eyes move to gaze at the spring where water washed gracefully over large gray stones, and then moments later returning to her face.

"You know, I'm smitten with you, too. I have been for a long time and only just now realized it."

She was totally and positively numb, yet a nerve in her soul blazed like the noon sun. She was dreaming! This couldn't be happening to her. John had just said what she had longed to hear without her having any hope it would ever happen. Was it real now? Was she really sitting here beside him in his buggy and surrounded by the fresh aroma of pines and yellow-leaf hickory trees? Here in paradise, with John saying such special words? He had just said he loved her, hadn't he? Well, that he was smitten with her, which must be the same thing.

"Did you hear me, Kathryn?"

She stared blankly.

"Remember when I got off the train and didn't know if I was in Arkansas or Texas?"

"I remember," she said, her voice so soft she wondered if John could hear her words.

"I think that's when it must have happened." He gently squeezed her hand. "I felt something for you, then. And it's always been like I've known you all my life."

"Why did you wait so long to tell me?" Kathryn thought about the way he often carried on with fancy-dressed women in town, and how Sharleen was often at his side. Were there more women?

John held his head back for a moment as if in thought, and then he pulled her close and touched his lips to her hair. "I just never felt the time was right. Not until now."

His arms embraced her tightly. She could feel her breasts coming alive against his chest. She could feel his warm breath in her hair.

"I've decided something Kathryn. You're going to be my wife." he said, his voice more tender than she had ever heard it. "I want you to have my baby."

※ ※ ※

Rowe didn't know if the outlaws were after him or not as he rode along the Louisiana and Texas border northward toward Texarkana. They may suspect he had come into Minor's store and stolen money from the cash register as well as Morton's gun. Or maybe they would think somebody else did it—one of them, perhaps. No matter, they had surely found they had been robbed by now.

Hopefully, the bad men believed he was dead. So far, he had no evidence of anybody on his trail.

He pulled at the reins, impelling the horse to slow its pace. He was out of the Caddo Lake wetlands now. The ride onward to the city would be easy.

Hearing water running over rocks, Rowe guided the horse to it and dismounted. Suddenly he realized how lucky he had been. First, he had escaped from the two gunmen who had come for him at the Texas jail. Then he had taken money and a gun from right under the noses of a band of outlaws in Minor's store. Now, he had gotten away from the gang again. And here was a creek of clear spring water. He loosened the bridle so the bit fell from the horse's mouth, and then pulled it over the horse's head and dropped it to the green earth.

Now, the idea was to take care of himself. He hadn't taken a bath in a coon's age, it seemed. He removed his tattered shirt and denim pants and dropped them on the rocks in the shallow creek waters. Then he waded in 'til he was chest deep. The chilled water was soothing to his skin. He ducked his head in and out of the water, over and over, and then dove into the flow. He came up, took a deep breath, and dove under again. After a while, Rowe retrieved his garments and hung them over a tree branch to dry. He went back into the creek and stayed there until he felt every pore in his body was clean, then he emerged and bedded himself on a patch of grass. The sun beat down on him, singeing his skin and warming his bones.

Rowe woke up rested and relaxed. He put on his crisply dry clothes, bridled the horse and mounted. "Let's go," he called lightly and shook out the reins.

"Texarkana, here I come!"

※ ※ ※

Patricia Lieb

This was the best it could possibly be—Kathryn in John's arms and him asking her to be his wife. But what had he just said? He wanted her to have his baby? Would he love her and still want to marry her if she told him she could never carry a baby inside? That her womanhood was destroyed years ago?

"John," she whispered, her eyes becoming moist. "When I was younger..." She swallowed. Through a knotted throat she said, "I long ago lost the only baby..."

Before Kathryn could say more, John's mouth covered her lips, kissing away fears she had of truth. "We'll talk about babies later. Right now, I just want to hear you say you'll be my wife."

He kissed her again and when her lips were free, the only words that came from her mouth were, "Yes, John. Yes, I will."

The remaining two-mile ride to the homestead was like a dream for Kathryn. It seemed the carriage was a chariot floating through fluffy white clouds, and she was riding to a castle in the sky. She clutched John's arm, almost afraid if she turned him lose the ecstasy would end.

At the homestead, Kathryn led Sugar to the pasture while John freed his horse, Blaze, from the carriage and tied it to a front porch post.

"Hi Mama. Look who I brought home," Kathryn said as she entered the front room from the kitchen, her hand clutching John's arm. Mama held the broom handle and was swishing the long straw bristles over the pine flooring.

"Hello Mister Allen," she said, greeting with a smile. She propped the broom upside the stone wall and offered her hand. "It sure is neighborly of you to come calling way out here."

Kathryn touched John's arm and guided his attention to the sofa where Aaron lay, his tiny feet furiously kicking in the air. "What's my boy doing this afternoon?" she asked, jabbering baby talk as she lifted the infant. "This is little Aaron. Aaron Zebadiah Williams."

John reached for Aaron's fingers. "Hello there, Aaron," he said, teasingly. "I'm pleased to meet you."

"Want to hold him?" Kathryn asked, a short time later as she and John sat side-by-side in the front porch swing.

John shook his head casually. "I'm not much for babies," he said, hesitantly. But Kathryn smiled and passed Aaron to him, keeping her eyes on him to see his reactions. The look on his face was indifferent. She figured he might be a little intimidated by a child so young. He surely would get used to Aaron, though, as he grew. *I'm sure he loves children*, she told herself. *But I wish he would show some expression. I wish I knew what he really thinks of this child. Oh stop it Kathryn!* she scolded herself. *John will eventually love him just as much as you do.*

"When we marry, Aaron will be your son, too," she said. She smiled, resting her hand on his arm. "I really do love you," she whispered, her reverie again riding in the slow moving clouds in the southern sky.

They remained in the porch swing for the longest time, the only sounds being the swing's screeching, while Aaron slept on John's arm. About the time the sun started to sink beyond the green hillside, Mama appeared in the doorway.

"Supper's ready," she announced, her voice inviting.

"I'll put Aaron to bed," Kathryn said, carefully lifting him from John's lap.

"Are you going to tell your mother of our plans?"

"Yes. Shall I give her a date?"

"Tell her we will marry soon," he said with a smile. "As soon as I get my shop operating profitably."

Kathryn's mouth opened in awe. "You didn't tell me you were opening a shop, John."

He grinned. "Kathryn, I was a carpenter in Ireland. I ran my own business. I built houses and the furniture to go in them. I'm doing the same here, just on a smaller scale. My business is growing more every day."

"I'll say the Blessing," Kathryn said as they sat down at the kitchen table. She glanced over the feast of black-eyed peas and ham hocks, okra, and cornbread. Mama, who normally said grace, glanced at Kathryn.

"Lord, bless this food we are about to eat." She hesitated for a moment. And her eyes searched over the red-and-white checked tablecloth as if she were reading a script. Then she continued. "Lord, I thank you for my family. For Aaron who has lit up my life. For Mama and our home," she groped again for words. "And thank you for bringing John to me. Bless our marriage."

Mama's eyes shot up, showing momentary shock. Then her expression cooled and she stared Kathryn in the eyes.

"John asked me to marry him. I said 'yes.'"

"This is a bit of a surprise," Mama said. "When did you decide this?"

"Today, Mama. John asked me to marry him this afternoon and I said 'yes.' I love him, Mama," she said, her hand finding John's under the table and squeezing it.

Without saying more, Mama got up from the table and kissed Kathryn on the cheek. Then she hugged John. After supper, she retired to her bedroom, leaving Kathryn and John alone.

Kathryn cleared the table, and then she and John sat together in the front porch swing. Kathryn said, "But John, we could marry now. We don't have to wait. I trust Mama to take care of Aaron while I work. I can go back to cutting pulp any time I want to, or I could even get on at the sawmill."

"No. When we marry, I will earn the living," he said, sternly.

She swallowed. Would John want her to change her way of life? The life she had always known? Maybe he had never known a woman like her, but with all its ups and downs, there wasn't a gal alive she would change places with. Actually, she liked cutting pulp in Milton's Woods with Leonard.

"You're quiet, Kathryn."

"Just dreaming, I guess."

Her smile played in the blue of his eyes. She knew she could be happy with John. After all, she was deeply in love with him. She would be a fool to do or say anything that would cause her to lose him now. John was the only man for her, the only one she had ever hurt for. She would never leave him; never let him down.

But what if he wanted to live in town? That would be out of the question. They would live at the homestead with Mama and Aaron. That's how it would be. On this matter, John would have absolutely no say.

Then John spoke, breaking her contemplations. "I want you. I want to hold you in a special way." A lingering tingle spread from his hand to hers and on through her whole body.

"But we aren't married yet."

He moved closer to her. "I know we aren't married." He squeezed her hand even more tensely and rested it on his lap. "Kathryn, I need you now. I hurt for you all the time."

He lifted her chin, cupping it in his hand. "Let's not wait, Kathryn. Marry me tonight."

※ ※ ※

On that same moonlit night, Kathryn stood with John in front of Pastor Adam Grayson on the front lawn of his big redbrick house on College Hill, a part of town across the railroad tracks from the city.

She wore her pink flowered dress and carried a bouquet of colorful mums that had sprouted up alongside the front porch at the homestead.

Kathryn was unaccustomed to feeling so special, and wearing the fancy dress Mama had made for her, she must even be pretty. And she was about to marry the handsome John Allen—the catch of the town, she marveled, glancing up at him. He honestly looked like Sunday in his ironed gray-and-white striped three-piece suit. Mama looked nice, too, with her hair rolled into a neat twist just above the wide collar of her ivory attire. And Aaron, in a long white dress with tiny white flowers embroidered on it, was a might fitting for the occasion. At nearly three months old now, he could look around and take notice of the goings-on.

"And do you, Kathryn Williams, take John Allen to be your lawfully wedded husband, to love, to cherish, to honor and obey, from this day forward, as long as you both shall live?"

"I will."

John's mouth covered hers with warmth, sucking her up in affection.

Then, in the light of the full moon they traveled down the trail heading for the homestead. Aaron slept all the way in Mama's arms. As they passed the spring where John had proposed, Kathryn remembered the preacher's words, "Love and obey." She felt John's ring on her finger and she knew she would always, always love John. But, to obey—she really wished she had not taken that vow.

At the homestead, Mama went right to bed. Kathryn tucked Aaron between covers in his bassinet. He didn't budge.

"I have lived this night many times in my dreams, Kathryn," John said. He blew out the lamp so only light from the moon and stars fell into the room. He put his arms around her and held her close, his mouth falling over hers. Slowly, he twisted the buttons on the bodice so the pink lace flowers lay over her chest. Kissing her, he pushed the fabric from her shoulders.

Kathryn needed John's love making. It had been so long since a man had touched her. She closed her eyes while his hand played a game of seek over her skin. His touch was good and made her so womanly and so vulnerably sexy.

He kissed her mouth, first with his lips, then his tongue. His kisses trailed to her ear, down her neck, to her nipples. She moaned in ecstasy and tightened her arms around his back, her hands pressing hard against his skin.

"Oh my God, I love you, John," she whispered, feeling his male hardness. Her body was in a whirl. It was like a storm rolling in to cover her, its waters coming in huge waves, rolling over her, rolling over her faster and faster, twisting her this way and that way, and then delivering her to a high of ecstasy until she couldn't hold back any longer.

Kathryn opened her eyes with a start the following morning when the rooster delivered its bold crow before sunrise. Remembering the night before, she lay on her side and looked at John's sleeping face. She smiled and got out of bed to push open the window frame so the cool air could penetrate the room.

"Ah, that feels good," John said, then inhaled long and deep.

"I though you were sleeping," Kathryn said, shyly. She eagerly submitted to his arm wrapping around her and pulling her onto the bed, forcing her face to his and kissing her lips gently and completely.

"We can't do this," she teased, although her body ached for him as it had last night. "Mama's moving about in the kitchen," she whispered.

"Then I'd better stop thinking of how much I love you," he said with a grin. He kissed her again. "That what you want, Kathryn?"

Before she could say anything, her body succumbed to John, taking him in completely and whole-heartedly, as if it would be the last time she would find completion with the man she so dearly loved.

"I'm going to town today to get some work done on the shop. I'd like to have you come along. And bring Aaron. He'd enjoy the ride," John said. He buttoned his shirt and pulled on his pants.

Kathryn smiled and nodded. "We can leave right after breakfast. Let's take Sugar. She needs the exercise."

Kathryn was pleasantly surprised John had invited Aaron to come with them. Oh, she felt sure John cared about the baby, but he generally kept his distance. And more than once she'd caught him frowning when she was lavishing attention on Aaron. But it wasn't like John played second fiddle to the infant; she loved them both. And in time, John would understand that the love a woman has for a man and the love a mother has for her child are of equal stature, but totally different; like comparing figs and grapes. She found the taste for both fruits equally desirable. One thing for sure, though, Aaron was here to stay. In time, John would get over any jealousy he might harbor.

In the kitchen, Mama stood beside the wood-burning stove. A rag protected her hand as she clutched the handle of a black iron skillet and pushed it back and forth over the hotplate. Already the aroma of ham and biscuits floated through the room. Now the eggs were about done.

"Ah, does that ever smell good," John said, sniffing.

Mama grinned. "It'll have to do for your wedding breakfast."

"It's a splendid breakfast, Mama Williams," John said, and kissed her on her cheek.

As they prayed over their food, Kathryn couldn't keep her eyes off John. She was so proud to have him. Mama was happy for her, too. Kathryn knew she was.

"Mama Williams," John said, forking ham onto his plate. "Why don't you ride into town with Kathryn and me? We're taking the boy."

"Well, son, I really would like to, but I think I'd better stay around here and try to get a few things done."

"Why, Mama?" Kathryn butted in. "What's to be done that can't wait?"

"I'm sewing you a dress. I had planned to have it ready before you married."

They all laughed.

"Let it go," John encouraged. "Come with us."

"Not this time. You young folks eat your breakfast and go on."

It was almost eight o'clock when they finally reached town. Kathryn glanced toward the sawmill as the carriage rolled by. She would go back there and call on all her friends later. She clutched Aaron tightly in her arms as they drove down Broad Street and across State Line Avenue.

"And here we are," John said. He helped Kathryn from the carriage, and then he started right to work. Kathryn walked about examining materials. "I should have left Aaron with Mama and worn my overalls. There's lots of work I can do here."

John grinned. "But I like you dressed up. Being a woman becomes you," he said with a smile.

She didn't know if it was pride or embarrassment that caught her up in a whirl of excitement when John complimented her. Whichever, though, she liked it.

"I'll tell you what, Kathryn. You take the carriage and ride around town. Shop for a while. I heard that Smith's Dry Good Store has a shipment of hats in from St. Louis. Get yourself one."

Her lips tightened, and she tried to conceal her smile. John wanted her to buy a hat, one from St. Louis! She wasn't like the so-called fashionable women wearing hats on the city streets. And since she hadn't been a go-to-meeting person since she divorced Alex, she wouldn't even need a hat on Easter. Maybe now that she was married to John, she should consider going to church. Aaron would need direction during his growing up years.

"Go on," John insisted. "I'll meet you at the State Line Café at ten for cider."

"Okay, John."

She held Aaron on her lap, securing him between her arms while she clasped onto Sugar's reins and headed toward the sawmill. As she guided the mare through the gate, Leonard was the first person she saw. An unexplainable feeling of sadness ran through her. As happy as she was, as much as she wanted the world to know of her marriage to John, she wished her good news could go unsaid for the time. There was no way to tell Leonard without hurting him. She pulled the reins and climbed down from the carriage.

Leonard's mouth opened, a grin overtaking his face as he walked in long strides toward her.

"Why, my goodness, Kitten, I didn't hardly recognize ye," he drawled. "Guess it's yer clothes. I ain't seen you dressed up like this in a decade." He removed his hat and began scratching through his thinning hair.

Kathryn choked. She held Aaron tighter and nervously began to sway.

"I'll be getting out to your place in a day or so," he said. He paused, and patted Aaron on the head. "This little feller sure is growing. Need me to bring anything out to ye?"

She shook her head. She had no words for Leonard, this man she had known all her life, the man she had shared both good and sad times with, the man who had always loved her, the one she could always depend on.

"How's that boy doing? He sure did give us a scare when he went getting sick on us," Leonard said, chuckling, and rocking his head back and forth. "Think ye'll be coming back to work now that he's 'out of the woods'?"

She had to tell Leonard of her marriage. Lord-a-mercy, she had to tell him. She looked onto his anxious face and wondered if she would ever have to face another task so difficult. She took a deep breath.

"I don't think I'll ever be coming back to work for Milton."

"Never, Kitten?"

"Maybe not, Leonard." She swallowed. "John and I got married last night."

Leonard's face suddenly flushed red. He surely must feel the same hurt now that she would have felt if John had married Sharleen. He touched her arm and was silent for the longest time. Finally, he spoke, "I hope ye'll be happy, Kitten. If there's ever anything I can do for ye, ye call me?"

Tears filled Kathryn's eyes. She nodded.

"Well, can I kiss the bride?" he said, his lips brushing lightly over her cheek. "Take care of yer self, Kitten," he said, then turned and quickly walked away.

She watched him disappear into Milton's office. She wanted to go after him and hug him. But she knew she had caused his hurt. She could do nothing to help him now.

"It's okay, baby," she whispered, as Aaron became restless. "We'll walk."

Tightly clutching Aaron on her hip with one arm, she hurried across the sawmill yard toward the area where Billy Don was stripping logs.

"Hey there, Billy Don," she called. He glanced up and waved quickly.

"Wait 'til I tell you this, Kath-ern," he drawled. Dropping his saw, he hurried toward her waving his index finger in the air.

"Did you find out something about the calf?"

"Boy, did I! Yesterday after I got through here I moseyed on off down to Kibler to see old man Jones." Billy Don caught his breath and spit out a generous amount of tobacco juice. "It's no fooling. Old Moldie sold him that calf all-right."

"Yeah, I figured as much. Why, he's liable to do anything."

"Dad-gum-right-a-tooting. Alex gave old Moldie a nickel to sell that calf."

Kathryn sighed. "Who told you that besides Moldie?"

"Old man Jones told me, that's who. Old man Jones said he wouldn't have even bought that calf from Moldie if Alex hadn't been with him."

"With him?" she screeched in agitation.

"That's right." He spit again, the sun seeming to set in the upper row of his lemon-yellow teeth. For a young boy, his grooming was slack. She stared a minute in silence. Aaron's teeth would never yellow, he would be taught good hygiene. Billy Don spit again. "Yep, Alex was with him okay."

"But why would Alex do that?" Her gaze now on the thin lips covering those yellow teeth somewhat held back the anxiety spreading through her.

"Who knows? Your guess is as good as mine."

Kathryn was silent. Why in the world would Alex do such a ridiculously stupid thing? And if he had really come to town, where was he now? Why had no one seen him except Moldie and old man Jones? It just didn't make sense.

Suddenly, Kathryn turned from Billy Don and started to the carriage. The idea of Alex being in town and the confusion he could create ran like a river of stress from her brain through her chest to her legs and into her feet. She felt she would drop before the river curved and returned to her head. *If he is here, I don't want to see him*, she thought.

Right now she needed to be with John, safe in his arms. He had told her to meet him at the café but it was too early for that. She would kill time by stopping at the dry-goods store for some oatmeal. Oatmeal was good for babies.

✳ ✳ ✳

Bridged By Love

Alex's pockets bulged with more cash than anybody needed as he got off the eastbound train at the Texarkana depot. Yes, he had money. Lots of money. But he would have more as soon as he found Kathryn, married her, and turned the Williams homestead into a fortune. It was good to be back in the city. He stepped across a set of tracks, then stopped and pulled from his jacket pocket the walnut pipe Lilly had given him when he stopped by her place before boarding the train from Dallas. He shook tobacco into the bowl, held the stem to his mouth and sucked in. Nothing was more relaxing than a good smoke, he marveled. And the pipe was aristocratic, like him.

Casually puffing as he walked, Alex meandered through the train depot, pausing near the newspaper stand long enough to catch the news headlines on the ***Daily Independent***. But who cared about a gunfight between local cowmen and a gang of outsiders; or that some gambler was found dead in a ditch outside town, or that telephone service had been added to more city locations? Damn, though, sure a lot of trouble and shootouts and knifings commencing at the gambling halls over the last three months. He would have to keep this in mind. It could be a little hairy for a gambling man like himself. *Lots been happening here since I been gone*, he thought, his eyes becoming narrow at more information than he needed to see. The next line really caught his eye:

Burglaries are becoming of too frequent occurrence in this city and it may be necessary to increase the police force. It cannot be expected that 2 or 3 men can do the work of a half dozen officers. It strikes us that Texarkana is large enough to have a regular organized police force.

Alex's mouth twitched at one corner. That was too much. The city didn't need police running around everywhere meddling in everybody's business. This town was fine as it was. No need for more marshals.

The recently completed five-story Warren Hotel located across Front Street from the depot would be a place to linger for a while. At the modern hotel he could even use a telephone if he needed to call the furrier back in Dallas. Right now, he just needed a clean room to rest up in while he plotted out the proposal he would put to Kathryn.

Alex laughed, expelling smoke. No doubt about it, by now Kathryn would be totally dedicated to Squaw Girl's baby. He'd play his cards right now and he'd have Kathryn doing anything he asked her to. Not like before when she refused to sign the homestead over to him. Now, he had a plan. She'd give him what he asked for and he'd let her keep the kid.

He grinned, and raising his brows, marveled at his own clever scheme.

Twenty-one

IT WAS MID-MORNING when Rowe rode into Texarkana from the south. He guided his horse across a wide group of railroad tracks and on to the train depot. He dismounted and lapped the horse's reins over the tie post at the side of the long plank building and walked around front.

"Where's a place a Mexican can get a room?" he asked a black man wearing a red cap and stacking baggage alongside the train depot.

"Ought to can stays over there. The Warren Hotel might works, if yas got money. That's what I'z hears."

"Thanks man," Rowe said. Turning on his heels, he returned to his horse.

Rowe rode across the street but hesitated when he caught an image of himself. He would be thrown out of the fine hotel the moment he set foot inside. He rode on west on Front Street to the hotel stable. The groomsman there took money Rowe offered. He looked at Rowe through squinted eyes and directed him to the elegant hotel's back entry. "Might be better accepted if yas gos in the back door. Tell 'em yas looking for a job-of-work."

"I got money."

"Better have lots of it. There's signs all over town that says "white only" and "we have the right to refuse service to anyone," that means Negroes, Indians, Mexicans and idiots."

"I don't want any trouble."

"Yas don't have to want it. 'Round here, trouble just comes."

"Is there someplace else I can stay?"

"Don't think anybody gonna rent yas a room." The groomsman paused. "Yas can stay here in the stable. Yas can sleep on that bunk up there. If anybody asks, tell 'em yas working here. Yas pay me two-bits a week."

Rowe pulled a half-dollar from his pocket. "Here's for the first week," he said, and tossed the coin to the groomsman. "Name's Rowe."

The groomsman grinned, his teeth as big as the seeds in a cotton bowl. "Grimes, be me," he said with a nod.

"I got a good horse here but I want to trade for a Pinto. Got one?"

"Yas be a horse thief? I'z ain't dealing with no horse thief. Townspeople don't take kindly to rustlers. No horse trading here."

Rowe knew he couldn't be riding around town on the stolen horse. Somebody might very well recognize it as belonging to one of the bad men.

Bridged By Love

He needed to distance himself and his involvements from the outlaws who had held him captive for months. He'd be hard pressed getting justice for the wrongs they'd done him. He needed to concentrate on getting his life back.

On Front Street, Rowe walked towards State Line Avenue. He dearly wanted a bath and a shave, and a good barbering, but first there was a man he needed to talk to. Someone who would be less inclined to speak freely to a well-groomed gentleman than the ruffian Rowe appeared to be.

The stable attendant had suggested he might get a job with a Mexican who had a food wagon and prepared hot tamales. Rowe wasn't looking for a job, however, he needed to talk to somebody he could trust, and the only person he could put faith in was an honest working Mexican.

Rowe crossed State Line and continued on east until he spotted the food wagon parked on a lot near the end of Front Street. He hurried toward it. The attendant peeked up. He was rolling tamales in corn shucks and putting them in a bucket over a cooking fire.

"I'm looking for a girl. A young Indian girl with black hair hanging to her waist. Have you seen such a person?"

"No Eng-ga-lish," the man said.

In Spanish, Rowe repeated the question.

The man pointed at a poster stuck on the side of his wagon. A rider, who the Mexican claimed he didn't know, had put it there earlier in the morning.

Rowe walked to the end of the wagon. Someone had drawn a picture of an Indian girl, clearly Shanna. "Wanted," the sign read. "$1,000 reward. Wanted for attempted murder and gun theft."

"Attempted murder!" Rowe said. This was unbelievable. Shanna wouldn't hurt a snake. Who had she tried to kill? He read on. "Deliver her alive to Minor's Fish Camp."

Hopefully, nobody in town could find Shanna. One thousand dollars was a lot of money, though. A heck of a lot of money. Too many people would snag an Indian girl anyway they could for much less. They wouldn't even consider why she had run. Rowe rubbed his forehead. How many more signs like this were scattered around town?

Steam with beef, corn meal, and hot spices filled the air. Rowe turned back to the Mexican. "I'll take one," he said, nodding as the Mexican took cooked wraps from the pot. He pulled a coin from his pocket and laid it on the table.

Rowe rolled back the corn shucks and bit into the tamale as he walked slowly from the Mexican's wagon. The food was tasty, and as he bit, memories came of his boyhood days in Southwest Texas. His mother's tamales had tasted and looked the same as the one he was eating now.

Beginning sometime in early childhood, Rowe had been curious about land and its natural resources. The study of minerals had led him into the Louisiana marshlands. That was how he had met Shanna at Minor's Fish Camp. After that, he had found trouble galore.

Walking along Front Street, Rowe hesitated at a men's store widow and studied a mannequin dressed in a tailored gray suit and white shirt with full gathered sleeves. Then he saw his own reflection. His black hair long and shaggy, months of growth on his chin and hair hanging in long strands alongside his lip; his shirt and denims faded and tattered, shoes clogged with dried mud. He knew he must clean himself up if he were to be accepted anyplace. Especially here in the city, where high rollers drifted in droves to gambling halls and whores wore silk dresses and carried parasols.

Rowe turned into the store. A well-dressed clerk approached him. "I think you're in the wrong shop," he said, his eyes moving over Rowe suspiciously.

"No mistake," Rowe said quickly. He reached into his pocket and brought out a roll of bills. "The suit in the window; I wish to purchase it."

While the clerk undressed the mannequin, Rowe tried on black rawhide boots, then a gray hat with a tall trunk and a jeweled pin on the silver band above the wide brim. From a grooming rack, he gathered a straight razor and soap mug.

"Got a place I can clean up," Rowe asked as he paid for the items and handed an extra buck to the clerk.

The clerk stared at him. "Clean up? Here?"

"Been riding. Got business in town." Rowe showed the money wad again; this time offering the clerk five bills.

"There's a room in back."

Clean, shaved and dressed in new duds, Rowe thanked the clerk and passed him another folded bill. His heels clicking on the marbled floor, he strolled from the storefront and walked along Front Street, thus seeing a familiar figure. Morton was nailing up a notice. Without looking, Rowe knew the outlaw was still circulating wanted posters for Shanna. He stood back and watched. A well-dressed man with a black mustached walked toward Morton.

"Morton," the man called. "Who you looking for?"

"Jake Minor's squaw."

"Squaw Girl?"

"Yep. She knifed Minor and left him fer dead. Stealed all his guns, too." Morton turned. "Ye seen her?"

"No. How much you offering for her?"

"Thousand bucks."

"Where you getting that much money?"

Morton laughed. "Who said we'd pay?"

"If I found her, I'd get paid one way or another."

"Sure ye would, Alex. I know ye. Ye find her and we can deal."

Alex, huh, Rowe thought. He had heard of the man named Alex who had dealings with Jake Minor, but this was the first time he had seen him.

Rowe pulled the hat brim close to his eyes. He stood back until the two men parted. Alex headed westward down Front Street and Rowe fell in step behind him. He couldn't let him find Shanna first. He might just be after the reward, but his comment—I'd get paid one way or another—suggested he was the type of man who wouldn't stop at that.

They crossed State Line Avenue and Alex turned into the Warren Hotel.

Rowe waited outside for a moment to make sure Alex didn't become suspicious that he was being followed. Seconds later, he went into the big luxurious hotel. Dressed as he was, he wouldn't go back to the stable but would get a room here. Clothes and money talks; this he had come to know.

Inside, the middle-aged woman behind the desk gave him a curious smile. "Come in from east or west? You get off the train today?"

Rowe smiled and winked. "Come in from Texas," he said. He paid the woman and then signed the register. While he wrote, he glanced at the preceding signatures. There: Alex Andrews, room 322. "Can I get a room on the third floor?" he asked, and again winked at the eager woman.

※ ※ ※

Aaron had become more restless by the time Kathryn reached the State Line Café. Rocking him in her arms, she looked past several men to see a clock on the wall. It was a quarter-to-ten. John would be in soon.

She sat down at the table facing the open window and tried to pamper Aaron by pulling a biscuit from her purse and pinching off small bites, but he seemed more tired than hungry. "Come on baby boy, everything's okay," she whispered, her lips rubbing gently over his soft black hair.

She glanced out the window. A commotion had suddenly begun on the plank sidewalk. A police officer was overtaking a woman quite familiar to her, as she had often seen her intoxicated and fighting with the law on the streets. Kathryn's eyes moved back to Aaron.

"I think that kid wants something that's worth eating." The voice was that of a ghost from her past. "Give the papoose some of these black beans and rice."

Kathryn felt her own heart stop beating. The last man she'd ever want to meet again on this earth.

"My God, Alex," she said without turning. "What do you want?"

"Say hi to your husband," Alex said, sliding a bowl of steaming bean soup across the table toward Kathryn and Aaron. Without an invitation, he pulled over a chair for himself.

※ ※ ※

At the back end of the counter inside the State Line Café, the young Mexican sat stirring a cup of hot apple cider with a cinnamon stick. Trying not to be conspicuous, Rowe turned just enough to glimpse Alex, who had just perched at the table across from a red-haired woman and a dark-skinned child.

Twenty-two

HUSBAND? THE CRAZY fool!
Kathryn stared at Alex. What could he possibly want here? Why had he returned to the tri-states after all these years? Didn't he know they were divorced? Surely he knew. And surely he knew she had good reason to legalize their split. Not only had he deserted her, they had come to learn that he had sold livestock that belong to Mama and her upon his leaving.

"I'm sure glad to see you, Little Gal." His voice was devious. "I've missed the likes of a wife."

Kathryn's face twitched sharply and her eyes burned all the way to her brain at the sight of this man. She despised his sarcastic attitude. She loathed the wavy black hair and midnight-black eyes that had once turned her on. She detested the straight-faced devilish smirk on his face. To sum it up, she just didn't like Alex.

Aaron started to cry. She turned her chair to the side, bouncing him in her arms.

"I told you to feed the kid beans," Alex said, arching one brow. "The kid's hungry."

"He's too young to eat beans," she snapped angrily.

"Is that a fact?"

She nodded once, her face twitching again. Then glared at him with an evil eye. "Why did you come back here? What do you want Alex?"

"My family brings me back," he said, leaning across the table, so close she felt his hot tobacco breath on her.

"Your family doesn't live here."

"Who are you?" He leaned back in his chair and slid his fingers into his shirt pockets, and then he pulled out his Prince Albert and a package of cigarette papers. "You're my family."

Kathryn glared harder at him and tried to swallow the bitterness that rose like a fungus on her tongue.

"Aren't you my family?"

"Alex, surely you have brains enough to know I divorced you! I divorced you a long time ago."

His black eyes peered at her from his unsmiling face.

"Well, don't you know we're divorced?" she said, raising her voice in anger.

"Don't get so excited," he whispered harshly. "You're still the same little wild flower, the one with the bitter yellow blooms—my own little bitter-weed."

"Oh please spare me your poetry! I know you're after something, Alex. Let's hear it."

"Just my family," he said, putting the just-made cigarette to his mouth.

"Unless you've married somebody in recent years, you have no family here. You know I've divorced you! Now you can't tell me you don't!"

"Sure, I heard something about it." He moved closer to her and rested his elbows on the table edge. "But now, let me tell you something. I didn't sign any papers. So, as far as I'm concerned, you're still my wife."

"We're divorced, Alex! And I'm married to another man now." She turned and began rocking Aaron.

"Married to somebody else. Well, now, that's just real cute, Kathryn," he slurred, and his frown dropped to Aaron.

"Ah, Little Gal, we really have us a problem now."

"What you mean 'we'?" she snapped. "I'm sure your problems don't involve me."

"Well, you're not expecting me to let you keep the boy if you're going to be another man's wife," Alex said calmly, and again leaned back in his chair.

"What a rotten thing to say! How utterly rotten!" Kathryn said, her eyes widening in outrage.

"My dear, why are you surprised? You ain't the kid's mother. I told Shanna to go to your place and have it. I told her you're my wife. Why, I didn't know after you got my boy you'd up and marry someone else. Who's the lucky fella? Leonard?"

"You're sorry, Alex!" Kathryn yelled, her arms tightening around Aaron. "You're a sorry, sorry excuse of a man. Let me tell you something right here and now. This is my son! Mine! And not yours! No one will ever take him from me! Do you understand? He's mine!"

"He's my boy, Kathryn, and I think you know it," Alex said, his voice still calm and his eyes moving from Kathryn to Aaron. "I would have let you keep him if you hadn't married somebody else. But you did, and now I'm forced to take him."

"You leave us alone, Alex!" she demanded, standing up quickly and holding Aaron tightly to her breast. "You leave us alone! Do you hear me! I'll kill you before I allow you to take Aaron. You'd better hear me good, Alex. I'll kill you for sure. I mean it. If you dare try to take Aaron from me, I'll kill you so quickly you won't even have time for a prayer."

"Good-Lord," the cafe owner said, walking toward Kathryn's table. "What in the hell is going on here? Is this man causing you trouble, Kathryn?"

"Yes, Mack, he sure is."

Turning to Alex, Mack put his hands on his hips. "Look here Andrews. I don't know much about you, don't know your business here, and I personally don't give a damn. I think you'd better be hitting the trail 'cause I'm afraid if you stay here, you and me will have a personality conflict. Get it?"

"It's this little wild flower here that's making the fuss. I'll quiet her down."

Tears of anger fell from Kathryn's eyes. She screamed out again, "I'll kill you, Alex!"

"Look here now, mister," Mack said, easing closer, his muscled arms flexed. "Kathryn's been coming in here for years. She's never had any trouble with folks. Now, I want you to get on out and don't you be fooling around here anymore. There're a dozen other stops between here and Front Street. You best be using one of 'em."

Alex stood up. "Okay. I don't want trouble. I'm a peaceful man," he said calmly. "I'll see you later, Little Gal. And I'll take my kid."

Kathryn shook all over. Aaron, obviously feeling her fear, cried louder.

"I just want to know one thing, Alex!" she screamed out at him. "What is it you really want? Don't tell me it's this baby. You don't want him and you know it. You've never wanted anyone."

"I want my gal back," Alex said, the grin on his face deepening the wrinkles near his mouth and eyes. "My own little wild flower. I want my wife back. Divorce your new man and marry me." He tilted his head. "We can be a cozy little family. You and me and this kid. We're blood."

"I don't believe you for one minute. All you've ever wanted was money. How much, Alex? How much money is it you want to leave us alone? How much is your blackmailing going to cost me?"

"You're underestimating me, Kathryn. Would I sell my own flesh and blood? No, I would not. Nor would I just stand by and let another man play house with my wife."

"You want something," she screamed above Aaron's cries. "What is it? You tell me!"

Alex neared the door, and then paused, one hand resting on the doorknob. He turned casually toward her. "You better think about what I said. Next time I see you, I expect you to be divorced from that new man you've found. Else I'll take the kid. Just that simple. I'll be talking to the judge."

✳ ✳ ✳

To Rowe, it was obvious the red-haired woman and Alex were involved in a domestic dispute. With all the yelling, he'd had to have been deaf not to hear their argument, at least the woman's side of it. Who was this woman? Alex's wife? Rowe thought he might have heard Alex call her that.

And his comment—"I'll be talking to the judge."—must be referring to the baby. According to the woman's shrieks, Alex planned to take the child from her, and she insisted the baby wasn't his. It didn't make sense that a man like Alex would want a child, but there wasn't time to worry about his motives right now.

Alex was leaving and he needed to follow.

Rowe dropped the cinnamon stick into the cup and slid from the counter stool. He hoped he was unnoticed as he walked passed the redhead and followed Alex from the café. Alex walked south on State Line Avenue, and then turned west on Front Street. About a block farther, he turned to the right and into the Warren Hotel.

Rowe assumed Alex was going to his room now. He thought for a moment. He needed a horse, one that wasn't stolen. He passed the hotel and walked the extra block to the stable where he had already rented space for the week.

"Looking to buy a horse. A healthy fast one," he said, walking up behind the stable keeper.

The keeper turned. "Gots a good Paint. Gots 'im at the stockyards. Best that is."

"How long you had him?"

"Couple weeks." The groomsman cocked his head to the side and eyed at Rowe.

"I knows yas?"

"Not really."

"Yas been here before?"

Rowe shook his head. If the groomsman didn't recognize him, no need to draw any attention to the change in his appearance, just in case the outlaws came looking for him here.

"How much for the Paint?"

"Six."

"Why so much?"

"Good horse," the attendant said. He walked to the horse's stall and grabbed its head. Getting a good hold, he pulled back the mouth so the horse's teeth became visible. "He 'bouts three."

Rowe reached in his pocket, took out his money roll, and handed a bill to the groomsman. "Bridle and saddle come with it?"

"Keeps the bridle. Yas can find yas a saddle down at Simmons. Over on East Broad. Aims on boarding with me?"

"Nah. Be leaving town."

Rowe felt the groomsman's eyes on him as he led the dark brown Paint from the stable. Outside, he jumped on the horse and rode bareback toward Broad Street. He'd buy a good saddle and a new bridle and be ready to ride should he need to follow Alex out of town.

❈ ❈ ❈

Kathryn swallowed a glut of tears after the cafe door closed behind Alex. She moved quickly to the window, watching until he was out of sight. Then, her boot heels clicked loudly on the marble flooring to the tune of her thoughts as she paced rapidly.

Finally, she forced herself to relax some. Aaron, not so frightened now that Kathryn was quiet, sucked on his thumb and snuggled his face to her shoulder.

"What am I going to do?" she asked, turning to Mack.

She was still angry, scared, and crying when John arrived.

"Kathryn, are you upset because I'm late?" he asked, confusion in his voice.

"Oh, no, John," she sobbed, unable to hold the tears. "Something terrible has happened."

John listened intently while she told him of her encounter with Alex. "He said I have to divorce you. He said I must do it immediately, before he sees me again. If I don't do what he says, then he'll take Aaron. He claims he's Aaron's father."

John stared out the window. Finally he said, "You're obviously frightened of him." His voice was vacant. "And you believe he really can take Aaron, but I don't think so. I think maybe we better just take it easy right now and call his bluff. See what happens."

Unable to comprehend John's words, Kathryn moved about nervously. She tried to stop crying, and when tears ceased, she started jabbering again.

"I can't wait, John. Something has to be done now. He means trouble. My God, I know Alex. I know he means trouble. He will take my baby from me unless I do something to stop him. I'll lose Aaron for good. I can't lose him, John. I just can't." She dropped to a chair and searched his eyes. "And I can't lose you," she added, her voice slightly above a whisper. "I couldn't bear to lose you, John."

"Don't worry, you won't lose me." John reached over and laid his hand on her shoulder. "And I won't let him take Aaron. I'll handle things. Just trust me, Kathryn."

John was telling her not to worry, but how was that possible? Her whole happiness was at stake. Alex was trying to force her to leave John. She couldn't do that. She wouldn't. And she certainly couldn't let Alex take Aaron. She would do whatever was necessary to prevent it.

No, she couldn't stop worrying and she couldn't let John handle this situation alone. She couldn't be dependent on anyone when it came to Aaron's future, not even John. She had to fight for what she wanted. And right now what she wanted more than life was her son...and come heaven or hell, she would keep him.

"Okay, Kathryn?" John gently patted her hand.

She shook her head. "What?"

"Will you let me handle this?"

"What will you do? What can you do? Alex claims he's Aaron's father. Promise me that I'll keep Aaron."

"I'll do what I can. You're my wife."

"How will you stop Alex?"

Bridged By Love

"I don't know. We'll wait and see what he does. I don't actually believe he's serious."

Kathryn gasped. "He is serious, John. He is threatening to take Aaron. I know the snake he is."

"I think he's just blowing hot air. If he really does try to take Aaron, we can fight him in court."

Kathryn didn't say anything more. She didn't want to argue with John. She would be silent for now, but she would not ignore Alex. She had a decision to make and she would make it without involving John.

After a bowl of chili and a glass of cider, John excused himself, saying he must get back to his shop. He tried one more time to assure Kathryn he was capable of handling everything. He asked her to stay calm and not to worry.

She just looked at him and said, "John, I love you. But I have to do what I have to do to keep Aaron. He's my son. He depends on me. He's my own little baby."

John pinched her gently on the cheek and went outside. For a moment he stood near the door, bending slightly and coughing as if he were choked. Kathryn stood silently. Had she hurt John to tears? Should she check on him? But before she moved to the door, his cough had ceased and he walked away.

Kathryn sat down and tried to think above the chatter of two cowmen who had just entered the café and were whooping it up. Right now, she had to do something quickly. She couldn't just sit there and worry.

Aaron had fallen asleep. She held him so his head rested on her shoulder and hurried across the shiny floor to the door. There was one person who could tell her what to do and that was Cavin O'Tool.

Heat from the sun penetrating Kathryn's skull was not nearly as hot as the anger for Alex frying like an egg in her brain. From the café, she made a quick turn north on State Line Avenue. Cavin O'Tool's office was just ahead in a modern, brick building.

"Just let him be here," she whispered to herself.

Without even kicking dust from her boots, she clutched Aaron tightly in her arms and ran, skipping steps, up the stairs to the second floor and flung open the door to the lawyer's office. Gazing at Cavin's young assistant, Gerald Thompson, she opened her mouth to speak but no words came.

"Kathryn," Cavin said, walking toward her from the adjoining room. "How are you?"

"Oh," she blurted loudly, tears again muffling her words. "My world is ending."

"Gerald," Cavin said, "take the baby to the next room so Kathryn and I can talk."

"Cavin, Alex is back in town. He wants to take Aaron from me. But I can't give him my baby. He's my son now and I love him and he loves me."

"Sit down here, Kathryn," Cavin said, dragging a chair from the desk. He sat on the edge of the desktop and lit his pipe.

"Now tell me, why does Alex want Aaron? A person can't just up and take somebody's child because they take a notion. It's just not done."

"He says he's Aaron's father," she cried, wiping her eyes with the back of her fingers. "He says he told Shanna to have the baby at my place. He told her I was his wife."

The lawyer rubbed his chin. "Doesn't Alex know about the divorce?"

"He doesn't accept it. Cavin, there's something else. Yesterday evening John and I got married. Now Alex says I must divorce John and take him back or he will take Aaron." Noting Cavin's perplexed expression, she hesitated, and then spoke softly. "What can I do?"

"I'm pleased to hear about you and John, but now you have to tell me if or not you want Alex back."

"Of course I don't. Not one bit. I love John with all my heart. I've loved him since the first time I saw him. But, Cavin, I just can't give up Aaron. Can Alex take Aaron?"

"I don't know. If he is the child's father, and if he means business, maybe. Don't know what to tell you. You just can never tell how a judge will rule. If Alex can convince the judge that he really wants his son, then the judge is very apt to see his side."

"I won't let Aaron go," she cried. "I'll leave this town. I'll leave Texarkana and take my son with me. I'll go find Shanna and her people. Aaron and I can live in the Territory."

"Now, now, Kathryn. You're not considering John. Don't be hasty. Let's talk this over and try to figure something out." He paused. "Let's see now, did the Indian girl—what's her name...?"

"Shanna. Her name is Shanna."

"Right, right." He snapped his fingers and stood up, propping his foot on a chair so the white stripes in his trousers flashed at Kathryn. "Did Shanna write anything down? Did she sign any paper saying you could have the infant? To keep him, or to raise him, or anything like that?"

Kathryn shook her head. "No. Shanna didn't write anything for me. I'm not even sure she can write. She spoke English well enough, though. But, no, she didn't write anything out for me. I never even gave the matter a thought."

O'Tool walked to the window and looked down on the street, and then he turned back to Kathryn. "Do you know where Shanna went?"

Kathryn closed her eyes. "I can't remember if she told me or not. Best I know is that she was going to find her people in the Territory. She couldn't take Aaron because it would be unsafe for him, she said."

"Did she say anything about the baby's father? Was he white or Indian?"

"I don't remember her saying one way or the other." Holding her hand to her forehead, she stroked hard, as if rubbing a crystal ball.

"Kathryn, do you suppose she could have left here with Alex?"

"Oh God, it's possible. Is that what you think happened?"

"Yes. But then, we have to figure out why Alex is here now and she isn't, unless..."

"Unless what?" Kathryn asked anxiously.

"Unless Alex really does want you back and thinks your having his child is the way to your heart." He paused a moment. "I think what we better do is find Shanna."

"And when we find her, then what?"

"When we find her, if we find her, we can get her to sign adoption papers, if she will."

"Is that all I have to do? Find Shanna and get the papers signed?"

"It's a start."

"What about Alex? Does he have any rights? Could he protest and take Aaron away, even if Shanna does sign?"

"It's possible." O'Tool reached for her hand. "I can't make you any promises. But I'll do my damnedest to help you."

"I'll find Shanna," she said. "I'm leaving right now for the Territory. I'd better take Aaron. If I leave him here, Alex will take him from Mama just as sure as sin."

"It's a long trip for the baby, Kathryn."

"I can make it up there in a couple of days. Aaron can sleep in the buggy. I'll take his bassinet. He'll be just as comfortable as he would if he'd stayed home," she paused, and noticed the sincere way Cavin was looking at her. "I couldn't rest for a minute if I left him in the same town with that snake Alex Andrews."

"Will John go with you?"

"I don't know." She shook her head worriedly. "I just don't know. I hope he will. But whether he goes or not, I must."

Cavin's eyes peered deeply into her, as if reading a devastating fortune. "I can go with you if you'll wait a week."

"I can't wait a week. Alex could do anything during a week! Can't you come with me now?"

"No, I have an important case coming up before Judge White this week. If I lose this one, well, it could be the end of the rope for Keith Gibson."

"Is he the man who swiped the steers from that big herd that came through town about a month back?"

O'Tool nodded. "He's pleading guilty, but I'm hoping the judge will just lock him up for a while. He was poisoned on moonshine when he did it."

O'Tool went behind his desk and pulled several pieces of paper in front of him. "Have Shanna sign her name at the bottom of each of these documents. There's a copy here for her to keep, one for me, and one for the judge. Now make sure she signs each one and then you get them back here as soon as you can. I'd like to present this to the judge before Alex starts any action."

"Thank you, Cavin."

He reached in a desk drawer and withdrew another sheet of blank paper, then reached for a pen in a stand beside an inkwell. "One more thing..." he said, seating himself and dipping the pen in the well. "Let me give you a map to help you find your way."

On the way home, Kathryn told John of her plans.

"I don't want you to go, Kathryn. You are my wife. I want you to stay here. Don't go off looking for an Indian girl you barely know in a land you don't know a thing about. You aren't even sure she went to the Territory."

"I'm almost certain she did. John, I must go. And I want you to come with me."

"No, Kathryn," he said, shaking his head once. "I'm staying here and that's what I'm ordering you to do. We will fight Alex in court and do what we have to. But we won't go to the Territory. That's savage country up there." He gazed straight ahead.

She stared at him. Couldn't he see this was what had to be done? They couldn't just fight in court. The judge might think Alex was a kind and honest man. He might think he really wanted Aaron. My God, the judge might allow Alex to take her baby. She couldn't let that happen. She would fight for Aaron. She would go and find Shanna and she'd get the papers signed.

John couldn't stop her. She had never taken orders from any man and she wouldn't do so now. She loved John with her heart and soul, but she must think of Aaron. It was his entire life at stake. And his future was in her hands.

During the ride home over a road that seemed miles longer than before, Kathryn's mind was in a state between love and confusion. She could understand John's fear in her traveling alone to the Territory, but she couldn't understand his refusing to accompany her. Was he afraid of the Bad Lands? He did want her to keep Aaron, didn't he?

It was not until they reached the homestead that she told John of her decision to go north, though he had already expressed his objection.

John climbed down from the carriage and started to unhitch Sugar.

"Just leave it hooked, John," she said, without first swallowing the tightness closing off tubes in her chest. She hated to tell him; God knew how much.

"Leave it hooked? Why, Kathryn?"

"I'm leaving soon. I'm going up to the Territory. If you mind my taking your carriage, just say so."

"What are you saying?" he demanded in a raised voice.

This was out of character for John. She had never heard him talk like this. She had never seen anger in his eyes.

"Do you mean to tell me you'll go through with this absurd idea even though I object?"

She lowered her head. "John," she said, uncertainties still buzzing through her mind with his sudden voice of anger. "Please understand I have to go. It's for Aaron."

He placed his hands on her shoulders, squeezing her to shame. "You aren't going! You're staying here where you belong! You're my wife and you'll do as I say."

"I'm sorry John, but I will go," she said, shrugging loose from his grip.

"Kathryn," he said, his anger turning to frustration as he followed her to the front porch. "Listen to me. You're my wife. You're supposed to do as I say," he hesitated briefly. And then, raising his voice again, said, "If you go, we're through. I won't be here when you return."

"Where will you be?"

"I'll be in town. Back at my old room."

Without turning to face John, still standing at the porch edge, Kathryn entered the house. So John would leave her and go back to Sharleen's place. Tears filled her eyes and her soul ached for her new husband. But she had to follow her heart.

Kathryn knew Mama sensed her troubles when she met her at the door, her arms reaching anxiously for Aaron.

Without a word, Kathryn surrendered the baby and hurried to her bedroom. She changed from the dress she had so proudly worn for John, to overalls, and packed an extra pair of trousers for herself and some diapers for Aaron. Carrying the bag, she hurried into the living room.

Mama held Aaron on her hip with one arm and nervously rubbed down the side of her dress with the other. "What kind of trouble do we have, Kathryn? Where you heading off to?"

"The Territory to find Shanna. Mama, Alex is back in town and he claims Aaron is his son. He says if I don't divorce John and marry him, he will take Aaron." She touched Mama on her shoulder. "I have to go."

Mama nodded. "But why are you taking Aaron?"

"I'm afraid if I leave him here Alex will seize him." She hesitated, and then smiled softly at Mama. "I know you can take care of Aaron, probably better than me during this travel hunt, but," she said soberly, "Alex is a snake. I'll feel better having Aaron with me."

"Shanna might decide to keep him," Mama said in a worried voice.

"Yes, Mama, she might. I've thought of that. If she does, well, I just don't know what I'll do. But Mama, Shanna is a caring young woman. I know she loves Aaron and wants what's best for him. It's Alex I fear."

"When do you leave?"

"Just as soon as I throw this bag in the carriage and give Aaron a bit to eat."

John didn't offer to help as Kathryn carried the bag across the porch. Instead, he sat on the steps rubbing his fingertips together. Kathryn glanced sadly at him and wondered if she were doing wrong to the man she so dearly loved. But the baby was innocent, helpless, and needed her help now.

Mama was feeding Aaron when she went back into the house. "Aren't you going to eat some supper yourself, Kathryn?" she asked, as she dipped

Aaron's spoon into a small helping of warm mashed potatoes. "There's fried chicken and mashed potatoes and chicken gravy. That's your favorite."

Kathryn tilted her head. She wasn't hungry but perhaps she should eat. Perhaps then she would feel more like traveling. Besides, it would give her longer to be with John. Maybe he would change his mind about leaving her.

"Yeah, Mama, I think I'd better," she said, spreading plates on the table. Then she hurried to the front porch to fetch John. "Supper's all ready," she said, forcing a cheery voice. "Mama fried chicken. It's still sizzling. Can't you just taste it already?"

John said nothing.

Stooping beside him, she whispered, "Come on, John," and reached for his hand.

There wasn't much talk during supper. Kathryn nervously chewed the white meat off the wishbone and tried to make eye contact with John. He avoided her completely.

"Kathryn, do you know the way up to the Territory?" Mama asked, a worried look on her face.

"Yeah, of course I do. I just take the Texas Trail north and cross the Red River. Then I ride 'til I find the Indians."

"You sure ought to have somebody going with you," Mama said, shaking her head in bemusement. "Never thought I'd see the day when my daughter would go traipsin' off to the Territory with a little baby and nobody to protect her." Mama glanced at John, who had barely touched his chicken.

"I have to go, Mama."

"I know you do, Kathryn. I'll pack you up what's left of the chicken and some smoked ham. We have a whole pan of biscuits on the stove that haven't even been touched. Here's a jug of honey water for you to take along for Aaron."

Kathryn felt awful that John was upset about her decision. She truly wished he would come with her. He'd promised to support her. She just couldn't understand why he was so dead-set against her making this trip. He had to realize the urgency. She carried the bassinet out to the carriage and secured it on the passenger's seat. Looking back, she saw John had followed her as far as the porch. Perhaps if she asked him again, he would go with her. She went to him and gently touched his face with her fingers.

"I wish you'd come with me," she pleaded. "I can't bear to lose you. My goodness, John, we've only been together one night. One beautiful night. You can't leave me, John. I love you."

John said nothing; he just stared aimlessly beyond her.

"Look at me," she begged tenderly.

"Kathryn, I asked you not to go. I'm the man of the house. You're my wife. You're supposed to do as I say."

Bridged By Love

"And I told you I have to go. Why don't you understand? You know how much I love Aaron." She lowered her hands and lovingly rubbed over his chest. "Come with me, please, John."

"No. I'm not going to cave in to you, Kathryn. You are not wearing the pants in this family. I'm not going and I've asked you not to. I've told you we can fight this thing with your former husband in court." He paused, his eyes becoming distant. "If you go it will be alone. And, as I've already told you, I won't be here when you return." He paused again, and this time looked into her eyes. "Kathryn, you're putting your obsession of the child before the needs of your husband."

She started at him. Obsession? Was that how he defined her love for Aaron? She wanted to grab him and hold him tightly against her flesh and squeeze understanding into his soul.

How could he have these bewildered feelings? And how could he even think of leaving her when he knew how much she loved him, when she had made love with him so completely last night and again this morning? She had wanted him desperately and had given herself so shamelessly. And now he was leaving her for doing what she knew was right. How could he? If he loved her, if he truly loved her, then he should want to make her happy. He should go with her.

If he loved her, he wouldn't leave her. He should support her and wish her a safe trip and a rapid return. She wanted to tell him this, to make him understand that nothing could stop true love. Nothing could cool the deep burning that flamed inside her for him, the deep burning love she hoped he had for her. But where were the words? What could she really say to this man? He had clearly made a statement.

She could only cry now. And already she had cried so much this day.

※ ※ ※

On the front porch, John watched Kathryn pull the reins to the side and guide Sugar from the yard and onto the narrow trail. Kathryn turned, her pleading gaze only adding to the aggravation forcing its way through his veins and plunging up anger. Evidently Kathryn was more concerned with finding Shanna and getting those damn papers signed than she was in being his wife. She surely took him for his word that he would leave. Lilly would have never done this to him, he was sure. He would have to leave anyway if Kathryn ever learned the truth about the Indian girl and him. If Shanna ever saw him she would recognize him and then Kathryn would know everything anyway. He had rather split with Kathryn, here and now, than allow the chance of her coming up with ill feelings about him—such the truth would most definitely generate.

John had never intentionally hurt Shanna. He had not known that at the time he slept with her she was only fifteen-years-old. But then, most girls were married and having babies at fifteen. Anyway, whether he had touched her or not, her fate was doomed. Jake Minor sold her to any man who would pay. Still, though she had been fondled by many, there was a genuine innocence about the young woman.

Actually, John never would have gone to the Fish Camp had Jake Minor not approached him offering more than he could get from the whore house in Texarkana. Minor had been outside the house when John approached on a night when he desperately needed a woman.

The bushes around the brothel were grown up covering the front so passers-by who didn't know what was there would never stop in. John had turned from the bushy alleyway into the domicile entrance. Hearing a nearby voice, he hesitated on the stone walkway that led to the long porch.

"Name's Jake Minor," the stranger said, appearing out of nowhere, it seemed.

John turned to the man seated in a stone chair built alongside the walkway. He reached to shake his extended hand.

"Ye come here often?" the fat man asked.

"No. I come occasionally. Why?"

"I got a young woman, young as any ye find here. I'll let you have her all to yerself for the whole month."

"And why would you do that?"

"'Cause I got to go on a mission with night riders. Be gone most hours of darkness fer a while. Can't leave her by herself; she'll take off."

"You mean you keep her captive?"

"Sure do. I own her. She owes me and she ain't going nowheres until I say so."

"How you know I won't let her go?"

"'Cause I think ye like living. Ye let her go and yer life won't be worth a plug nickel." John laughed. "I don't think I want to deal with you Mister Minor."

"Ye ever had a squaw?"

"You have an Indian woman?"

Jake grinned. "A pretty one."

"No. I have never been with an Indian."

"Ye don't know what yer missing."

"But you keep her captive, Mister Minor. I don't think I could be with her under those circumstances."

"Suit yer self. If ye don't help me out, somebody else will." Jake paused. "I'll hang around here 'til another trusty-looking dude comes along. Case ye change yer mind."

John turned from Jake and started up the stone walkway toward the porch. He turned. Minor had stopped a man who had just come through the gate. *Somebody is going to be with a young Indian. Though she is captive, it may as well be me,* John thought.

Oh Kathryn. If you only knew the story. Alex wasn't there with Shanna. I was. I was there the whole time. And the timing was right. John wondered why Alex thought he was the child's father? Perhaps he wasn't sure of Aaron's age. Perhaps Alex thought the child was older than he really was.

Searching for the Brown Girl

Twenty-three

SUGAR PULLED THE carriage into rolling terrain just north of the city. It seemed to Kathryn she had been on the trail for days, but this was only the first day and already the sun was crossing over Texas.

"You're doing good, Sugar," Kathryn said in a calm voice. Regardless of what anybody said about animals, she was quite confident her mare understood—if not the words, certainly her tone and mood. "You're doing better than I am about now." She held the reins loose to give Sugar freedom of gait.

She wiggled her toes about inside her boots. How many miles had she traveled in this wooded wilderness? Twenty? More than twenty? She'd allow Sugar to keep the pace as long as Aaron slept, then they'd take a rest stop.

Moments later, Sugar's stride slowed. "What's wrong, girl?" Kathryn called. Then the mare stopped and raked her hoof on the gravel. "Oh, heaven forbid," Kathryn said, raising her hand to her forehead. The foot Sugar had problems with a couple months back was ailing. She dropped the reins and climbed from the carriage. She was glad she had changed into her overalls before leaving home.

"Looks like you picked up a rock. We'll fix you right up." She reached into her bosom and brought out a knife she had placed there for extra protection. She had, since childhood, carried a knife on her person to have in case of trouble. She flicked open the weapon and gently dug into the mare's hoof.

Once she had scraped out the gook and matter, Kathryn dropped the hoof and stroked the mare's mane. "You'll be okay now," she whispered to the animal.

With her hoof cleaned, Sugar strutted on, covering more trail that evening than Kathryn had expected she would. But the more they traveled, the more the mare favored the wounded foot. And Sugar wasn't used to pulling a carriage. Kathryn definitely must find a place to stop. Her eyes searched the trail. It looked as if there might be a clearing ahead, if so, there would likely be a spring. That would be the perfect place for Sugar to rest and for her to catch a little shut-eye.

"It's all down hill now, Sugar," she said, rubbing the mare's mane before climbing on the carriage seat.

Sure enough, just prior to reaching the clearing, the spill of water onto rocks brought pleasure to Kathryn's ears and a smile to her face. She reined Sugar on the few thousand feet or so to where water fell over a hill of boulders then spilled over a long bed of brown leaves before venturing off into the forest. In the evening light, Kathryn unhooked the carriage and led Sugar to the brook. She stood alongside the mare while she drank. Then, knowing Sugar would never wander off, Kathryn removed the mare's bridle.

Hearing Aaron's restlessness in his bassinette, Kathryn returned to the carriage. "Come on baby," she pampered, lifting him into her arms. He was wet and hungry, she knew. She was thankful she had brought plenty diapers and that Mama had sent a goodly size tin of mashed foods.

After she fed Aaron, Kathryn spread a blanket over the cool earth. She brought out another blanket for cover and caressed Aaron under her wing and let him fall into dreamland. When he was sleeping soundly she put him in his bassinette, still secured in the carriage. Like at home, Aaron would sleep through the night.

Kathryn sat on a log of petrified wood a few feet from the carriage and allowed a brisk, cool breeze to brush her face. She watched her silhouette in the moonlight, watched as the wind sweep her hair from her face and thoughts of John into her mind. She longed to feel the warmth of his body, to pull him close and know he would stay.

She rubbed her hands over her face and slipped to the ground where she lay staring at the star-filled sky and the semi-full waxing moon. She remembered the day three years ago when she had first seen John. She remembered the polite way he had taken off his hat and bowed his head to her, and how he had smiled, and how his eyes had glistened when he looked at her as if he was hurting to hold her. Lord, she loved how he looked at her. She remembered the way he held her hand and gently squeezed it, making a want for him stir through her whole body. She remembered their wedding, the vows they'd made only yesterday.

What would happen now? Would John truly be gone when she returned?

"John," she cried out, burying her face in the grass. "John, I love you. I love you so much." He couldn't leave her. He just couldn't. Not now that they belonged to each other.

If only he could understand...

※ ※ ※

"Easy here Chief," Rowe said, pulling the reins to slow the Paint's pace. A voice from somewhere in his head sprang forward and told him to take precautions so that he not be noticed as he followed the white stallion eastward out of town. Where was Alex going tonight? Would he lead the way to Shanna? If he knew her whereabouts, he would likely go for her and try to collect the thousand dollar reward offered by the outlaws. That was a lot of money in anybody's pocket.

Staying out of sight, Rowe followed the stallion along a dark tree-canopied trail before turning onto a sandy moonlit lane several miles from town. Rowe pulled the reins enough to lead the Paint into the grasses along the tree line. The stallion slowed, then Alex guided it to a thicket of shrubs and halted it about a hundred feet from a lighted log house.

Rowe reined the Paint into a tree cover. He reached into his pocket and pulled out a plug of Red Man chewing tobacco. Used to patiently waiting, he could certainly hang here as long as it took to see Alex's interest in this house.

Less than an hour later, a man with a bag came out of the log house and approached a horse tied to the front railing. He tied the bag to the horse's saddle, and then he mounted and turned the horse toward the trail.

Rowe watched as Alex backed the stallion farther into the thicket. He reined the Paint higher onto the incline. Holding the reins steady, Rowe curiously watched the man pass. Rowe stayed put, keeping his eyes on Alex as he emerged from the thicket. Alex's horse fell into suit behind the man who had come from the house. Rowe waited for Alex to pass. He could now follow the two, or he could—one way or another—see who occupied the dwelling.

He glanced back at the lighted house just as a lamp went out.

Rowe rode from the grassy incline toward the quite house and stopped in the thicket where Alex had just moments ago waited. He dismounted and, avoiding as much moonlight as possible, hovered among the shrubs and slipped quietly to the front porch. He cautiously walked around the house, hovering low underneath window seals. He heard nobody inside. But someone was there; a person had shut off the light after the man had left. Careful he wasn't heard, Rowe peeked through one window and then another. He could see nobody. He went around the house and onto the back porch, then, hearing a noise from inside, ducked around the corner. The back door opened and someone walked out onto the porch.

"Who's here? Speak before I start shooting."

It was the voice of an older woman.

Rowe stayed totally still.

"You here somewhere, John?" the woman asked.

John. Maybe that was the man who Alex had followed off.

A few moments later, the woman walked back into the house. He heard the door latch behind her. Perhaps he was on a wild goose chase. Perhaps this was the home of a nice old couple that never hurt anybody.

But why was Alex spying on them, and why did the man leave the house? He could figure that out later. He'd keep a watch on this house to see who came and went. Right now, he would catch up with Alex and the man he was following.

It didn't take Rowe long to fall into procession. In single file and keeping their distance, the trio reached town. Rowe followed Alex. His Paint's hoofs clicking along on a bricked street. Alex stopped at a long brick building. Rowe slowed his mount until Alex was off the horse and inside the facility, then he rode forward. He dismounted, lapped the Paint's reins over a picket railing, then, lowering the rim of his tall gray hat to shadow his face, walked on the stone-covered earth through a garden patio. He walked casually to a door under an arch that identified the place as the Dixie House Saloon, on through swinging doors, and into a room of gay festivities. The chandeliered room was filled with tables of gamblers. Without hesitation, Rowe headed straight for the bar.

"Beer," he said to the bartender. Though he wasn't much of a drinker, he felt the need to fit in. "And a shot of shine," he said, taking special note of the expression on the bartender's face.

Sipping at the beer, Rowe glared around the gambling hall until he noticed Alex. He had perched at a table with three other five-card-stud players. Was the man Alex had been following one of the three? He couldn't tell, since he had not gotten a close look at the man.

But the woman on the log-house porch had called him John.

Keeping his distance, he watched the gamblers, also fancy-dressed women as they fondled around them. None were Shanna.

Nothing's going on here, Rowe said to himself. Already the clock on the wall showed 3:32 a.m. But then, as sudden as spit, one of the gamblers playing with Alex jumped from his chair.

"Yer a liar and a coward."

Rowe rose from his stool and inched closer to see what the ruckus was about. Alex jumped up. "I hope you're not talking to me, J.D."

"I'm talking at 'cha. Yer a liar and a coward. Yer a cheating."

"Now how can you say that? I don't cheat."

"Then how come ye got money I had marked just to catch ye with?"

Alex eyed the table. "Guess it was pushed over to my stack."

"Give it back here."

"You can have it. I don't want it if I didn't earn it."

The player sneered. "I'm saying it again. Yer a liar and a coward and a cheat." He pushed the barrel of a Colt .45-caliber pistol close to Alex's nose. "Ye ever try anything like this on me again and I'll take my gun and I'll shoot yer right eye plum out of its socket. Ye ever hear of Sheriff Dixon? Well, I may not own any gambling houses like he did, but I'm just as mean and just as crooked. If'n that sheriff can go shooting another gambler's eye out, so can I."

Rowe walked on past the gamblers, through the swinging doors and into the cool night. Outside, he waited in the garden. At nearly daybreak, Alex staggered from the gambling hall and mounted his stallion. The mount started to move, but Alex pulled the reins quickly, and the horse neighed. Then he geared the horse into the garden, practically running upon Rowe, and stopped. The horse neighed. "Hey Mexican, you been following me?" he asked, his voice slurred and nasty.

※ ※ ※

Before dawn, Kathryn hitched Sugar to the carriage. A little while later, Aaron woke up whining. The baby was hungry no doubt. Kathryn opened the food bag Mama had packed for them. She fed him mashed vegetables and spooned spring water into his mouth until he had enough. Then she ate a biscuit herself.

Soon, ready to leave the clearing, Kathryn climbed onto the carriage driver seat. "Let's go," she called out as she shook the reins. Again, she headed toward the Territory.

It was still morning when Sugar started limping again. Kathryn checked the mare's foot but found nothing wrong. As they traveled on, the limp became worse. Sugar stopped often and scratched the gravely earth. As she pulled the buggy on, her gait slowed more and more. Something had to be done. Kathryn couldn't expect the poor mare to keep pulling the carriage with a lame foot. Besides, she didn't know how much further she'd have to travel before reaching her destination. And once there, no telling how much running around she'd have to do before finding Shanna. Sugar couldn't make it. That was a fact she had to face. The next house they came to, she would stop and try to borrow a horse.

By mid-morning, Sugar had practically stopped walking. Suddenly Kathryn saw a store. There were horses posted to a log in front. "Thank God," she whispered.

Inside the store, an old man stood near a stone fireplace.

"My mare is lame," Kathryn explained. "I'd like to leave her here and take a horse. I'll return your horse and collect my mare on my way back through."

The old man scratched his head. "That'll cost you six-bits a day. And you have to leave something for security."

She raised her brows. "I can give you six-bits, but I need everything I have in the carriage."

He squinted, and his skinny, splotched face became overly wrinkled as he tilted his head and allowed his full attention to fall on Kathryn's hand. "You don't need to be wearing this do you?" he asked, pointing to her wedding band.

A lump grew in her throat. Her ring. The golden band John had placed on her finger only two nights before. She clasped her hand to her heart.

"What about my mare? Isn't she security enough?"

"You're crazy, woman. I don't need a lame mare. Leave the ring or it's no deal."

For a moment she stared ahead. "How much for that jerky?"

"Two-cents a strip."

"Gimme one."

She paid, then slowly slipped the ring from her finger and handed it over. Without looking up, she turned and hurried out to unhitch Sugar.

"I'll be back for you soon, girl," she whispered, rubbing the mare's mane. "You get all better, now, you hear."

※ ※ ※

From the window in his elegant room at the Warren Hotel, Rowe watched Front Street below—the vast milk wagons, horse-pulled trolleys moving hastily over iron tracks, a band of cotton wagons, dressed-up women with parasols, and an array of riders on horses traveling past the railroad station.

Many things had happened before he had returned to his room last night. Alex had confronted him. Of course, Alex was too drunk to remember the question he had asked two seconds after he had asked it. He had just hem-hawed around and had practically fallen from the stallion as he meandered it along the darkened streets to the Warren Hotel. What was Alex all about, anyhow? What did he have up his sleeve for today?

Rowe noticed a crowd gathering in the railroad yard around a man hanging from a trestle. The lynching had occurred the night before about the time he was returning to the hotel. It seemed that a band of masked gunmen had hanged the man after a judge had found him guilty of cruelty to his thirteen-year-old wife. The crazed fellow had strung the girl up by her feet and branded her twice with a cow iron. Seemed that except for one, the herd of police marshals watching the jailed man had gone out for a bit to eat and a group of masked raiders had overpowered the marshal and strung the man up.

They were probably eating in the depot café, Rowe though in humor. *Probably got what he deserved.*

Rowe watched the hullabaloo over the ordeal continuing on the street below. He wondered if the hanging man might have been one of Jake Minor's outlaw gang. Glancing from the mob of observers, Rowe noticed three men walking from the hotel entrance. They stood on the walkway talking for a few moments, and then crossed Front Street to the train station. Keeping his eye on the street below, he rubbed his clean-shaved chin. Moments later, he saw Alex step from the hotel. Rowe quickly grabbed his room key and hat, checked to make sure he had his roll of bills, and hurried down the three flights of stairs. He stood at the hotel entrance and watched until Alex had crossed State Line Avenue. Then he continued his pursuit.

※ ※ ※

It didn't take long for Kathryn to figure out why the horse she had rented was named Crazy Sam. The stud was all spirited and ready to move. After developing a trot, it would break into a gallop and then try to run. Repeatedly, in order to control the beast, Kathryn would have to pull it to a halt. In two hours time, it seemed, Sam had covered as much ground as Sugar had covered all evening the day before. She would reach the Territory before no time at all.

They reached the next spring about the time the sun moved somewhat past noon. Kathryn stopped Crazy Sam and slowly climbed from the carriage. She barely touched ground with one foot and then the horse reared and pulled and started to run.

Fear rushing to her heart, she held onto the carriage and ran beside it until she got a good grip on the seat rail. She pulled herself up behind the horse and grabbed the reins.

"Stop, you confounded despicable harebrain," she yelled, pulling the leather straps with all her strength. She tugged so hard the horse's head pulled to the side. Crazy Sam reared and neighed like an unbroken stud.

"You're a confounded fool! We're going right back to that spring whether you want to or not," she said to the horse, anger flushing her to tears. "You might as well learn something right here and now you crazy outfit you. I'm the ramrod and you're going to do as I say. Next time you pull a fool stunt like that I'm mighty apt to whap you upside the head with something. And don't you think I won't."

Realizing she was talking to a horse that could care less about her feelings, she breathed deeply through her nose and tried to still her trembling hands. Had she not been close enough to hold onto the carriage when Sam had taken off running, Aaron could have been hurt, even killed. She trembled even more at the thought.

After that incident she was careful not to let go of Crazy Sam's reins until she had found a place to tie them. She wouldn't chance this idiot stud taking off with Aaron again. The mere thought brought terror to her heart.

That evening, Kathryn held Aaron on the blanket with her through the night. The next morning, she had the carriage ready to roll before she climbed aboard with Aaron.

Evening was quickly approaching. Kathryn arched her back and peeped behind her at Aaron in the bassinette, kicking and waving his fists. Then, "Whooaa," she called, pulling the reins so hard the horse turned its head sideways and whinnied as it came to a stop. She reached into her knapsack and pulled out the map Cavin O'Tool had drawn. The trail was narrow, as he had noted it would be. Trees and hills fit the pattern to a tee. She put the map back into the bag and shook the reins. The Red River was close. She could taste the clayish mist as the air settled on her tongue.

She reined the horse around a bend. Yes, there—Drake's Ferry lay just ahead.

What a sight, she marveled at the large raft. As Cavin had noted, the vessel was plenty big enough to carry the horse and carriage across the water. The Territory lay just beyond this long body of red water.

Kathryn geared Sam to the small building. A middle-aged man came out to greet her. "Looking to cross?" he asked knowingly. "Cost ye a bit."

"Sure." Kathryn smiled at the gentleman and tossed him a quarter. "We're ready whenever you are."

"This way."

The man led the team aboard the good-sized raft. Kathryn kept one hand on the reins and the other on Aaron's bassinette. Should Crazy Sam leap from the raft, she'd have a hold on Aaron.

But her fears were unjust. In no time, the raft had reached the north side of the river and the man was leading the team off.

"Catch ye on yer way back this way," he said.

"Thanks." Kathryn smiled and waved good-by. She had reached the Indian Territory.

Now, on the fourth day of her journey, Kathryn steered Crazy Sam well into a pine tree thicket to hide the team from any possible bandits. She hopped down from the buggy and held her arms high in the air and then bent to touch her toes to force stiffness from her body. *This is the longest ride I've ever taken*, she told herself.

She walked a few yards from the buggy and using her booted foot, raked away brush to clear a spot for a fire. She placed stones around the small clearing and gathered sticks for the center. Hurrying to the carriage, she pulled a match from John's smoking tray.

She and Aaron would sleep here on a blanket atop the soft pine needles near the warm fire.

Before daybreak, Kathryn got Crazy Sam on the move again. The Territory wasn't exactly what she had figured. She had expected to see Indian folks running around all over the place. So far, she had seen none.

A short while before noon, Kathryn stopped the horse and looked from the hillside onto a village of a half-dozen adobe-type storefronts grouped in the valley.

"Shanna be here," she whispered. "Please be here."

Kathryn reined Crazy Sam toward the village and tied him to the railing in front of a trading post. This building, like the relay station where she had picked up Crazy Sam, was made of logs and muck that had aged to a weathered gray. She looked around, her eyes gliding over a couple teepees spaced closely to the right of the trading post.

"Won't know what's here 'til we go in," she whispered, lifting Aaron from the carriage. Holding the baby so his legs hugged her waist, she anxiously stepped onto the plank porch, took a deep breath, and entered through the open doorway.

Inside the store, she stood motionless for a few seconds, her eyes suddenly glued to the center of the room where three braves dressed in animal skin pants and vests stood in a leisurely fashion. Beyond the Indians, long shelves filled with commodities lined the wall behind numerous animal skins that hung from ceiling rafters.

A heavy-set middle-aged white man with beady brown eyes and brown hair hanging to his shoulders sat on a wicker chair near the long plank counter. The smell of peaches rose from the smoking pipe in his hand. As Kathryn walked toward him, he gazed up at her, raising a thick gray eyebrow as if he were intrigued with the sight of a woman.

Aaron must have felt the anxiety that suddenly rushed through her body. His tiny fist pulled at her shirt and he buried his face against her breast. She kissed him on his head. Swallowing, she walked on to the gentleman she suspected was the storekeeper.

"My name is Kathryn," she said, offering her hand and at the same time, feeling a new burst of courage. "I'm looking for a young Indian girl called Shanna."

The man's dark eyes seemed to bore right through her. "The name's Okie," he said finally. "Where ye be from?"

"Down in the Ark-la-tex," she answered. The man seemed quite friendly.

"That be near Louisiana parishes?"

She smiled comfortably. "Just down the road a bit to Dixie town."

Okie rubbed his unshaved chin. "I was down around there when I was a might-bit younger. I got my start trading with the Cadocochu tribe down along the Red River, near Dooley's Ferry." He shook his head and grinned. Now his face carried gentleness. "Tell me 'bout Texarkana. Is it really a big frontier town like folks says?"

"Yeah. It's big, too big really. Getting bigger all the time. Right now there's a bank building going up eight windows high. And the streets are so wide it takes a body might near all day to cross one, and streetcar tracks run everywhere." She paused. "There's enough cotton sold on the streets every day to cover the whole state of Texas."

"Is Texas really a state? I heared that's just hogwash. That it's really Mexico."

"The newspapers say Texas is a state so I reckon it is." She hesitated, and looked Okie in the eye.

"Okie," she said, changing the subject, "I'm looking for an Indian girl. She's a bit thin, yet she's taller than I am. Her hair hangs in a braid to her waist, and she's really quite pretty. Have you seen her around here?"

He held his hand up, moving it about and pointing at nothing. "Indian tribes living all around here. Indians in and out all the time. Ye can hang around if ye want to. Maybe ye see the squaw yer looking fer. Indian women all come across about the same to me."

Kathryn looked pleadingly at Okie. Should she tell him why she was looking for Shanna? She took a deep breath. "Shanna's my friend. She stayed at my house. She taught me to fish with my hands."

Okie snickered. "Ye mean to tell me ye comed all the way up here hunting a squaw 'cause she teached ye how to catch a fish. It's a long haul to Texarkana." He leaned back on his chair. "Ye got more of a reason fer finding that squaw than yer letting on. Ain't it got something or another to do with that little feller yer riding on yer hip?"

"Please, Okie. I need to find her. It's so very important."

Kathryn could feel the eyes of the three braves on her. She turned, catching the gaze of a tall, handsome young brave who had just entered the store. Except for a pair of buckskin breeches, his brown body was bare.

She turned back to Okie. "You see, I have to get Shanna to sign some papers for me."

Okie sucked on his pipe and his head nodded amusingly. The sickening taste of peach tobacco floating from the pipe and into her nostrils had become as thick as fog. How did tobacco get such a flavor? Okie surely mixed the tobacco with peach peelings.

Desperately, she turned again toward the Indians. "Do any of you know a young Indian woman named Shanna?" she asked boldly.

Nobody answered. They looked at each other and chattered among themselves.

Okie laughed out loud.

"What's so confounded funny?" she demanded.

"Ain't 'cha ever been round Indians before? Half of 'em don't know what yer saying."

"These men don't speak English?"

"Nah, not to brag on." Okie took the pipe from his lips and allowed smoke to trickle from his mouth as he talked. "Let me tell ye something. I've dealed with oodles of Indian tribes in my days. Mind-ye, none of 'em ever talked the same stuff."

Kathryn held her head back, her eyelids tightening together. Good-Lord-a-mercy. Shanna could be anyplace. Anyplace. She might never find her. What if Shanna had disappeared forever? How would she fight Alex then?

Would she have to go back home without getting the papers signed? Would she have to return now and do what John had pleaded that she do in the first place? Did she hurt John, and possibly lose him, without accomplishing her goal?

Perhaps, if she had not been exhausted, she could have dealt with anything that came upon her. But she was tired, too tired, and hurt, and defeated. Her wet eyes stared tearfully at a braided rug hanging from the ceiling and covering nearly a whole wall. Feeling she could not breathe, she opened her mouth just a little and when she did, sobs sprang forth.

"Hey, hey," Okie babbled. He stood up quickly and offered his handkerchief. "What's all the crying fer? I was just gabbing." He rubbed his whiskers anxiously and his dark eyes squinted. "Sure didn't aim on making misery fer ye. Yer apt to find that squaw yer looking fer. Blow yer nose gal. See if'n ye can be getting straight now, ye here?"

Kathryn wiped her eyes and looked around at the three braves standing in a huddle and the one who had entered the store after her. He walked to the three and said something. Then they all mumbled uneasily and stared at her and Okie.

"I'm sorry," she apologized. "I don't know why I started crying. That isn't like me at all."

Okie grinned.

"Well, it isn't," she snapped, wiping her eyes with her fingers. "I've never broken down like that. Never."

"Don't fret 'bout it. Sit here." He pulled forward a chair and placed it near the one where he had sat earlier. "Rest yerself and tell me why yer looking fer the squaw."

"Aw, what's the use? You can't help me anyway."

"What'd she do, drop that kid off on ye? If that's the case she probably ain't gonna be taking him back, not if he ain't got a daddy, even if'n ye do find her."

"What you mean?"

"Indian folks don't go in fer squaws having bastard babies."

Kathryn sat on the chair Okie offered and tightened her arms around Aaron. "It's nothing like that," she said. "I love this child and now Alex is going to take him."

Okie removed the pipe from his mouth, his eyes burning into Kathryn's face. "Alex? That's not yer everyday name. Alex who?" he asked.

"Andrews. Alex Andrews."

"Where's he at?" Okie dropped his hand on his knee and leaned closer to Kathryn.

"Do you know Alex?" Kathryn asked hopefully.

"Ye-mighty-right I know 'im. Where's he at?"

"Texarkana. Why do you want to know?"

"Well hell fire, I know a lots of folks who'd like to get they's hands on that rattlesnake."

Thoughts shook in Kathryn's brain. If Okie knew Alex, then he must know Shanna. "Was Alex here?"

"Ye can bet yer boots he was here." He put the pipe back in his mouth.

"Did he have a girl with him?"

"I heared he had a squaw. A pretty one."

Excitement stirred through Kathryn's veins. Relief, it was relief she felt.

"Ye think maybe she's the squaw yer looking fer?"

"Yep, she surely must be. You say she was pretty, that sounds like Shanna."

"I heared she's young and pretty. So most the squaws that's young be pretty. What about it?"

"Well, did Alex call her Shanna?"

"I never heared her called that name. Round here she be Yellow Bird."

"Yellow Bird," Kathryn repeated the name softly. "Please, where is she?"

Okie shook his head and frowned. "Don't know where the squaw be. Ye can let me tell ye a few things about Alex Andrews, though. When he comed here, he stealed from them Indian folks." He looked at Kathryn accusingly.

"I don't know much about the relationship he had with the squaw. I heared she was hiding out. He was s'posed to help the Indians some how or another and ended up taking off with they's furs and selling 'em they's own guns. I'm telling ye, he sure 'nough did pull the wool over they's eyes,"

Okie muttered, as if keeping the statement from the braves.

Kathryn shook her head regretfully. "I believe every word you've told me. That sounds about like something Alex would do. And what about Shanna, I mean, Yellow Bird? Was she gone, too?"

"Nah, he leaved the squaw here. I don't think she knowed what he was aiming to do." Okie leaned back on his chair and once again puffed on his pipe.

Kathryn felt she was getting closer to answers. She could endure the awful smell of stale peach if it meant finding Shanna. Shanna had been in this area, and not so long ago. Okie knew more. He had to. "What happened to Yellow Bird then?"

Okie took another puff of his pipe. "Ah, she's sommers 'round here. I don't know if she stayed with her people or not. They's was rightly upset after that deal Alex pulled."

Feeling uncomfortable, Kathryn looked around at the Indians. The handsome young brave was still staring at her. She wanted to ask Okie who he was, but she didn't want him to hear. He seemed to know exactly what she and Okie were saying. For-goodness-sake, Shanna spoke English very well. It was quite possible other Indians could do so suitably enough.

Aaron twitched on her hip. He had been quiet since she entered the trading post, but now he was becoming a bit restless and hungry. The poor baby was sucking on his fist. She had kept him fed throughout the trip, but without milk. Would be nice to find milk for him here.

"I got to go now," she said, looking down at Aaron. "Do you have a cow around here someplace? My baby needs milk."

Okie pointed. "There's an old Indian that stays in a teepee right 'round the corner. He got a Jersey. Jest go on out there and get ye some milk for the kid. Don't bother to ask him 'cause he can't talk no hows. Everybody takes milk. I think that's why he keeps the cow. That's the only time he gets company."

"How sad," she said, getting up. "How about letting me have a piece of that jerky?" She reached into her pocket and pulled out two pennies.

"Just smile at that old Indian. Makes him feels real good. He be thanking yer his friend," Okie jeered.

"I will be," Kathryn said, politely, and tilting her head.

She hurried to the carriage and pulled out Aaron's tin dish and a quilt. Then she went to the teepee that was partly hidden behind a stand of small pine trees. She spread the quilt on the hard, red earth and lay Aaron on it.

The old Indian was sitting on the ground in front of the teepee. She smiled and nodded. She really felt she should say something, but she didn't. She went to the cow and knelt beside it. She looked back at the Indian and, seeing a pleasant smile on his face, waved. She smiled and winked, and then held the dish under the cow's teat and pumped milk into it.

When the dish was filled, she again smiled at the old Indian and nodded her "thanks." She then returned to the quilt where Aaron lay.

Kathryn had almost finished nursing Aaron when a noise coming from behind seized her attention. She jerked around quickly. There, standing straight and tall was the handsome young brave who had stared at her while she had spoken with Okie inside the trading post. His face was straight and his brown chest glistened golden in the sunlight.

Twenty-four

IN THE CITY, Rowe followed Alex to at least a half-dozen gambling halls spread over areas on both Arkansas and Texas sides of town. It was beginning to looks as if he had nothing better to do than throw money around like he owned a gold mine. Rowe was beginning to wonder if he knew anything of the whereabouts of Shanna, or if he was just bullying the outlaw riders.

Rowe sipped lightly at a mug of beer, all the while keeping an eye on Alex as he gambled for big stakes at a seven-card-stud table. He watched as pretty painted ladies swooped around the gambler as if he were a tree shaking off golden leafs. Occasionally, Rowe detected a few words of the conversation between Alex and the same three men he had gambled with at different times in different saloons. He kept moving over stool-by-stool to get closer to the action.

"We're going into this together. I don't want to hear any crap after you get the land," the dealer said to Alex as he dropped a card on the table.

Alex tapped the card and eyed the dealer. "Don't you trust me?"

"Shoot! You ain't talking to a woman now," the dealer said with a mordant laugh. "You don't come through with the deal, I'll shoot your poker fingers off."

Then a pretty blond-haired lady in pink stopped rubbing Alex's shoulders. She looked at Rowe and, puckering her thick rosy-lips, walked toward him.

Just what I need, Rowe thought, *one of Alex's women to attract attention my way.*

Rowe quickly tossed a coin on the bar and hurried toward the swinging doors. The woman followed him. Outside, he stopped and turned to the woman. "You need something?" he asked, pulling a Red Man plug from his jacket pocket.

"I was about to ask you that," she said with a smile. "I know you've been watching Alex."

Rowe looked into the pretty woman's blue eyes. Perhaps she knew something. "Did Alex sic you on me?"

"Alex just pays us to rub his shoulders, that's all," she said, her sexy voice maintaining a drawl.

"So why are you here?"

"You want to know about Alex. I know a little about him."

"Ever see him with a young Indian girl? Long black hair?" He raked his hand across his lower back to demonstrate length.

The woman raised her brows. "You one of 'em who's after the reward? I've noticed the wanted posters around town," she said, maintaining an insinuative tone.

"I'm looking for the girl. I'm not after the reward."

"I haven't seen her," the woman said, again puckering her lips in a teasing way. "I can do anything for you she can, Poncho," she guaranteed, a smile forming under her raised brow.

"The girl's my friend. She needs my help."

"And you think Alex might know where she is?"

"Possibly."

"That why you following him." The painted woman swayed as she talked and kept her eyes curiously on him.

Rowe wondered whether this woman could be trusted, but what did he have to lose? If she knew he was tagging Alex, there was a good chance others knew it, too.

"That's why I'm following him. Seeing if he goes to her," Rowe said, finally, his eyes studying the pink lady.

"Sure I can't do anything for you, Poncho?" she said, reaching her hand to his cheek.

"Not if you don't know Shanna."

"Shanna?"

"The Indian girl."

"I've heard the name," she said, a bit skeptically.

"Now we're getting somewhere." He pushed his hat back on his forehead, reached into his pocket and pulled out a money roll. He freed two greenbacks and swished them over the woman's powdered nose. "Find out what Alex knows. I'll give you two more just like them."

The woman took the money. "You got it, Poncho."

※ ※ ※

Kathryn stared at the good-looking young brave with an analyzing eye.

"You hunt for woman?" he asked.

"Yes. She's called Shanna, or Yellow Bird."

"Why you search for Yellow Bird?"

"I need her. Yellow Bird is the only person in the world who can help me," she said, her nerves twisting into the usual knot in her stomach.

The brave's narrow eyes were like those of a yellow wolf protecting cubs. Kathryn braced herself for anything that might come. Could this Indian help her find Shanna, or was his intention to harm her? She swallowed again, painfully, as she gulped down a ball of air. "Please, can you tell me of Yellow Bird?"

"Whose papoose you tend?"

"This is my son. His name is Aaron."

"Let the papoose drink. When finished, I come back. Take you to Yellow Bird." With those words he turned and his long strides carried his lean frame from her to the store porch where he joined the other braves.

Kathryn sank to the quilt. Finally, something good was coming of her trip. "Everything's going to be okay, baby," she said, touching Aaron and allowing his hand to grip her finger.

The old Indian's eyes stayed on her while she fed Aaron. There was a chance he'd understand if she said something to him. She stood up. "I'm going over to my carriage to fetch a pail." She pointed. "I'm leaving here soon and I want to take extra milk for my baby."

The lines in his leathery cheeks deepened and his face, turning into an ear-to-ear grin, pleased Kathryn.

Reaching the carriage, Kathryn untied Crazy Sam and led him to the water trough. "Drink up, you crazy stud you. This might turn out to be a long journey."

After watering Sam, Kathryn filled a pail with milk, then sat down on the ground next to Aaron and waited for the brave to return. She tickled Aaron and played coo-chee-coo, making him laugh out loud, and every once in a while she spoke casually to the old Indian. She knew he was getting great pleasure from her visit and she wished she had more time to give. He was surely a lonely soul, living there all the time, watching different tribes come and go. He must be starved for companionship.

Half-an-hour lapsed before the brave returned. "We go now?" he asked, his voice stiff.

"I'm ready," Kathryn said, lifting Aaron. She followed the brave toward her carriage and, turning briefly, she waved good-bye to the old Indian.

"You follow," the brave said, and leaped onto a bareback Paint.

Kathryn guided Sam close behind the Paint, up the trail northward, for more than an hour before he turned onto a narrow trail where tree limbs leaned close to the wagon-wheel ruts. Every once in a while, her eyes would drift from the trail to a framed house with grass growing from the roof. The further she followed the Paint, the higher the hills became and the slower the carriage moved. After about an hour of manipulating the buggy through the deep ruts, the brave bent forward and steered the pony's head northward again.

Holding onto the reins, Kathryn eased her hips from the seat and moved about to relieve her back of stiffness. She arched slightly, her curves deviating from one side to the other. Then she sat again and stretched out her legs.

Suddenly the brave turned the pony into a large clearing.

She followed.

Goodness, she thought, this is some settlement. It was much larger than the one back at the trading post. Small houses built mostly of logs and mud spread spaciously about the area. Several Indian men, women, and children clothed in animal hides walked to and fro among storefronts and pines.

The brave rode deep into the settlement between two rows of small log houses. Near the end, he called out "Whoa!" to his Paint, bringing the horse to a halt. Several barefoot children ran to him, giggling and pulling at his legs, as if begging him to join them in play. Dismounting, he muttered a few words and they scurried off. Feeling completely safe now, Kathryn watched as the brave moved toward her.

"We here," he said, pointing at a small house to the right of the carriage. "Yellow Bird here. Come."

Kathryn suddenly lost all feeling in her body and her mind spun in an unusually odd whirl. She shook her head to bring focus to her brain. She had come all this way to find Shanna and now that she was here, she was terrified. *Oh God,* she said to herself. *What if Shanna has changed her mind about Aaron? What if she won't sign the papers? What if she takes Aaron from me?*

Fears sweeping her mind, she stood silently and closed her eyes. "Lord, Your will be done," she whispered devoutly, though she didn't feel too Christian nowadays. She opened her eyes and focused on the house before her, and then on Shanna standing in the opening. She was clothed in a long burlap-looking garment draped from her shoulders and her hair was pulled to one side in a long braid. She tilted her head slightly and her eyes peered into Kathryn's.

Kathryn cleared her throat.

"This who you search for?" the brave asked, shifting his weight from thigh to thigh.

Bracing herself, Kathryn nodded. She started toward Shanna, and then suddenly she remembered she had not tied Sam. She quickly grabbed the reins and went to the front of the carriage. There she tied the ropes around a tree trunk. Inside the carriage, Aaron was sleeping soundly. She reached for the papers her lawyer had drawn up; then again she turned to Shanna.

"Hello Shanna," she drawled, honestly pleased to see her.

Shanna nodded, consternation showing on her face. "Why you come here, Kathryn?" she asked restlessly.

"Shanna," she said, her voice stammering in her own ears. She raised her hand to wipe sweat from her forehead. "I need your help."

"You need help, Kathryn? You helped when I needed. My turn is to help you. Come," she said, motioning Kathryn into her hut. "Sit here," Shanna said, pointing to a hand-woven chair. She pulled up a seat for herself also.

Kathryn moved the chair so she could see out the doorway. "I must keep a watch on the carriage. Aaron is sleeping inside."

Shanna's head jerked.

"You want me to bring Aaron inside so you can see him?" Kathryn asked in apprehension.

"Kathryn, you care for Aaron. I keep Little Soul here," she said, her hand pressing her heart. "What you want from me?"

Kathryn unfolded the documents. "You must sign these papers saying you gave Aaron to me. You can write can't you, Shanna?"

"Yes," Shanna hesitated. "Miss Shearon taught me to write long ago. Why should I sign? I already give my son and my word."

Kathryn shook her head sadly. "Oh, Shanna. Our laws don't have the human factor that we have. It is a white man whom I can't trust. A white man is trying to take Aaron from me."

Shanna's eyes squinted to a slant, her gaze intense while she absorbed the bewilderment in Kathryn's face. "White man?" she asked, her worse worries coming to surface. The white man would either be somebody Jake Minor had promised a slave, or Alex was up to one of his conniving maneuvers.

"Yes, Shanna." She hesitated for a moment. She really didn't want to mention Alex to Shanna after what he had done to her people, but she had no choice. She turned her head slightly, biting at her lip, and then she looked back at Shanna. "Alex is trying to take Aaron."

Shanna's face stiffened visibly and a large vein protruded in her forehead. She had tried to keep Alex away from Kathryn and Aaron but her attempts obviously had failed. But why did he want to take Aaron? He had no use for him, unless he planned to sell the child into servitude, like Jake Minor had vowed to do.

"Why does Alex want Aaron?"

"Because he says he's Aaron's father. He says I must leave the man I've married and take him back or he will take Aaron."

Shanna stared at Kathryn. "Leonard is your man now?"

"No, no. I married John. You didn't meet him."

There was a long silence. Bafflement showed on Shanna's face. "Why does Alex say he is Aaron's father?"

"Well, he is Aaron's father, isn't he?"

Shanna's head dropped forward. "I disgrace my people when Alex came here."

"Shanna, Alex is Aaron's father, isn't he?"

"No. Not Alex. Father of Aaron was a fine boy. He's gone," she said, the confusion in her voice turning to that of pain. "Maybe to the Glory Land in the sky. Rowe was good." She smiled slightly. "First time I see Rowe, his brown face lit up like the harvest moon. I see it now," she said, hesitating for a moment, and then she divulged her secrets boldly to Kathryn.

"Shanna, how can you be sure who made you pregnant if Jake Minor had made you a sex slave? How can you be sure some other man isn't the father?"

"When I was touched, I took my spirit away and didn't return until it was safe. I was not there when men touched me. When I found Rowe, I was there. I stayed. That's when we made the new soul."

※ ※ ※

On the day they met, Shanna, behind the butcher block at Jake

Minor's store, chopped furiously at a half a steer that would be picked up that afternoon by Mike Ramsey, a storekeeper with his business just off College Hill in Texarkana. The second half would be Jake's pay for the butcher job.

The sharp hatchet in her hand, Shanna looked up to glimpse the young customer's face. He stopped halfway across the driftwood floor, his lips slightly parted and his black eyes fixed on hers. Then he walked closer, an awesome smile on his face, as if he had never before seen a girl.

"What'cha doing?" he asked, though he saw very well she was butchering a steer into pieces to be salted down and taken to market in town.

The young man talked faster than most people who wandered into the Minor's store. He pronounced his words too fast. *He must be from far away*, she silently told herself.

"Don't understand."

Her gaze lowered back to the hatchet and beef parts on the table before her.

"I said, 'what are you doing?'"

"Butchering this steer. My job."

"You cooking it, too?"

"I cook some of it soon," she answered, her voice lowering as Jake neared.

"Why ye talking at my squaw?" Jake asked, his voice stern and demanding.

"Don't mean any harm. Hoping to eat here."

"Cost ye two bits."

Shanna didn't look up anymore then. She knew what was about to come.

"Cost ye two bits fer supper and another two bits to bed my squaw."

Shanna felt the stranger's eyes linger on her.

"I didn't know she was for sale."

"If ye don't bed her, somebody else will. Don't make no mind to me." Jake turned and headed across the storeroom.

Leaning against the butcher block, the young Mexican asked, "Want me to bed you?" His voice was little more than a whisper.

She nodded.

"My name is Rowe. What yours?"

"Shanna."

That night, Shanna found Rowe was different than others who had taken her. He treated her with courtesy, holding her and allowing his fingers to play through her hair. He spoke of himself.

"I come from Texas. I'm researching land. Looking for minerals." He touched her cheek. "You're beautiful. What tribe you from?"

"Don't know. Been here so long."

"How'd you get here?"

"Masked riders got me. I woke up here."

"Oh Shanna," he said, cuddling her in his arms.

She wanted to lay with him forever.

A couple nights later, after paying Jake Minor for another night with her, Rowe whispered, "I love you Shanna. I want you to leave here with me."

She didn't answer. She knew she couldn't get away. She had tried and failed so many times. And each new punishment from Jake was always worse than the time previous.

"I know you heard me, Shanna. I know you don't like being here with that boss man of yours." Rowe touched her face and rubbed gently. "I want you to leave with me. Will you?"

"Can't go. I'm afraid."

"I'll help you."

"Can't go."

"I want to take you away, Shanna."

Two weeks later, while the two made love, she agreed to leave Caddo Parish with Rowe. And that night, after spending time with her, Rowe left the back room and went into the store where Jake and a half-dozen other men sat cussing, gambling and drinking fresh brewed beer. He pitched Jake the two quarters he owed for bedding Shanna, then hastened outside, got on his Pinto and hurried around the building to the storeroom window. Shanna climbed through the tight opening. Rowe held her hand and pulled her onto the neighing pony. He slapped the reins and the stud galloped though the night, fleeing into its own shadow.

❋ ❋ ❋

"We travel far through swamps and trees. Rowe is Aaron's father."

"Are you sure?"

"I know such stuff. I keep track of woman's curse, like Miss Shearon said I should do."

"Miss Shearon?"

"Woman who taught me to read. To write." Shanna hesitated, and her eyes looked as if they might draw tears. "Miss Shearon went away. Everybody I care about leaves me. Rowe went away, but Rowe wanted to take me. Rowe is the father of the soul that grew here," she said, placing her hand on her belly." She hesitated again. "Why did Alex say he is father?"

"I don't know, but you can bet he has a reason. He's after something. That's the kind of man he is." Studying the agony lingering on Shanna's face, Kathryn said, "Shanna, I know what Alex did to you and your people. Okie told me everything."

"I made a mistake. I disgraced my people when Alex came here."

"You're not the only one who's made mistakes."

Shanna held her head high, her eyes seeming to search for something. "What you saying, Kathryn?"

"I was suckered in by Alex myself many years ago. I was foolish enough to marry the confounded rat. A few months later he was gone."

Shanna was speechless, but Kathryn knew hearing of her experience with Alex made the girl feel less culpable. "Shanna, you did know Alex when you stayed at the homestead, didn't you? Isn't he the person who sent you there?"

Shanna nodded. "He said Kathryn and Mama would take my Little Soul."

Kathryn closed her eyes and nodded forgivingly. "Okay, Shanna. It's okay now."

He had a reason, Kathryn thought. Alex Andrews had a reason for sending Shanna to her. But what was it? He wasn't thinking of Shanna or the baby. He wasn't thinking of her, either. But it was something. It was money. It had to be a way to get money. Money was the only thing that had ever been important to him. But why would he use her? She wasn't wealthy by any means.

Her reverie was interrupted by neighing outside. It was Crazy Sam. "Guess that horse has cooled off enough for water," she said. "I better fetch him some."

"Get water at the creek back of my hut," Shanna said.

Kathryn untied Crazy Sam and led him, still pulling the carriage, toward the clearing. A fat white man stood near a storefront holding a rifle and pointing it toward the sky. The brave who had brought her to the settlement was standing beside him. Kathryn gripped the horse's reins as she passed them.

Suddenly, the fat man fired the gun generating a roar like thunder. Crazy Sam reared, knocking Kathryn from her feet and kicking her so she rolled over the dirt. The fat man fired again and Crazy Sam took off in a wild gallop, as if he were running from a beating.

"Stop shooting, you fool!" Kathryn screamed. "You've stampeded my horse! My baby's in that carriage."

Twenty-five

"WHERE YOU BEEN?" Alex asked as the blonde clad in pink rubbed his shoulders.

"Drinking at the bar," she said, her sexy voice whispering in his ear.

"Oh. Did my girl find another man?"

"Your girl?" Again the whisper made his ear hairs tingle.

"'Course you're my girl. Who brought you that dress?" he said, his fingertips caressing the bulk of fabric just below her waist. "So, who were you drinking with?"

"A good-looking Mexican."

"A Mexican?" Alex turned quickly, his eyes boring into hers.

"What'd he want?"

"Looking to collect a reward, I reckon."

"What makes you think that?" Alex seemed to recall confronting a Mexican who had been following him around. The incident, vague in his mind, had occurred here at this gambling hall. Hadn't it? The fellow after the reward must have seen him in the past with Squaw Girl. Otherwise, why would he single him out to follow now?

"What makes you think the Mexican was after a reward?"

"He showed me a wanted poster. Wanted to know if the Indian works here?"

Alex laughed. The Mexican was obviously barking up the wrong tree. "Well, does she?" he asked, though he knew the answer. He laughed, and turned back to his cards.

"She might," the woman whispered.

Alex turned again. "Then why don't you collect the reward yourself?"

She leaned closer and whispered in his ear again. "Maybe I will. Maybe I'll share with the Mexican if he runs into her."

"That's not about to happen."

"Why not?"

"'Cause you know as well as I do she don't work here."

"Maybe I know where she is, though? Maybe I saw you with her. Maybe I saw you with her in Dallas."

What the hell? Alex thought. How did this gal know he had been with Squaw Girl in Dallas? He turned to face her again. He frowned and looked hard into her ice-blue eyes. "What you mean, you saw me with the Indian?"

"I was there. I was leaving Lilly's flat when you and the girl came."

"What the hell?" The woman's grin aggravated him. This woman must know something. "You know Lilly?"

"Sure I do."

"You tell the Mexican?"

"No."

"Good girl."

"Wanted to see if you aim to share with me."

"Share? I'm not collecting any reward." Alex stared at the woman a moment longer. "You keep your mouth shut. You tell anybody you saw me with the Indian I'll shoot you both."

The woman shuddered. "If you're not collecting the reward, then what'cha doing?" Her face turned from its puckered lips and wise grin to anger.

"It's not your business. Now, you either rub my shoulders or get yourself lost."

Alex watched as the woman in pink sashayed to the bar. She put her arms around an off-duty marshal who was drinking whisky shots. Just because the bitch had seen him at Lilly's place with Squaw Girl didn't mean she knew where he'd taken her. He'd have to keep an eye on this conniving gal, though.

Alex raked up money. "Count me out," he said. Keeping his eyes on the woman in pink, he pushed the greenbacks into his pocket, then, his eyes staying on the woman who had confronted him, he hurried to the swinging doors.

※ ※ ※

Outside the gambling hall, Rowe watched as Alex headed quickly toward the swinging door. He backed into the bushes. The woman in pink must have rattled Alex to the point of checking on his investment. Rowe watched as Alex mounted the white stallion. He waited until Alex was a ways down the street to mount his Paint. Following cautiously, Rowe's horse made it's way east and then turned in the same direction as it had the last time he had followed Alex from town. This time, however, the day was bright with sunshine, making it more difficult to remain out of sight.

※ ※ ※

Within the Indian settlement, Crazy Sam galloped wildly, his hoofs digging in the dirt and kicking up thick clouds between the two rows of houses and storefronts.

"Help! Somebody stop that horse!" Kathryn screamed.

Alongside the buildings, a small group of ponies neighed.

"Shanna! Help! Shanna!" Everything blurred. The young brave, who had led Kathryn to Shanna, jumped on a horse and took off in the same direction as Crazy Sam.

"Shanna!" Kathryn screamed again. She couldn't wait for the brave to save Aaron. She ran to the ponies and grabbed one around the neck. Jumping on its bare back, she kicked furiously at its belly and slapped at its front shoulders. The pony neighed angrily in the swirling dirt, and then it galloped through the thick clouds made by the brave's Paint. Reaching the trail, she bent forward and slapped at the left side of the pony's neck so it turned into the dusty path behind the brave's Paint.

Dust rising from the trail flew onto Kathryn's face, creating muddy tears. "Aaron, Aaron," she cried breathlessly as she kicked at the pony's belly.

Suddenly she felt the presence of a horse running wildly beside her. And then, as the horse flew past, she saw the woman's long dark braid whipping behind her. Kathryn kicked the pony harder.

The pony ran faster through the thick dust than any horse she had ever ridden, still, the animal wasn't catching the carriage. And then a clog of dirt, or a piece of shrub, or something out of the blue slapped her across the face, ripping her skin and blinded her. The pony neighed, standing up straight in the circle of thick dirt so he nearly reached the sky. Kathryn grabbed a tighter hold of his mane and he quickly turned a half circle. And then she saw an object lying a few feet away near a stand of shrubs.

"Aaron," she cried sliding from the pony's back. She ran to the object and grabbed the broken piece. "Aaron! Aaron!" she screamed. Turning on her toes, her eyes searched frantically for the rest of the bassinette and, most of all, for Aaron.

"Aaron!" she called. "Aaron!"

In a state of shock, she began to run in the direction the carriage had gone. She didn't know how far she had run, but suddenly she stumbled over something. She stopped. It was the rest of the bassinette. "No," she screamed, and continued running in a record-breaking pace.

And then, Kathryn ran into a fast swirling tornado of hot dirt. There, the carriage. The brave was holding Crazy Sam's bridle and Shanna was holding onto the horse's reins. Kathryn ran toward Shanna.

"Aaron," she cried. "Where's Aaron?"

The most wonderful sound she had ever heard then emerged from the carriage—that of a baby coughing. "Aaron, Aaron," she cried, lifting the stunned child from the flooring between the seat and the buckboard. He coughed again. Maybe he was too startled to cry.

Kathryn stared at Shanna, at the relief blooming on her face. She squeezed Aaron closer. "I'll never let anything like this happen to you again, Aaron. Never," she whispered, tears still streaming down her face.

Kathryn held Aaron on her lap during the ride back to the village. "Thank you Shanna," she whispered over and over. She wondered what would have happened if Shanna and the brave had not been close enough to hear her cries. She wondered if she could have caught Crazy Sam, or if he would have stopped running, before something dreadful happened to Aaron. Would she have reached the carriage before it turned over or wrecked? She shivered to ward off the cold tremble passing through her at such frightening thoughts.

❋ ❋ ❋

The sun still beating down on his head, Rowe's Paint trod the soft earth where grass had yellowed from lack of rain. Keeping out of sight, he gently pulled the reins and guided the horse to a patch of brush. He wondered what interest Alex had in this same log house he had previously followed him to. He watched as Alex halted the stallion a short distance from the dwelling. Alex waited twenty or so minutes, then guided the stallion past the house. Staying out of sight, Rowe followed. A couple minutes later, Alex dismounted and walked about looking at the ground, as if he had lost something there. Then he took an object from his saddlebag and dug something from the earth, wrapped it in a cloth, and placed it into his saddlebag. Without further ado, Alex mounted and rode back the way he had come.

Rowe waited until Alex was out of sight, and then he rode to the spot where Alex had dug. He got off the Paint and studied the earth. It was black and bubbly. He, as Alex had done, scraped a hand full of the messy black mush, wrapped it in his handkerchief and placed it in his saddlebag.

Who lives here? Could Shanna be held prisoner here? He studied the idea for a moment, then seeing a woman step out on the porch, he reined the Paint toward the house.

The woman raised her hand to shield sunlight from her eyes. "Hi-dee, there," she said as Rowe neared the porch. "Looking for somebody?"

"Actually, I am," Rowe said. "Okay if I dismount?" He didn't want to scare the older woman.

She nodded. "How can I help?"

Rowe dismounted, and smiling at the woman, removed his tall hat. "I'm not sure you can help me."

The woman pushed strands of hair from her face. "Won't 'cha sit down," she offered, pointing to the porch swing.

"I'm tolerable. Been riding. Need to stand a while. Name's Rowe."

The woman extended her hand. "Mrs. Williams. Called Mama. Mama Williams," she said with a smile. "Who you looking for Rowe?"

He pulled the wanted poster from his pocket and unfolded it. "I'm looking for a young Indian girl. Thought maybe you've seen her."

Glimpsing the drawing, Mama gasped, holding her breath.

She knows her! Rowe watched Mama's expression. *Yes, this woman knows something.*

"You're a bounty hunter! Oh my!"

"No, no. I'm a friend. I want to help her."

"A reward. A thousand dollar reward. A bounty," she hesitated, her fingers suddenly trembling out of control. "You better go," she said, hurrying to the doorway.

"No, no. I'm not a bounty hunter."

The woman reached inside the house and, before Rowe knew what was happening, had a shotgun aimed at him. "Okay, Mister Rowe. Start talking. If you ain't a bounty hunter, or one of the outlaws that's been looking for Shanna, you better talk quick before I start shooting."

※ ※ ※

Shanna and the brave had already reached the settlement when Kathryn reined Crazy Sam toward Shanna's cabin. Still clutching Aaron as if afraid to turn loose, she got down from the carriage. "I won't leave you with that beast again," she swore.

With Aaron resting on one hip, she tied Sam to a tree post and hurried into the hut, though she knew it would hurt Shanna to look at the child she had birthed, and whose life she had now saved.

"When you leave?" Shanna asked, her eyes moving from Kathryn and Aaron to the door opening.

"Soon. I need to get these papers back to my lawyer so he can get the adoption started. Shanna, you gave Aaron to me. And your word is fine enough for me, but it has to be made legal or government people won't accept it. Some folks, Alex for one, might try to take Aaron from me. If you sign these papers, Aaron will be legally mine in everybody's eyes. No one under the sky could take him away."

"And if I don't sign what will you do?"

"Well, Shanna, if you don't sign," Kathryn commenced, raising her brows, "I shall have to go away someplace far. Maybe I'd try to head off to California. I couldn't go back and fight for Aaron without any rights."

"But Alex is not his father. Alex was gone. He returned after Rowe and I had run off together. He returned after I was captured. I had life growing inside already." Shanna paused. "For one whole moon before I left with Rowe, only one other man came to me. He was decent to me. But he wouldn't let me leave Jake's store. And he bedded me. But I know he didn't make a new soul. I know when the seed sprouted. I was with Rowe." She paused again. "Aaron's father is Rowe."

"Never-the-less, Alex claims he is. Everyone would think I'm lying if I say he isn't. They'd think I was just saying that to keep Aaron. I'd be forced away. I'll never give Aaron up, Shanna. I'll die first." She extended the papers and charcoal pencil forward. "Will you sign?"

Shanna didn't move.

"Shanna, turn around here and look at me. Look at Aaron. Please, just take a good look."

Shanna held her head high. She turned, her eyes dropping onto the infant.

Anxiousness came over Kathryn. She knew this was the most important thing that would ever happen in her life. Right now, Shanna would sign the papers, giving her every legal right to Aaron, or although she had given her solemn word, she would reclaim him. Kathryn held her breath and kept her eyes on Shanna.

"I'm not the person you think. I'm a killer squaw," Shanna said, her voice low.

Kathryn gasped, and she felt her own eyes widening before she finally spoke. "What you mean, Shanna?"

"Jake Minor died. I—" she said, pointing at her own chest, "I killed him."

"Oh my Lord, Shanna! Why'd you do something like that?"

"Jake Minor made the outlaws take Rowe. He said he put Rowe in a pit so he can't get out. I don't know where."

"Oh, heaven forbid!" Kathryn clutched Aaron even tighter and sank to the chair near the door opening.

"I tell you how it was." She hesitated. "It was the day we made the new soul."

※ ※ ※

It had happened in the swamplands adjoining Jake Minor's store: Shanna's arms clamped tighter around Rowe as he slapped the reins so the Pinto trotted through the mush.

She rested her forehead against his shoulder blades. She loved this human whom her God had sent as her personal salvation. She would forever thank the Almighty. She would hold Rowe, care for him, and love him. She would protect Rowe as he was protecting her now. Two suns after her escape from Jake Minor, Rowe dismounted the Pinto and then helped Shanna from its back.

"Where you think we are? he asked, spreading his pony blanket on a patch of green where the lake and river met.

"Out of swamplands," Shanna said, rubbing her arms. "I got stung by poison plants, poison bugs in swamp."

Rowe turned to her, picking up her arm for a closer look at the tiny blisters protruding the skin. "Looks like poison ivy." He then put his hand on her forehead. "You got fever. We'll rest."

Shanna knew the fever would be more than she could deal with alone. "The way to cure the rash is with the poison that caused it," she explained to Rowe. "Don't touch the leaves or vines. We must dig roots and cook them in water, and then wash the blisters."

The fever must have gotten to her brain then, for the next thing she knew she was awakening, her body and mind relaxed. There was a soothing on her arms. Still dizzy, she opened her eyes. It was Rowe rubbing her with forest medicines. "Welcome back to life," Rowe said, his eyes squinting as they peered into hers. He smiled. "You've been hallucinating for two days. I was afraid I'd loose you."

"Two days!" Her body jerked, and she wiggled up. "Two suns!"

"Yes. Two suns."

"No! It can't be. The outlaws will find us."

"Hush. Don't talk. We'll go now."

She felt so very weak but she couldn't let her body hold up their journey any longer. She didn't want to lose Rowe and she didn't want to fall back into the hands of Jake Minor. She would rather die than to do either.

By nightfall, Shanna and Rowe had followed the Red River far south into Louisiana. "Need to rest?" Rowe asked.

"Not tired. We'll stop when the time is right."

Rowe pointed, "There're fishermen ahead. We'll talk to them.

Shanna held onto Rowe's waist as he reined the Pinto on toward the two men standing on a log at the river edge.

"Howdy. Got any ideal how far to the next town?" Rowe asked.

The men looked at them and one said, "There's a fishing camp on down the river a ways. Not much else on the river 'til you get to Shreveport. Hope you got money if yer going there."

"Maybe we'll find us a place to bed down alongside the river," Rowe said. "The girl here's just recovering from a poison ivy breakout."

"There's an empty house about a mile down that there trail. Nobody lived in it in quite a spell. Got a good well there."

Rowe nodded, and turned the Pinto in the direction the man had indicated.

At the well, Shanna couldn't get enough of the cool clear water and didn't stop drinking until Rowe took the dipper from her. "Too much too fast," he said. "You can drink more later. Rest now."

She watched Rowe drink. Then he led the Pinto to the nearby trough.

"Maybe we'll bed down here," Rowe said. "We'll be by the well and can fill up with water before we get on the trail again."

That night, lying on the pony blanket inside the vacant old home place, Shanna was engulfed by tenderness. Rowe's arms around the small of her back pulled her body into his so the two connected as one. Her mind and spirits circling in a galaxy of moons and stars, Shanna passed out of this world into one of ecstasy.

At dawn, while the two lay in each other's arms, barking dogs neared the house. "Let's go," Rowe said, pulling on his pants.

Shanna yanked up the pony blanket and ran, skipping down two porch steps at a time. Reaching the Pinto, she lapped the blanket over the animal's back. Rowe, right behind her, grabbed the saddle from the porch railing and quickly fastened the buckles underneath the Pinto's belly, then mounted. He held out his hand and Shanna grabbed hold. He pulled her up behind him just as the pony neighed, rearing straight and moving about in quick steps on its hind legs.

Then the Pinto galloped away, with Rowe's weight riding the stirrups and his head and shoulders leaning just above the pony's mane. Shanna gripped Rowe's waist, holding on for life.

The barking dogs neared, seeming to take shortcuts through the brier thickets.

The river—if the Pinto could reach the river the dogs would lose their scent. Rowe steered the pony toward the water, slapping the reins at its neck rapidly.

"Heia, heia!" he yelled. "Heia, heia."

Moments later the Pinto was huffing through a bayou.

"Heia, heia!"

And then, pounding on them all at once, dogs appeared from all directions. And behind the dogs came the outlaws, tossing ropes at Shanna and Rowe as if they were cattle.

One horseman whirled his rope so it hissed and cracked like a bad storm through the morning light and then he threw the noose, looping Shanna's shoulders and pulling her to the soggy earth. She didn't see Rowe after that. One outlaw tied her hands and, while he rode horseback, pulled Shanna to Jake Minor's dreadful fish camp at Caddo Lake.

❋ ❋ ❋

"Is that why you killed him Shanna? Because he took you from Rowe?"

"No. I kill Jake for what he said he would do. He said he would take a wire to me. Bring my baby out before time. He had a buyer. He said he would sell him. Make him a slave boy."

"There's no slavery in the United States any more, Shanna." Kathryn said, gazing into Shanna's eyes.

"Jake made me slave."

"Oh Shanna. Shanna."

"I killed Jake after thinking about it for long time."

"That's pre-meditated murder." Kathryn thought for a moment, and then said, "You say you thought about it for a long time. Want to talk about that?"

"Yes. I'll tell you about it. I thought about killing Jake for many suns and moons before my chance."

❋ ❋ ❋

Shanna lay on her cot for weeks recovering from the beating Jake Minor had given her after the outlaws had returned her to the fish camp. After a period that seemed years, Jake allowed her to return to work chopping meat in the storefront. Still, he watched her almost constantly. And then he noticed her tummy had started to swell.

"I'll take a tin clipper to ye," Jake threatened, his eyes shooting daggers at her.

"I'm being good Mister Jake," she begged. "Please let my Little Soul come."

"Ye don't need no kid. Ye ain't no good to me with a fat ugly belly. Nobody wants to bed ye now. Ye mind me and don't try no funny stuff, and I'll let the kid live. But mind ye, the little bastard will be sold 'fore it's a day old."

Shanna took the threat seriously. She didn't make a fuss when Jake talked with different customers about selling them a half-breed Indian kid. She would lose the child into slavery and she would again be forced to bed with dirty men. There had to be a way she could prevent this, a way to save the child, the child made from the love she and Rowe had shared.

The baby grew inside her quicker than she had expected. Soon she would give birth. Time was running out. She had to act fast. What could she do? She was locked in the storeroom at night and chained to the butcher's block at day.

And then she saw her chance. During the late evening, and with her time nearing, Shanna stood at the butcher block and allowed her eyes to freeze on the bloody hack knife in her fist. And then she knew the only thing to do.

She slipped the knife into the waistband of her burlap dress and stood stiff, barely breathing, for fear the knife would make her waistband stand out as Jake unlocked the chain at her ankle.

"Eat yer supper and git on to yer room," he ordered, apparently noticing nothing different.

That night, Shanna was too frightened to sleep for fear she would not wake before Jake came in the morning to let her out. She sat on the bed dazed at what she was about to do. But she knew backing out would mean a life of torture for her child.

❋ ❋ ❋

"So when he came to let me out, I killed him. After I killed Jake, Alex comes to the store," Shanna said, her eyes meeting Kathryn's.

"Alex was there? He was in the area then?"

"Alex did business with Jake for long time past."

"What did he do? Did he know what you did?"

"Alex knows everything. He saw Jake there on the floor with blood all around. Alex says, 'you better get out of here before the outlaws come.' He says, 'go to Kathryn. Kathryn will take your baby.' He said how to find the way to your homestead."

This was difficult to comprehend. Why would Alex tell Shanna to come to her? He was right about her taking the baby, though. She raised her brows. "So, when did you get back with him?"

"Alex found me on the trail. He promised to leave me alone. Alex brought me to the Territory. He says my people are his friends. He showed me the way. I couldn't get away from him until finally a brave named Snakeskin helped me run off from Alex. But Alex found me here. Then he steals furs from Moon Hunter and sells my people their own guns. Then he goes away. Not seen him any more."

With Shanna's eyes fixed on Aaron, Kathryn could feel love energy filling the room. She knew it was all Shanna could do to keep from sweeping Aaron up into her arms and holding him there forever. If Shanna should do this, then Kathryn could not fight her. After all, Shanna had given birth to the infant. Though she loved him with all her heart, with all her breath, she would understand.

There was silence for the longest time. Then Shanna looked at Kathryn with wet eyes. "Give me papers," she said, reaching.

In silence, Kathryn handed the papers to Shanna. She really loved this brown girl.

After Shanna had signed, Kathryn stood up and started out the door. "Shanna, please, hold Aaron," Kathryn said, a smile on her face.

"For what reason?"

"Because you love him the same as I do," she said, gripping both hands around Aaron's waist and lifting him toward Shanna.

"But I'm being hunted. Not a good life for Aaron." She stood straight and placed a hand on Aaron's head. "Ayimat Caddie, let Aaron be wise and good," she said, and then she turned away.

Shanna's words stayed with Kathryn as she bathed Aaron in the creek, and then walked dazed back through the settlement, back to where Shanna stood near the carriage. Kathryn touched Shanna's shoulder and put her face close to her cheek.

"I guess this is goodbye, Shanna," she said softly. "Anytime you want to come and live at the homestead, you just come right on. There's no reason why you can't be with Aaron, too. There's no such thing as too much love."

"I put a basket on the floorboard for Aaron to sleep. You can watch him while you drive horse. I put food for you and Aaron. Plenty to eat."

Kathryn nodded. "Thank you," she whispered through a blur of tears.

Unable to stop crying, Kathryn moved forward and untied Sam. She climbed onto the carriage, put Aaron in the basket, and reined Crazy Sam through the settlement. She knew Shanna would not want her to see the tears collecting in her eyes, too. She looked back to wave goodbye once more, but Shanna had already disappeared into her little cabin.

Kathryn felt good as she drove along the trail. Now Aaron was truly her son in every way. No one, positively no one, could take him from her. She shook her head and cried out in happiness. "Nobody under heaven can take him from me now."

※ ※ ※

I did right, Shanna told herself after entering her hut. Kathryn would be a good mother to Aaron. She would teach him right and send him to school. Kathryn was settled in so many ways.

Shanna couldn't tend Aaron regardless of how much she loved him. Even if by some God-given miracle Rowe were alive and wanted to find her, he would never know where to look. And on top of everything, Jake Minor's friends, as well as lawmen, were looking for her. Should they find her, she'd hang. If she had Aaron, what would become of him then? Not to mention the Nation didn't take too well to fatherless births.

But Kathryn's offer that she come live at the homestead was tempting. They were good people, Kathryn and Mama. She would be welcomed. *Maybe*, she thought, *maybe someday I can slip back there. Maybe someday I can see Aaron. Maybe, maybe I can be with Little Soul again.*

Shanna turned to gaze out the wall opening. "Oh Aaron," she cried, unable to prevent a flood of tears. "Oh Aaron. Oh my baby. I love you so."

※ ※ ※

Time passed smoothly on the road leading home. Aaron slept a lot. When he was stirring, Kathryn held him close while she drove Crazy Sam. On several occasions, she pulled the carriage into a thicket to avoid men riding over the hills on horseback. Not that she was afraid, but there was no use in taking unnecessary chances. And often she would stop the carriage and take the adoption papers out just look at them. She was so very happy.

Night camps went with ease, too. Kathryn always found a good clearing to stop where she could pull out some grub to feast on.

The morning she reached the relay post where she had left Sugar, sense of time had escaped her. She paid for Sam's use and the post keeper returned her ring.

For a moment, Kathryn held the ring in her hand before she slipped it on her finger. She thought of John, the way he had given the wedding band to her. Now, a voice in her head said, "It's over."

She kissed Aaron as she walked from the relay post. She had won him while she had lost her husband. But she had been right. It was John who had been wrong. She had done the right thing; she knew she had.

At dusk the next evening, Sugar stopped at the front steps of the homestead and Kathryn got down from the carriage. She arched her back and held her arms up in a stretching motion, and then she lifted Aaron from the basket.

"Mama, we're home," she called. "John, John are you here?"

And Her Name Was Kathryn

Twenty-six

AT THE HOMESTEAD, Mama grabbed Kathryn, hugging both her and Aaron at the same time, as they entered the living room. "Thank God you're safe." Then, turning Kathryn loose, she reached for Aaron. "I think this little fellow here needs a bath and a nap," she said, starting into the kitchen.

Her breath hanging in her throat, Kathryn looked about the room. John couldn't be gone, he just couldn't. How could she live without him? She glanced stealthily toward the open door to her room, then not seeing John, she followed Mama to the kitchen.

"How'd everything go?" Mama asked, turning to glance at Kathryn. Holding Aaron with one arm, she poured hot water from a kettle on the stove into a pan on the counter, and then dipped in enough cold water to cool it for Aaron's bath.

"I got the papers singed, Mama, that's what I went for. I didn't have any trouble finding Shanna. But I'll tell you, I sure wouldn't want to go through the whole ordeal again." She stopped and pushed away hair that had fallen to her forehead, her eyes lingering on Mama's curious glance. "Sugar's foot went lame so I boarded her at a relay station and rented a wild stud. When we got to the Indian settlement he got scared and stampeded off with Aaron in the carriage. Mama, Shanna saved Aaron's life. She caught up with the carriage and stopped the horse. I'm afraid I couldn't have done it myself. I can just be thankful it all happened in Shanna's presence.

"Sweet Jesus," Mama said, as if she had been in the Territory and witnessed the ordeal.

Kathryn held out the adoption papers so Mama could see the signature. "There for a little while I was kind-of frightened that Shanna might not sign these papers."

"What did Shanna think of Aaron?"

"I could tell she loves him more than she wants to admit. I told her she could come down here and live with us anytime she wants to."

"Good. Maybe if she does want to come, she will. She's so young."

"Yep, Mama. But she's been through more in her young life than one needs to endure in a lifetime."

Kathryn rested her elbow on the table edge and dropped her chin into her hand. She was afraid to ask about John, yet she had to know what he'd done, and it was obvious Mama wasn't going to volunteer information. She swallowed, and then asked, "Did John leave?"

"He did. Same night you left."

It was all Kathryn could do to keep from screaming, but she would not allow herself to do so. She was too tired to cry. Besides, if she should start now, she knew she would never stop. She sat up straight. "Did he take his things?"

"Everything he had here."

"Well, guess I'd better get his carriage back to him tomorrow. I have to get these papers to Cavin O'Tool anyhow," she paused, her eyes lingering on Mama. "Will you feed Aaron his supper?"

"Sure, I will," Mama said in baby talk, and splashed water on Aaron's legs.

"Then I'm going on to bed." She kissed Mama and Aaron on their cheeks and left the room.

Mama turned to Kathryn. "There's something else you need to know."

"Can it wait, Mama? I'm so weak I could cry."

"Guess it can. You got enough on your mind."

Kathryn stared curiously at Mama for a moment. "It can wait, can't it?"

"It can wait," Mama replied, and splashed more sudsy water on Aaron's chest.

Unable to sleep, Kathryn tossed restlessly. How she wished John were lying with her now, holding her, whispering words of passion, and making love to her. "I need you, John," she whispered into the still emptiness that shadowed her room. "I love you so." Maybe nothing could damage what they had shared. But now, as her eyes traveled to the window, she knew John was as distant as the stars in the heavens. She could never touch him; she had probably really never done so anyway.

She stretched her legs—her aching legs—dozing off every now and then only to awake with the haunting agony that John was gone—maybe forever. She looked toward the corner where Aaron slept but the bassinet wasn't there. Remembering the bassinet had flown away when Crazy Sam had gotten spooked, Kathryn's heart pounded. In panic, she jumped from her bed and whirled toward Mama's room. Relief came as she looked through the doorway and saw Aaron sleeping on the bed next to Mama. Still, her heart pounded hard. There was no use trying to sleep. She turned and entered the kitchen. She allowed her mind to linger on John and figure ways to get him back to her: *I'll go to him and throw myself at his feet. I'll tell him I love him so much and that I can't live without him. I'll promise him anything.*

At break of dawn, I'll take John's horse and carriage to town. I'll see him then.

※ ※ ※

Bridged By Love

Rowe waited for word to come from Chester Everett, whom he had located two days prior about his findings in the filthy dirt he had collected at the log house property. The property, he later had learned, belonged to the Williams women—the woman he had talked with at the log house and the redhead he had seen fussing with Alex Andrews at the State Line Café. Rowe had also discovered that Alex Andrews had presented his ground samples from the property to Chester Everett. Alex had claimed to Everett that he was married to Kathryn Williams and that he owned the property. Yesterday, Everett had left town with the samples. Now, a curious attorney in town, Cavin O'Tool, had left word at the hotel desk that he wished to see Rowe. It seemed Mr. O'Tool was working on a civil case for Kathryn Williams. It all had to do with Kathryn, Mama Williams, Alex and Shanna.

Rowe looked out his hotel window. Dawn hung over Front Street like the dim lamp lighting his room. Still, many hours would pass prior to his morning meeting with the interested attorney.

❋ ❋ ❋

Kathryn reached her lawyer's office building just as daylight lit the town; she held her skirt just above her ankles and climbed from the carriage. She was glad she had worn the pink dress Mama had made for her. John liked her dressed up.

Clutching the papers Shanna had signed, she hurried inside. Cavin O'Tool didn't answer her first knock. She banged again and the door flung open.

Cavin pushed his rumpled hair back from his face with a small black comb. "Damned if it isn't Kathryn," he declared. "You're back. After today, there wouldn't have been any need in you coming back at all."

"Why's that?"

He removed his suit jacket from a rack near the doorway and slipped his arms into it. Walking across the room, his eyes gripped hers. "I'm afraid you'd have lost your case if you hadn't made it back here today."

"How come, Cavin?"

"Sit down, Kathryn." He pointed to a chair near the window. "I might as well tell you what's going on. Alex hired a lawyer to come all the way down here from Fort Smith. This fancy dude has talked the judge into hearing the case today so he can get on back north. Alex has given him a big line of bull. And the judge seems to believe it."

"Brace yourself," Kathryn said, holding the papers forward.

"They signed?"

"You bet they are."

"Good," he said, taking the papers and glancing over them approvingly. "But now, Kathryn, you better prepare yourself for whatever happens. Even though Shanna signed, there's still Alex. It might not have been a legitimate birth, but the judge could still rule in Alex's favor."

Kathryn breathed deeply. "There's something else. Alex Andrews isn't Aaron's father," she paused, raising her brows. "Alex is just after something. I don't know what it is but you can bet your boots he has a reason for all of this, and it isn't because he loves Aaron. Alex has never loved anything, except money," she paused, rubbing her hand over her forehead. "But God knows I don't have money."

Cavin paced back and forth across the floor while Kathryn talked. "You know, he was just using Shanna. He sent her to my place so she would leave the baby there. That rat went up to the Territory and stole furs from the Indians."

"Is that right?"

"Yes sir, he used her to come by furs. That's the truth."

"An idea of mine is getting stronger," Cavin said, rubbing his whiskers. "Everything you've been telling me is making it look more and more like—" He stopped talking and gazed out the window.

"Like what?" Kathryn hurriedly rose from her chair. "Do you have something to go on besides what I've told you?"

"I just might have. There's a man in town right now from Kansas City named Chester Everett. He's been digging holes, been trying to find something in the ground, I guess. If my hunch is right, Alex knows what it is and that's what he's after."

He looked at his watch. "Kathryn, meet me in the courtroom. If I'm not there by ten, get on the stand and tell the judge everything you've learned about Alex. No matter what, keep talking until I get there. Don't let the judge close the case on us."

"Sure, Cavin. Whatever you say." She tilted her head, wondering what the lawyer had up his sleeve.

She followed Cavin out the door. She would return John's carriage before going to the courtroom, but first she would go to the State Line Café and have the cup of black coffee that she so needed.

※ ※ ※

At the Warren Hotel café, Rowe sipped at the cup of strong black coffee a hostess had placed on the table before him. He kept an eye aimed at the hotel foyer while his mind wandered. He couldn't dismiss from his thoughts the things that Mama Williams had told him when he had called on her at the log house.

So Shanna had come to the Williams women's homestead out of the blue, bringing with her an infant. She had left the child with the women and had then taken off to the Indian Territory to find her family. And now Alex Andrews was claiming the child as his own and trying to take him.

Rowe shuttered. Jake Minor had sold Shanna to so many men. How could a man who had so dishonored Shanna want her baby?

Rowe's coffee had cooled. He got up, went to the big modern iron stove, and helped himself to another cup full. Returning to his table, he waved to the lawyer who had entered the foyer. "In here," Rowe called.

He watched the lawyer walk toward him.

"Chester Everett's joining us," Cavin said as the man from Kansas City entered the hotel café and followed O'Tool over the tile flooring.

※ ※ ※

Upon entering the State Line Café, Kathryn met face to face with her worse nightmare. Her blood gurgled in the veins swelling with hot anger through her whole body. She bit her lip and quickly walked by Alex to the counter. "I'll have a cup of coffee, please, Mack," she said, sliding onto a barstool.

Mack poured the coffee and at the same time, his gaze moved to Alex, who had come to stand behind Kathryn. "Look here mister, I thought I told you to stay out of here"

"I'm not doing wrong," Alex said, holding both hands out in front of him. "I just want a drink."

"All right," Mack said, pushing a cup toward him. "But one false move on your part and you're out."

Lifting the steaming cup to her lips, Kathryn sipped quietly. She must not let Alex's presence bother her. She would get him in court. He would bleed at all the evidence she had against him. She could not prevent grinning.

"Kathryn," Alex's voice interrupted her thoughts. "Why don't we settle this whole thing out of court? I've already let my lawyer go on back to Fort Smith."

She couldn't believe what she heard! Turning, her eyes stabbed at Alex's stiff, sullen face. Was he serious? Did he really want to call off court?

"I hate to drag you through the mud," he continued, keeping his face perfectly straight. "I know all about John leaving you. He didn't stick by you when the going got tough," Alex jeered.

Kathryn took another sip of coffee.

"Since John's gone already, there's really no need to fight me. We belong together. That's the way it should be. Think about it: you and me and my son."

She bit her bottom lip so hard it brought blood, but that didn't hold back her anger. "Alex, you must think I'm a fool. Can you possibly think you can get to me with your confounded, smoothing-talking deceit? Just because I fell for your lying ways once, when I wasn't much more than a kid, is no sign I'll ever do it again," she quipped, angrily slamming her cup on the bar.

She wished she could hold her temper but it just wasn't the Lord's will. "Alex," she blurted, "I've been up to the Territory and I've found Shanna. I know Aaron isn't your son. His father is a Mexican down in Louisiana.

Alex jerked, as if hearing this news for the first time, but surely he knew all the details.

"That's a lie, Kathryn. Who'd believe the word of a squaw tramp against the word of a respectable white man?"

"Respectable, ha! Old Moldie told me all about how you baited him into selling Thatcher's calf."

Alex remained calm and looked at her soberly for a moment, then said, "Everybody knows Moldie's a fool."

"And the Indians you stole from, Alex, what about them? Did they lie, too? And, by the way, I just happened to have met Okie. Did he lie on you, Alex? Why is everybody trying to persecute an 'innocent' man like you? And what about the goods you took from Mama and me years ago when you deserted me? How about that, Alex? Or is that all my imagination?"

"That was a long time ago, Kathryn. I was young and sought the world," he said, his black eyes as devious as ever. "You know we belong together. I was your first man, Kathryn, and I know you can't forget that."

She stood up and reached into a pocket inside her sash. "You sicken me, Alex," she said, bringing out a nickel and flipping it onto the bar. "Memories of you in my bed make me want to throw up."

She turned from Alex. Noticing the clock, she saw it was already nine. She had wasted enough time here when she could have been with John and trying to renew his love.

Outside, Kathryn climbed onto the carriage. "Let's go, Sugar," she called, taking the reins and heading down the busy avenue. Already traffic was buzzing with cotton wagons and horse trolleys.

Standing on the front porch of S. Wagner's Boarding House, a strange feeling crawled under Kathryn's skin; it was a sudden vision that she had lost John for good. She knocked anxiously on the square post that helped support the long white porch. John must return to the homestead with her. He just must.

She braced herself and knocked again. Soon Sharleen appeared behind the screen door.

Kathryn swallowed. "Is John here?"

Sharleen unlocked the screen and walked out onto the porch. "Indeed, John is here."

"I'd be obliged if you'd tell him I'm here," Kathryn said, peeking past Sharleen into the front room.

Sharleen raised her finger to her lips. "John is sleeping," she whispered, authority in her voice. "He's ill. I'd rather not wake him."

Kathryn's heart stopped, then it pounded hard and slow. "John, sick? What's wrong?"

"It's that cough of his; it's been out of control. He's spit up blood and been running a fever since day before yesterday. I've been keeping him wrapped up in blankets. Put a potato compress on his chest, but that ain't helped none."

"Oh, my goodness. What can I do?"

"Nothing. The doctor's already been here. You might as well just go on about your business. John needs rest. I can take care of him."

"All right. I guess that's best. I'll leave his carriage here." She started down the porch steps and then turned demandingly toward Sharleen. "I'll come back to pick up my horse and to be with my husband after court."

Kathryn flagged down a horse trolley for the short ride to the Courthouse. She could have walked but she didn't want to chance being late.

The courthouse was packed with people. Other than civil court, where her case would be held, a murder trial was being heard this day. It was something to do about a man who gunned down a marshal on a train in Texas.

Inside the civil courtroom, Kathryn glanced at the clock on the wall. It read exactly ten. She next quickly searched the people present. No Alex. Nor did she see his attorney. *Thank the Lord.* She took a deep breath and, looking around, saw an empty space on a long bench near the front of the huge walnut room. A bit of anxiety ran through her but she quickly dismissed all negative feelings. Her purpose was to get in, be heard, and be awarded legal custody of Aaron. Then she would go fetch John and she'd take him home. She would win him back. He had loved her before. He would love her again. She smiled, sinking deeply into her reverie.

Kathryn's head jerked upward at the sound of the bailiff's hammer rapping on the legal table. Her suddenly weakened body trembled, and sweat sprang from her pores.

"All rise," the bailiff said. And everyone in the courtroom stood up. The judge walked across the platform and perched himself on a stool behind the bench.

Kathryn shook. She had never talked in a courtroom before. When she divorced Alex her lawyer had done all the talking for her. Now, here she was. She turned to see the door at the back of the courtroom. Her lawyer had not arrived. She watched the bailiff lift his hands, then lower them, as if he were directing a church choir.

The judge picked up a docket sheet. "Let's see what we have here," he said, reaching into his shirt pocket and pulling out his eye glasses. He began to read off the cases: "We have the case concerning Thatcher's calf; and there's a complaint filed by Barney Johnson against Sally Johnson." He studied the document a moment longer, then said, "Barney here claims Sally shoots at him whenever he takes his dogs to drink at the pond near her place."

Immediately after the judge had spoken there was an outburst by Sally. "Near my place heck! That pond is on my place. That Barney screwball brings all them old hound dogs over to my place and it don't do a dang thing but scare off the wild life. I ain't having any darned killer dogs drinking from my pond."

The judge removed his glasses. "Come on up here Sally. You too, Barney."

All was quiet as the two enemies approached the bench.

"Do you swear to tell the truth, the whole truth, so help you?" the bailiff asked, directing them to put their hands on the Holy Bible.

They both nodded at the same time and, as if twins, their look-alike eyes narrowed in strict attention.

"All right now, who owns the pond?" the judge asked, his head rocking back and forth.

"I do," Sally quickly said. "Our daddy left that pond to me."

"Is that right, Barney? Does Sally own the pond?"

"Sure enough. Recken she does. But there ain't no law against my dogs getting them a drink of water there, mind ye."

"Well now Barney, if the pond belongs to Sally, you got to get her permission before you use it."

Sally spoke up. "I say he ain't bringing them darned killer dogs on my place. I'll shoot 'em. I tell you, I'll shoot every lastin' one of 'em."

"Hold it Sally. Hold it. Barney, do you have a spring around your place?"

"No. I sure ain't. The nearest spring to me is a mile down the trail. And I ain't got no well. And it jest seems like a lot of hog-wash for me to go all that ways when all I need to do is jest go right over to Sally's pond. I can tolerate a little shooting."

The judge sat up straight, a disdained look on his pale face. He raised his hand, and then quickly slammed the hammer down on the bench top. "Barney, from now on you are ordered to get water for your dogs from the spring, or dig a well, or dig a pond, or let them starve. I don't want to hear of you bothering Sally anymore. Case is closed."

The judge put his glasses on again and read from the trial document, "Alex Andrews verses Kathryn Williams Allen."

A hush fell over the courtroom.

The judge raised his head, looking over all the faces. "Is Cavin O'Tool in the courtroom?"

Kathryn stood up. "No sir. He asked me to go ahead and tell my story if he didn't make it here by ten.

The judge scratched his head. "Sit down for now. We'll take this other case first."

Kathryn sank to the long, oak bench and placed her hands on her lap. Her face was so hot she felt her hair might catch fire.

"Thatcher verses Saul Jones," the judge's voice echoed.

"I didn't do a blasted thing wrong," Saul Jones roared as he got up from his seat. He sauntered to the platform near the judge's stand and took a position near George Thatcher.

The judge had them swear to tell the truth, and then he said, "It says here that Saul Jones has possession of a cow that belongs to George Thatcher."

Saul propped his foot on a chair in front of him. "I didn't swipe that calf. I bought it. Old Moldie sold it to me fair-and-square for fifty cents."

"Easy, easy." The judge raised his hand. "This is a court of law. Is Moldie here?"

"Right he-he-here," he stammered, his voice emerging from somewhere in the back of the courtroom.

"Come on up," the judge said.

"How did you come by the calf, Moldie?"

"Al-Al-Alex told me to sell Th-Tha-Thatcher's calf to Sa-Saul Jones."

"Alex in the courtroom?" the judge asked.

"I am Your Honor."

"Join us up here," the judge sing-songed. "This case is so trivial," he murmured.

"Do you swear to tell the whole truth in this case?" the bailiff asked.

"I do sir," Alex said, nodding.

"Is it true you told Moldie here to sell Thatcher's calf to Saul Jones?"

Alex held his hat in his hands and cocked his head to the side, and then he began to incite his reasons. "You see, Your Honor, I knew about this Indian girl, Shanna, who was about to have a baby. I knew she planned to leave him with my wife."

"I'm not your wife!" Kathryn interrupted, the tone of her voice that of bitterness. All of a sudden her fears had disappeared and she felt incredibly very brave.

"Silence!" The judge slammed his hammer down. "You said, your wife. Explain."

"That little wild cat over there," he nodded toward Kathryn, "well, she divorced me, Your Honor, but in my belief she always will be my wife. 'Til death do us part.' That's what the good-book says."

Kathryn shook her head in disgust. Alex Andrews never had a belief except to grab what he could from whomever he could. And she could tell by the expression on the judge's face that he was taking him seriously.

"What does that have to do with the calf?" the judge asked, his facial expression hopeful.

"Well, you see, Your Honor, I knew Shanna was going to leave the baby with my wife. And I knew she would need milk for him. That's why I told Moldie to do something with the calf. I knew if Thatcher's cow didn't have the calf hanging on her, my boy would get his milk."

"Your boy? I don't understand."

It was all Kathryn could do to keep from yelling out at Alex then.

"Well, sir, with no wife to go home to, I found this little squaw girl. You know how it is, Your Honor."

"That's not the case," the judge quipped, quickly preventing more words demeaning to his character. "We're here to determine ownership of the calf. It seems Saul Jones has the calf now," he paused, looking at George Thatcher. "Guess it's a young cow now. Thatcher, how much do you think you should have for it?"

"I'd say fifty cents would be fair enough. Saul's been feeding it all this time."

The judge rubbed his chin. "Moldie, do you still have the money Saul paid you?"

Moldie shook his head, "We-we-well, no sir.'"

"Okay, okay. Alex, since you're the ramrod of this whole shrewd deal, you pay Thatcher fifty cents."

Kathryn watched Alex dig into his pocket. She watched the judge as he looked down at his document sheet. Then she heard the judge's words: "Next case. Alex Andrews verses Kathryn Williams Allen."

※ ※ ※

Rowe shook hands with Chester Everett. "Mr. Everett, I may see you in Kansas City before too long. I appreciate the job offer." He then reached for Cavin O'Tool's hand. "I'm heading up to the Territory shortly," he said. "I'm glad to hear Shanna is safe with her people. It'll be good to see her again." He smiled. Things would be good now. For everybody concerned.

"The Williams women are in for a surprise. Their land is going to be worth plenty of money," Rowe added.

"They aren't the only ones in for a surprise," O'Tool added.

Chester Everett grinned. "Yeah. They'll be some wealthy people here someday soon. Looks like Alex Andrews won't be one of them, though."

"People to benefit are those deserving," O'Tool noted. "Kathryn and Amanda Williams are only two of many good folks with lands in the boggy parts."

Outside the hotel, the men went separate ways. Rowe went to the stable where he already had the Paint saddled and ready to ride.

"Ye heading out of here now?" the groomsman asked, his head leaning knowingly to one side.

Rowe grinned. "Just might be."

"Where ye be heading?"

"Lots of places." Rowe thought for a moment. Sooner or later, he expected to return to country alongside the Rio Grande. That was home. First, he wanted to look at more country on this side of Texas, though. More land. Perhaps even take Chester Everett up on the job offer, at least for a while. He would enjoy going out collecting land samples from across the country. First, he'd ride up to the Indian Territory. He'd come this far looking for Shanna, he wasn't about to stop now.

Rowe whistled as he mounted his horse. This was a good day.

Twenty-seven

Hearing the judge call her name, Kathryn blushed. She looked around, and then slowly stood up.

The judge removed his glasses, his eyes searching. "Is Cavin O'Tool in the courtroom yet?"

Kathryn shook her head.

"You can sit back down, Mrs. Allen. We'll start with the plaintiff. Think you can find your way back up here, Alex?"

The judge held a handful of papers. "This complaint is filed by James Osman, lawyer from up at Fort Smith," he mumbled. "Says here that you plan to state your own case. That right?"

"That's right, Your Honor."

"It says here you're claiming one infant child, known as Aaron Williams, as your son."

"That's true, Your Honor."

"And that you wish to gain his custody away from Kathryn Williams Allen."

"Your Honor, it's the only way I can have my son. I've begged Kathryn to take me back, but she won't. Maybe after I get my son she'll marry me just for him."

The judged leaned forward. "Do you mean to tell me you plan to use the child if you win guardianship?"

"No, no, not at all. I want the boy whether I can have Kathryn or not. But if she should only come to me because of the boy, I'll gladly take her back. I love her that much, Your Honor. I want my family."

Alex had the fake-serious look on his face that Kathryn knew he could draw up anytime he so chose. Why was he doing it, though? He didn't love her and he didn't love Aaron. She took a deep breath and shook her head.

"How long have you been divorced from Mrs. Allen?" the judge asked.

"Kathryn got her hair-brained lawyer to draw up some papers a bunch of years ago," he paused, his face wrinkling in thought. "'Bout seven, more-less, while I was away on a business trip. You see, I had to keep the little gal there in style the best way I could, and that was to hunt buffalo and sell the hide. Had a pretty good business going. But the little gal there, she got the crazy idea that she needed a divorce. But, Your Honor, I've never accepted it. In my belief, divorce is a sin."

"That's all my questions," the judge said. "Anything you want to add?"

"Just that I love my son and I love my wife."

"Okay, you can move along." The judge waved his hands. "Kathryn, do you still want to start without your lawyer?"

"Yes sir," she said, her voice betraying her anger. She walked hurriedly to the stand.

"Do you swear to tell the truth?" the bailiff asked.

"Yes, I certainly do," Kathryn answered quickly. "And everything I said before was the truth, too."

The judge rested his arms on the bench. "Tell me, Kathryn, just how you came about getting that child."

"Sir, in September this Indian girl came up to my homestead and asked if she could stay with Mama and me for a few days. She had an infant with her. Naturally, we invited her to stay. A day or so later Shanna, that's the Indian girl, she asked me to take the baby. I did and I've had him ever since."

"Did Shanna ever mention Alex Andrews being the child's father?"

Kathryn bit nervously at her lip, and then said, "Alex isn't Aaron's father. That was one of his lies. Aaron's father is a young Mexican. He's somewhere in Louisiana, I guess. Shanna doesn't know if he's alive or dead, though."

"Wait a minute. Answer my question first, then you can tell me anything else you want to."

"Sorry, Your Honor." She hesitated, her eyes pleading with the judge. "Shanna never once called Alex's name while she was at the homestead. I didn't even know she knew him."

"Now why do you say the baby's father is not Alex Andrews?"

"Because Cavin O'Tool gave me some papers to have Shanna sign and I went up to the Territory, just Aaron and me. I found Shanna and she signed adoption papers. I told her what Alex was doing and she said Alex was not the father."

"Of course that squaw would say that because I left her to come back here—to my wife and son," Alex's calm voice interrupted. "And, incidentally, Kathryn is a good liar herself, Your Honor."

The judge rapped his bench again. "Order. I only want to hear from one person at a time, and that's the one who's on the stand." He turned back to Kathryn. "Now, where are these papers you had the girl sign?"

"Mister O'Tool has them."

"Is this all you have to say?"

Kathryn hesitated a moment. "No, Your Honor, it isn't."

"Then proceed."

"Alex stole valuable furs from the Indian people and even sold them their own guns before he left the Territory."

"How do you know this?"

"I met a fellow by the name of Okie running a trading post up in Oklahoma. He told me everything. And then Shanna confirmed."

"Kathryn, that's hearsay. It can't be used."

"Well, Your Honor, Aaron is my son now. He doesn't belong to Alex. He's mine. Shanna gave him to me. I won't let Alex take him," she said. "Never."

"Take it easy here."

Tears of anger burned her eyes, and hearing loud talk amongst people in the room, she looked over all the blurred faces. Good, she thought. Cavin was walking toward her. She wanted to jump up and grab him and hug him, but she didn't. She just sat there.

"Cavin, do you want to ask Kathryn any questions?"

"No, Your Honor, she's probably told you everything already. I'd like to recall Alex Andrews."

"You're dismissed, Kathryn. Alex, come back up."

"I already said all I need to say. I've told you all I know."

"You're finished when the case ends, and it hasn't ended yet. Please, take the stand," the judge roughly demanded.

Cavin pulled the documents Shanna had signed from inside his vest and handed them to the judge. "These are adoption papers signed by Shanna, also called Yellow Bird."

Cavin's hand slipped into his vest again and brought out more documents. "These papers are some files I borrowed from Chester Everett. Now, I'll explain who Chester Everett is. He's a fellow here from Kansas City who is beginning to lease oil rights from landowners in these parts. Alex Andrews claims he owns one-hundred-and-sixty acres that are actually owned by Amanda Todd Williams and Kathryn Williams. Alex has committed fraud here. Pure and simple."

Kathryn's mouth flew open. Why on earth would Alex say he owned the land? And why such a big deal over oil?

"What are you getting at, Cavin?" the judge asked.

"I'm saying Alex thought he could pressure Kathryn into marrying him before oil drilling commences in this part of the country. It's already been found in California and Kentucky. They say it's here, too."

The judge scanned over the papers. "Is this your signature?" he asked, turning to Alex.

Alex opened his mouth but before he spoke, Cavin butted in. "I can bring in a hand-writing expert from the east in a matter of days."

"Is this your signature, Alex?" The judge asked again.

"Well, yes it is. Certainly," Alex said, tilting his head and maintaining his poised personality.

"I don't understand, Alex. You signed this document claiming you owned the Williams property. Now why did you do that?"

"Oil. The oil that's on the Williams' place!" Cavin said in a raised voice.

"I'm asking Alex Andrews," the judge informed, raising his brows as the spoke.

Alex groped for the first time. "Judge, Your Honor, as I already told you, I never accepted the divorce. As far as I'm concerned, Kathryn and I have always been man and wife although we've been apart. And, well, I just knew we'd be getting back together and business did need attending. I was only trying to take care of things without involving my wife."

The judge peered over his glasses. "Alex, you and Kathryn are legally divorced. Every time you refer to her as your wife, you are perjuring yourself." He held the files toward Alex. "This looks like a sure simple case of fraud all right."

All was silent for a moment, and then the judge said, "Cavin, do you have any more questions?"

"No, that's my case, Your Honor."

"Alex, is there anything more you want to tell the court?"

"Only that I want Kathryn back."

The judge glanced at Kathryn. "Well, it's quite apparent she doesn't want you. Alex, you can't make a woman marry you." He paused, a disgusted look coming to his face. "You may step down."

An outburst of chatter sprang through the courtroom. The judge rapped his hammer. "This court has come to a decision. This court grants Kathryn Williams Allen legal custody and the adoption of the infant child Aaron Williams. This case is closed."

Kathryn jumped from her seat and ran to her lawyer, swinging her arms around him and hugging tightly.

"Better let Chester Everett know this lease isn't worth a plugged nickel," the judge said. "He might be wanting to press charges against Alex himself."

The judge then looked up from his paperwork and addressed the court clerk. "Notify the Federal Government that it needs to investigate Alex Andrews. The government might want to file charges, as well."

Joy sweeping through her, Kathryn walked alone through the corridor. She had won the battle. It had been hard and troublesome but she had won. She could barely wait to tell John.

Smiling and lifting her shoulders in joy, she started out the door, suddenly coming face to face with Sharleen. "Sharleen," she said in surprise.

Sharleen was breathless. She made an effort to speak, bringing words out slowly. "John's in a bad way. The doctor's with him now. He's calling for you, Kathryn."

John! For a moment Kathryn was in a state of confusion, and then she ran from the courtroom and flagged down a horse trolley. Reaching S. Wagner's Boarding House, she fled up the steps to the front door. She stood there, catching her breath for only a second, and then she opened the door and swung into the front room.

Through an open door, she could see the doctor standing over John's bed. She hurried toward him. "John," she whispered, falling to her knees.

He raised his hand toward her.

"I love you, John," she cried. "With all my heart, I love you."

"Tell me what happened in court," he whispered.

"I won. Aaron is legally my son now. Our son, John. He's our son. No one can ever take him away."

John's lips parted into a slight smile. "I'm glad," he said, and raised his head upward a little. "You're some gal, Kathryn. I'm never going to try telling you anything again. My goodness woman, you wouldn't listen anyhow." His voice was gentle, yet weak.

"I once knew a girl who was as head strong as a bitch dog, stubborn as a mule, pretty as sunshine." He raised his hand and touched her lips. "And her name was Kathryn."

She smiled, tears rolling down her cheeks. She held John's hand to her lips. "I want you to come home with me, John. I want to have your baby," she whispered, and realized she meant it, though she had been warned pregnancy could cost her life.

"You already have my baby," John said.

"Oh John, you sound as if you mean it. I knew you would come to love Aaron as your own," she said, suddenly sobbing.

All of a sudden, John's hand was limp. She looked at his face and then at the doctor. A haunting stillness enveloped the room.

The afternoon sun was warm at the back of her head as she staggered from S. Wagner's Boarding house. She couldn't cry. She could never cry again. She had cried all her tears out already.

Stumbling over the stone sidewalk, she saw Sugar tied to the back of a wagon parked alongside the street. Beside it, Leonard stood tall, his straight face seeming to carry her load.

Nothing was said as the wagon rolled over trolley tracks south on State Line Avenue, then along busy Broad Street. She gazed at sudden clouds hanging low over the city. She was here, with Leonard coming to her side as he always had when she needed him desperately. He loved her. He always had. And she loved him, too. Not with that fiery, urgent passion she had for John, but she loved him.

20th Century Epilogue

A YOUNG JOURNALIST IN every respect, Kathryn, so named for her grandma Williams, got off the westbound train in Texarkana. She was home for a while—not sure how long—after developing her chosen career at Southern Illinois University—the college her Uncle Aaron had insisted she attend. "If you're ever going to be anybody this day and age," he proclaimed.

Now, she was here as well as on the payroll of Arkansas' *Uncensored Magazine & News*. But she wouldn't write about the olden days in the Ark-la-tex, when cowboys drove cattle herds through the city streets and sometime right into the saloons. Or about these booming modern times and the way people carried on—the days of short skirts, radio, and the Ford automobile. She wasn't really here to write at all, she thought, the January sun beating down on her blue woolen dress as she cross some three or more sets of railroad tracks leading to the elegant depot on the boundaries of Texas and Arkansas.The thing was, if she had come here to write, the city itself was a story and the longer a journalist thought about it the more pages would flip through the brain.

Walking through the huge modern entrance and across the depot lounge, Kathryn's black paten leather high-heels clicked on the shiny gray marble flooring. She went to the luggage pickup where a redcap attendant had delivered her trunk—a trunk that contained all she owned. "Thank you," she said to the gray-haired black man, and handed him a dollar bill. Then, "Oh," she said, catching the attendant's attention. "The Warren Hotel—can somebody take this trunk there for me?"

"Sho 'nough," the eager assistant said with a grin.

Kathryn walked across Front Street to the hotel on the west side of State Line Avenue. Perhaps she should have telegrammed home to let folks know she was arriving early rather than book a room at the Warren. But she had heard so many stories of her ancestry, and now her heart ached to spend time in the modish inn—"Preferably a room on the third floor," she had told the hotel clerk when she made reservations. Right now, she just wanted to be alone, to gaze out the window and look down on the goings-on in the exhilarating city.

She would see her relatives soon, all her aunts and uncles, and cousins—the Shipps and the Fishers and the Williamses—and even Grandma Shanna and all the kinfolks from the reservation. First, though, she must remember her last trip home and her favorite person—the one they were coming together now to celebrate—Grandma Kathryn:

> Grandma, I miss you this cold January day,
> But it is not as cold as it was that day,
> That January day
> The southern sun brought sweat beads
> Up on my back
> Underneath that deathly blue dress
> I wore;
> The day I listened
> To the preacher say
> The last words
> From his *Holy Bible*,
> I do not remember one word he said.
> My eyes,
> Wet as they were,
> Gazed at your bronze coffin.
> Thoughts swam in my scared brain.
> Your warmth embraced me.
> But I was so cold,
> And you were gone.
> You would have done anything for me,
> And I had come to expect it.
> What could I have done
> To make your life better? I wonder.
> Was a mere squeeze around your fragile
> Shoulders enough?
> You deserved a million times more.
> There was no snow
> At the Rose Hill Cemetery
> The day they laid your body
> In the Texas dirt;
> But it was cold.
> Grandma, it was so dreadfully cold.

❋ ❋ ❋

Patricia Lieb

Born and raised in Texarkana, Arkansas, my career as a journalist included working 10 years (1991-2001) as an award-winning reporter and feature writer for *The Suncoast News* in New Port Richey, Florida. Awards I received from press, municipalities and clubs include the Florida Press Association, The Dunedin North Rotary, the Countryside Kiwanis, and the City of Dunedin, FL.

As the crime reporter for the *Daily Sun-Journal* in Brooksville, Florida, (1987-1991), I learned enough about murder to write for the true crime magazines, RGH and Globe, (on the side, of course, and using the name Patty Shipp) for some 10 years. In addition, (again moonlighting) I wrote for Vocational Biographies during a 10-year span.

As well as writing features for the *Daily Journal* in Kankakee, Illinois, for three years prior to moving to Florida, I was an original writer at the *Bourbonnais Herald* in Bourbonnais, Illinois, in 1976.

In the early 1980s, I was the co-editor/co-publisher, with Carol Schott Martino, of the literary magazine *Pteranodon* and the *Pteranodon Chapbook Series*; and in the 1990s co-editor/publisher of the online *Write On Magazine* with Evelyn Manak.

I have served as a speaker at various writers' conferences including the annual Florida Suncoast Writers' Conference at the University of South Florida in St. Petersburg; the National Federation of State Poetry Societies annual conventions (for some 10 years held across the U.S.); Illinois State University; Nichollas State University in Thibodaux, LA; the Chicago Chapter of the American Pen Women; the College of St. Francis in Joliet, IL; Columbia College in Chicago; Central Illinois' Writer's Conference at Millikin University; and for some state poetry societies special events in Illinois and Ohio. To talk about my true-crime book titled *Murders In The Swampland*, I have served as guest speaker at William Carey College in Gulf Port, MS, the GFWC Spring Hill Service League and The United Way Author's Luncheon at the Brooksville Golf and Country Club in Brooksville, FL, the Suncoast Information Specialist (SIS) in St. Petersburg, FL, and at other events.

My fiction, articles and poetry have appeared in numerous literary and national magazines as well as publications for teenagers including *Scholastic Scope* and *Star magazines*.

Also available from Patricia Lieb...

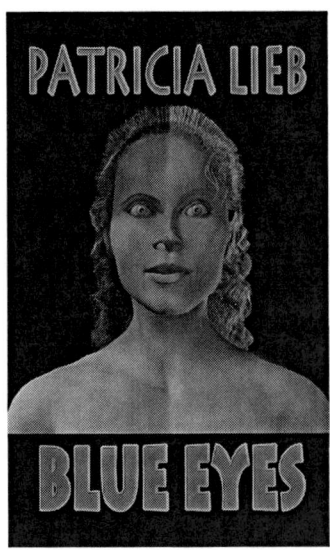

BLUE EYES
Paranormal by Patricia Lieb

Mary is starting to remember things. Things she couldn't possibly know... because they never happened to her.

ISBN 1-934337-13-7

Available as a Download, on CD, or in Print format.

MURDERS IN THE SWAMPLAND
True Crime by Patricia Lieb

A collection of true murder cases and crimes that took place in the swamplands of Central Florida from the late 1970's to early 1990's. Reported by Patricia Lieb for The Daily Sun-Journal, Ms. Lieb includes personal notes from her own journals as well as 2007 updates on many of the convicted felons.

ISBN 1-934337-47-1

Coming Soon from Patricia Lieb...

WAYS TO SAY I LOVE YOU - Poetry
DANGER IN THE CLIFFS - Romantic Suspense

Recent Releases from Tsylett Press...

GEE-WHIZ MEETS SHAFT
Romantic Spy Thriller/Comedy
by Valerie J. Patterson

Milton Gee, the only surviving partner of the Gee-Whiz Detective Agency, is determined to solve the murder of his partner, Chaz Whiz. When he's approached by two gorgeous dames—er, women—who want to enlist his talents to save the life of a Canadian Mountie, he's not overly interested. But a man has eyes and babes have gams and Milton's were fixed on these babes' long, shapely legs... when he wasn't gazing deep into their bedroom eyes. His resistance begins to crumble once they use their powers of persuasion...some of which might actually be considered violent.

ISBN: 1-934337-49-8

DEMON INSIDE AND OUT
BOOK ONE OF THE HERETIX CHRONICLES
Dark Fantasy by Jason Jeffery

In a world where magic and nightmares hide beneath the surface, Talbolt McCreary discovers his dark side can transform him.

Even a wizard can hit rock bottom. Talbolt McCreary's self-loathing drags him into the abyss of addiction. And he would have remained there, if not for the mafia boss who enlists him—against his will—to assasinate the competition. Stripped of his magical abilities, taking on vampires and werewolves will be hard enough. Add in a sudden unpleasant physical transformation, and the return of his powers with a dark twist, and Talbolt's life just got a lot more complicated.

OPEN HOUSE ON MURDER
Romantic Suspense by Lavada Dee

Recently widowed, Aimee has returned to Woodsville to rebuild her life. A positive step in that direction is buying into the real estate company belonging to her best friend, Sharon Phillips. Another step is managing to avoid Quin Martina, the sexy onetime love of her life.

Then the unthinkable happens – one of their agents is murdered. Now Aimee now must deal with Quin, her own uncertain feelings and the serial killer who soon has her in his sights.

ISBN: 1-934337-37-4

More Speculative Fiction from Tsylett Press...

ALIENS FOR SALE
Sci Fi Comedy by Randy Lankford

It's invasion by persuasion when a race of aliens tries to convince their neighbors to let them move in.

Elderly spies and seeing-eye Chihuahuas, ALIENS FOR SALE is a rollicking farce that skewers marketng, politics and pop-culture.

ISBN: 1-934337-31-5

GHOST KISS
Paranormal/Horror by Kris Ashton

A woman struggling to conceive suspects she may have been impregnated...by a ghost.

ISBN 1-934337-20-X

HOSTAGE
Horror by Paul Wilson

How well do we know our neighbors? How well do we know ourselves?

ISBN 1-934337-15-3

SANCTUARY
Paranormal/Horror by J. A. Cerullo

Who knows what demons lie in wait...?

ISBN 1-934337-03-X